I0675146

BLOOD AND WEEDS
A CLARKE LANTHAM MYSTERY

J. Daniel Sawyer

Blood and Weeds
A Clarke Lantham Mystery
by J. Daniel Sawyer

AWP Mystery
A division of ArtisticWhispers Productions

Text Copyright © 2015 J. Daniel Sawyer
All Rights Reserved

Book Design by ArtisticWhispers
Digital painting "Figures In The Brush" © 2015 Kitty NicIaian

This book is a work of fiction. Names, characters, events, and locations are fictitious or are used fictitiously. Any resemblance to actual persons or events, living or dead, are entirely coincidental.

This file is licensed for private individual entertainment only. The book contained herein constitutes a copyrighted work and may not be reproduced, stored in or introduced into an information retrieval system or transmitted in any form or by any means (electrical, mechanical, photographic, audio recording, or otherwise) for any reason (excepting the uses permitted to the licensee by copyright law under terms of fair use) without the specific written permission of the author.

Dedication

Dad, this one's for you

BLOOD AND WEEDS
A CLARKE LANTHAM MYSTERY

J. Daniel Sawyer

3:00 AM, THURSDAY

THE HIGH, DRY WINTER AIR had coated the Kawasaki Ninja and its rider with more road dust than any human being could be reasonably expected to endure, but the failing moon and the three-horse town didn't promise much relief.

The bike pushed itself on little more than idle power from one shut-down gas pump to another, in vain hope of finding something to drink.

Not even the computers were up this late on a Friday night. Not here. Maybe there were labor laws or something. Well, it was possible. The northwest was supposed to be ultra-progressive.

Not that this was really the northwest. Not for another stretch of road yet. This was still California. So, maybe the robot's rights revolution was already starting up here. Or, maybe looking up at Mount Shasta's barely-snow-capped top was enough to drive everyone here just that nuts.

The gas tank was so empty that shining a light inside it didn't show anything but fumes.

"Come on, Carmen," Rachael said to her bike, "Let's find you a drink."

Even with rice rocket mileage she got, if she didn't find a working gas pump in the next few minutes she was going to have to huddle up against the side of a building and wait until the mini-mart opened for the morning commute crowd, if they even had morning commutes around here.

Rachael saw one option, almost all the way to the north end of town, just in the shadow of I-5. An Arco, with an AM/PM attached. All the lights still on.

The computers even worked, but Arco didn't take Visa. They were a debit-card and cash operation, had been as long as anyone could remember. That suited her just fine. She wanted to keep her pre-paid Visa for emergencies, and she didn't want to use the other cards, which might be tracked by any one of the several people she knew were looking for her.

So, she thought, *cash it is.*

Rachael took her helmet off. The cold air rushed in and fogged it up, along with her breath. She reached up underneath the nape of her no-longer-purple hair, and pulled the chain on which she carried her wallet from the back of her neck and lifted it over her head.

She fed a twenty into the kiosk, hit the obligatory buttons, returned to the pump and squirted five gallons of premium into her tank, went inside for her change.

She got a beef jerky and an Arizona Peach Green Tea, on the grounds that she hadn't eaten since Reno. She found a rack with maps on it—nearly empty, probably hadn't been re-stocked since the Terminator lived in Sacramento—and looked at one of the west coast. Someone had written "Jefferson" over the border between California and Oregon and then drawn hard Sharpie lines at Medford and Chico.

"How far to Portland?" She thumbed through. Portland was a good place to get lost. She'd thought Tahoe would be nice, but there wasn't anything there. Reno was worse. Cameras everywhere. Not the kind of place to go when you didn't want anyone to find you.

Not that it had made a difference those first few days. She'd found some trouble to get into, enough to drown out the memories for a little while. It wasn't much, but it gave her what she needed at the time. A month or two lost here or there, out of a life of ninety years, in the end didn't cost much if it bought her some piece of mind.

Too bad it hadn't. Not yet.

She checked the scale, did a little math.

Three hundred fifty miles to go, give or take.

"Hey, hey!" She waved at the clerk, who was pretending not to sleep behind the till. He started awake. "Any snow on the pass?"

"I don't know. Check your phone."

"Don't have a phone. Can you check?"

He shrugged, pulled an iPad out from behind the till and started tracing shapes on it. He muttered something like "Funny, you don't look old enough to be my grandmother,"

She ignored him. Took a bite of the jerky and a slug

of the tea. It's not like she could eat it on the road under the helmet.

"No chain requirements. No fresh snow, but they've had six accidents. It's cold out there. Probably some black ice. I'd watch it on that crotch rocket." He gave her the kind of look that might have been a come-on if he'd been awake enough to muster up any enthusiasm. As it was she felt like she'd been leered at by someone half-under anesthesia.

"Thanks a bunch." She tossed a dollar bill on the counter as she passed it on the way out of the store. Just another late-night customer, nothing out of the ordinary beyond the bike and the Kevlar suit. Before leaving Reno she'd made sure to take out the extra piercings, re-dye her hair, get new ride armor, and make sure anything that might make her stick out in anyone's memory was covered up, tamped down, or otherwise hidden under ordinary.

She'd had good training. The product of two mentors who knew as much as any spy or master thief. As much as anyone could disappear anymore, she would pull it off, as long as she needed to.

Her bike was warm between her thighs. She took the kickstand up and sat astride it, feet on the ground, while she finished her dinner. Out of habit and training, she watched her mirrors and casually checked her sight lines. Just in case.

The tea washed the road out of her throat, at least. The jerky gave her something to think about besides her own grinding teeth. She tossed the wrappers in the trash and turned the ignition on.

Before she could kick the starter, something crossed behind her. She only caught a flash of it in her mirror. Her hand went to the bulging pocket on her right hip, opened the zipper so she could get to the Ruger SRc concealed inside, just in case.

She turned. Saw the faintest rustle of movement retreating behind the mini-mart. Could've been a deer, way up here. Maybe a homeless guy trying to find some kind of shelter from the irregular wind that ripped her breath-fog from her face.

But it was making a sound.

Deer didn't sob.

Homeless men didn't sob at that pitch.

Women didn't either, not adult women.

The rider re-set the kickstand, left her helmet on the bike. She circled around the far side of the mini-mart, weaved her way around the disused pallets, the battered brown dumpster, the milk crates, the slick of slime seeping out from a trash bag left loose. Coming up to the last turn, she could hear the choked sounds of someone trying to breathe through tears, and not to cry out loud, for fear that someone would find them.

She peeked around the corner. There wasn't anybody there against the wall. But across the way, under the bushes, she saw a child's dark back. Scratched, naked, shivering.

She ducked back behind the store and unzipped her

jacket, stripped it off. It smelled like she'd ridden in it all night. But it would keep the kid from freezing. If she could catch it before her tits froze off.

"Hey," she whispered. "Hey. Are you okay?"

The child jumped. It looked over its shoulder at her. Deer in the headlights. Eyes wider than the sockets. Dark pits in a dark, grime-streaked face. Hard to see in the shadows. Couldn't quite tell if it was a boy or a girl.

She squatted down. "I'm not gonna hurt you. Really. Are you cold?"

It nodded.

She scooted toward it. Kept eye contact. It looked away. Watched her hands. She kept them hidden underneath the jacket. She had to get her hands on this kid. Had to get it to someone who could help it.

She got within a foot.

The kid shrank back. The boy. It was a boy. He was all goosebumps and shivers. Scratched up. Dirty. Like he'd been crawling through bushes. He was naked from the waist up. From the waist down he had what looked like yoga pants, or hospital pants maybe. Blue, pale, cut all to ribbons.

She scooted forward again. He jumped back.

She jumped forward, grabbed his wrist.

He squirmed. Started to shout, stopped himself.

"Stop. I'm not gonna hurt you." *And I'm now officially a cliché. Brilliant.*

The boy tried to bite her. She tossed the jacket over his head, then tackled him. Like a zoo animal.

"Stop. Shh. Stop. I'm not taking you anywhere you don't want to go, okay? Just calm down. You speak English, right?"

"Y...yeah."

"Okay. So sit up and put on the jacket already." She let him go, sat back on her haunches, waited while the boy tried to find the arms.

She caught a glimpse of his left arm. Covered in track marks like a heroin addict. He didn't catch her looking. He was too busy trying to figure out why her jacket was so big. He looked like he was maybe eight or nine—old enough, if she remembered right, to imagine he was a lot bigger than he actually was and be frustrated when the world didn't agree—and didn't know which way was up.

He got it on, clutched it tight around him, like it could protect him from the monsters out there.

"Are you okay?" She asked, kicking herself again for asking goddamn stupid questions. "Are you hungry? Can I get you something?"

He nodded at her. Something in his eyes looked a little hopeful at the offer.

"What's your name?"

"Zarek," he said. "Zarek W...w...Woodfork," he shivered. "What's yours?"

For a minute, she thought about giving him one of the dozens of aliases she'd used in the last month, but she was gonna be talking to someone soon enough who'd be able to ID her.

It'll put me back on the grid.

Well, it would have to then, wouldn't it? She wasn't about to leave this kid out here to freeze to death. Or for some yahoo to pick up who didn't know a thing about who to go to. She was here, this was her problem. She'd disappeared once, she could do it again. One appearance on the grid was just a single data point. She could go any of six directions from here and get well and truly lost. She could make it all the way to the border without spending any more time on an Interstate, if she wanted to. She could even make it across. She'd need to get a Canadian ID. Or a passport. But that was tomorrow's problem.

She stuck out her hand and told him something she hadn't told anyone in weeks.

"Rachael Oldman." She shook his hand. "Ever gotten to ride on a motorcycle?"

3:24 PM, Thursday

THEY STONEWALLED HER, BECAUSE of course they fucking did. First it was for the weapon.

Yes, the permit was genuine. They could call the Santa Clara County Sheriff and run the number if their computers were...well, she forced herself to say "down" instead of "too old to shit," because she really did want to get out of town instead of borrowing trouble.

Then it was for her presence in town. What was her business here? 'Just passing through' wasn't an acceptable answer. Armed drifters weren't welcome here, so where precisely did she intend to go next?

She wasn't prepared to say, because it was none of their goddamned business. She wound up doing breakfast all the way down in South Weed at a place that wanted to be a Denny's when it grew up. She was too pissed off to want anything other than bottomless coffee. But it took her a while to get there.

She should have been back on the road already. But the kid lived in Weed, not Yreka, so the first thing the Yreka cops had done was truck him and her and her bike all the way down to the Weed department to set up a "Joint Interdepartmental Task Force." And she'd better stay close, because they still had more questions for her.

That was fine. She had more questions for them, too. The ones she'd asked already had gotten her a bag full of fuck-all.

Were they going to call the FBI? Of course not. Why force someone to come all the way up here when it was just a local matter anyway?

A local matter? Well, of course. This was Old Man Woodfork's grandson, a good boy by all accounts. Nobody had even reported him missing. Where had she found him again? Behind a gas station? Must have been out running around town with other boys from school on a dare. Nobody had reported him missing.

She'd demanded to talk to the Chief of Police, but the Sergeant wasn't interested in her demands. She played the "brother officer" card (well, daughter of one, anyway), but he wasn't impressed with that either. Even less impressed with the Private Investigator card (she didn't mention that she only used to work for one, she didn't have a license herself). No, the Sergeant didn't fancy the big city folk getting all up in his business over a little matter of a boy that got himself in trouble roaming around at night.

So where, she'd demanded, had he gotten those track marks on his arms? Those weren't from a thorn bush.

Didn't matter, he said. Everyone experiments with drugs around here. Sure, he was on the young side, but they started young out here, on everything. What the boy needed was some looking at by a doctor, just to be sure, and then going home to his grandpa.

And that's where it sat. She left her phone number and reassembled her cell phone—she hadn't had it turned on since the night she left Castro Valley—and resigned herself to the fact that the people who wanted to find her would be able to find her now, if they were still looking.

Maybe she'd get lucky and they weren't. Maybe they'd butt out of her business.

But this was Lantham, and her dad. Two more nosy motherfuckers she'd never met. So it was only a matter of time. Maybe that was a train she ought to get out in front of. Call them before the got around to calling her.

It was a mid afternoon. If she'd have minded her own business, she would've been in Portland eating some kind of interesting ethnic meal off the side of a food truck. Falafel would suit her just perfect right now. Something with more tooth and more real-feeling vegetables, sharper flavors, than anything on the menu in dinerville. She'd be chilling on the side of a street, watching all the pseudohippies walking around, checking out the local alt-culture papers down in the strip club district, scoping for some good places to go tonight. Somewhere she could dance herself half to death. Maybe find a sub who'd be interested in a bit of flogging. That was what she needed after a long road trip. Center herself. Help her de-clench after all that bullshit in Nevada.

But instead she was here, in a nowhere town halfway between somewhere and somewhere else. A place named after the kinds of plants you didn't want in your garden. She hadn't gotten back on the road like she should have. Even with the detour to the police station she could have been back on the road by nine AM, still plenty of time to make a late lunch in Portland—she wouldn't've have gotten there yet, but she'd be well on the way. Not stuck in a diner in Weed.

But she didn't like the way she'd gotten the brush off from the locals here. Maybe it was big city prejudice. Maybe she'd read too many Stephen King books, and expected rural cops to be a bunch of inbred whiskey-swilling good ol' boys who cared more about preserving the image of an idyllic community than they cared about finding out who'd kidnapped this boy and what they'd done to him, and how he'd escaped. Maybe she expected them to be worried about bad publicity costing the town money. "A lot more people in town would suffer if this got out," that kind of thing. One little boy was important, but maybe not enough to upend the whole town and maybe put people's livelihoods in danger.

Maybe she was wrong about all of that. Maybe the case really would get a fair hearing, and they really would find the perp.

Maybe.

But she didn't believe it. She and her big city prejudice needed some fucking satisfaction before she'd leave the locals to do their job. She'd found that kid, and as far as her moral compass was concerned, that made him her responsibility.

Okay, then, so what did she know?

He couldn't have gotten far in this weather, half-dressed like that. Whoever had kidnapped him had to have locked him up somewhere close to that gas station.

Or had him in a car, dammit. Okay, so she couldn't know anything about his abductor based on where she found him.

She thought of calling her Dad, who was Deputy Chief of the Santa Clara County Sheriff's Department back home, but she knew exactly what he'd say: Call the FBI.

The coffee was bottomless, but the food wasn't. A good thing too. It sure as hell wasn't going to leave her ass-less. She could feel her hips spreading just looking at it.

Maybe she could call Lantham.

Lantham. Clarke, technically, but she couldn't remember ever having called him that herself. It wasn't his fault that she didn't want to see him, or even hear his voice, but she still wanted to be able to hate him for it. She didn't have the energy for lying to herself, and she wasn't all that good at it in the first place. She knew she'd left because she couldn't handle it anymore. Seeing them together, him and Erica. She should have been happy about it, since she'd set them up and pushed for it, but she wasn't.

Because she was an idiot.

Because she should have known better.

But he didn't need to know that. She'd be damned if she'd let him see her, salamander-weak, crawling back, asking for her job back, asking for help. She was not, under any circumstances, going to listen to him gloating about her needing his help. She'd shoot him first...but then, he never would. That wasn't the way Lantham did things. He'd be pissed at her for leaving, or happy to find out she was alive, but he wouldn't be gloating.

But he didn't need to. Her own head would do that job on its own the second she actually heard his voice.

Maybe...

No. She could figure things out on her own. There probably wasn't anything she could do, but she would at least make sure that kid got home safe, and maybe ask him a few questions of her own.

Buzz buzz.

Her left arm's pocket buzzed. She unzipped it and pulled her phone out. Felt weird, answering the phone again after so many months without one.

"Rachael Oldman."

"Ms. Oldman, this is Darren Coben. I'm the Detective here at the WPD," Rachael figured that had to mean Weed Police Department.

"Detective Coben."

"You wouldn't still happen to be in town would you?"

She thought about lying, but then thought better of it. She wasn't going to be leaving soon enough that she might not get spotted walking around. She didn't exactly blend in with the bike and all the Kevlar. "Yeah, I decided to stop for some breakfast and a rest before I hit the road again."

"Oh, good, so pleased to hear it. Look, if you wouldn't find it imposing, I'm looking over the transcript of your interview this morning and I'm noticing a few irregularities. I can't tell you how much it would mean to me to be able to talk them over with you before you get on your way. Mind stopping by the office this afternoon before you leave?

She sipped her not-really-coffee. The time with Lantham had really fucked up her definition of coffee. "Nope. Wouldn't mind. I can be there in about fifteen minutes. That work for you?"

"It does indeed. Thank you."

He ended the call.

She flipped the phone over. Now that she actually had the attention of somebody professional, she ought to be on the road by tonight, with nobody the wiser that she'd blinked back into the twenty-first century for a few hours. Fate blinked, she got lucky. Her father, Lantham, Nya, nobody at all had noticed that her phone was on. Maybe everyone was out at lunch, and they'd get an email this evening showing that she'd connected to the network, but by then it would be too late. She'd be off and gone again, as far away from Weed as they were. No way to find her again.

She should have been using a pre-paid, but cargo space was at a premium, and would be at more of a premium once she crossed into Oregon and had to stow her weapon until she could apply for a non-resident carry permit.

The back popped off, she reached inside to pull the battery.

And she hesitated.

She actually had a chance to call home. To let everyone know she was alive, at least. It was the decent thing to do. A month ago, she wouldn't have even considered it. Last night, even, it might not have occurred to her. But now she was brushing up against the one thing that had always united her with the people she loved most: a monstrous crime. It made her long for home, a kind of hunger she hadn't allowed herself since she'd left.

What could it hurt?

Well, aside from the obvious.

"If I'm gonna do this," she muttered, "Might as well go for the fucking gold medal right up front."

She re-covered the back, flipped the phone over, and dialed Lantham's cell phone.

The phone went to her ear. The cell network took its sweet goddamn time routing the call. Long enough that she had to take a second breath, which is when she realized she'd been holding the first.

Then, that stupid chime. The call had connected.

But it didn't ring.

"Hello, you've reached Clarke Lantham of Clarke Lantham Investigations. Please leave your info after the beep. If this is an urgent matter, please call our main line at 510 582 4268. Beep."

He actually said "beep" before the phone company's computer came on and delivered its typically insulting narration before dignifying her phone call with a genuine computer-generated beep.

She hung up, on the grounds that she had nothing whatsoever to say to his voice mail. She didn't even know what to say to him, she just knew she ought to say something.

But she was due at the police station in another couple minutes, and it was a five minute ride away. She could call him later. Now that she'd gotten up the nerve once, she wasn't going to puss out again.

TAB PAID, STARTER KICKED, roads rolled over. She rumbled behind the police station, out of view of anybody and of all the security cameras she could spot, and stowed her weapon in the lock box under the seat next to her emergency toilet paper, tampons, and fire flint—she'd been caught out by a breakdown in the boondocks before—then cruised around and parked her bike at the front of the police station.

The front desk actually had a dispatcher at it this time of day. She asked for Detective Coben, got waved to a door toward the back of the building. If Lantham had been here he'd probably have waxed lyrical on how the building was a stunning example of mid-century yadda yadda yadda, and then looked all hurt when she didn't give a fuck. And then laughed at himself.

He didn't know he did that. Always gave her a little smile, which she made sure never to let show.

Then again, not even Lantham could find the charm in this building. They must keep it locked up in the drunk tank or something. It looked shockingly like a city office at the ass-end of nowhere.

Detective Coben's name was on his office door in one of those brass brackets with the slidey brown plastic name tags. The door was half open, so she clutched the jamb with one hand and leaned the top half of her body around the corner.

A thin, completely bald Chinese man sat behind the desk, his body curled over the surface of an iPad. She could hear the muted sounds of the Angry Birds soundtrack.

"Detective Coben?"

He stared, looked up, a little blush creeping up into his face. Then he caught up with himself and brightened. "Ms. Oldman?"

"That's me. Is this the right place?"

"Come on in," he waved at the black Naugahyde Austin Powers-looking chair on the visitor side of his desk.

She set her helmet next to the chair. Her armor creaked almost as much as the upholstery as she sank into it. As soon as he did, he stopped looking at her and moved his iPad out of the way, then started studying the manila folder underneath.

"It says here your father is a cop, right?"

"Yes."

"And you're on a...trip? Business?"

"Not yours."

"That's not a good attitude, Ms. Oldman."

"I get that a lot. Didn't you say you need something?"

"Give me a minute, give me a minute..."

"You said you noticed some irregularities."

No response. Rachael had been around cops her whole life, she knew all the games in the book, and knew how to play them on both sides. That didn't mean she was going to play just because someone invited her.

"Are you intending to detain me?"

"What? No, no, nothing like that. Just...you said you found him at the Arco?"

"Yes."

"And what were you doing there?"

"Setting up a drug deal. I make my living trafficking in Tylenol."

He looked up from his folder, gave her a pointedly mild squint.

"Ms. Oldman, please." Like a schoolteacher who caught her passing notes in class.

"You're right, I'm sorry. Mind if I ask something?"

"By all means."

"Have you called the FBI?"

"Why do you ask?"

"Signs of violence on the body," Rachael ticked her

fingers off, just to reinforce the point. "Reactivity to assistance. Mistrust. Signs of trauma. This boy was kidnapped, Detective."

He closed the manila folder. "He's been recovered. Thanks to you."

"Kidnapping is a Federal crime, not a local one. Federal Kidnapping Act, 1932. You need to notify the FBI..."

"He's recovered and he didn't cross state lines..."

"....get their help in here—this is *not* the first time this fucker's taken a kid, I guarantee..."

"Ms. Oldman..." He raised his voice, but she kept right on going as if she hadn't heard him.

"...and if you can find the perp, you'll find more victims. There'll be a case with the Federal prosecutor. That's above your pay grade, Detective. And I don't see why you're all so preoccupied with confirming everything I ever saw in a *Twin Peaks* episode..."

"Ms. Oldman." He didn't raise his voice anymore. The eyes did it. The mild exterior was gone, and for just an instant she saw something else underneath. Worry, maybe. Something else too, but it was gone too quickly for her to get a good bead on it. "Doctor Harris has examined the Woodfork boy, and we've reunited him with his grandfather. He's going to be all right. We will be calling the FBI this afternoon once we have the file in order and can hand over the clean case. That's why I needed to speak to you."

"Oh." She actually blinked a couple times. *Reality reset*

in three, two... "Good." She sighed theatrically. "Okay, so, what do you need from me? And, uh, sorry about the *Twin Peaks* crack."

"Forget it. Never saw it." He opened the folder again. "As I said, the doctor confirmed your suspicion. Zarek—that's the boy's name, by the way—Zarek displayed symptoms of hypovolemic shock, hypothermia, and psychological trauma. The injuries to his back and stomach are consistent with having crawled or slid over a smooth surface."

"And the track marks?"

"Consistent with repeated frequent intravenous needle use, but he didn't have any bruising or false start scars that you'd expect with a habitual drug user. No scars of any kind, in fact. Everything fresh. That doesn't excuse your harassing the Sergeant last night, or your implicit threats, but we can overlook that. I just need to know what he said."

"What?"

"When you found him. What did he say to you? Anything."

"I...uh...not much. He was pretty spooked."

Detective Coben sighed the sigh of a beaten man. "I was afraid you'd say that."

"Why?"

"Zarek. He's non-responsive."

"Like, a coma?"

"No, just catatonic. Won't talk to anyone or look at anything."

"Can I see him?" The words were out of her mouth before she realized she was saying them. *So much for Portland.*

DETECTIVE COBEN WAS SURPRISED she offered, then suspicious, but on balance he couldn't see any reason not to. He didn't seem to suspect her of being involved with the kidnapping, and, with a little cajoling, couldn't produce any reason it might be considered evidence tampering, as long as she didn't ask the boy anything about where he'd been or who he'd seen.

She agreed to the terms, and twenty minutes later they were at a disco era double-wide that backed up to a wilderness of scrubby hills. She left her bike at the side of the road. Didn't seem quite polite to pull into the driveway like the Detective did in his official car.

The old man who opened the door didn't have much hair left on top of his latte-colored head, and his beard had gone well past salt-and-pepper frizz to all-salt foam, but he looked sturdy enough to go up and wrest a living from the wilderness—which, it turned out, he had done in his youth. The Doctor was in as well, and stepped out onto the porch to speak to Detective Coben, leaving Rachael at the front door with the old man to make small talk.

"And thank you for finding my grandson. I didn't catch your name?"

"Rachael Oldman." She extended her hand.

"Dennis Woodfork the Third," he took her hand, but rather than shake it, he kissed it gallantly, then gave her a wink.

"The Third? You're from the Irish Royal Family in Exile, right?" Rachael winked back.

"Better. Dennis the First got himself emancipated at five years. Dennis the Second joined the Army and got to be a test pilot in both World Wars."

"Nice! What about you?"

"Oh, I got Nancy and went up in those hills back there," he pointed off toward Shasta, "and got myself a big haul of pay dirt. Bought this very spread here, got to retire and spend my life with my books and my family." He invited her inside.

As she stepped through she said "Nancy is your wiiiiiat the fuck? Oh my god. You weren't kidding. Whoa..."

The living room was stuffed floor to ceiling on every wall with paperbacks. Some names she recognized, most she didn't. She wasn't as well read as Lantham, but she was no slouch in the bookworm department. This old man looked like he'd read everyone from Aeschylus to Ziegler, both alphabetically and temporally.

"'Where your treasure is, there your heart will be also.'"

"And you sunk all your gold into books?"

"Mmm...most of it. Sent my son—Dennis the Fourth—off to school with some of it. Helped my daughters with their weddings. But mostly, yeah." He ran a satisfied, unweathered hand across a shelf full of memoirs "These don't tarnish."

"You've read them all?"

He pointed to a lone shelf a the top of a bookcase, next to the portal to the kitchen. "Haven't read those yet. Saving them for a rainy day."

She wandered over, out of courtesy more than anything, and gave it a look. There was a Bradbury, a Crichton, something by John F. Kennedy, a book about walking across China by a guy named Jenkins, that new Tolkien book that came out a few years ago. "Why these?"

"The last book I haven't read by my favorite authors. Guess I'll have to give in one day, before the years take the chance away from me, but there's something about having that one last chance to hear your favorite voices all fresh and new. Gives you something to live for when the days get dark." His face fell a bit. "Like today."

"I like it. I might have to try that myself." Rachael looked for a good segue into asking investigative questions. This was the part of the job she wasn't sure she was good at yet. Everything else—following up clues, doing the book work and research, running suspects to ground, solving the puzzle, understanding motives—that was all stuff she'd gotten her teeth into. Interrogation, though, she'd not really gotten the chance, either in school or during her time working for Lantham.

And this is one of the reasons I didn't set up my own shop to compete with you, Lantham. Lantham always used to joke that she'd quit and start her own agency and run him out of business, but that was only because he had no idea how much invisible expertise he'd pulled together over the years.

"She wasn't my wife, you know," Dennis said.

"What?"

"Nancy. She wasn't my wife. She was a nag mule I got for twenty-five bucks off of government surplus from the construction gang at Shasta Dam. I was fifteen, just run away from home to try to fight in the war, but they could tell I wasn't near old enough. So I did the next best thing. Great old girl, was old Nancy. Kept me company through some awful scrapes. Saw me safe home with my haul, too." His story had a practiced wistfulness to it. Rachael wondered how much of it was true.

How much gold could a fifteen year old prospector haul out of the mountains a hundred years after the big gold rush, anyway? Enough to last him for life? She had her doubts.

But it was a great story.

"What about Dennis the Fourth?"

He shook his head sadly. "Cancer. Early, too. Small cell. Smoked like a chimney, even though we all told him not to. Bad stuff."

"And his wife?"

"What wife? Had a girlfriend, she was Zerek's momma. Nah, she didn't stick around. Got her own things to do." He shrugged. "Boy was just supposed to be camping..."

"When did you..." She heard footsteps on the porch, coming to the door. "Never mind."

The Detective and the doctor opened the screen and made themselves at home.

"You can speak to him," the Detective said, "as long as you don't mention anything about the incident this morning, or ask him any questions about the case. We," he pointed his finger between himself and the doctor, "will both be present to witness, and the meeting will be recorded to protect the chain of evidence. Agreed?"

At last, some fucking professionalism. It didn't even bother her that it was basically the same thing Detective Coben had said before they left the police station.

Rachael gave a curt not. "Agreed. Anyone mind if I leave my jacket in here? It's getting hot under here."

Zarek was sitting with his back against the wall. A cartoon was playing on a laptop on the nightstand, but all his attention was fixed on the raggedy home-made green gingham teddy bear in his lap. Rachael watched for a moment before she was introduced, and wished she'd taken child development or child psychology rather than just focusing on abnormal and criminal psych for her criminal justice degree. *Note to self: call the admissions department and get my classes for this semester suspended.*

Not that she wanted to drop out, she just wasn't sure

she wanted to finish it up now. One of the things she was trying to decide, and trying to avoid thinking about.

He was posing the bear, whispering unintelligibly to it. Sounded like soothing words. But she couldn't be sure. He was kneading its arms, maybe like massaging them, but, again, she couldn't be sure.

"Zarek," the doctor said, "Do you remember Rachael?"

Zarek nodded, but didn't look up. Kept right on playing with his teddy bear.

"She's come to visit you."

He looked up at that, found her with his eyes, and stared at her. The kind of eyes that you saw in horror movies. Wide, and deep, and full of the kinds of questions too frightening to ask out loud.

Rachael didn't know what she was doing here. She wasn't any good with kids. She wasn't ever going to have any, so she'd figured it was a good idea not to get too worked up about them. Last thing she needed was a maternal instinct, so since high school she'd pretty much had steered clear of anyone too young to drive. She tried to think of a time when she was a kid and she'd been that scared. Big fat blank. So she gave up trying to figure out what to do, and just did the first thing that came to mind:

She sat down on the bed. "Remember me?"

"Uh-huh." He looked down, shame faced. "I lost your jacket. They took it away. The policemen."

"It's okay. They gave it back to me."

"Really?" He looked up at her again. She nodded. "Okay. Good. Yeah. Thanks. It was warm."

"Gotta be when you're driving on the freeway. Lots of wind."

"I like the wind." He perked up. "You ever flown a kite?"

"Yeah."

"My dad gave me this kite. He made it himself."

"You still have it?"

"No," glum again. "I lost it on some power poles. The spool, though. I kept the spool." Excited again. Big eyes, a little bit of a smile. "He made it out of a Lando Calrissian figure. You know the one from Jabba the Hutt's palace, with the disguise and everything?"

"Yeah. With the big teeth on the helmet..."

"That's it. Yeah. You like *Star Wars*?"

Rachael grinned. "Sure, who doesn't? Can I see?"

"Oh..." Zarek's face dropped, like a storm just broke right over his head. When he looked back up, his eyes were swelling with tears just waiting to break. "I don't have it anymore."

"What happened?"

"I lost it." He shrugged. Looked down again.

"I'm sorry."

"If you see it, will you bring it back?"

"Well, I don't know how I would, but if I do...sure."

"Thanks." He sighed. Started grooming his bear.

"Really."

"Promise?"

"Even if I'm a hundred miles away."

That made him smile. Then he got a perplexed look. "Why are you here, anyway?"

"Oh. I just wanted to ask you something."

"What?"

"Are you okay? I mean, last time I saw you, you were pretty shaken up and everything." In one of her psych courses her prof had said that mirroring someone's cadence was a good way to make them open up. If she could get him to remember something...

He pulled the ears of the little bear. "Yeah, I'm fine."

You just backed yourself into a conversational corner, you idiot. Maybe she should get sales training. Open ended questions, leading the witness, eliciting trust, all that kind of thing. Had to be useful in interrogations, right?

Rachael waited a full twenty seconds, hoping something would come to her, but nothing did. Instead, she patted the bed and said:

"Well, I guess that's all. I just wanted to make sure you got home to your grandpa okay. Take care of yourself, all right?"

He nodded, slipping back into his sullen self-isolation.

Rachael shifted, to get up, and suddenly the kid was in her arms, wrapped around her like a capuchin dangling from its mother.

She hugged him back, since she didn't know what else to do.

"Thanks for letting me use your jacket," he

whispered.

She patted his back. "You're welcome."

He loosened his grip on her neck, looked at her right in the face, and in a voice too low for anyone else to hear it, he said "Don't let the vampires get ya."

Then he let go and nodded firmly at her, waiting for an answer.

"Okay," she said, "I won't." Because she didn't know what else to say.

Zarek went back to looking at his bear. Rachael slipped off the bed and followed the professionals back out through the panel-veneered hallway into the libraryish living room.

The doctor was thrilled that she'd gotten through to him. The detective was flabbergasted. The grandfather was fighting back tears of relief. She'd been such a help, was there anything they could do for her?

Not really. Permission to leave town would pretty much do it. And the name of a good health club or a community center where she could shower off the road grime and change before the next section of the trip.

There wasn't anything like that up here, what with it being a small town and all, but there was a shower in the department locker room if she'd like to come back to police headquarters.

As showers went, it wasn't exactly luxurious, but it had hot water and soap and clean towels, which was about all she needed out of it. A place to sleep would have been good, too, but she figured she could catch a nap along the road. Wal-Marts were good for laying out her sleeping bag and getting a few dozen snores in relative safety. Once she got to Portland, she'd get an AirBnB and plan her next move or two.

No rush. No worry. Not when there was hot water unwinding the knots in her wrists and neck. Her fault for taking a crotch rocket on a road trip. Her ass was still sore, too, more sore now that it was getting a proper warm up. No padding on the seat. She resolved for the fifteenth time since she'd left home to spring for a padded seat cover next time she was near a good custom shop, a promise to herself she knew she wouldn't keep.

There was snow up on the pass—it dropped this morning. It wasn't socked in, she wouldn't need chains, but it was going to be chilly. She might need to get a second cowl to protect her neck from the wind—the one she had wasn't thick enough to stand up to real cold, and she didn't much fancy getting frostbite on her throat.

All the little details of the next leg of the trip made it easy to slip back into the anonymous life she'd carved out for herself, a life that would last until her money ran out. If she could keep picking up the odd modeling job like the one she'd done in Reno, or some dominatrix work, the kind of stuff that paid cash, she could extend the three months of remaining reserves. She didn't know for how long—sooner or later there wasn't going to be enough to pay the insurance on her bike or the rent on the apartment back home, and she'd either have to return and get a real job or go home and pack up all her stuff.

Or maybe she could get Nya to help. It wasn't Nya she wanted to avoid, not really. Sure, she was embarrassed at slipping out like she had, but Nya understood. Lantham wouldn't—or, she couldn't afford to have him do it, cause she couldn't live with doing that to him—so she didn't want to get him involved, but maybe...

Well, maybe when she got out of the shower.

First she had to work the knots out of her forearms and wrists. Crotch rockets don't come stock with cruise control, and Rachael had never fitted an aftermarket—an oversight she was paying for now. Holding her right hand at tension for a few hundred miles tended to make her grow little golf balls up by her elbow. And she wasn't even paying for the hot water. And she didn't have to worry about it running out.

"...and the one in Fort Bragg? That makes eleven 'back country disappearances' in five counties, and the assholes still don't have any idea where they're all going." A woman's voice, over the row of lockers that separated the shower cubicles from the rest of the place.

"Hell, Sue, I thought it was bears until this morning."

"You would." A locker opened. "You hear about this IDF thing?"

"Yeah, they woke me up with it. I don't know what the hell they think we're supposed to do about it." A man's voice. Small enough police station that they shared a locker room—old enough that it was probably built before there were any women on the force. Rachael had no clue what sexual politics were like up here in the land that time forgot, but she figured they had to lag behind a fair bit. Why else would anyone move out here except to stay as far away from the churn and change of the big city as possible? Standing astride history yelling 'stop', like her poli-sci prof used to say.

Locker rooms are great for eavesdroppers. No such thing as a private conversation in a locker room. No way to keep your voice from bouncing off the hard metal lockers and the concrete floors and the grout-and-ceramic shower walls, especially in a place this old where everything was poured concrete instead of bolt-in partitions.

She kept rubbing her forearm, and kept quiet, hoping nobody would look around at the cubicles and notice her suit and silks and duffel hanging just outside. *Just another brother officer in here, guys, nothing worth noticing at all.*

They didn't come around to look, but she kept her ears strained for anything else interesting.

"Yeah, well," the woman said, "if Honey doesn't get his shit together on this IDF thing we're gonna have the whole world landing on top of us. You're keeping copies of your notebooks, right?"

"Just like you said."

"Maybe we won't need 'em, but just in case. Only a matter of time before this sicko starts shopping out in the open." A locker door slammed, followed by another. Then the soft, hard-metal click of weapons being load-checked. "You catch the score last night?"

"Yeah, yeah, I saw it," the man said, "I've got lunch covered."

"You didn't watch, did you?"

"Are you kidding? My girlfriend brought over *Game of Thrones*. Gotta catch up before next season..."

Their footsteps carried them around the corner and out of earshot.

Hell of a coincidence, hearing that kind of talk after what I saw this morning.

Rachael gave up on getting rid of the knots in one session, figured she'd get a masseuse to go over them once she got to Portland.

But she had to figure out what to do before she blew town. If this was the eleventh disappearance they knew about, and they hadn't called the Feds in, maybe there was some weird kind of Twin-Peaksy thing going on up here.

Still, there were right ways and wrong ways to do things. The wrong way would mean rattling the cages of people that could put her in one.

Rachael got dressed as quick as she could. New underwear, her second set of silks so she wouldn't smell like a barnyard and wreck the armor, then her long-sleeved thermal shirt, then her leather pants, boots, and jacket. The cowl was in the seat compartment back in the bike.

She hoisted her bag, took her leave—thanking Detective Coben on the way out for the use of the shower—secured her gear on her bike, slipped on her cowl and helmet, and headed out of town to a rest area about forty miles north, and not very well populated. She found the furthest spot, away from anyone, took out her phone, put the battery in. She was a member of the twenty-first century for the second time today.

No messages waiting for her—well, none new since the eight thousand "where the fuck are you" messages that she'd found this morning and ignored. She kept ignoring them, since the entire point of being out here on the ass end of nowhere was so that nobody would know where the fuck she was.

Now, of course, she was going to tell everyone exactly where the fuck she was, whether she liked it or not. Some things were more important than her stupid wangsty bullshit.

This time, though, she wasn't going to call Lantham. Not at first, anyway. Not until she had the lay of the land.

"Oh. My. God." Nya's thick low alto crackled with excitement on the other end of the bad connection. "Twatmonster! Are you really calling? Tell me it's you and not some jerk off who stole your phone?"

"It's really me."

"You're alive and not dead and everything?"

"Well, as far as I know. No ghosts, no zombies, no fucking vampires." What had that been about, anyway?

The longer she let it sit, the creepier it sounded. What kind of sick fuck had done what kind of sick fucking thing to that poor kid to make him try to warn her about vampires? "What's going on down there? Lantham still mooning it up over Agent Ellis?"

"Lantham's been shot."

Rachael nearly dropped the phone. "What? He's alive, right?"

"Yeah, he's alive. Sleeping in his office."

"What? Why isn't he in the hospital?"

"He got in a big gunfight this morning. Mercenaries, he said. They had a shotgun, but not a good shot..."

"What, did they just wing him?"

"Yeah. Anyway, he was doing this job for your Dad..." Nya filled her in on what little she knew—something about a courier job, and a car accident, and a gunfight in the mountains by Pescadero. Rachael sighed as she listened. If she'd been there, none of this would have happened—she'd have run the errand herself, since her Dad's little black bag jobs were the kind of thing Lantham would pass off on her.

But, according to Nya, Lantham didn't let it get him down too much. He'd done his job, saved the day, and made it home in time to get a nap before planning his next move. Wound up with a couple clients in the bargain, even. By the time Nya finished telling it, Rachael was holding onto her bike in order to stay up, from laughing so hard.

First good, hard laugh she'd had in weeks. She didn't

much want to think about what that should tell her. Besides, she had other priorities at the moment.

"Look," she said after Nya finished with a second story involving Lantham's dog Klepto and how he'd scared FBI Special Agent Erica Ellis out of the shower and almost out the front door naked two weeks ago, "I was wondering, I mean, I know I got no real business asking, but could you do me a favor?"

"Twatmonster..." Nya had that tone that sounded like she was gearing up to give a lecture, so Rachael headed her off at the pass.

"I know, I know. Okay, fine. I just landed in the middle of a big pile of weird shit up here," Rachael quickly filled Nya in on her morning. "Could you have a poke around and see if there's any rumors or stories or anything about missing kids or serial kidnappers or killers or anything up here? Look all over NorCal. This whole business smells a lot more complicated than the cops are trying to make it look, and I don't feel right about leaving it alone. And don't tell Lantham."

"Of course, but you have to promise me something."

"What's that?"

"You'll call him. He's worried sick about you. He hides it by pretending he's still angry, but he walks around like he's missing his right arm. Please, let him know you're okay, at least? I don't think he's gonna be right again till he hears from you. *Really* hears from you."

Rachael swallowed around the lump of sand that had suddenly formed in her throat. "Okay. I guess I can do that. I just...need a few minutes."

"That's okay, he's still asleep. Hey, did I tell you what happened with his nephew?"

"Tricia's son?"

"That's the one. Oh man, this guy is something else. He shows up here in this van..." Rachael didn't even listen, really, to the rest of the story. She just laughed along, enjoying the moment with Nya's voice, and trying not to wreck it by breaking down. It made all the parts of home hurt for not being there.

She missed her bed. She missed her cat. She missed the way the bay breeze cooled things off in the early evening, even after a hot day. She missed Nya. And Klepto. And Sir Seligman, and Scuttlebutt. And her Dad. Her Mom too, even though they weren't all that close. Even Lantham. The whole world felt like a bruise all of a sudden, but at least it was a bruise wrapped around a bad joke, and a good laugh.

She went with it. Let it hurt. Let it fucking throb like a hangnail as big as Mount Shasta. You wait too long for a bone to knit, it doesn't heal right, it can't take your weight, and you're crippled for life. After this morning, Rachael figured she'd pretty much run out that clock. Which was why she stayed on until Nya said, "Uh-oh, it looks like...Hey boy!"

"Kelpto?" Must've been. She could hear his tale beating against the floor.

"Yeah," said Nya, now keeping her voice low. "Clarke's up. I better go."

"Email me that stuff I asked for?"

"Course. You know you don't even have to ask."

"Yeah, I know."

"You'll call him right?"

"Yeah. In a bit. I love you."

"Oh. He's got a temp. I'll text you the number. Love you too. Bye-a." Nya whispered the last bit, and Rachael heard Lantham's voice in the background before the line went dead.

She took a breath. Realized that she needed a few more, decided that it had to be the altitude. And her complete lack of anything resembling a plan.

What are you doing, huh? Why aren't you on the road up to Portland? You think you're going to just breeze into town and save the world?

Well, yes, that was basically what she was thinking, and now that she'd caught herself at it she was pretty goddamned embarrassed about it, too.

The rest area parking lot followed a finger of land next to the Klamath river. Rachel jumped the fence and went down to the river proper, sat on the bank for a little bit, tried to sort herself out.

She was going back. Eleven missing kids, and no FBI involvement yet? That was heavy duty creepsville stuff. She had to assume that nobody was going to do anything about it—maybe they had something standing in their way. Maybe they were all in on it.

Or maybe there just wasn't anything to go on, and there wasn't any pattern they'd put together. A missing kid wasn't a kidnapped kid—her Dad had told her that once. Some kids run away. Some kids get lost. Some kids die. That one cop said he thought it was bears—the bear population had been making news even down in San Francisco, so that wasn't stupid on the face of it. And out here with all this wilderness around, those things all had to be possibilities. Maybe mountain lions, too. And avalanches. And caves and cliffs. So maybe the cops were all honest. Maybe they were even competent.

But she couldn't take that chance. Maybe she was only twenty-one. Maybe she'd only been in the snoop business for a year and a half. And maybe, yeah, okay, just maybe she was trying to fix her personal problems by sticking her nose into other people's business, but, goddammit, that didn't mean that the job didn't need to be done, or that she couldn't do it.

The river seemed to agree. Or, at least, it didn't seem to notice. The world was like that. Didn't give much of a shit as long as you didn't get in its way.

Well, she gave a shit, and she was about to get in its way. So she needed to do this the smart way. She couldn't just ride back into town on the bike, dressed like an action figure, and start poking around. It was a small town. They'd recognize her. Bikers stuck out at the best of times. A girl on a race bike on the open road stuck out double.

Okay, so she couldn't go back right away. She needed to change her look. Pick up a different vehicle or hitchhike in, maybe. She'd need somewhere to store

Carmen. She'd need different clothes, different hair. Maybe some glasses.

Some different ID wouldn't be all that bad either. She'd need to get a job. That might be tough in a small town, but she could figure something out. Somewhere she'd be able to pick up gossip and plug into the town. A bar, maybe.

And then...

Well, then she'd need to wait. Maybe for a long time. Wait and listen. Until she had enough to prove something really was going on. Enough that the FBI would listen.

At least she knew a couple friendly agents.

Rachael scrambled back up the bank, hopped the broken-down cyclone fence, got to the bike. First thing she had to do was get to Medford, pick up some supplies. She broke down her Ruger into inoffensive pieces, locked them all together in the lock box under her seat, stowed the ammunition in a saddle bag. Then she threw her leg over and unhooked her helmet from the handlebars, and...

Well, she *had* promised she'd call Lantham. Might as well do it now. She pulled her phone out, found a text from Nya. Dialed the number.

It rang a couple times. Then:

"This is Clarke Lantham." Scratchy. Digitized. Just at the edge of good reception.

"Lantham?"

She waited.

He didn't say anything. Or, at least, she couldn't hear him. The silence dragged on until she was shaking down in her gut.

"Lantham? Can you hear me?" She wasn't sure if she hoped he did or not.

"Yeah," he said.

She took a breath to ask how he was doing, when he said:

"You've got a hell of a nerve, you know that?"

In the kind of voice he used around dead bodies. Cold rage.

She closed her eyes, took a breath.

"I know."

"Do you," he hissed, "know how long..."

"I'm not an idiot, Lantham. I know." Like she'd been able to think of anything else, with all the energy she put in to staying off his radar.

"So what do you want?" He hated her. It was all there in his voice. He had about as much time for her as he did for a telemarketer.

"I...I heard you were shot." *Brilliant scintillating conversation, Rachael. Why don't you ask how the weather is next?*

"Yeah, that happens when my partner isn't there to watch my back. One of those things you learn when you take your job seriously."

She couldn't snap back at him. She wanted to, oh god did she want to, but she couldn't. He was right, and he wasn't saying anything that hadn't been going through her head. All she could do, really, was beg him:

"Lantham...don't."

"Don't what? Don't..." He stopped. Like he was doing everything he could not to yell at his phone in public. "Look, I'm on a case right now. Your life isn't in danger, right? You're still breathing? Not locked up in a basement anywhere?"

"No," she said. And hoped, for just a second, that they'd actually get to talk. "Nothing like..."

"Then fuck you." And he hung up.

Rachael wiped some tears off her cheeks, stuffed the phone in her bra, and kicked the bike to life.

"Well fuck you too, Lantham. See what you think when I find the asshole who's stealing these kids."

The road north was as clear as it needed to be. Traffic moved slow, but it moved. In forty minutes she was over the border and into Ashland, with California well behind her.

For the moment.

1:00 AM, FRIDAY

BEFORE I GET STARTED, you have to understand, I just wanted to take a walk with my girlfriend and my dog. That's all. I still had prickle-pain from where I'd caught the edge of a shotgun blast a couple months back.

The cool air helped with that. That's why I went out. I never thought that taking in the neighborhood's wee hours with my girlfriend would tip over the first domino in a chain that would end with everyone I love running for cover. That's just the way my luck runs.

"Clarke, Jesus, you'll wake up everyone." The buff, willow-limbed redhead in the blue suede jacket said it without laughing herself. She was walking next to me, trying her best not to have a sense of humor. That's her job, though, keeping the straight face. Erica Ellis, the woman who officially makes me the luckiest doofus this side of Pee Wee Herman. Took her work not to laugh, too. She had to bite her knuckles to pull it off, one of the little things she does that breaks that cool-as-steel FBI facade they trained into her at Quantico. Kinda like watching a tiger get all cuddly when you give it a beach ball. And she wonders why I put up with her work schedule.

Silly tiger.

"Serve you right, to get hauled in for disturbing the piece." I kept my voice low so it didn't, in fact, wake up everyone in the houses we were walking past. "You think Nya could bail us out? Or would we have to call Rivers?" That would be Special Agent-in-Charge Ronald Rivers, for those of you joining this torrid tale in progress. Her boss, and apparently born with an abnormal affection for alliteration. After his parents saddled him with initials that make him feel at home at every railroad crossing in America, he went and hired Erica Ellis as his chief advancement agent on special assignments, and one time when I got her drunk enough she let slip that there was a Leslie Lawrence and a Daniel Dartmouth on the team too.

She flared her eyebrows at me. "If you ever so much as..."

"Cross my heart, hope to die, stick a thousand needles in my eye," I tried to hold up my right hand, but Klepto was pulling, so I had to switch his leash before making with the solemnity. "I wouldn't dream of it."

"Be careful when you say that. You talk in your sleep."

Well, she's right, I do. I've recorded it. I sound like an aphasic who's been filled with the Holy Spirit. Probably a good thing. My dreams aren't something I'd willingly inflict on an enemy, much less a bed mate.

"You didn't read the part of the license agreement

where it says 'listen at your own risk.'" I smiled at her. She smiled at me. Sometimes, that's all it takes to make a too-warm summer night into something special.

Or, at least, I thought so. Sir Klepto the Maniac, my teenaged pit-mastiff cross, had other ideas. For him, it takes a really interesting tree, or fire hydrant, or—in this case—juniper bush, overgrown with African daisies and filled with interesting urine deposits and little creatures he can chase. When he was a puppy, not that long ago, all it took to make him ignore the canine community bulletin board and come to heel was an encouraging noise. Now, it took a stout leash and a goodly amount of patience. Another year or so, and he'd be all grown up, and subduing bad guys by drowning them with kisses.

I clicked my cheek and jiggled the leash. "Klepto, come on. Leave the daisies alone. That's not your flower bed."

He looked back and whined at me. I cocked my eyebrow, which he took as some kind of permission, and dove back into the bush.

"Aieee!" The bush seemed to have an opinion about this.

"Um..." That's me being intelligent at one in the morning. Impressive, eh?

"Who's there?" Erica was all business. Reached for her gun, which she wasn't wearing, then rolled her eyes at herself.

A shame. There ain't a lot sexier in the world than a redhead with a gun.

"Just me. It's just me." A hand poked out of the bush, a little hand. Not easy to see whose hand it was in the as-dark-as-it-gets-in-the-suburbs.

But I knew the voice. "Teddy? That you?"

"Yeah. Yeah, Mister Lantham, it's me. Ow!"

"Who? Wait..." Erica said, "Is this the kid from..."

"Yeah." Neighbor kid from three houses down. We met when I asked him to stop doing rail slides on the retaining wall at the front of my yard, on the grounds that I had a migraine and didn't want to get arrested for shooting a child in the head. After that, he started shadowing me. Evidently, when you're ten, having a private detective in the neighborhood is the next best thing to living next to a spy or a Nazi war criminal. I gave up and decided to like him when he opened up his own detective agency catering to the other kids in the neighborhood, and started coming by for consults on Saturday afternoons. "Teddy, what are you doing out at this hour?"

"I snuck out." He climbed out between the branches, came out covered in crumbs and prickles from the juniper bark. He wasn't more than ten—I didn't know for sure cause I'd never actually asked him his age, and he never volunteered it. He seemed to think that if he didn't mention that he was less than twenty-five, I wouldn't notice.

"Won't you get in trouble?"

"Not if you don't turn me into the Gestapo."

"Hell of a thing to call your mother. Teddy Stride,

this is Erica Ellis, Special Agent with the FBI."

His eyes went big as saucers. "FBI? Really?"

She nodded. "Really."

"Are you Mister Lantham's big squeeze?"

She chuckled. "Big squeeze?"

"Well, that's what Nya calls you."

"You know Nya too? That can't be safe..." She gave me the kind of look that said *You've explained to her about the age of consent, I assume.* Erica has some pretty traditional ideas about relationships, and she thinks anyone that has Nya's ideas about them must be a barely-contained sexual danger to self and others.

Which goes to show you that even really fabulous people can be a bit dippy around the edges.

"It's *fine.*" It was my turn to roll my eyes, and not really care is she saw. She wasn't going to pick a fight about it in front of the kid, and it was now officially on my list of things to talk over with her at length and over bourbon.

"Yeah, she's great. Why?"

"Forget it, Ted. It's a thing."

"You say that a lot..."

"Hmph." Erica was still smiling through the harrumph, which I took to be a good sign. "You've got no idea."

"Ted, dude, why are you out?"

"Oh! Well...um..." It's never a good sign when a kid like this goes sheepish.

"You're screwing up my date. If I don't get laid

tonight it's your fault..."

"Clarke..." Note to self: Don't mention sex in front of the girlfriend and the prepubescent at the same time. She has a thing about that, something she calls 'propriety.' My mother used to use that word sometimes, and I still don't think she knew what it meant. Erica doesn't either.

"...so make with the syllables, or I will call the Gestapo."

"Okay, okay, just...look, can we talk in your office?" He was looking around like he was afraid the fence might overhear him.

"Why?"

"Well...I kinda need to hire you."

I sighed. "Look, Teddy, really, just come by this Saturday and I'll consult like usual..."

"No, no, it's not that. It's..." He stopped talking, closed the distance between us, then stood on his toes and whispered in the general direction of my head, which was in orbit a few miles above his. "It's my Dad. Something's wrong with him."

"Like, medically?"

"No. Like, I think he saw something...awful."

"Like what?"

"Like somebody got beat up. Or killed maybe."

I blinked. Then I did it again just to make sure that my eyes were still there.

"Where?"

"At work."

"Teddy...he works at a college." He didn't just work at a college, he worked at Trubody Bible College over in the City, which is only a little bit less uptight and freaked out than a traffic warden who's been strapped to the front of a stock car on free beer night. People that boring don't commit murder, except by euthanizing their congregations with deeply probing readings of bible verses like Deuteronomy 23:12.

Okay, so I spent a little time in Vacation Bible School when I was thirteen. In my defense, it was the only way for a good Catholic boy to have any chance at kissing the cute girls from the Baptist church across the road.

"I know. But there's things going on there. Big things, and I ain't supposed to tell anyone, but..." He looked at me with this kind of solemn panic, like he was willing me to believe, and willing me to believe I was the only hope.

"All right, kid, you got yourself a snoop. Do you mind if the Fed listens in? It's not technically in her jurisdiction, but she might have some tips."

Teddy squinted at her, like he was trying to get the size of her. "I guess so."

"Well, then, best way to stay ahead of spies is to keep walking. Come on." I coaxed Klepto back onto the sidewalk, and the four of us crowded the place up.

It's about half a mile around the block I live on. Klepto'd ferreted out our interloper about halfway down the first leg, so we had plenty of time to talk.

"It started last month. Dad stopped coming home

until real late, after Mom was in bed. Didn't matter how late she stayed up, he just wouldn't come home. Like he was circling or something, waiting for her light to go out, you know? Well, they got in a fight, and I heard it cause I stayed up to find out what was going on. He was saying we might have to move, *like* way up north. It's a lot cheaper up there, you know? We could buy a house and everything, maybe even have a horse!"

Teddy paused. Then scowled. "But Mom wasn't happy about it. Dad talked and talked, trying to convince her, but the more he talked the more it sounded like he was scared, not happy.

"Well, the next morning he was gone again, and wouldn't come back for anything. Even when I called. And he kept doing that. Just never coming home."

I didn't make the obvious observation, but I shared a look with Erica. She thought the same thing I did, but how do you tell a fifth grader from a good churchgoing home that his father's cheating on his mother?

Instead, I said "How does that add up to him seeing someone get killed?"

"That wasn't how I found out. Duh."

"So how did you find out?"

"Well, it was last night. I got up to go to the bathroom, and, well, you know how our back bathroom has that window that looks out on the lawn, right?"

"Yeah." I'd never actually been to his house, but he'd told me about how it was one of his favorite escape hatches before. His family's back yard stretches half the length of the block, so if he wants to get to anywhere in the neighborhood, all he has to do is get out to the back of the house, run out to the yard, and hop the fence into an apartment complex parking lot. Since his parents sleep at the front of the house, they never know he's gone on his secret missions. That setup's gonna serve him really well in a couple years when he finds out about girls and creative driving and all the other fun ways you can get in trouble when you're in high school.

"Well, I was looking out while I was taking a leak, and I see him out there in the back yard, just sitting on the tire swing. All bent over, you know? I mean, you know Dad, you know he never does that."

"Sure." Tom—his father—actually had a generally depressive air about him, but he was one of those stiff-upper-lip types who didn't want anyone to see anything but the smiling veneer.

"Well, I went out to see what was wrong. I took my phone, like you taught me. I recorded it. Glad I did too, cause wow..."

"Hey, wait a second," Erica said, "Did you ask him if you could record him?"

"No, of course not."

I could feel Erica's eyes drilling a disapproving hole in the side of my head. "You know it's a felony in California to record someone without their knowledge, right? It's called wiretapping, and they can send you to jail for it."

"But you do it all the time Mister..."

"That's because I'm an idiot." I risked a glance up to Erica. Yeah, I was in trouble. I decided to hold off on explaining how to decide which laws are flexible and how to avoid getting caught until we were safely away from Federal surveillance. "I'll explain later. You got the phone with you?"

"Sure."

"Mind if I borrow it? I'll give it back tomorrow."

"Okay..."

"Come over, say, four o'clock. After school..."

"It's summer vacation."

"Okay, so come over at two. I'll give you your phone back, we'll talk."

"I've only got twenty bucks."

"We'll figure something out."

"So you'll take the case?"

"If what's on that recording squares with what you're telling me, I'll think about it."

We shook on it. He slipped me his phone, then ran ahead to get back in bed before the Gestapo did a bed check. Before he was even around the next corner, Erica said:

"You shouldn't be toying with that boy that way, you know."

"Who's toying?"

"You can't possibly think he's serious."

"Sweetheart, he just gave me his phone." I held up the none-too-cheap HTC. "He's serious."

"There's a difference between serious and right.

What are you gonna do when you catch his father schtupping the secretary?"

"I'll figure it out. Trust me."

I can't be sure, but I think someone once said that right before getting hit by a train.

APPARENTLY, MOST PEOPLE HAVE this thing they do after a good walk in the night air with a woman like Erica Ellis, and it's something I've never understood.

No, I don't mean peeling her out of her clothes and feasting on every inch of her like she was a ripe mango. I don't mean upending her at the edge of the bed and painting a smile on her face as wide as the sky, or laying in a tangle afterwards and feeling the summer night air playing in eddies through the sweat sheen, or tasting her salty skin when you nuzzle her cause she's shifting against you, half-delirious, like she doesn't know whether she's dreaming or wants to have another go. I don't even mean trying to keep the hellhound on the floor even though he resents that there's a woman laying in the spot he usually sneaks into when I'm not looking.

No, I mean the other thing. That thing Erica did when she came down from all the excitement. That part where she closes her eyes and starts in with the soft breathing and the occasional twitching. I hear the normals call it "sleep."

I don't do that, at least not very well. Never been

able to. Most people seem to have brains that need to recharge so they can figure things out. Mine doesn't turn off unless it has just the right amount of noise. If there isn't anything for me to worry about, my lizard-brain hunts around like a skittery wolf trying to find its way out of a cage. But if I go to bed without putting all the really interesting puzzles to rest—say, for example, I've left a Rubik's cube half finished or I've lost a piece to the holiday jigsaw or I left a game of Tetris on pause—then I get locked in these loops, round and round, trying to solve the puzzle so I can relax and get to sleep.

Ever since I was a kid, near as I can tell, I've been this way. Half the reason I got into police work in the first place was so I could have a steady stream of arms-length problems to solve, because my insomnia was killing me. Worked pretty well too, right up until I tried to solve the Chief's domestic troubles by sleeping with his wife so that she wouldn't henpeck him to death. Once they threw me out on my ass for that one, I tried doing other jobs, but wound up getting stuck in the PI business. It was the only way I could get any sleep—I still don't sleep well when I don't have a case, even though I've settled down a bit in my old age.

Never could figure out why, either. Doc Samson—my therapist—told me once that it's because I was trying to solve some kind of trauma in my past, and that I should take a break from everything and try to work it out, so that I wouldn't be so driven by things I didn't understand. But I don't actually remember being molested by a goat while drunk off my ass on bad whiskey I'd scored from a local tramp who needed directions to the Satanic Child Sacrifice festival, and if I can't remember something like that than I figure that my brain's too corroded to do anything useful in a therapist's office anyway, so I solved that problem by firing her ass.

Now, this neighbor kid, Teddy, the hero-worshipy one, he was probably imagining things. His parents were probably on the outs, maybe about this move they might have to make, maybe because they just stopped talking for the normal reasons people do that when they've been together long enough. When not rocking the boat is more important than being honest.

Important skill, that one. I might be married now if I'd ever learned that one.

Then again, dating Erica, it might not matter. She's got the same kind of "can't keep her mouth shut" problem I do.

But he was a sharp kid. Really sharp. And he was going to be a lot of trouble someday, probably not too long from now, and if there's one thing about a kid that makes me sit up and notice, it's when they're trouble. Kids that are trouble are the kinds that grow up and don't ever forget how to be themselves. They're the ones that write books and invent things they saw on *Star Trek* and generally make life safe for weirdos everywhere. Crazy-determined sharp kids grow up to be batshit-crazy determined adults who can reorganize the planet before breakfast, and then have the nerve to invite everyone else to come play with them.

And, on top of all that, he really wasn't a half-bad detective. He had a good people-sense, and after three months in business he was actually earning some money at it, which, trust me, is not as easy as it looks.

So if he was really this freaked out, and convinced something bad was going on, he might just be on to something. Probably not actually murder, but maybe his Dad was having to do something he found distasteful at work, or maybe he was trying to figure out how to move the family, or whether to look for another job. Whatever it was, it had changed the behavior patterns of Tom Stride, and Tom was a pretty solid guy. Not exactly my wheelhouse, what with the whole Bible College thing, but a solid guy anyway. Told you what he believed, stuck to it, wasn't an asshole about it.

If he really was in trouble, I wanted to know how. It wasn't just that his kid was my client, or that I liked the kid and didn't want to see him go nuts while his parents split up. It's that, when a kid like Teddy gets worried, there's usually something to worry about.

And that worried me. And it wasn't the kind of worry that got my brain to settle down at all.

So what do you do?

Kiss the girlfriend on her sleepy head, make sure she's really well gone.

Slide out of bed. Poking around might wake the girlfriend, so don't worry about clothes. You haven't got anything the roommate hasn't seen before a hundred times.

Besides, she's asleep anyway.

Pad your bare feet through the house, head down to the basement, pick up some knock-around clothes from the laundry room.

Remember that you left the kid's cell phone up in the living room, head back up the stairs, through the kitchen, to the living room, get the phone.

Stop and pet the Klepto so he doesn't bark at being ignored as he trails your not-quite-naked-anymore ass.

Exit the building through the back door, cross the lawn to the office, set up at the desk and enjoy the early morning quiet.

Then, when all that's done, and you've got the smell of fresh Costa Rican coffee tickling your nostrils from the office drip-brewer, then you fire up the computer, copy the eavesdropping files off the phone, and start to listen to them.

Most recent file. Looked to be about twenty minutes long. I popped my studio phones on and pulled the thing up in Audacity.

I'm not dumb enough to try playing a cell phone recording straight through a player. Any time you jostle the phone, any time your clothes brush by the pickup, you get bass spikes that can blow your eardrums out. Even if it doesn't it can make your ears hurt like hell if you're listening closely on ear phones—and, if you're wanting to make out finer points of a badly mic'd conversation, you have to listen on good cans.

So I ran a standard high-pass/low-pass EQ on the thing to cut out the ambient noise, then did a few experiments randomly on the timeline to make sure I was getting both voices nice and clear—wound up boosting things around 400hz so that I could bring Tom's voice a little further to the front. A little muddy, because I couldn't boost his consonants, but still perfectly intelligible.

Now that I had something I could listen to without making my ears bleed, I filled my "Grouch Fuel" mug with some el cheapo Colombian that would make Juan Valdez request Bolivian citizenship, sat back in my chair, and queued the cursor up to the first part of the waveform that looked like it might contain a human voice, about forty seconds into the twelve minute recording.

"Hey Dad..." Teddy's voice. Very tentative, almost meek. None of the brash he habitually used when he was talking shop with me.

"Oh. Hey. You should be in bed."

"So should you." There wasn't a challenge in his voice. Just concern, exactly the right pitch to disarm any reasonable man. Either the kid was really worried about his Dad, or he was already a hell of a grift. "What's wrong?"

"Nothing, nothing. Just enjoying the night."

"Dad, come on. You gotta talk to somebody, right? I mean, you won't talk to Mom. You don't come home for dinner. You don't come home when anyone's awake. You aren't even singing at church. Are you...I mean...are you..."

"Teddy, I mean it. You need to go inside." Tom's voice was a lot closer to the mic now. Ted had to be standing within arm's reach now.

"I can't sleep either." He huffed. Sat down.

"Why? What is it?"

"Oh...you know, just this thing." Bored, petulant. Ashamed, almost.

"What thing?"

"Nothing, I guess. Hey, you remember how you grew up on the farm, right?"

"I seem to remember something like that." A smile in Tom's voice here.

"Well, I've always wondered—I heard you tell Uncle Arthur about how you got in trouble this one time when you were herding cows, cause Grandpa thought you would ruin the milk, and he made you clean the stables for a month instead."

Tom laughed. "Oh, wow, I haven't thought about that in years. When did you hear that?"

"Christmas, when we went to visit."

"That was six years ago..."

"I was waiting up to catch Mom playing Santa Claus. You guys were laughing, so I hid behind the curtain and listened."

"Right."

"Wait, you had this joke you told Uncle Arthur, I

didn't get it. How'd that go...right. What's a 'hair lip on a knob polisher' mean?"

"Uh...I'll tell you when you're older."

"Dad, come on, I'm almost ten." Okay, so I guessed him a little old—in my defense, the kid's good.

"Trust me, some things you won't get even if I explain them to you."

"Daaaad."

"You said you wanted to know the story about the cows, right?"

"Yeah."

"Well, every day after school I had to drive them in from the pasture to the barn so we could milk them in the morning."

"On a horse?"

"Yeah."

"Did you get to use a whip?"

"Well, actually, two border collies and a stick."

"That's lame."

Tom laughed. "That's what I thought. It took *forever*, every day. I had trouble getting enough time to do my homework, and time to watch *The A Team*? Well, forget it. So, for my birthday when I was about your age, I got a BB gun. I figured that when a cow got out of line, I'd just shoot it on the rump..."

"Rump?"

"Butt."

"Oh."

"And it'd sting it, and it would come back in line, and

I wouldn't have to keep running around, and trying to remember all the whistle codes for the dogs, and getting close enough to whack the trouble ones."

"It's really that complicated? I mean, they're cows, right? That's like...you know...live hamburgers."

"Jerseys aren't bad. Not like Brahmans or Angus. But they can still kill you."

"Wait, *cows* can kill you?"

This provoked Tom down a long and pretty dull explanation of cattle breeds and which ones were ornery, which then took a left turn into tales about trying to collect eggs from Rhode Island Red hens, which are evidently not so much chickens as they are feathered switchblades with attitude.

Eventually, he wound back around to: "So, anyway, I had the BB gun, and I'm shooting the cows..."

"How did it work?"

"So well. Like a charm. They got out of line, I popped them, they came back in line."

"Cool!"

"Yeah. But Dad—your Grandpa—saw me the second day out. He got home early from his construction job, and he *completely* lost it. And...well, you heard. I got grounded, and had to clean the stables, and your Aunt Ginger got to do the herding for the next three weeks."

"Why? I mean, it worked, right?"

"He was sure I'd miss, and hit an udder or something."

"Like...the cow's boobs? But a BB gun wouldn't put a hole in them..."

"Nah, but it'd bruise them, and that makes scar tissue which make the cow produce less, and that makes us lose our farm and...well, you've heard how your Grandpa gets."

"You mean the part where he hates kids?"

"Oh, come on, Teddy. He doesn't hate kids. He just...doesn't get them."

"Uh huh."

"Okay, so he's kind of a jerk sometimes. But he's, you know, he's from a different world."

"Well, I know what that's like." Ted said it with just the right amount of hopelessness in his voice that I wanted to reach for my wallet. There was only one thing his Dad could say to that.

"What do you mean? What's wrong?"

Set the hook, kid. Set the hook. He had me cheering him on while I listened to a recording. That takes a special something.

"I'm not supposed to say..."

"Why not? Did someone do something to you?" That kind of worry that comes from someone who tries to keep their stranger-danger paranoia under control, which means they're looking for any excuse to bust loose with the who's-been-touching-my-kid shtick.

"Uck, no, Dad, come on, get real."

"Okay..." Clearly confused.

"No, no, I mean...okay, I guess...look, what do you do

when you found something out, something you're not supposed to know, and knowing is making you go all sour in the stomach, but if you say anything, people are gonna get in trouble, even the people that didn't do anything?"

Goddamn, this kid's good.

"That's tough. That's really tough."

"Yeah..."

Nobody said anything for about a minute and a half. I could hear Tom breathing, and it was the kind of breathing I'd learned to listen for in interrogations. The kind that told me the mark was just about to turn over, but was looking for a way to do it without losing face. I could almost see him looking around, checking over his shoulder, trying to make sure nobody was listening.

"Let's walk."

"What?"

"Let's just walk."

"Okay..."

They walked. I could hear their footsteps on the flagstone path, then snapping the occasional twig as they got out into the back yard that ran about three times the length of mine.

After another couple minutes, Tom worked up the nerve.

"That's tough, when you can't talk about what's going on."

"You ever had that happen?"

"Yeah..." A big sigh.

"What do you do?"

"I suppose it depends."

"On what?"

"Well, it depends on whether not saying anything is worse than saying something."

"How can you tell that?"

"Well, is anyone going to get hurt if you don't talk?"

"Um...well, I don't think so."

"Has anyone gotten hurt already and doesn't know about it?"

"Like how?"

"Well, like this one time...there was this friend of mine, he found out that his friend was, um...well, doing something her husband would get very upset about."

"What, like screwing around?"

"Teddy?"

"Dad," I could almost hear Ted's eyes rolling, "I watched Perry Mason with you all last summer, remember? I know what it means when people have affairs and stuff. I'm not some kinda retard, you know."

"Oh. Right. Sorry."

"So what did your, uh, friend do?" Establishing shared knowledge without actually saying so out loud with that "uh." The semantic code for "This'll be our little secret." I had to get trained to do what this kid was doing on instinct.

"He...well, he didn't tell anyone, I guess. But maybe he should have. Maybe if he did, then he wouldn't have had such a hard time. Maybe if he'd said something or done something, he wouldn't have had so much trouble later on?"

"Like what?"

"He...well, I guess he didn't tell me, not exactly. But he found out some more things, bad things, and since he'd already kept that first secret when he wasn't supposed to, he didn't know what to do then, except worry what else might happen."

"Sounds bad."

"Yeah. It is."

"So who's having an affair at your office?"

"What? Now look, son, I never said..."

"You don't *have* to tell me, Dad, but, I mean, you're always telling me I shouldn't lie to you, so it's only fair you don't lie to me. And it's not like I can even get to your office to tell anyone. I don't know any of them, right? I mean, okay, except the ones that come over for barbecues. It's not Glenn, is it?"

"No, no, it's not any of the faculty. It's...it's complicated. And..."

"And this is what's got you all worried." He had a sagacious tone in his voice, like he'd already figured everything out.

"Yeah."

"And that's why you keep not coming home. You're not cheating on Mom or anything, you're just worried about what's happening at work?"

"Yeah."

"It's pretty bad, huh?"

"I can't prove anything."

"So you can't call the police, even though you want to."

"Right."

"You know you can tell me if you need someone to talk to. I won't freak out like Mom."

Tom clapped Ted on the back, the kind of encouraging pat fathers give to sons who are growing up faster than they know how to handle. "I know, son. I know. Want to throw the football around a little before we go back in?"

There was a little more after that, but nothing that sounded relevant. When Tom exited stage right to turn on the lights so they could play catch, Teddy fumbled with the phone, and stopped the recording.

"AND YOU THINK *MY* job eats *my* life."

My feet slipped off my desk, but that isn't what let me know that I'd been asleep. It took tumbling sideways out of my office chair onto the floor for that. "Note to self," I grunted, "thicker carpet. Ow."

"You all right?" Erica laughed. She has the kind of laugh you can recognize from halfway across a loud party. It's just-barely-controlled, the same kind of laugh you get out of veterans who learned that the only way to cope with death is to take life in big bites.

"I don't care know who you are, but you better have coffee."

"What, you mean like in this pot here?"

"Fresh coffee or death." I scraped myself off the floor and tried to make a show of dusting myself off, which clued me in to the fact that I'm not thirty anymore and sleeping at my desk like that makes my joints ache.

"Mmm...a serial killer who operates at Starbucks. You know, we haven't gotten one of those yet."

"Cute." I shuffled around my desk and figured out how my legs were supposed to work, then I got hit with the biological end of the early morning. I made an excuse and ducked out of the office. I didn't really want to walk all the way across the yard, so instead of veering left I hooked a right around the corner to the part of the yard that you couldn't see from any street or window, and watered the plants.

"Clarke? Where did you..."

"Hey, can't a guy get some privacy?"

"What the hell are you doing?"

"Agriculture." I shifted my body so she was directly behind me. I don't like being watched when I pee. I know, guys are supposed to be all cool with it, cause we water bushes with our buddies when we're ten, and have lightsaber fights with the urine streams with our brothers, and all that good shit. But some of us actually grow up, and some of us never really got the whole bonding-through-urination thing. You know those long trough toilets they've got at ballparks? Well, they give me the sudden urge to sit down in a stall. "This is my 4-H project."

"Uh huh."

"Come on, Erica, this is not my kink. Get the hell out of here."

"Fine, fine..." she strolled away, which let me de-clench enough to finish shaking off.

I found her again in the main house. She was giving Klepto his breakfast, which I noticed before I even topped the rear stairs—there's something unmistakable about the way that canned dog food slightly sours the aroma of a perfect drip-brewed medium-roast Costa

Rica.

"You didn't have to do that," I said.

"What, the coffee?" She handed me a fresh mug. "You never look in the mirror in the morning, do you?"

"Nah." The first sip hit my tongue. The thing about medium-roast Costa Rican is that it tastes like it's half made of sweet lemons, without being sugary at all. Tastes kind of like smoky sunlight. Puts a smile even on a craggy face like mine. "After they drummed me off the force, I made a promise to myself that I'd never do anything that might drive me to suicide."

"And now you're a cop again."

"Part time. And don't remind me."

"I thought you missed it."

"Yeah, but it's hard to be a sexy hard-boiled cynic when you've got a day job as Mister Law-And-Order. You headed back up to Napa today?" Her current assignment had her up there on *Operation You're-Not-Cleared-For-That*, but at least her relatively local locale meant that she could visit for a few days a week.

"Yeah. I'm on for the next three, maybe four."

"Gonna stay at the apartment?"

"I think so. It's a bit of a drive." She had an apartment in Sausalito, which was where she parked her stuff. Better drive for her to Napa from there, but that meant I wouldn't see her for...

"You know, I take this job for Teddy, I'll need to be in the City for a while. I could visit you up there..." I sat down at the table and propped my elbows on the old varnished wood. Belonged to the previous owner—had all the hallmarks of something he'd made himself. None of the pieces fit quite right, and it wobbled a little, but it was made out of solid oak and would probably hold its own in a fight against a big rig.

"You could, huh?" Her lip curled a bit around her mug. She'd picked the dark green mug—she does that when she wants me to notice how red her hair is, as if I could forget. She wasn't quite fully buttoned-up yet, and the half-finished Men-In-Black Fed look, with the top three buttons still undone and her stray hair, not yet pinned, up, teasing round her jawline and falling on her collar bone, made me wonder if breakfast was strictly necessary in a job like hers.

"I think so. I've heard about this weird thing called a 'car' that lets you go places without even pedaling."

Her smile broke over the rim of her cup, then she cradled it in both hands and set it down. "So you heard something interesting last night."

"Oh, yeah. Teddy might be a little in love with the drama, letting his imagination running away with him, but there's definitely something going on, and if my Dad talked that way..." Technically, he never would have. He didn't think enough of us to stick around past my fifth birthday. "Well, if I was him and my Dad talked that way, I'd be worried too."

"You never told me about him."

"Who?"

"Your Dad."

"It's a short and sordid story. Ask me sometime when I'm feeling maudlin, you'll get the best version. Your parents—they're in Reno, right?"

"Mmm. It's a dry heat," She rolled her eyes a bit. The kind of thing she wore the ultra-black shades to conceal. Without her Fed Armor, she wasn't as intimidating—dressed like this, she could only stare down a dozen well-armed men hopped up on meth, rather than a hundred.

"Yeah, but it ain't got nothin' on the city and all the weirdos therein."

Then she looked at me, and her eyes weren't happy anymore.

"What's wrong?"

"You know you can't take this job, right?"

"Why? I don't see a conflict of interest."

"Because you're going to wreck that boy's life. You know that."

"Eh. It's wrecked already."

"Hmph. And if you find out his parents are cheating on each other, what do you do then? Are you going to tell him?"

"He's the client."

"So then he has to live with the secret."

I gotta admit, she made a hell of a point. "Okay, so I don't tell him."

"So you're going to lie to your client. A little boy, at that. You're going to just take advantage of him."

"Look, Erica, he's a good kid. He asked for help.

He's a friend of mine."

She just looked at me with those Federal eyeballs, like she was trying to see if I was really as stupid as I looked.

I hate it when she does that. So I hid behind my coffee for the last half cup.

During those four swallows, the table seemed to grow on its own, until all I could see of Erica was how alarmingly official she looked, even without her shades.

I got up to get more coffee, decided to bring the pot back to the table.

"Look," I said, "The difference between your kind of cop and my kind of cop is that you've got rules and procedures for everything, and we don't. Private or public, a detective solves problems, and the hell of it is, not all the problems in the world have tidy solutions. I wish they did. I'd sleep a lot better. But they don't." I decided to top her mug up before I did my own, and I ran my fingers across her shoulders where I did, more to remind myself that she was a person and not just a Fed, and a person I loved at that. "You're going to have to trust me. I've been dancing this dance a long time, and I know my business."

"Clarke, he's a little kid, and you've got no business wrecking his life."

"I've got every bit of business. That IS my business. Look, your job is to unfuck things that are fucked up, right? You come in when people are breaking the rules and you straighten it out, and sure, you've got political pressure, but you're a good cop, and you try to do your best by the people you serve, right?"

"Right."

"My business is to find out what's fucked up. I don't fix anything. I don't have the authority. When I'm really lucky, I find out things that are fixable. Most of the time, I find things that are so twisted round that you couldn't un-knot them with a hundred Boy Scouts. But I find them out, and that means the people involved have choices that they didn't have before."

"No child that young has choices like that."

"Of course they do, and they make them all the time, whether adults want to admit it or not. I learned this one the hard way, dear. I had to get shot to learn it, and it cost two kids their lives in the bargain. Never again." I wasn't getting through to her. Her body was closing up, her shoulders squaring off, her jaw getting more tense the longer I talked. I knew she really gave a shit, or she wouldn't have said anything in the first place. But she also wasn't used to being disregarded. She expected that just bringing it up would make me back off. In her defense, we haven't been dating *all* that long.

But maybe I oughta take a different track, in the interest of domestic tranquility.

"Look, it's not easy for me either. You come into this house, every time you come in, and a part in the back of my brain wonders if I've accidentally committed any Federal offenses lately. I know that since you're here by invitation, you could completely screw me over if you had a mind to. You could rifle through my shit without a warrant, and trump up something. You have that power, and you do that kind of thing as part of your job. You're carrying concealed nukes where people's lives are concerned, and most people you run into don't really understand it, but I do, cause I'm a cop too. I know the game, and I know the rules. But you know what? I trust you. I trust your character. I know that even if you might fuck up—cause, hey, we all do, right?—you're not malicious like that.

"So, I trust you. I need you to trust me. I know what I'm doing. You're worried about good things, but this isn't a Federal ethics board. I can't just back off something because it could get messy. That's not in my job description. In your job, that's what you do to get out of a compromising position. In my job, sometimes, the only way out is through."

She nodded, and relaxed a bit, but the hardness in her eyes stuck around.

And when she kissed me goodbye, her head was somewhere else.

Me? I had work to do, and I wasn't going to solve anything by worrying.

Besides...she did kind-of have a point.

NYA, THE OTHER REDHEAD IN my life, caught the frisbee, then crouched in front of Klepto. The afternoon sun lit up her a-line hair—next to Klepto the Hellhound's brindle blue, it made a hell of a picture. She smiled at him, jumped back and forth across in front of him like she was doing a ceremonial dance. The grin slashed across her face a little farther than looked natural. Her doctor called it a birth defect, and, with her flat face, heavy brow, and big anime eyes, it made her look like she came from one of the nice neighborhoods in the uncanny valley. "You want me to come on the job with you?"

Nya swooped the Frisbee over Klepto, ducked under his jump, and jumped herself. She threw the Frisbee across the lawn to me. Short limbs like she had, it was like watching a linebacker do an interpretive dance.

Klepto galloped after it, managed not to trip the whole gangly awkward way, then skid to a stop in front of me and cocked his head crooked, like he was trying to figure out how I managed to make the bright neon orange disc disappear.

"Yes, boy, the big monkey eats the magic frisbee. Yes,

yes, yes." He started hopping in place. I flipped the disc out from behind my back, sent it flying toward Nya. "Yeah, I want you along. Why not?"

"Well, you never really did before. I mean, not on my own." She had an edge in her voice.

"Sorry. It's just..."

"Just that you remember what happened the last two times." The only two times she'd wound up in the field with me, she'd wound up a hostage. The first time, she stabbed her own father to get me a window—the second time, I shot her to get her out of the way. She could read people like nobody I ever met, but she trusts too easy, and she doesn't know how to stay out of trouble.

And, especially with Rachael gone, I'm not sure I could stand to lose her. "Yeah, something like that."

"So what changed?"

"It's a job."

"You know what Rachael would say."

"What, something like 'Goddammit, Lantham, what the fuck are you thinking taking a job from a client who can't pay you? What, did I fix your books for nothing?'"

She laughed. Dodged around a little bit just to get Klepto a little more wound up.

"I think we could use two people on this. Three, really, but we've got two, so..."

"What about Erica?" She tossed to me.

"I, uh, think she'd get in trouble with her boss." I caught it, flicked it back. Drove Klepto nuts not being able to even get all the way to me. Nya caught it again. "Besides, can you imagine her going undercover?"

Nya shrugged, which was kind of my reaction about it too. Erica was a Special Agent, not an undercover agent, and she had the posture and body language that screamed "cop" from about four miles away. Damn sexy, sure, but not exactly subtle.

"So I'm thinking if we can both get jobs there, and keep our ears open..."

"How are we going to do that?" Nya threw. I let it fly by so Klepto could get a little satisfaction. Important, you know, letting the mutt get a bit of satisfaction now and then. Keeps him from eating the furniture. "I mean...do they even need people?"

"Actually..."

"Mr. Lantham?" Teddy vaulted over the parking gate and rushed into the back yard.

"Ted!"

Klepto dropped the frisbee and barked. Tail swinging like he was fixing to mow the weeds with it.

"Sorry I'm late." Ted went from sprint to stomp to stop not too far away from Nya, still far enough back that he could peek at her out of the corner of his eye. "I had to...I had to...this thing at school they..."

Klepto broke his alert stance and charged the kid. Teddy got buried under a pile of dog while still trying to figure out how not to look at Nya's ass.

"Dude, Ted, settle down." I scooped up the frisbee. Klepto was entirely absorbed with attempting to identify the interloper by taste alone. I whistled. "Klepto! Come here!"

The hellhound's head popped up, and he stopped trying to drown the kid, turned on a dime and started bounding at me like he was trying to win the Kentucky Derby all on his own. Teddy stood up and straightened himself out, still a couple feet behind and to Nya's left, and trying like hell not to let on that he was looking at the sweet spot where her yoga pants turned into spray paint over her ass and hips.

I was reading a few weeks ago how the boomers were a huge generation, and the millennials are another huge one, and the one coming up after the millennials is another small one, like the X-ers. That means that there aren't a lot of kids Teddy's age hanging around. Looking at the way he was looking at my assistant, I guess that means the Puberty Fairy's getting ahead on her workload and visiting kids younger and younger.

Then again, I had my first crush when I was nine. The Puberty Fairy and me, we had an understanding—she fucked with me, and I walked around holding a jacket in front of myself. You can stop AIDS with a condom, but you need a heavy jacket to keep from catching a terminal case of embarrassment.

Klepto sat in front of me, looked up, his tongue lolling out of his mouth. When a dog gives you the look that says "Hey, man, the only thing that matters is this moment. Embrace it," it reminds you about life. Makes you feel good.

In my case, it also stings, because of who bought

him for me.

But, like the pup's face said, that's in the past, right? You gotta move on if you're gonna remember to throw the frisbee. I squatted down and gave him a good tousle, then said "Go long, boy!"

He started running. I shouted "This one's for Klepto," and flung the disc way out to the driveway gate. It sailed high enough that I started kicking myself before it got halfway there. It was gonna go over, and the pup was gonna follow it, and in the process he was going to figure out that he could actually jump that fence—or he'd bounce off the fence cause he couldn't quite clear it. I wasn't sure which was worse.

Sir Klepto the Maniac got his name because, since the first week he lived here, he's been a very effective thief. If it could be snatched and chewed, Klepto snatched it and chewed it. It's taken me months to make my shoes, and Nya's corsets, and Erica's holster safe (and, trust me, you haven't had a heart attack until you've caught your four month old puppy trying to find the peanut butter hidden down the barrel of your girlfriend's olive drab Glock 22), but that doesn't mean he's lost the gift of grab.

That not-so-little monster jumped a good five feet into the air, stretched his neck out the whole way, opened his yap, and snapped shut around the plastic like it was his dinner plate.

To be fair, it was. He ran it back to me, then, while Nya and Ted applauded and yelped like a proper cheering section, dropped it at my feet, and then started licking my hand.

"Okay, boy, come on in." I picked up the frisbee, headed inside. I waved Ted and Nya in after me.

"So, I listened to your recording," I was climbing the stairs, started talking once I heard Ted clear the door behind me. I'd hate for him to miss anything, but I'd also hate for him to think I was patronizing him. With a kid like this, you do the "crouch and look them in the eye and be ultra-earnest" thing at your peril. Do that to Ted and you're liable to find toothpaste on your doorknobs. Doing the walk-and-talk, and expecting him to keep up, that makes him feel like one of the guys.

"Yeah?"

I rounded the corner into the kitchen. "Yeah."

"What did you think?"

"Well," I tossed the frisbee onto the table, ducked into the fridge to grab Klepto's dinner, "he's definitely hiding something."

"Like what?"

"That's gonna take some doing to find out." I peeled off the saran wrap and rubber band that was keeping the doggy stew fresh, and the smell of cold soup hit my nostrils. At forty degrees, your nose can't tell the difference between dog food and leftovers. Same thing's true when you grow up with my mother's cooking, but that's another story.

"So you'll...hey..." Teddy scowled a little bit. "You know, you do that a lot."

"What's that?"

"Say something without saying something. It's really annoying."

Nya sporfled.

"What'd I say?"

She cupped her lips with one hand and waved the other one like these weren't the droids he was looking for.

"What?" Teddy sounded like he was half four years old and had been left out of the clubhouse, and half like he was a college student who didn't understand why people kept mentioning the Spanish Inquisition whenever something unexpected happened.

I emptied the can into Klepto's frisbee and put it on the floor for him, then patted him on the head and told him he was a good pup for waiting so patiently. One of my neighbors gave me the idea—teach him to associate frisbee time with food, get him to work out harder. Important for big dogs, since they're prone to getting overweight and losing their joints.

Me, with neighbors. Living in a neighborhood, talking to people. Getting life tips. Borrowing a cup of sugar for a late night batch of cookies. How the hell did I turn into this?

How did I turn into this and like it?

Guess life takes some interesting twists when you're not looking.

"Nothing, nothing," Nya said.

"Yeah, yeah," I said, "Just you keep ragging on the

ragged cop, see what happens." I chucked the can into the bin, dove back into the fridge for drinks. "Anyone thirsty?"

Nya got enough of a handle on the suppressed laughter to say "Beer?"

"Belgian?"

"Sure."

I tossed her one.

"Teddy, how bout you? Coke? Iced tea? Water?"

"Um...tea, I guess."

"Good choice. Think I'll join you." I pulled the glass pitcher from the fridge, set about the business of pouring a couple glasses while I talked. Plenty of ice, because tea without ice is like a grizzly bear without a tutu—sure, you can have one, but it's not going to do a hell of a lot to liven up the place, so what's the point? "So, tell me, what is it, exactly, you want me to do?"

"I want...huh...I want you to fix it."

"Fix it. You mean, you want me to find out whatever's bugging your Dad, and make it go away?"

"I guess..."

"What if what's bugging him is a person?"

"Well..."

"You know I don't kill people, right."

Nya stifled an incredulous laugh.

"Wait, what?" His eyes went big as silver dollars. "You *kill* people?" Like he wasn't quite sure whether to be scared or impressed.

"Yes, I've killed people, but only in self-defense. I

told you I used to be a cop, right?"

Nya cleared her throat.

"Oh, right. Am a cop, am a cop. Gotta remember to tattoo that on my ass so I don't forget." Ever since Carl Oldman deputized me for his little witch hunt down in Silicon Valley, I've technically been a member of the Santa Clara Sheriff's Department, at least, part time. "And wipe that look off your face, it's not cool. I only kill people in self-defense, and it takes something out of you even then."

I didn't raise my voice, I just looked at him. If I could keep this kid off the wide and crooked, he might have a chance at some kind of life that didn't involve departmental politics, shitty paychecks, and long-term relationships with licensed rent-a-friends that hang fancy degrees on their walls over their desk, just so you won't forget that they're only on your side cause you're writing the checks.

He took the hint. Nodded, then broke into a goofy smile.

Maybe I should qualify that, because Teddy was many things, but he wasn't exactly the epitome of style. Goofy was his default. He could persuade, cajole, manipulate with the best of them, but I wouldn't be surprised to find out that he got picked on at school. He tended to wear hand-me-down Charlie Brown striped T-shirts, pants that were half a size too big, and he had one of those haircuts that screamed "my mom used a bowl and a pair of scissors and all I got was this lousy haircut."

So this smile he broke into, it was goofy by Ted standards.

"Anyway," I handed him his tea and took a swig of my own, "If I'm going to take this case, there's a few things you need to understand. You ready?"

"Yes sir." He didn't say it ironically. He was just from one of those families.

"Okay." I pulled a chair out, set down at the table. He and Nya joined me. "If I do this, I want you to know what's involved. This isn't exactly the same kind of job as the kinds of things you've been doing. Your most common case at your agency is, what, lost wallets?"

"Actually, it's phones."

"Stolen, lost?"

"Yeah. And they always leave their GPS on, so..."

"Hell of a racket you got going there. Anything else? Ever had to solve a mystery?"

"Mmm...well, kinda."

"Tell me about it."

"Well, one of the girls at school, she had this problem with someone peeping at her window and drawing on it to freak her out. So she hired me, and I found out it was some of her friends who wanted to scare her for Halloween, so I got pictures of them doing it and told them I'd tell their parents if they didn't stop."

"Nice work. So, you, what, snuck out and staked her out?"

"Yeah. Took two whole nights, but I got 'em."

"So, that's one of the things we might have to do. I'll be honest, kid, we don't have a lot to go on, here. I'm going to have to find out what's going on with your Dad, then find out if there's anything I can do about it. On a normal case, I'd give you a report on the whole thing, but..." I really didn't want to say what I was about to say.

"But what? Mr. Lantham?"

Nya decided not to let me dangle on the end of the line. "We might find out things about your Dad that we can't tell you about."

"What? Hey..."

"It's not personal," she said. "He didn't tell me anything, either."

Now there was a road I wasn't eager to go down. "Nya, I don't think..."

"What didn't he tell you?"

"My Dad killed a friend of mine."

Which is just a great thing to tell a kid who's worried about his Dad. "Nya, his dad hasn't killed anyone..."

"You don't know that, Clarke..."

"Yeah, I kinda do, now come on, you're gonna spook him."

"I'm not spooked!" Teddy said it with the kind of brave-man quaver in his voice that I spent my entire teenagerhood trying to learn how not to make when I was so scared I could've fertilized an entire soybean field.

"Nya, come on..."

"But I found out anyway when he tried to kill me, so..."

"Nya! Stop. This isn't helping."

"Um...yes it is. Look."

So I looked, and the kid was completely rapt.

"Okay, fine, tell him the story," I said, but with my eyes I was begging her to censor the shit out of it. The kid did *not* need to hear the whole story, not coming from the world he comes from. Plenty of time for those kinds of nightmares later on.

She told him the story. She left out the sex club part, which just goes to prove how wrong Erica is about her. Even Nya has some sense of decorum, but if I had to lay money I'd say it was because of the kid's age, not because of his religion.

The blood and guts, though? She kept that in. She spun a hell of a yarn, had Teddy sitting right on the edge of his seat.

"Look, look, look," I stopped her before she went on to talk about how she wound up living with me, because that's a story that would have filled about four books, "This isn't a social morning, this is a business meeting. We have a client trying to hire us, we don't need to sell him, you can fill him in on our greatest hits later."

As soon as I said it I knew it was the kind of thing I'd wind up regretting, but if she *was* going to become the neighborhood's assassin of youth and privacy, the very least she could do was not do it in front of me.

"Okay," then she winked at the kid, "Ask me later, I'll

tell you about the time he got a spider bite and almost started a war."

"Really?"

"Really."

"Sweet!"

Just what I need: Nya as the local black-sheep uncle. Except, well, not a man.

"If I can sort-of wrangle this conversation back around to some semblance of order..."

"Sorry, Clarke."

"Sorry, Mr. Lantham."

Iced tea is a remarkable beverage. Centering. Refreshingly devoid of the kind of insanity that was cluttering up this particular conversation. Not as good as scotch, but it is cheaper, and you can drive after you drink it, so it's got that going for it.

I could use a good drive about now.

"Now, here's the deal, Teddy. I can try to find out what's bothering your Dad, and if I find it out, I'll do what I can to fix it. But I'm not a miracle worker, and I don't have the power to force him to do anything..."

"But you said you're a cop."

"Cops have to follow rules, too, and I don't have a lot of authority in San Francisco, or here, for that matter. But that brings me to problem two. If I find out what's wrong with your Dad, the chances are pretty good I won't be able to tell you unless it's so bad that you wouldn't want to hear about it."

"What do you mean?"

"Well, if he's breaking the law, or covering up for someone breaking the law, I might have to arrest him, and everything that went on could wind up on the news. I know you love him, Ted, so think hard about this. Even good people can have some pretty dark secrets."

"And what if you don't have to arrest him?"

"Well, then whatever's bugging him might be really personal, and not the sort of thing I have any business telling you."

"But...I'm your client."

"Yes, and that would normally entitle you, but you're also my friend, and your Dad is my friend." Not exactly true, but we waved all neighborly-like when I walked Klepto. "And I can't tell you his personal business."

"But..."

"No, stop. This is a condition. I will not take the job unless you understand that I will protect your Dad's privacy, from you, if I think that's the best thing to do. I'll encourage him to talk to you, and I can be very persuasive..."

"Trust me, he can."

"...but it will be his choice. If you can't live with that, you can take the case yourself. But I won't. That's my condition."

He nodded, very serious. "What else?"

"Only one other thing, and I want you to listen to this because I like you. What you're about to do, hiring me to help your Dad, it's dangerous."

"Dangerous, how?"

"There are certain things in life you can't undo, and this might be one of them. This could have consequences, things that will change how your life works from this point forward."

"What do you mean?"

How do you explain regret to a nine-year-old?

"Let me see if I can explain. As you get older, you do things you're not proud of. Everyone does. It doesn't matter how good a person you are. Your Dad works at a Bible college, you go to Sunday School, right?"

"Yeah." He shrugged, like it was a stupid question.

"That thing they tell you about sin, about how everyone sins? Well, Jesus might forgive you if you say the right words, or have the right attitude, or take communion, or whatever, but people don't. People don't forgive each other, people don't forgive themselves. It's hard to know what kind of things you're willing to forgive until you run up against something where you just can't do it anymore. When you're in the business I'm in—both businesses, private snoop and cop—you spend a lot of time finding out the kinds of things that people do when they're not on their best behavior.

"I could find out things about your Dad, or about your Mom, or about people your Dad works with, or you, and even if I don't tell you what those things are, the fact that I find them out, the fact that I'm asking the kinds of questions that let me find out...well, that can change things. It can wreck people's relationships. It can ruin things so that even God can't put them back together. If you have us do this, we could find things out that everyone wants to keep secret, and that's a decision you can't un-make. Do you understand?"

"I think so, yeah. I think so." His brow was furrowed. All concentration.

"Do you know what you want to do?"

"Yeah."

"What do you want to do?"

"I want you to find out what's going on. And I want you to fix it."

"The job will cost you twenty bucks, and it might take a while. Deal?"

"Deal."

"Great. Now, there are a few more things I need you to find out for me so we can come up with a plan..."

7:30 AM, Monday

THIS BUSINESS—AND, PUBLIC or private, law enforcement is a business—is a business for civilized people. Normal people don't drag their gargantuan carcasses out of bed to tail their neighbors in a rented car for a job that doesn't pay anything. Something's wrong with you if you do that kind of work, even for a good day-rate. Down deep in your gut, something turned sour at an early age. Maybe you had a sneaky best friend. Maybe your mother didn't breastfeed you enough. However it happened, you wound up on the outs. The mentality of a tabloid reporter and the sense of humor of a loan shark.

One thing you come to grips with sooner or later: you're not fit for civilized life. You don't have a "moral compass," and if you're lucky you'll never get one in a box of Cracker Jacks. You're the kind of person they make rules for, and penalty boxes, because you don't care what they want you to do if they aren't going to rap you on the knuckles for ignoring them.

And they have a lot of rules. Rules about ethics, and conflicts of interest, and eavesdropping, and felonies. Rules about strong-arming people, and how many guns you're allowed to carry, and when. Rules about consumer protection. Rules about the difference between investigating and stalking. Rules about how you follow the rules.

All of them you can pretty much ignore if you can get away with it. I've broken all of them at one time or another, and I'll keep on breaking them if I want any kind of career, right up till the day they put me away like they did Pellicano.

But there is one rule that matters. Only one. The one you don't break, no matter what, unless you go soft in the head:

Money talks.

This isn't a charity auction. If you want to do charity work, join the peace corps or find a soup kitchen or volunteer at an animal shelter or something. Law enforcement is a mercenary game, and the PI is the most mercenary of the bunch next to a cop on the take. Sure, you get genuine public servants in the mix, but a good cop doesn't stay a good cop if he can't make rent.

So why the hell was I dressed in fake sideburns and tie-dyes like a pot merchant from nineteen seventy-nine, with my hands on the wheel of this rented Impala and my eyes glued to the rear-view trained on the driveway of Tom Stride waiting for him to make his move?

Well, I didn't have anything on my plate for the Santa Clara Sheriff's Department, at least not today. Sure, I had that open IA investigation Rachael's dad suckered me into—yeah, I know his name is Carl, but he'll always be Rachael's dad on the grounds that I'm basically a charity case, which doesn't exactly ring my bells about being there—but I was waiting on a set of records subpoenas that were going to take forever. I didn't have any insurance work on the table, and the adultery case I was working for that guy out in Blackhawk was waiting on a DNA test that was backed up behind real paying clients at a local crime lab, so I had a couple days to kill.

This was just recreation, really. I wasn't breaking the rule. Not if I squinted hard enough while looking at it in the mirror.

Truth was, I figured I had to make a good showing for Teddy. I wasn't actually gonna be able to help him, but I had to make him feel like I was taking him seriously. There's nothing worse in the world than being ten and not having anyone take you seriously. That kind of thing is why those two kids that went missing from our neighborhood in '89 only turned up in pieces on the beach the week after the cops gave up on them.

Call it a favor to my younger self. And those kids I used to skateboard with.

Tom's faded green '95 Grand Cherokee rolled out of the driveway at about a quarter to eight. I had to juggle with my laptop in the passenger seat—Tom knew what my car looked like, and he knew what Nya's car looked like, so I didn't have a ride that had my usual set of toys all set up. I missed my computer mount.

But Teddy's phone was definitely in the Jeep. I'd told him to stash it there with the ringer off and a full charge the night before. Now I didn't have to risk being noticed in the rear view. I could just hang back a ways and not worry about losing him. The little blinking blue dot let me know exactly where he was at all times. I just needed to stay close enough to see who, if anyone, he interacted with. Maybe I'd get lucky and find out he was shtupping the pastor's wife or something.

Well, it's better than catching him with a contract killer. And a lot harder to explain to a ten-year-old kid.

The Grand Cherokee headed north, then hung a right on Somerset, then jogged north again on Redwood before settling on course due east toward the middle school. The line for dropping off kids stretched a full mile before the actual school, and I killed my time in line listening to a playlist of old TV theme show songs that Erica gave me for a three month anniversary present. I waited through the interminable line of parents waiting to drop their kids off, but opted out of actually cycling through the parking lot.

I turned left and flipped a u-turn, parked myself in a turnout a little ways from the traffic out-flow.

Then I waited. Couldn't do a hell of a lot about it. Sometimes, you wait. Part of the business. Sometimes, you wait for a dad to drop his kid off at school. I just hoped Teddy kept up his end. With no phone in that Jeep, this'd turn into kind of tail job that gets police attention.

You know how you see movies where someone tails someone else for a long time, and the person in the car in front doesn't notice?

It's bullshit. They always notice.

Always.

Just like they always notice long-term stakeouts, when a strange car parks in the neighborhood to keep a house under surveillance. People aren't stupid. And they don't like strangers spying on their neighborhood. PIs get beaten up, mugged, and sometimes shot pulling stunts like that.

Hell, undercover cops do too. Had a buddy that bit it once that way. Hell of a thing.

The little dot on the screen snaked up the hill. Took about ten minutes before it even hit the main parking lot. Times like this, I could've used an assistant to talked to, but my protégé hasn't been around for months, and I haven't talked to her for a good chunk of that time. One of these days, I'm just gonna have to face up to the fact that she isn't coming back. Move on with life.

If there's one thing Irish Catholics are good at, it's moving on in life. We never said a word about the way the British occupied the homeland. We're never plagued with guilt about how many shamrocks we've stepped on or how much sex we have. Nope. We're among the best-adjusted cultures on the planet. Just look at how low our alcoholism rates are.

Doc Samson—department therapist that got assigned to me after I took down the Broadway Slasher—used to harp on about that. Moving on. Letting go. Getting in touch with my feminine side. She'd get a kick out of me thinking about moving on. Good thing I fired her before she could work her witchery on me. I decided back then that I'd rather keep the sickness in my melon than try to bleach it out. Live long enough, see enough of the right things, and your scar tissue is the only thing you can depend on to hold things together when life turns nasty on you.

No sickness, no Lantham. And, screwy as it sounds, I'd miss me.

And I probably wouldn't be mobbed by a certain canine monster or another certain redhead Fed. *Don't look now, Lantham, but for the first time in years you've got something to lose. How the hell did that happen?*

The things that happen when you're not looking. Next thing, I'm gonna start finding gray hairs, bald patches, and children I never knew I had. Might even wind up with a winning lottery ticket and find myself in the priesthood. Price you pay for concentrating on mysteries in order to avoid the rest of life, but it's worth it. Things that don't fit piss me off, so solving puzzles puts the universe in order, at least in my little corner of it.

I wound up waiting for over twenty minutes while Tom wound his way through the soccer mom frenzy and found his way back to the relative sanity of the surface streets. The phone tracked the whole way. *Teddy, you've just earned your Junior Woodchucks detective's merit badge.* Assuming Teddy knew anything about the Junior Woodchucks, which he probably didn't unless his parents fed him *Duck Tales* on nostalgia home video. Maybe I'd have to get him a set. He was still young enough that he'd probably dig 'em.

He headed downhill to Crow Canyon. I merged out into traffic a fair few cars behind him. Gave him a good long lead, since I had the tracker on him. Didn't want to lose visual on him entirely, in case Teddy had forgotten to charge his phone last night, but for the moment I had enough invisible rope to get well and truly lost in the traffic behind him so he wouldn't spot me.

That was the theory, anyhow.

He headed toward 580, hopped on the freeway westbound. Then, at the other end of Castro Valley, instead of heading north into Oakland and across the Bay Bridge like I expected him to, he veered left onto 238 and proceeded down toward that special kind of hell that you can only find on 880 at rush hour.

What are you up to, Tom?

He couldn't be trying to avoid traffic. As nasty as things got through the Macarthur Maze and over the Bay Bridge, that was nothing to the river of crap he'd have to wade through heading either up 880 to the Bay Bridge or south to the San Mateo, across, then north on 101.

But that's exactly what he did. And I did it too.

Every agonizing mile of the way. Took long enough that I started wishing I'd brought Klepto along, then lasted longer enough that I figured I'd have had to stop for a doggy bathroom break and wished I'd brought Nya, then lasted long enough again that I figured she'd have gone nuts from over-stimulation, so I gave up and wished I'd brought an audiobook.

K-Hear-BS was wall to wall with a breaking story about the geopolitical ramifications of Dennis Rodman's marriage to Kim Il Sung's second cousin. I switched to them after I finally got sick of KGO's fucking with their format all the time. Biggest news station west of the Mississippi, and the yahoos that owned the thing couldn't figure out what to do with it. But I switched over anyway, cause I had nothing better to do. Got rewarded with a news story about a big car accident last night on I-5 near Redding. In an area with close to eight million people, you don't get slow news days very often. Wish I'd been in the kind of mood to appreciate the novelty.

By the time I got up to the exit for the Coyote Point Gun Club, I was starting to miss the good old days of the Great Recession, when you could actually get anywhere in the Bay Area in forty minutes, if you knew what roads to take. Then again, even in those days, nobody but an idiot would ever dream of getting on 101 during rush hour without a damn good paycheck waiting at the other end of the drive.

Or an airport pickup. Tom Stride was about a mile ahead of me, and the tracker showed him shifting rightward just in time to take the exit for SFO. *Let's hope he's a circler, and his passenger's running late.* I might just be able to lap him on the inside and get a look at whoever he was here to pick up.

SFO is a little outpost of San Francisco stuck on the border of San Mateo and San Bruno, and the only reason it matters is that San Francisco City Cops hang around there looking for people to bother. Of the dozen or so police departments around the Bay, they're not the worst. Oakland gets that honor. But SF doesn't like playing second fiddle to Oakland on anything, so they're working on it.

Not a bad airport, though, as airports go. They managed to grow it from a little hub to the sprawling supercity it is today without making it feel too big or unwieldy when you're walking around in it.

Driving the loop, though? That's different. Two major highways pour in, two pour out, all funneling down into four five mile-per-hour lanes to the domestic terminal. The turn-around is an afterthought. Going in there at rush hour is like taking a journey through a hypodermic into the veins of an atherosclerotic with a barbiturate problem.

I lost tracking as soon as he went in under the superstructure. That meant arrivals level, not departure level—the departures level is open to the sky. Downstairs at arrivals, all that concrete and steel makes a pretty good Faraday cage. They have repeaters underneath for cell service, sure, but GPS doesn't work under there, so close-order tracking's useless. So I got into the jam, kept left, got in the taxi lane. It was moving faster, figured it would give me a chance to close in and get a visual.

Had to circle once. Didn't see him on the first pass, didn't get a signal when I came out from under the tangle of concrete ribbons, so took the turn-around.

Second time, I spotted the Grand Cherokee crawling up to the curb by the United arrivals terminal. I pulled right at the next crossover, got over to the curb a few doors down, parked the car.

Too many other cars dodging in and out behind me for me to get a good view of who Tom was picking up. Exited the vehicle, made to go around to the back like I was gonna get my luggage, but then I saw a skycap coming toward me.

Dammit.

No, officer, I didn't realize that I couldn't stop here without having someone to offload. Yes, I was here to pick up a friend. I was just getting ready to wait for him, you might have heard of him, Jimmy Nolan, the famous romance writer? No? He was scheduled to come in on 1608 from Atlanta. Yes sir, I'll get out of here right away and circle with the other schlubs.

I almost played it like an asshole, would've been more believable, maybe, but I only needed to get out of there, and being an asshole at an airport is a good way to earn a cavity search these days. They can actually put you in jail just for mouthing off. Some fucking free country, right?

The longer I'm not a cop anymore, the more I start thinking like a civil liberties lawyer. Gotta get my head out. Now that I'm technically a cop again, I gotta go back to thinking like one. Bad habit when you're a private snoop—got me in all kinda trouble, took years to break.

Oh, well.

I circled once more so that I cold follow Tom's Jeep when he got out. He popped back on 101 North, which I found out when I cleared the airport for the last time. That sound you heard was my inner child weeping at the thought of getting back on that asphalt ribbon of misery, but where the little blue dot on the computer goes, I go.

He got off at Silver Avenue, turned left under the freeway, and headed uphill to the west. Old San Francisco here. As south as south gets in the city. Lot of buildings from before the 1906 quake, and the rest of them built right after.

Top of the hill, about a mile on, on the right, he turned right into a circular drive with a football-field sized lawn in front of it, and a circular drive with parking spaces swooping around in a big arc from curb front to curb front.

Trubody College. Hell of a building. The kind you find in the older parts of the city. Woulda made the architecture geek in me have joygasms if I didn't have more important things to focus on. Like that Grand Cherokee and the white-haired fellow just ducking out of it. Had darker roots, like maybe he bleached. Pinstripe suit. Walked like a young guy who worked out a lot.

He didn't go inside. He got his bags out of the back of the Jeep and then walked around to the driver's side and leaned his arm on the window. Gave me enough time to drive past them, pull into a parking spot, get my camera out.

Always bring a camera when you're following someone. You never know when you might witness something you need to document later. Just don't let anyone catch you doing the actual clandestine photography.

I aimed the 400mm zoom out the rear window and got in tight on white-hair's face. His mustache was trimmed, neat, the kind of thing you'd see on a motivational speaker or a politician. Come to think of it, he looked a little bit like Ted Turner, but without the cowboy hat. And in the close-up, it was really obvious that he was bleaching his hair. His roots were about a quarter inch long. If he was a younger guy trying to pass for a good old boy, he was doing a lousy job. Maybe he was an actor or a rocker come to give a motivational talk between tours.

But I didn't like that theory. Didn't smell right. The way he leaned up against that Jeep and talked to Tom Stride told me everything I needed to know about the relationship. Pulling my zoom back to get Tom into frame confirmed it. Without the polarizer I wouldn't've been able to see it, but he had that plastered-on-smile that yes-men get when the head honcho is threatening them and making it sound like a joke.

White-hair was a big deal in Tom Stride's universe, and Tom wasn't all that happy about it.

And if I stayed here much longer I was gonna attract attention. What am I doing taking long-lens photos in an Impala without a parking permit? Oh, nothing, I just got this great bug smashed on my back window and loved the way the light was playing on it. Thought it'd make a great modern art piece.

Not my idea of fun, those conversations. So I got out of the car and walked across to the lawn, got an angle where I could plausibly be taking shots of the building for the historical society, and then took a few more of White-hair, getting as many details as I could. Hands, for wedding rings or evidence that he normally wore one. Shoes, for relative wealth level—if he was part of the same subculture Tom came from, you could judge that kind of thing pretty directly—and suit details for the same thing.

And a better shot, over the shoulder, of Tom Stride's face. Figured I was tempting fate by getting into his eye line, but hoped the disguise would do its job. Should be enough—most people don't notice when they see familiar faces in places they're not expecting to, so even a minimal disguise would do—but you never really know until it's too late.

Fate had better things to do, I guess. Or Tom was just too worried about not looking like the perfect toady to take his eyes off of White-hair. I got out of sight again before he even flicked his eyes my way.

Packed the gear into the car, folded myself in after it, turned it on and moved the rest of the way around the circle-drive, took the last spot on the right, right before the driveway dumped back onto the road, and hunkered down so nobody would notice me. Just an older student taking a nap in the car for all anyone knew.

Angle the mirrors. Get a good bead on Tom's Jeep.

The conversation continued for a good two minutes more, then White-hair headed inside.

Tom started moving, picking up speed, not looking like he was trolling for a parking spot. Blew right by me and stopped, California-style, where the driveway met the road, then hung a right out onto Silver.

I followed.

He curled around the next right as well, heading steep-down to behind the school.

280 cut a concrete ribbon across the valley about another quarter-mile on and a couple hundred feet down. Was he heading home?

Wherever it was, it wasn't the faculty parking lot. Found that one out when I rolled by the "Trubody College, Faculty Parking Only" sign next to a driveway below and behind the school.

Stop sign at the next intersection. The road pitched at a thirty degree angle, and didn't level out until past the sign. Tom sat at the sign, fumbling with his phone, hadn't looked back at me, but soon as he did...

Before I had to brake to a full stop, he shot off the line like someone had shoved a wasp's nest up his butt.

I couldn't follow him like that. Didn't need to, either. So I parked at the stop sign and gave him some lead.

Waited about two minutes before another car pulled up behind me wanting to use the stop sign.

Well, Lantham, you'd better hope he's not running errands all day or you're really gonna wish you'd grabbed an audiobook.

HE DID RUN ERRANDS all day. But they weren't his errands. Tom Stride doesn't shop at Hermès or deal with Sotheby's, not unless he's got a secret oil well somewhere. He also made a couple stops at high-priced addresses near the Fairmont Hotel and in Seacliff—neighborhoods that show up in a lot of movies because of how well they photograph and how many tens of thousands of dollars per square foot their real estate lists for. I counted ten stops in all, like a delivery route. And at each address, he carried what looked like a bento box in, and then carried the same bento box out.

Ring ring.

Not the ringtone for unknown numbers. So it was someone I knew but didn't like enough to give them their own ringtone. I popped my earpiece. "Lantham. Go."

"Clarke, this is Cal." Cal Oldman. Rachael's father, or he was, back when there was a Rachael. Guess he still is, as she apparently isn't dead yet. Just cut me out of her life for no reason I know about.

"Hey Cal. I'm on a stakeout right now. Is it an emergency?"

"Not yet."

"Make it tonight."

"All right. Might have to be late. Marisa's on a schedule these days."

"I can live with that, just call the cell after ten. Should be home by then."

"Will do." He hung up.

IA work. It paid well. Made me a real cop, too. Can't say it blew my skirt up.

AFTER HIS DELIVERY run, Tom Stride drove out through the sunset to the Great Highway, then due south. Past the zoo. Daly City. Left on John Daly Blvd, heading inland.

Westlake. America's prototypical suburb. Every gated community, HOA, subdivision, and planned community in the world has a little Westlake DNA in it. It wasn't the first, but it was the place where it all came together. You know the song "Little Boxes"? That was about Westlake.

And, even if you're not a big fan of the 'burbs, Westlake's got some charm that you just can't shake. Weird blend of sterile mid-20th century architecture with earlier, grander Victorian sensibilities. It all adds up to something that looks offensively inoffensive from the outside, but on the inside they've got a nice amount of space and a good sense of flow. You could do worse, even for a million bucks a pop on the used-house market.

Stride's Jeep settled down in front of a yellow house on Fairway Drive, but he didn't. He was feet-on-the-tarmac as soon as he'd shifted into park, gym bag in hand, jogging up the walk to the main door—it wasn't a front door, being as how it was on the side of the house just forward of the back-yard fence line—and ringing the bell.

I pulled over a few houses in front of him, got my rear view angled back.

A willowy, older blond woman answered the door. The two of them talked, but she didn't invite him in. The conversation stretched for a couple full minutes. *Lantham, you forgot the parabolic mic.* It was back home in one of the secret hide stashes in my Subaru, not in my bag of tricks.

I hate using strange cars. Fucks with my chi.

Stride handed the gym bag over to the woman, she handed him an envelope—receipt or payment of some kind?—and he hot-footed it back to the road and flipped a U straight off the line.

"Stride case, tail job, first day," I said into my phone. Had to make some notes before I took off to follow him. Needed to give him a bit of lead. Needed to make sure my impressions were fresh. The mind plays tricks on you when you let memory sit for too long. It gets colored by things that have nothing to do with it. Great for nostalgia—not so great for collecting puzzle pieces and sticking them all together. "One thing's for sure," I said once I finished the recap, "With all these drops, he's carrying something, and it's something he's nervous about. Coke, maybe. Whatever it is, he isn't happy about the work." I stopped, thought for a few more seconds. "Let's take a look at his financials. Use the kid on that one. Pull his credit score and rap sheet too, just in case there's something there." I clicked the phone off. Leaned over to look at the track.

The school was only five miles down the road from here, but he was crawling up the eastern hills like he wanted to circle around by Burlingame. I didn't have much option but to catch him up, see what he was doing. If he stopped to make another meeting, especially to drop that envelope off to somebody, I wanted to know about it.

If he did it, he slipped it in a mail slot while I was giving him lead. I caught up to him about twenty minutes later. The afternoon commute was ramping up and things were getting ugly everywhere.

Then, around 4pm, by a route so complicate that it could only have been planned by Google Maps, he landed square back at the college where the whole thing had started.

Parked. Got out. Took his laptop bag with him. Tied his tie as he went. Just another professor going in to host his evening classes.

So who are you schlepping for, Tom?

I TRAWLED THE NEIGHBORHOOD for a good parking spot that would give me a good bead on Tom Stride's ride, found one up the hill on Yale, which t-boned right into the college.

Not a great spot as stakeouts go, seeing as how it was right next to an elementary school. Middle-aged men sitting out in front of schools with long lenses tend to send the helicopter parents into overdrive, so I had to retreat back up the hill when I realized I was attracting attention. Wound up having to keep watch with the rifle scope from my bag of tricks (don't ask). Balanced it on the dashboard, set my phone up against it with the video camera turned on, and then just tried not to sweat to death while I waited all that long and stupid evening for Tom Stride to come back out.

Music made me antsy. I tried the news again.

"...reaking news twenty miles south of Redding on Interstate 5. The fatal accident this morning between a pickup truck and a big rig *still* has 5 southbound choked out. KGO motorists calling in to tell us of a massive police presence blocking both lanes, with traffic routing around the accident on the shoulder. The CHP has refused to comment, but KGO news has received unconfirmed reports that the pickup was carrying more than two dozen crates of biological material. We understand the FBI and the Department of Homeland Security have agents on site, but details remain sketchy at this time. Stay tuned for further updates to this breaking story..."

I switched it off. One day it's drugs, the next its organ runners. Somebody crashes, somebody burns, either way you've heard it all before. Should've brought an audiobook. Made up for it by installing a podcast app on my phone and catching up on Hacker News.

Around eight I got too hungry to think straight and ordered myself a pizza with a two liter bottle of coke, since I was running out of water bottles to piss in. Sitting in a rented Impala on the side of a residential street at the south end of San Francisco, I figured this wasn't a stake out, not anymore, so much as it was a staring contest between Tom Stride's car and my lower intestine. If he was in there much longer, I was going to have to give up and find a gas station.

About the time I was considering quitting the detective game and going in to the fertilizer business, Tom Stride stumbled out of the school's front door, looking like he'd just had the shit kicked out of him.

At this point, I'd pay good money to get the shit out of me even if it did involved getting kicked.

He was worn, like he'd just stood up to a police grilling from an old time film noir. And he had a guy behind him. The guy with the white hair.

The light wasn't very good, but it might just be good enough. I pulled my SLR out, stuck the 400mm prime on it, opened it up wide, and got what shots I could. I needed to find out who this clown was. If he was pulling Stride's strings—and the body language, plus this morning's delivery escapade, sure made it look like it—then I had to find out what his deal was.

I got a couple bad pics. Not sharp enough for facial ID through any of the government databases—which I couldn't get to without paying Earl Whitaker my left nut for anyway—but good enough that I might be able to match him to another picture, once I figured out where to look for this guy.

They opened the Jeep and got in, then de-parked. I needed to follow them, but I figured I had about three minutes, maybe five, before I was gonna need fresh underwear.

Well, I did have a tracker on his car. And there was a Shell at the bottom of the hill. As long as he didn't head down the peninsula on 280 I could probably find him again without attracting too much traffic-cop attention.

I took the gamble.

And that move probably cost me an extra three weeks on that case, right there, and a whole hell of a lot of trouble, too. When I got back to the car from dropping my load, I saw them making a b-line south down 101, about ten miles ahead of me. Way too late for any traffic to hold them up, they were flying at-the-limit, all the way until they got to the San Carlos Airport, and then Stride's Jeep came out again, headed for home.

If I'd been able to follow him in, I might have seen the plane that White Hair got into. I might have figured out where he was going. And I might have saved a few lives, and myself a shitload of trouble.

But I didn't.

And, of course, I didn't know that at the time.

At the time, I only thought *Oh, hell, now I have to do this the hard way.*

"MY NEPHEW QUENTIN," Mrs. Molly Parks said over the brim of her nearly-empty white diner mug. "He was the kind of boy who'd spend hours trying to set off all the dogs in the neighborhood at once, just to see if it could be done."

"Was? I thought, I mean, he didn't die, did he?" The waitress behind the blue-flecked Formica counter, a large-nosed blond woman in her late twenties, topped off Molly's coffee. She was new to the job, at least compared to the longtime veterans that staffed the town's most successful family eatery, and spilled a little, as she was wont to do. A bit of a klutz, but such a good conversationalist that the customers really didn't mind. She reflexively wiped up the spill, but she did it like she had to think about it.

Molly had seen a lot of new faces come and go on the wait staff at Murphy's over the years. She figured this new girl, Daisy, wouldn't last more than six months before she was off to greener pastures.

"Oh, well, there's no way to know that, is there? My sister thinks that if he survived the measles after she was too stupid to vaccinate him, and he survived that tumble into the river when he went fishing with Nathan," Mrs. Parks nodded to her son, a twelve-year-old boy at the end of the counter who was studiously avoiding his lunch in order to slay the monsters threatening to take over his phone, "then he'll live through whatever happened to him. But she's from Hoopa, so she'll believe anything..."

"But she's his mother, and needs to believe he'll come back?"

"Yeah."

"Daisy!" the cook barked. "Order up!"

The waitress excused herself and bustled to fetch the order and deliver it to the last of the lunchtime crowd, leaving Mrs. Parks alone at the counter with her unsettled memories.

NOT EVEN CLARKE LANTHAM would have recognized the blond girl behind the counter. Her birth certificate claimed she was Daisy Pickford, born twenty-five years ago in Seattle, Washington, and her driver's license attested that, until recently, she was a resident of Spokane.

She had sun-damage around her eyes, and looked like someone who had grown up around smokers. She wheezed a little bit when she stopped moving, but she didn't stop moving very often.

The staff at Murphy's Family Eatery in Yreka, where she worked, knew her as friendly, outgoing, but private—the kind of person who moved out to a small town in order to get away from the kind of hell only big cities can generate.

She said she wanted to get a degree in wilderness management and become a park ranger, and the local community college had some courses that looked promising. Meantime, she enjoyed meeting all the families that came in, and accepted her co-worker's invitations to church, and did everything she could to sink roots into the community.

Her only real problem, and it did get her whispered about from time to time, was that she was a little bit racist. Not enough that it would make anyone feel guilty about being kind to her, but enough that nobody was inclined to introduce her to any black friends they might have. Better for everybody that way.

Well, that, and she swore a lot more than you were really supposed to, but at least she knew how to keep it under control when there were kids around.

The racism was the hardest part of the role to keep up. It wasn't something that she understood well enough to feel comfortable faking. But she couldn't risk somebody introducing her to Dennis or Zarek Woodfork. They, she was sure, *would* recognize her.

If she was recognized, the game was up.

At night, when her shift was done—and she'd bucked hard for the undesirable shifts, so that she could eavesdrop more easily on the sorts of town gossip that people didn't discuss openly—she walked the mile east to the converted detached garage that she rented for three hundred bucks a month.

When the rickety thin-panel door closed behind her, and she turned the key in the patina-laden bronze lock, and threw the security bolt, only then did she let herself be Rachael Oldman again.

For a little while.

There was only one room, not counting the closet and the bathroom. Just enough for a double bed, a low rough-hewn oak dresser, a garage-sale wood rocking chair, a mangled pressboard-and-veneer coffee table, and an end table with an old CRT-style TV on it in front of a big blue curtain covering the south wall.

At least there was cable, and WiFi, just barely strong enough to be serviceable out here, when she couldn't stand the ruralness anymore and had to dive into the Internet and get lost for a while.

The laptop? She'd picked that up at a used computer store for twice what it was worth.

When she got home, every day, every night, she'd shimmy out of the diner uniform, or the church clothes—or whatever other nondescript duds she'd worn that day—shower off the makeup that covered her tattoos and piercings, take off the latex nose and scrub the mascara out of her eyebrows.

Then—when she had a good glass of red in her hand, and the heater going, and a tank top and boxer shorts or sweats on to keep her skin from freezing from the drafts that wafted in through the shoddy insulation—only then would she take the blue curtain off the wall and stare at the murder board underneath.

Well, more a "murder-patch-on-the-wall," but "murder board" was what they called it on TV.

She'd never seen a real cop use one, not exactly, but her Dad's gig wasn't homicide, and he was her main point of reference. But whether Hollywood just invented it to help out with exposition or they actually pilfered it from real cops, it worked for her. Good for data visualization.

And there was a *lot* of data piling up.

She'd put it up after she called the FBI field office in Sacramento. If the locals weren't going to call them, Rachael damn well was.

It turned out the locals had been in touch with them, they just hadn't seen fit to tell her. The case was open, but they hadn't every found a way to connect the disappearances. Until she found Zarek, it looked like a normal and predictable, if regrettable, up-tick in predator activity in the wilderness. The recovery of wilderness areas came with inherent risks, and people didn't properly appreciate them. Now, if she had any more information beyond what she'd already told the local cops, they'd be happy to take it down, but otherwise she should go away and let them do their job.

So it was up to Rachael to find enough for the FBI to believe there was really a connection between Zarek and the other missing kids.

And she was getting close.

The board had slots for eleven missing children.

That was the figure she'd heard back in the police station in January.

One recovered: Zarek Woodfork. The remaining ten still missing.

In her undercover time, she'd run into eight more of the names: Denny Winkleman, Nicole Adams, Philip Blackshire, Jason Chan, Kim Morgan, Barack Collier, Chris Perry, Orrie Park. That left two.

One, now.

Rachael set down her Cabernet—in a mug, since she didn't own any bar glass and didn't really want to invest that much in this cover—and opened the drawer in the end table. Retrieved a pad of paper and a pen. She wrote the new name on the pad:

Quentin Greenaway.

One push-pin from the same drawer, and it joined the other names, lined vertically in the middle with pictures next to them, when she could find them.

Quentin didn't have a picture yet. But he did have stats.

Eight years old. White—or white-ish, since his mother was Berber, and on the dark side—and tall for his age. Gaining fast on his mother at four-foot-five.

His name didn't have any connections, yet, but she would fill them in. That's what the post-it notes were for. They were clustered to the right of every name. They had the last seen date, whether or not, and when, there was a police report. The name of the school, the teacher, the parents.

Then, to the left, immediately by the name, were more post-its, this time the names of the other missing children. How many of them knew each other? Did they all know each other? Were they friends? Enemies?

Of the missing kids whose name she had, one was from Eureka. Another was from Calistoga. One from Yreka. Two were from Weed. Two from Red Bluff, two from Redding, one from Weaverville, and one from a place called Happy Camp—which Rachael hoped meant that they grew a *lot* of skunk weed up there.

They were all within three years of each other—the youngest was five, the oldest was eight. They were too spread out to share the same school, or the same hospital, or the same church or recess ground.

They didn't all go to public schools—three had been enrolled in private schools, two had been home schooled—so they couldn't have been poached from some central database in Sacramento.

Had they all gone to the same summer camp? That had been her fall-back. The green church house off the main drag in Yreka was advertising a fundraiser for the "premier summer camp in Northern California." She'd picked up a brochure when she'd first started attending. It advertised a place in Eureka run by something called the Evangelical Missions Association. She'd been going there for six weeks now, getting to know the families, listening in at the prayer meetings, recording them when she could. Taking notes when no one was looking.

A lot of the children had gone to the camp. Even

Zarek Woodfork, whose grandparents were not churchgoers, had attended at the invitation of Nicole Adams, the other missing child from Weed. Nicole had disappeared on a backpacking trip in September—search and rescue eventually found some torn clothes with her blood on them, but no trace of her.

Nicole's mother had told the local paper that Nicole and Zarek were "boyfriend" and "girlfriend," and spent their time giggling at each other from across the room, when they weren't working hard at their mutual quest to beat the latest Halo installment on Nicole's X-Box.

Now that she added Quentin to the mix, that blew the summer camp theory straight to hell. His parents were Krishna Consciousness devotees.

Rachael raised her mug to the board. "Well, I guess that means I don't have to keep going to that church."

If only. Truth was, every time she went, she had something new to put on the board. The local gossip network seemed to extend from Roseberg, Oregon to Arcata to Susanville. Lantham had warned her, over and over, that real detective work was like boredom had sex with dullness and they had children named after all flavors of obnoxious. Now she was learning first hand.

"How do you fit in to all of this, Quentin? Who else do you know?"

It wasn't church. It wasn't school. It wasn't the Boy Scouts or 4H. They were all different races, some were different religions, different sexes. They were almost all working class, except for Philip Blackshire, whose father owned a small-scale mining concern, and lived like it had paid well.

Rachael took most of the bottle going over the board again, trying to find anything that might connect the kids to each other.

No matter which way she turned the puzzle, some piece fell out. One or another kid didn't fit. Whatever it was connecting them, she hadn't found it yet.

Besides their age.

Could their age be enough? Everything she'd ever read about serial killers, kidnappers, and other garden-variety sickos told her that there had to be something particular the perp was looking for. But that left child molesters.

But Zarek didn't say he was molested. Not that that meant anything, with the little bit of contact she'd had with him, but in a town this small she'd hoped to hear details through the grapevine as they came out.

And she had. Stories about a scary dark room, and a doctor with a mask, and experiments, and the voices of other people.

Some people were saying that he'd been grabbed by organ thieves who'd stolen his kidney. Some said human traffickers, who hadn't been able to keep him sedated because none of the men in that family responded to anesthesia, and everybody knew that after what happened with Zarek's father after the hunting accident (which we don't discuss with outsiders, dear, sorry about that).

So what connected them? She'd already nixed hobbies, cities, parents' jobs, schools, churches. What was she gonna look for next? How many of them had parents that belonged to the same super-secret underground charismatic satanic Nazi sex-and-cookies cult?

How the hell was she going to find any of that? Was she going to just have to hang around until the next kid turned up missing?

She had one more trump in her back pocket. Might be time to play it.

Rachael fished her phone—her real phone, the disassembled one—out from the motorcycle armor she kept hanging in the closet. This was a bad idea. This would put her right on Lantham's map for sure. But she had to do it. She had to find some way to connect these kids. Something the FBI hadn't thought of yet.

She put the pieces back together, fired it up. Ignored the beeping that told her that her box was over capacity. She opened the VPN app Lantham had installed for her.

And then she logged into his server to take a look around his databases.

GETTING A BEAD ON WHITE Hair wasn't easy. That kind of work ain't sexy, either. Lots and lots of web surfing—if he was a Christian rocker or a motivational speaker, like I'd thought he'd have to be with that hairdo, he wasn't into publicity. No website that I could find. Nothing turned up on my pet facial recognition database. Two weeks later, I was pretty damn sure, this guy wasn't in the system anywhere.

That left the control tower. Control towers keep logs of the flights that come in and out of their airports, even the little general aviation airports like the one that White Hair flew out of. If I could ID the plane by the tail number, I might be able to track him through the registered owner.

Nice theory, but the brass at the airport weren't gonna let me see their logs without an official Sheriff's department request—and I couldn't get one. This was a private snoop job. So I'd need a subpoena, which I had no way to get.

Back to square zero.

When my client—the ten-year-old Teddy Stride—asked me about what I found, I told him it might turn up something, but it was too soon to tell.

When he pressed me, I admitted I was pretty sure his Dad wasn't cheating on his Mom, but that was about all I knew. Anything else, he was going to have to wait.

I had rent to pay. Well, a mortgage. Couldn't believe I had a bloody mortgage.

Most of my days I was splitting between interviewing the relatives of a dead oil millionaire for Lloyd's (some of the insured items in the estate hadn't turned up—basic insurance job), and working for Cal Oldman.

Oldman. He was why I was drawing a government check again. Deputy Chief of Santa Clara County Sheriff's Department. Hired me on for this big secret corruption case he had a hard-on for. Lucky old me got to scrub thousands of hours of surveillance video and then drag my ass down to Silicon Valley where I could sit in the Sheriff's Department office pretending I'm a real cop again.

If I can stick with it for another twenty-odd months, I get my Federal concealed weapons permit and don't have to worry about renewing my civilian one ever again.

Respectable, right?

Slow, too. Tar drips faster than an IA probe moves. By the book, all of it anal-retentive as hell. All so that when you finally bring charges—if you finally bring charges—against the dirty cop with the serial murder habit, you don't just have enough evidence to convict, you've got enough leverage to make sure the police union doesn't try to strike over your decision to prosecute.

So I was collecting dirt on the union organizers, too. Cute, eh?

Can't say it made me feel all fresh and shiny and happy with myself—the union saved my ass a couple times when I was on the Oakland force before I crossed the line into indefensibility—but what are you gonna do? I mean, if I was just a serial killer on the city payroll they'd have backed me until the apocalypse, but sleeping with the Chief's wife is something even the union can't get behind.

Now?

Well, maybe it's a cliché, but I've got a job to do. That's me. It's what I do. So, if I have to choose between nailing crooked cops and playing nice with the union, then the union can go to hell.

I guess it comes down to why you get into this line of work in the first place. Some people get into it for the power, some people get into it for the civic duty. I'm not either of those.

I got into it because I've got a screwy brain. It can't relax unless it's got a problem to work on. I figured making detective on a police force in a high-crime city would give me plenty of puzzles to solve. When that went bust I went independent. As long as the problems keep coming, and they're not too close to home, I'm a happy guy.

Well, more or less.

Anyway, with all that going on, I only had so much time to sink into Teddy Stride's little problem. So I put Nya to work for me, on the grounds that if I didn't have Rachael around, I needed to train my remaining assistant as best I could.

It started with chasing down that plane.

I sent her out there to talk to them in person. Took her three days to get a bead on the weak link on the ATC staff, pick up on him, get him to give her a tour of the tower, get him to leave her alone with the log book long enough for her to get a picture of the right day.

Smooth operator.

The plane was registered to International Sierra Charters, and they didn't share their client list with nosy PIs, random strangers, no-court-order-holding cops, or assholes on the phone. Took four phone conversations in four different accents to establish that.

Goose egg city again.

I put Nya on Tom Stride next. That didn't work out so well. She's a social engineer, and a damn good one. But tail jobs and stakeouts? She goes bug nutty.

But she kept at it like a trouper, even though she lost him the first day that White Hair came back into town and he went on another delivery route. Same cooler. Same little boxes.

So I let her off the hook, went to plan B.

For the next week, I walked Klepto by the Stride house late every night, and eventually I caught Tom parking in the driveway instead of in the garage.

Probably to keep from waking his wife up with the garage door opener. I stuck a real-time GPS tracker inside the trailer hitch receiver where he wouldn't notice it—he never goes boating and doesn't even own a trailer—and hoped the steel in the hitch housing didn't act like a Faraday cage and keep any data from leaking out.

Then I waited.

After a few days, I checked the stop log. The transmitter was doing its job, so I checked it every few days after that. Some days he did his delivery route, some didn't. When he did, some of the addresses repeated, and some didn't.

About three weeks on, I got a couple days of downtime, decided I needed to follow get a look inside his delivery cooler, somehow.

NEVER UNDERESTIMATE THE magical powers of water, soap, and gratuitous nudity. I figured out the "somehow" in the shower. Makes you wonder how many more crimes would get solved if cops actually showered, right?

Water in the face makes me see things. Always has. This time, I saw GPS squiggles across the map of San Francisco.

Tom Stride's delivery routes.

All laid over each other.

He'd been taking different routes, hitting different stops, but there'd been a pattern I didn't spot.

He was driving three different routes, on different days and different weeks, like whatever he was delivering was operating on some sort of subscription service.

Drugs. Had to be. Maybe one of the old happy standbys? Maybe a new designer something that wasn't quite illegal yet, but still wouldn't look good on his resume.

So how do you turn a guy like Tom Stride into a drug dealer?

Good question. One I ought to answer before I actually Fed any more info to Teddy. I'd need to find out if they were in any kind of financial trouble, or if there was something else that Tom might get levered on.

"ONE THOUSAND?" I didn't quite manage not to laugh at the guy in the traffic-cone orange grease-monkey suit in the parking lot in front of me. Even a mechanic's repair yard looked gorgeous in the Outer Sunset on a day like this. Late afternoon light hits here like nowhere else in the world, even in the rainier-than-the-rest-of-the-year season. "I'm bringing *you* business."

"Hey, man, this is Google Country," he looked like Darth Vader and talked like Cheech Marin. Welcome to the Bay Area. "It costs like fifteen dollars for a fucking soda down in SOMA. A thousand'll barely get me and my boyfriend a pair of tickets to the opera and some good pizza, and you're asking me to help shake down your friend for a practical joke, which gotta be some kinda illegal you know? He get pissed, how'm I gonna 'fford an attorney?"

This guy was a hell of a find, and I wasn't gonna let him not say yes. But I wasn't gonna pay him a grand for it either. I might be a masochist (opinions vary), but that's just too much pain.

"Look, Jorrey, Les Frees said you were the best guy for this job." Les is my mechanic out in Stockton, does all my custom work. I sent him the routes, asked if he knew anyone in his line of work that might work with me on a swindle-for-a-good-cause. "Said you'd be down with it. Look, this guy's been nothing but trouble ever since his boss started working him like he was in a start-up or something, and, well, what kind of friend would I be if I didn't knock him down a peg or two. You know what these tech company dickheads are like, am I right?"

"You sure don't got that wrong."

"Two hundred." Usually I've got a client who's either very rich or very stupid or both. Now I've got a kid who can barely afford the price of a Snickers. "No harm'll come to him, swear to god."

"Hey, man, that doesn't even cover my time."

This was gonna hurt. "Three hundred. Come on, I'll take all the heat if he gets pissed. I swear."

Dude shook his head. "Four."

"Fine. But it's gotta be tomorrow afternoon, right? Two-thirty, and you gotta keep him in here for ten minutes."

"Yeah, yeah, I got it." He held his left hand out, palm up, gave it a quick wipe with a red shock rag. "You said four bills. Gimme."

I dug into my pocket, got my bribe wallet out—which I keep full of cash and nothing I actually care about losing, in case some street source decides to roll me. I pulled two, held them up. "You get the other two tomorrow."

"I can live with that."

NOW I HAD TO make sure Tom Stride's ride had a reason to inexplicably break down right in front of Jorrey Johnston's Jeep Stop. On a newer car, I'd poke around for an exploit that let me hack it with my cell phone and then just kill the engine from a distance.

Tom Stride couldn't afford a newer car. This thing was from the late 90s, which meant no remote exploits in hackerville, so I was gonna have to get creative.

Now, don't get me wrong. I'm in love with an FBI agent. Sometimes I even think about asking her to marry me. I used to be a cop—am a cop, technically—and I've got a lot of respect for the law.

But, like anything, the law's got its limits. Sometimes you gotta bend it a little.

I was bending it a bit when I got myself an after-market ignition kill switch with full premeditation.

I tiptoed along that line that evening when I wired up the switch to a pre-paid cell phone, found the wiring schematics for Tom's Grand Cherokee, and packed it along with my my wire cutters, knife, and electrical tape together in a kit

And that night, when I broke into Tom Stride's garage, jimmied his driver's side door, and wired my device into his under-dash ignition assembly so that I could disable it on command and force him to do business with a certain repair shop...well, at that point I basically just pissed on it.

6:00 AM, TUESDAY

THREE NIGHTS AGO, A STORM dumped six feet of snow on the parched high valley. With nowhere near enough snow plows in the town, Rachael had to negotiate her walk to work on her own the next morning.

A two-hour trudge through the snow in her leather biking boots, because she didn't have any other boots tall enough to be worth the trouble. Growing up in the Bay Area had left her ill-prepared to deal with anything the rest of the world casually referred to as "weather."

The snow muffled everything. The storm had swallowed everything alive, the nearby interstate just a whisper in its gullet. From rim to rim, up and down all the cinder cones, the big valley answered her eyes with an impossibly loud, impossibly bright blaring white.

Hold on, Rachael. This isn't a real job. Stop thinking like that.

She had to keep her mind on the puzzle. The impossible-to-solve puzzle. She had to find out where Zarek Woodfork had been held, and what the hell was done to him—and how many of those other kids were really involved. And why.

The forced march gave her time to think without going stir crazy. Living as herself for only those scarce hours when she was alone in that little converted garage was starting to drive her around the bend.

She wasn't cut out for undercover work.

Lantham seemed to have no problem with it. He'd do long stakeouts, switch accents and apparent cultures at the drop of a hat. He must have had some acting training at some point.

Then, when he wasn't on the job, he'd come back to the office and take the face off like it was another one of his fedoras.

He'd just had a lot of practice. That's what she kept telling herself. He'd been doing this for more than half as long as she'd been alive. That's why he was better at it than she was.

But not her. For her, it seemed to eat away at her insides. Sure, when she was actually in character talking to someone, finding more things she could pin to her murder board, that part was fun. But coming home, the moment she dropped the mask, she was tired all over.

For the first time since she'd left Castro Valley, she wished she hadn't. But the thought of going home, or going on, without actually finding the asshole who was taking these kids—the fact that she hadn't been able to prove a connection yet only showed how good this guy was—and finding out how many of them were left alive...well, that was a level of humiliation she wasn't prepared to cope with.

Not that the snow underfoot gave two shits about any of that. It just wanted to stop her getting to work.

Well, the snow could go fuck itself.

Crunch.

Crunch.

Crunch.

So she'd been driving herself further and further into exhaustion. Staring at that board. Pouring through Lantham's databases. Working all the public records she could get at.

One great relief: Lantham hadn't called Rachael after Rachael had started stealing his database time. Which meant he didn't know about it.

Which meant that he was getting sloppy about his network security.

Or, to put it the way Nya had on the phone: "He's just too damn busy since your Dad hired him."

Rachael wasn't sure whether to feel pleased or guilty about that.

So she just concentrated on the board. And the databases.

She couldn't reasonably expect to find anything.

She hunted for weeks trying to figure out what, if anything, the kids had in common.

Children don't show up in criminal databases. They don't show up in national or state records. Their feet haven't been walking the earth long enough for them to leave bureaucratic footprint. Rachael figured that one out after a couple hours of work.

Children don't leave many footprints.

But their parents do.

Perhaps their parents had something in common.

Not a church.

Not a social club.

Not a workplace.

Not a religion.

Not a hobby.

Not even a favorite cigarette brand. None of them smoked.

And, after almost a month of searching, she'd been about to give up.

Until someone at work had mentioned about Philip Blackshire having had an appendectomy.

Crunch.

Crunch.

Crunch.

She hadn't checked surgeries. Had all the kids had surgeries?

HIPAA requirements meant that getting her hands on their medical records was going to be next to impossible, at least without going and volunteering as a candy striper at every doctor's office they'd ever attended, and then waiting for a chance to hack into the system—which left the problems of finding their medical numbers and the fact that she didn't know the first thing about hacking.

She thought about calling Earl Whitaker, the guy Lantham outsourced his serious data mining to. But he was way too expensive, and he had a big mouth—might blab to Lantham that she'd been in touch. Hell, he might even track her down and give Lantham her current off-the-books address based on cell triangulation and IP access logs. The man could find any piece of information that had ever been connected to the Internet.

She couldn't get access to their medical records, so she had poured over all the news reports again. Several of the parents had given interviews to Siskiyou Daily News and the Mount Shasta Herald and the Times-Standard and the North Coast Journal talking about how wonderful their kids were, and how much they missed them.

Three sets of parents had been smart enough to talk about identifying marks and scars.

Nicole Adams had a hernia surgery scar near her navel.

Quentin Greenaway had once had re-constructive surgery on his forearm, after a fall while rock climbing.

And Jason Chan had gotten stitches on his forehead after a skateboarding accident. The scars were still visible.

There was more: Nicole, Quentin, and Jason had all done their hospital time at the same place. Maybe that wasn't so unusual, since there weren't that many hospitals up here in the back-country, but it did make four of the missing eleven with major hospital activity in their not-too-distant past.

Crunch.

Crunch.

Crunch.

But four kids with something that specific in common? That was a real connection.

So how could she connect the rest of the kids?

Well, if she couldn't get to their medical records, she could maybe find out about their health insurance.

So she started calling around to workplaces. Finding out the sorts of health care they offered employees. Posing as a telephone survey taker, or a job-seeker, or just a bored customer with too much urge to chat.

It worked.

Lantham was really on to something with the social engineering shit he was always talking about.

All of the parents' employers used the same insurance company. The Woodforks were retired, but a call to the office of Samaritan Sanctuary Insurance confirmed that they had a variety of ACA-compliant plans for retired individuals, that made full use of Medicaid and Medicare benefits, and allowed for the listing of a limited number of dependents for a small additional fee, and if she liked they could email her a complete brochure, no obligation.

So there was at least a chance that the Woodforks were on the same insurance plan. Which meant they probably also took Zarek to the same hospital at some point.

More pins in her murder board.

Crunch.

Crunch.

Crunch.

Big break, right? She'd thought so.

For three days.

Then she'd realized that narrowing her search to an insurance company meant that she'd run headlong into a corporate wall.

Insurance companies had thousands of employees, each of them with theoretical access to the kids, their medical records, anything they'd need to hunt for victims in their nefarious whatever-it-was.

Any one of those people could be the bad guy.

Try as she might, she couldn't think of any way to narrow it down further.

Hell, she couldn't even figure out what kind of thing she'd want to look for. If she knew why the kids were being taken, she'd know what to look for the commonality, and she might be able to find the suspect. And if she knew what the commonality was, she'd be able to figure out why the kids were being taken, then she might be able to finger the suspect.

Too many possibilities. All of them equally attractive.

All of them equally unattractive.

Crunch.

Crunch.

Crunch.

The deadest of dead ends. That's what this was.

The chances of her finding anything else out by

listening to town gossip were next to zero, unless another child was taken—and no new children had gone missing since Zarek had disappeared less than a week before Rachael had found him behind that gas station.

Going back to work now was almost a waste.

Crunch.

Crunch.

Crunch.

Not many customers made it in that day, the day of the big storm. The few that did were truck drivers and regulars, all of them talking about how happy they were there was finally a break in the drought, and giving her advice on how to survive her first winter in town.

A quiet shift, followed by another frustrating evening staring at the murder board hoping for some kind of idea.

Then, yesterday, a busier day at work. Lots of chicken soup on the stove, selling to customers even more than the butter-and-fake-maple-drenched French toast. The roads had melted enough for regular traffic to flow a little easier than cold strawberry sauce.

About ten o'clock, truckers stopping in for midmorning coffee were bitching about a bunch of CHP screwing up traffic a ways down south. Blocked off a whole lane, didn't even have a flagger out. Looked like a goddamned cop convention, and nobody was saying a thing.

Then, one in the afternoon, the word came over the speakers that piped classic rock in for the customers to listen to while they ate. The kind of news update that tears small towns wide open.

Another child had turned up. Nicole Adams.

She was picked up on the side of I-5 sixteen miles north of South Weed, the second-to-last town on Northbound I-5, near the Oregon border.

She was wearing a pair of sweat pants three sizes too big, and an old Coors Light T-shirt.

The trucker who spotted her wandering on the shoulder at four in the morning called the CHP, not the local police.

The girl was being treated for hypothermia.

Rachael stayed glued to the radio until the end of her shift.

Afterward, she ran back to her house and updated the board.

She checked the Internet.

Over the course of the day, the police had turned up eight more children.

Counting Zarek, that made ten. One more was missing.

Rachael's murder board got a lot more pins.

And the questions multiplied.

BRIGHT DAY. NO CLOUDS. Not the kind of day it was easy to melt into the scenery, and it was the day I had to tail Tom Stride again.

Me waking up at eight is a like the Pope conducting a Black Mass. Not a pretty sight. A clashing couture catastrophe. But I did my bit for the neighbor kid, hauled my ass out of bed and slammed my head against the shower wall a few times until I was in fighting shape.

Had to wait till noon before Tom Stride rolled out of the driveway. Straight to SFO, just like last time.

Bottom deck, the tunnel of perpetual night with the bile-yellow sodium lights where even Mickey Mouse could look like a skid-row drug dealer. This time at the US Airways pickup, that same white-haired guy with dark roots—except this time the roots were longer. He was gonna need a new dye job soon.

What kind of guy dyes his hair white? The kind of guy who wants to project authority in a culture where being an old white guy still gets you extra street cred, that's who. If the lines on his face didn't say fifty, I'd have pegged him for thirty-five and faking the gray.

Guess he could be doing that anyway.

Who are you, White Hair?

Something about him bugged me, and it wasn't just the obvious hold he had on Tom Stride.

Stride drove from the airport to the school. Dropped off White Hair. Left on his run.

He looped north to John Daly Boulevard. Same delivery schedule through the Westlake district. Same shift out to the PCH. Same troll through the Outer Sunset.

His route jagged around as he hit three stops down there. I took a more direct route to the Jorrey Johnston's Jeep Stop. Head him off at the pass. Pulled up next to the curb in an illegal parking spot three buildings before the cracked-and-faded blue cinder block garage nested between two gorgeous old Vics.

Now I had to wait and pray no meter maids spotted the blood in the water for at least five minutes. In a city like this, that's only three steps shy waiting for the Rapture inside an active caldera and betting that Jesus shows up before the volcano god gets indigestion.

Took him more than five minutes.

Seven minutes in, I see the meter maid on patrol, coming up the street my direction, three blocks back.

Then, a minute later, that ratty old road-film-ridden green Grand Cherokee. Glory glory hallelujah.

Come on, Tom. Keep coming. Don't look at the parked cars.

I knew he wouldn't. They never do. But there's always that minute when they pass you by, when there's just the slightest chance they'll look sideways at the wrong time. And someone like me, who's tall enough to startle grizzly bears, well, it's not like I could hunker down or anything. Best I could do was turn my face away.

Needed to do it anyway, to dial.

One pre-paid dials another. No tracing either of them back to me if Tom got huffy and called the cops.

Ring ring went the other end of the line.

And, just like that, Tom Stride coasted to a stop, about a dozen yards past Jorrey's place.

I dialed Jorrey.

"Jorrey, this is Lantham. You're a go."

"Give me two minutes after we push him in here, man, then come in around the back."

"Mind if I block your driveway?"

"With that piece of garbage? Shit, man, I gotta make a living here, you know?"

"I'll take that as a yes." That meter maid was only half a block back now, writing up a ticket with her hand and pointing her eyes at my car like she was diabetic and it was made out of chocolate. If Jorrey wanted my other two hundred bucks, he'd just have to deal.

Hung up.

Got myself out into traffic, cut right in front of a Corolla so that pseudocop couldn't get my plate. Hung a right again, right into the driveway west of the building, the one that went around the back into the yard. Jorrey's shop had two bay doors that opened onto the street, and that's where he'd push Tom's car in. I just had to sit tight and wait for Stride to take the bait.

Probably ought to get out of view, too.

I drove through, parked in the back behind a dirty cream MGB convertible and a sparkling new metallic blue Maserati GranTourismo. Guess Jorrey did more than just Jeeps. Talk about underselling things on the sign.

Got out of the car. Hot-footed it across the three-hundred-year-old tarmac with all its loose gravel, made it to the building.

I leaned against the faded blue wall, about two inches from the corner. This time I had my bag of tricks with me, including the dental mirror I usually kept strapped to my left forearm when I went on a tail.

I squeezed my left hand, bent my elbow, then threw my fist forward and opened my had. The mirror popped out. I flicked the handle, the whole thing telescoped to twenty inches long.

Then I dropped it down low, poked it around the corner, and played like I had a periscope.

And I waited. I hate waiting.

That meter maid, though? She—well, turned out to be a he, but who can tell the difference anymore anyway—pulled up to a stop right in front of the driveway and got out, waving at him. Shouted loud enough that I could hear.

"Sir! Sir, you can't park there, I'm going to have to write you a ticket."

Then, probably Tom said something like "I can't get

this thing to start."

"I don't care, sir, you can't leave it there. Vacate the street."

Tom must have said something like "Can you help me push it into that shop there?" Because the meter maid hopped back in his go-cart and parked it in the driveway, then hopped out again, and a minute later Tom Stride's Jeep rolls backwards across the driveway mouth with two men, one meter maid, and one woman in high heels and a business suit pushing it.

I decided to run the risk of shorting my time in the garage in the interests of not being caught burgling Tom Stride's car. There aren't many things in life that look worse on a PI's rap sheet than "Arrested for Petty Theft by a Meter Maid." They put that kinda shit on your tombstone so that future generations of private snoops can learn not to be you.

Lantham, you're cowering behind a wrench-haven whose owner you bribed in the Outer Sunset so a Meter Maid doesn't catch you looking through your mark's mail. And you're doing it on purpose.

These are the kinds of life-choices that you make when you're thirty-seven and trying desperately to stay relevant in your own mind.

The meter maid climbed back into his go-cart and went.

To my right was a regular door, then a few feet beyond it were the bay doors. I leaned out and peered around the corner. Across the bays, on the west end of the building, were the offices. I could see Jorrey through a service window talking to someone—who, though I couldn't see him, had to be Tom Stride—on the other side of a counter.

Couldn't see the Jeep, though.

I leaned in, tried the handle of the people-sized door.

It gave.

I stepped in to find myself surrounded by racks full of tools and short stacks of old tires. Natural light blared in from the open double-bay doors on the north and south sides of the building, and two portable racks—one for each bay—held SUVs suspended eight feet up.

Tom Stride's Cherokee was underneath the nearer one, blocking any view he might have of me and my vehicle-burgling ways.

I crouched low, glad I'd left my hat in the car—given that I already look like a signal tower for wayward aircraft, I hardly needed anything adding more height and visibility to my silhouette at the moment—and shimmied between the piles of tires to the driver's side rear door.

Trip the latch and...

Locked.

For this I was paying four hundred bucks out of pocket?

Lantham, you need a new business plan.

He wouldn't have locked up a car that he was going to be getting repaired right away, would he? The repairmen needed access, after all.

Driver's door?

It clicked open. Goddamn selective automatic door de-lockers.

Check across the cab through the window. Still couldn't see Tom Stride from here, which meant he couldn't see me.

Leaned in, braced myself on the console. The cooler was in the passenger foot well in all its blue-and-white Colemany goodness. Next to it was a pair of brown bento boxes—checked those first, both empty.

The Coleman was one of those little picnic coolers designed to drive senior citizens to suicide. The one that has the pointy swivel top that unlocks when you press a button on one side and is about as easy to open as a sixteenth-century chastity belt.

Well, I opened it with my meat mitts and found dry ice packed around stacks of little boxes, each big enough to hold a spark plug. I picked one up. Brown paper, labels with bar codes and numbers—could be serial numbers or sort codes—and sealed with round blue stickers.

Took my phone out, brought up the camera, got it ready to take pics.

Stole the buck knife from my pocket, flicked it open, slit one open...

...and got the surprise off my life.

It was filled with four vials with rubber stoppers in the end. Like they were designed to load a hypodermic needle. I tapped one out far enough to see the contents.

Pale yellow. Viscous like glycerin. Nothing interesting on the label. Just a customer number on a white slip of paper with an impressionist-looking maroon plus on it, made out of four stretched out oblongs. I snapped a picture.

I really needed to find out what was in these. A picture might not do the trick.

"Just sit tight there," Jorrey's thin Mexican accent pierced straight through the side of the Jeep. "I'll take a look and tell you what we're dealing with. No, really. I can't have you out in the garage, the insurance won't like it. Watch some tee vee or something, okay?" Then, I heard him grumbling, but couldn't hear what he was saying, except that it was getting louder as he approached the Jeep.

Well, I wasn't going to be able to take a picture of the vials, and I needed to know what they were. I flipped the little spark plug box shut, pocketed it.

Slid back out of the cab just in time to get out of Jorrey's way.

He reached in, under the dashboard, popped the hood. "What the hell you do to the guy's car?"

"Ignition kill switch. Under the dash here. He'll need some wire splicing. Pretend his distributor cap failed or something." I was already digging in my BDUs for my wallet. Essential to a job where you gotta go fully loaded, the humble BDU. Got more cargo space than a sixteen foot box truck.

"You're one sick motherfucker, man. You got my bills?"

"Here you go." I forked over.

"You get your surprise planted?"

"All set."

"Then get the fuck out of here before your boy sees you."

I STOPPED AT AN AM/PM, got an empty donut bag and a glass full of ice, then I sealed the vial in as best I could with a plastic drinks top and stashed it inside my bag of tricks on the back seat. I could worry about how to ID it later.

Right now I needed to figure out who White Hair was, and figure out his deal. Time to engineer a meet and greet when Tom Stride wasn't around and couldn't ruin things by asking me why I was nosing around in his workplace.

I slid out of there and high-tailed it back to the edge of South San Francisco, to Trubody College where the visitor slots in the parking lot were as empty as the should-have-been-raining-winter-sky.

But I parked across the street anyway. Didn't want Tom Stride spotting my car when he came back. If he spotted me without expecting to, chances were good his brain would just edit me out. Tomorrow I'd get a shout across the front lawn about how "the funniest thing happened, I saw this tall guy at work who looked just like you."

People don't see what they don't expect to see. It's

the human evolutionary superpower. It's why we can survive in cities.

I figured that gave me just enough wiggle room to try to bump into Mr. White Hair, or at least find out what his deal was. Just had to ratchet up the charm, be the world's most amusing, likable nosy bastard.

And get lucky. Maybe really lucky.

Charm can work for a day, but if I didn't play this just right I might have to actually infiltrate the place, and that'd take a couple weeks, maybe months. I might have to try to get in as an adjunct professor and play the long game, except that I'm not a a Protestant. I'm not even properly religious enough to be able to fake it. When it comes to theology, I don't know my Assumption from my holy ground.

No good going in as to teach any of my specialties either. Bible colleges don't usually offer any courses in criminology or private detection. Even asking about adjunct positions would get me eaten alive. It'd also take way more time than I could give a job that didn't pay.

The idea of doing that kind of long con made me about as stiff and itchy as three-day-old cooked spaghetti.

But a short con I could do. I mean, what college doesn't like a prospective student, especially an older, non-traditional one with a lot of spare cash to throw around?

I threw my jacket on, even though it wasn't really cold enough for it, skipped across Silver, and strolled across the lawn, nice and slow, dodging between groups of students playing Ultimate Frisbee and taunting each other.

Gorgeous old building. Built way the hell back before the first world war. Looks like a Spanish Mission designed by the Army Corps of Engineers—which is more or less what it is. It started life as an Army office, then got turned into an internment center during WW2, then sold out to the Salvation Army, which then sold it on to some church group or other. The place had shifted hands among various bible colleges, Christian high schools, and churches since then.

You can still see the fingerprints in the hand-made bricks that make up the structure, and it's got a colonnade on the west end and a gigantic domed annex in the middle.

The facade is marked by fortress-style towers with painted archways recessed into the brickwork. It runs about a hundred yards from east to west, and if you think that's big, that's nothing on what happens when you get inside and find out that it's built on the edge of a cliff. Around back, the building stretches seven stories from top to bottom, with three wings jutting out so that it looks kind of like a giant capital E when viewed from orbit.

When you tell the Army you need a serious headquarters building, the Corps of Engineers doesn't screw around.

Inside that main entrance, history jumps out and

sticks its fingers up your nose. Creosote and plaster and lead paint and the salt that had soaked in from a hundred-odd years of San Francisco fog gave the place a sense that, around the next corner, you're going to find a gigantic forgotten library so filled with old books that you'll spend the next five years just getting used to the smell.

And then the rest of your life figuring out how to live without it.

I posed as a new convert who wanted to audit some classes. Figured it was the only thing that might look convincing on me, unless I stripped to a loincloth and said I was here to audition for the part of Goliath in the school play.

Yes, the Lord's work was very important to me now after my life of sin. Wanted to figure out what field of ministry He was calling me to. Wanted to learn about the history of my new religion. All that good stuff. I wasn't sure I wanted a degree, not yet. I definitely didn't want to go for credit until I knew what it was I was doing, because college is expensive. So I wondered, could they do anything to help me?

Evidently they could. The roundish blond work-study girl behind the half-door pass-through that served both as a front desk and the back door for the bookstore kiosk on the other side handed me a sheaf of publicity materials and encouraged me to take a look around, then warned me that the next round of classes started in three weeks and that I was almost past the enrollment deadline, even for auditing, so I'd need to move fast.

I peaked inside one of the brochures and my wallet had a very small heart attack. Classes for enrolled students came at the price of your immortal soul—you expect that from any private college—but just auditing a class still required sacrificing three virgins, two goats, and your firstborn child.

Better make the most of this, Lantham. Hanging around here regularly will seriously piss off your accountant.

I looked around. Got my bearings. Checked the map.

The annex had four exits, all on compass-points. Directly south was the door I came in through. North took me into an old, flat meeting hall-style theater with pews for maybe three hundred people. East and west both led down impossibly long hallways with green carpet, lime-wash white plaster walls, and dark stained oak trim around the doors and windows. Sure, it made my inner architecture geek sing, but I was definitely in a maze of twisty little passages, all alike.

So, I backed up to the center of the annex, decided that I liked being right-handed, and hung a right to head east.

It wasn't exactly an inspired bit of navigation. I wound up jockeying for shoulder space in a corridor that had been built back when everyone was malnourished and a lot shorter than me.

Okay, a lot shorter than most of today's people, who are still a lot shorter than me. So we're talking ancient

San Francisco munchkins built this place.

The windows to the left looked down on the rest of the campus sloping down the steep hill behind, then across the ass-end of the city to 280 cutting through the valley before it crossed 101 and headed down into the Hunter's Point neighborhood. All the doors leading off the corridor toward the front of the building—and there were a lot of them—seemed to lead into narrow book closets with desks in the middle.

There was no way you could actually use one of those desks for anything. There was no elbow room and you could barely fit a laptop on one. I figured they must be there solely for earthquake safety, so the poor bastards who had to squeeze in there to work had somewhere to dive before the world dumped the sum total of its published knowledge on them.

At the far east end there was another annex, this one set up like a big lobby, lots of glass looking out on the front lawn, and a couple other doors leading north—peeking through the wired glass windows in the doors, I saw stairwells, and beyond those, long halls.

Some place they've got here.

Don't ask me how it happened, cause I don't really know. Maybe it was just osmosis, from being around the Bay my whole life, but somewhere along the way, without any formal training at all, the architecture bug bit me.

This place? I could spend two whole years exploring it and never get bored. I was so in love with the architecture on display that it didn't occur to me to actually look at the map.

"Excuse me? Are you all right?" A silver fox, somewhere in his late sixties based on the fringe of white wreathing his distinctly Captain Picard-y scalp, accosted me with a creaky layer of Bronx. I looked over my shoulder to find him sitting at one end of a button-studded maroon leather chesterfield, using the arm as a prop for a notebook.

"A little lost, actually."

"What are you looking for?"

"Well, frankly, I'm not quite sure." I soft-padded across the carpet and sat in a matching low-backed chair that, together with the couch, formed half of a conversation pit around a long low glass-topped coffee table populated with a vase full of tulips. "I think the building got the better of me."

"Don't feel bad. Lots of folks get lost in a place this big."

"Oh, it's not the size." I waved at the nine foot French doors that opened south onto the front lawn. "It's the building. The design. Look at the trim on these doors here. You'd usually find these in an arts-and-crafts building, but they're used here in a Spanish Mission fortress. Kind of move that only an Army design board would have the temerity to make, especially back when this place was built, but it works, and it's gorgeous. And...well, I guess I got a little distracted."

The old man pursed his lips. The corners twisted up

a little bit. "They don't give architecture degrees here, you know."

I chuckled. "Well, there's all my dreams out the window. Clarke Follett." I stuck out my hand. He gripped it—a sturdy grip.

"Roy. Kids around here call me Grandpa Roy." He settled back into his seat with his notebook.

"You're not a professor." Obviously not. Just mentioning the fact that he probably wasn't drew a little flicker of amusement from his eyebrows. "Student? Working on your second degree, maybe?"

He shook his head, then pointed with his eyebrows—an old man superpower reserved for those who don't trim their eyebrows, one of the things I'm looking forward to about being too old to give a shit—at the vase of tulips.

"I grow these."

"And hang around with the kids all day?" I pulled my phone out of my pocket. My friend Earl Whitaker hooked me up with a Blackphone last month. Turns out that I've gotten enough of the right kind of attention that having something even the NSA can't tap into is a reasonable security measure—which is another way of saying that my life seems to be defined by Me and my big mouth...

Or would be, if I actually made a habit of blabbing to anyone. Maybe Me and my damn questions is more accurate.

Downside of the Blackphone is it doesn't have a

stylus, which means I have to use the touchscreen keyboard like a rube—not as easy as it looks when you've got hands big enough to palm a small planet. There's a reason why I carry a weapon that weighs more than most jogging weights and fires a slow moving cannonball instead of one of the fancier high-capacity Europop guns that all the fashionable cops are carrying these days.

"One thing you learn when you get to be my age, son," Grandpa Roy said, "You stay young by being around young people. Have you seen what most folks my age do for fun?"

"Canasta?"

"Hmph. Most of them still think playing cards are tools of the devil."

"In San Francisco?"

"You're too young to remember, but there was a time when this place was Catholics and EMA from one end to the other. This very building used to be an internment camp. We had segregation here, too, and the toughest eugenics laws in the country. Hitler based his on us, you know that? Called California the model for progressive scientific racial purity."

As a matter of fact I did know those things, but I made like I didn't so he'd keep on. I had to get down the details of the false persona I'd invented since walking in the door. Might need 'em later.

Trying to keep one ear on Grandpa Roy, though, made me write my assumed name as "Clarke Hitler" rather than "Clarke Follett," and it took me another sentence before I realized what I'd done.

"And under all that, we had the military. More military bases per square mile than you've seen in your lifetime, I guarantee. More even than there were at the end of the Cold War. That's what this building was originally. You know that, right? That's why the architecture is the way it is. My grandfather helped build it, when he was in the army back in 1908, right after the big earthquake."

"Really?"

"Yup. This place was bone-deep conservative right up until the Summer of Love, then everything started to go to hell."

"Doesn't sound like it was exactly paradise before then." I gave him a little twinkle, to see how serious he was.

He twinkled back. "Oh, it wasn't. Pleasant enough, I suppose, for most folks, but pretty dull. I shipped off to New Guinea in forty-nine…"

"Military brat?" The big French doors opened to admit a knot of about eight students—three men, five women—laughing and talking excitedly. You could smell the pheromones, and the sweat didn't help either. Judging by the Frisbee and the soaked clothes, I figured they must be one of the groups I'd seen out on the front lawn.

"Not for that move. No, that was following the Lord's calling."

"Missionary?"

One of the kids scooped up a tulip as he passed, saying "Thanks, Grandpa Roy," and joined his friends back by the door to the dormitory, where they kept up their game of gossip-and-grab-ass, except without any actual ass-grabbing as far as I could see.

"I was with a group trying to make contact with the last of the cannibal tribes," Grandpa Roy said, "and learn their language. Stayed out there in the jungle for the next thirty years. Can't tell you what it was like to come back."

"Just as AIDS was popping up. Hell of a culture shock." Watch your language, Lantham. People here think that hell is a real place and it's blasphemous to mention it. Better be careful or I'd blow the "new student" ruse.

"Different place than I ever knew as a kid. But that's when I noticed that my friends, a lot of the ones that went with me, were old, even then. I made a pact with my Josephine—my wife, you know, we met in the field—that we'd do whatever we could to stay young until the Lord calls us home."

I did a bit of quick mental math, realized that he had to be pushing ninety. "It's working. I wouldn't have pegged you for a day over sixty-five."

"Flattery don't buy much."

"Ah, but hanging around the young buys youth. I should stick here with you, and we can feed off their life-energy like vampires."

"That's a little morbid." He didn't say it with any levity in his voice. Time to step back and re-up on the charm.

"It beats cannibalism."

"I hate to tell you, son, but I've seen it up close. Broccoli beats cannibalism."

"Broccoli isn't sturdy enough to beat much of anything."

He narrowed his eyes. "You were the kind of boy that read Mad Magazine."

"And watched Monty Python. And hates the smell of broccoli, so I'm with you there."

"You don't want to know about the things I smelled the first couple years with that tribe."

"I believe it. In my old life...well, less said the better. Important to stop and smell the flowers after smells like that, right?"

He waved at the tulips. "Have one. I grow them in my front yard. Always have more than'll fit. Don't know what I'm going to do if His Grubbiness gets his way."

"His what now?"

"Oh." He chuckled. "His Grubbiness. It's what everyone calls him behind his back, but don't let him catch you calling him that, or he'll find some excuse to expel you. Tin-pot tyrant, a real rascal." Grandpa Roy must have noticed the confused look on my face, cause he rushed to clarify: "The president of the school here. Frank Gruber."

"Cute nickname."

He smiled. "Don't tell him I repeated it to you."

"How do I know it's him?"

"Oh, you can't miss him. Older guy, wears Chicago pinstripes all the time." Roy's tone sounded like he was remembering some rotten cabbage he'd once smelled. Then he snorted. "Crazy white hair, looks like something you'd see at a rock 'n roll show."

Bingo.

So why does the college president have Tom Stride delivering hypo vials?

Roy noticed I hadn't said anything. "Sorry. Family business, I guess. Not anything you'd care about. So, you said you were lost. What is it you're looking for?"

So I spun him my cover story, while I flipped through the menus on my phone. I started the recorder app and left it running so I'd be able to rehearse it on the drive home tonight.

"You're looking to find God's calling for your life, you're not going to find it in the halls of an institution."

"Maybe not, but I don't know enough yet to know the difference between his calling and mine. I figure on learning a bit more about it all, more than you can learn listening to a pastor just read from the Bible."

"Well, we do have some good people in the history department, if you can judge by how much the kids complain about their term projects."

"Any recommendations?"

"Oh, I don't sit in on classes."

I made a slightly-disappointed face, rather than

chasing him down verbally. I figured he'd take pity on me and throw me a bone.

"Professor Carpenter makes them miserable. And Professor Stride. Doctor Course, of course. You'd like him. Archeology and ancient history of the Holy Land."

"Where do they teach?" Find out where, I'd have a better chance of not running into him.

"Oh, it varies. Each class, a different room, a different time. Haven't you ever been to college before?"

I shrugged.

"Trust me," this wasn't Roy, this was a voice from the knot of kids in the corner. Tall kid, almost as tall as me, preppie hair cut, built like he was here on a basketball scholarship. "Doctor Course is the worst."

One of his compatriots—a soft-but-well-shaped coed with a gaudy maroon-and-silver sweatshirt dangling from her shoulders—hit him. "That's because you've got about as much interest in history as a rhino has in sports cars."

I looked at Roy. "English major?"

"Think so." He closed his eyes like he needed the extra processing power to search his database. "Betsy, I think. Betsy Kaufman. Or is that Bridget? It's hard to keep track of all of 'em."

"It's Betsy, Grandpa Roy." The young woman had her ear on the conversation. Gotta respect a good eavesdropper.

"I guess I'd better get moving, see if I can sit in on some of those classes before they wrap up for the day."

I stood up, made a show of collecting my stack of pamphlets and maps from the table.

"Son, do me a favor," Roy said. "If you run into His Grubbiness, don't let him know you heard it from me. I'd kinda like to hang around here until its all over with."

"Cross my heart. Why was he bugging you again?"

"He's got some fool notion to move this whole school up to the back of beyond, for no reason that makes any sense to anybody."

"Back of nowhere is a long way to bring tulips."

"You know, the thought occurred. Good luck with the professors."

Betsy swooped over and smothered Grandpa Roy in a hug, then bounced herself back to standing and lunged—politely—for my arm. She slipped an arm into it and escorted me back the way I came—west along the length of the campus, back to the annex.

"So you're a freshman, huh?" Her voice had a flirty lilt that reminded me, more than a little bit, of Nya. It made me double-check her face for the telltale signs of Nya's particular deformity, but there weren't any.

Guess she just liked using her charm to make people feel welcome. Certainly was making me warm all over. "Well, not really. Not yet, anyway."

"What are you interested in?"

"Umm..." I felt a lot stupider rattling the whole conversion story to the young woman on my arm than I had to the old man or the coed in the kiosk. But I rattled it off anyway, and finished with a "Guess it sounds kinda silly when you say it out loud."

"Nonsense." Big smile in her voice. When I said I needed to get lucky, this wasn't the kind of thing I had in mind, I swear. "Now, if you're thinking of coming here, you're going to need the grand tour. It's easy to get lost in a place like this."

"They gave me a map..." I held up the packet they'd given me at the kiosk.

"Map schmap." She snatched the packet out of my hand and tucked it behind her back, presumably into the waistband of her sweat pants.

Just then we crossed into the annex, then marched straight across it.

"Where are we going?" I asked. This was the right place to jump off. Now that I knew that White Hair was the President of the school, I could get back to doing my job the way it should be done: from behind a computer screen where nobody could see me or make me put on pants.

"My dorm room."

I didn't have to fake being nervous. "Umm..."

"Oh pfft. In your dreams."

"Not really. I..."

"Yeah, yeah, whatever. You need a tour. I need a clean shirt," she pointed at the dirty grass-stained oversized t-shirt she was wearing.

It's hard to artfully extract yourself from an intelligent young woman who's determined to play hostess. "No, I mean I have to..."

She squeezed my arms. "Relax. I'm not gonna bite you. Geepers."

The 'geepers' is what got me. Hadn't heard that word since watching old Dennis the Menace reruns. And here I thought I was gonna pour the charm on.

Fifty yards later we reached another large lounge—this one with deep green wall-to-wall carpet and white canvas furniture—with doors in the back. Betsy hooked a right and pushed through a vintage institutional-looking stained-and-varnished oak door with a wired-glass square window in the middle of it.

"This is the women's dorm," she said. "Floor hours go until nine, so it's okay for you to be in here."

We passed through a stairwell, I couldn't resist looking down and up. I could count two floors up, and more down. It got dark down there after a while. Guess there weren't enough students to use the bottom levels.

A second door—this one flat brown with metal over-paneling—gave way to a straight hallway, maybe thirty yards long, that dead ended in a window overlooking Bernal Heights.

Betsy led me to the third door along, right side, and said: "Stay here, I'll be right back."

Then she reached down the neck in her t-shirt, retrieved a key from her bra, opened the door, and slipped inside.

I cooled my heels. Spent my time studying the geography. This place felt like something out of a haunted building movie-of-the-week. Lath and plaster walls, with the hand-texturing still obvious after all these years, washed white as bleached bones. Dark hardwood crown molding and skirting boards and door jambs, expensive looking, almost black, like someone'd dipped seasoned oak into motor oil and let it soak for a week before nailing it up.

God, I'd hate to get lost in a place like this. Gorgeous as it was, the whole thing came over as ancient and creepy, like someone had imported a haunted castle and gave it a fresh, all-American coat of paint.

The fact that it had electrical outlets every ten feet, and dry-erase boards on each door, and bulletin boards spaced periodically down each side of the hall, didn't make it seem any more modern.

Betsy emerged, wearing jeans and a fresh-looking oversized Trubody College sweat shirt. She took my arm again and walked me down to the end of the wing to the window looking out over the valley.

"So, you know San Francisco," she waved out the window like Vanna White.

"Mmm. We've met."

"Ooh," she twittered, "I sense a complicated relationship."

I didn't have anything good to say to that that wouldn't blow my cover story out of the water, so I gave her a half-smile and half-shrug.

She narrowed her eyes a bit and lifted a brow, but it was just a quick thing as she turned away to lead me through another institutional door.

It led to another stairwell, and we went down.

In modern buildings, stairwells are architectural afterthoughts. The people who build them figure that everyone's gonna take the elevator, so why bother making the stairwells interesting or pretty?

Old buildings like this, the stairwells have plenty of natural light, and they're finished every bit as much as the hallways. Dark hardwood moldings, beautiful carpets, lime-white plaster walls. I'm not the kind of guy who pines for the good old days, but sometimes...

The next floor down, we doubled back down the wing.

"More dorms?"

"Nope. The other women's rooms are on the top floor. This is study rooms." She leaned against the nearest door. It opened. A room, about ten-by-twelve, with a single desk stretching all the way around it, a couple power strips, and a couple non-rolling orange plastic chairs.

"No latches on the doors?"

Betsy put on a voice that could've come out of an older-and-holier-than-thou Nashville vice cop. "Well, must not create opportunities for our upstanding students to be tempted with sins of the flesh."

"That's hardly fair, they're just trying to do what's best, right?" I figured I'd wind her up more by playing the semi-sympathetic fuddy-duddy. A gamble. When they don't clam up tighter than a nun's twat, annoyed people tend to get diarrhea of the mouth. When I was at school, there was always a healthy trade among the students about the very private lives of the worst teachers and administrators.

"You're gonna fit right in here." She pushed herself off the study room door and led me along the hall toward the main building again.

"You think so?"

"Yeah. As a prof."

That's what it sounds like when the temperature drops fifteen degrees.

She didn't say anything else till we got to the far end of the wing, in the stairwell. On this floor, there were doors on all four sides. Betsy slipped around the banister toward the left door.

"Hold on, what's down there?" I pointed down the stairwell, into the dark.

"Storage, I guess." She shrugged. "It's locked anyway."

"And those?" I pointed to the other doors.

"Boring stuff. Offices, copy room, supplies, that kind of thing. Oh, except through here." She wound around the stairwell to the door on my right—the west side, if I still had my bearings. "This is the TV studio. Lots of fun toys in here," she jiggled the lock. "They locked it up a couple years ago when some upperclassmen made a porno in there."

Now I didn't have to play fuddy-duddy. "Here? At Trubody? I thought...well..." I ground to a stop, because I didn't know how to say "So much for family values" without coming off like the outsider I was.

Those narrow eyes again, and a dramatic sigh for good measure. "I guess you were a virgin till you got married, then."

I held up my left hand, wiggled my fingers. "I'm not married."

"Riiiight." Another strange look. I was not getting the responses I expected.

Time for the quick two-step. "Sorry. I'm kinda new at this."

"How new?"

"Um...well, I only got saved about four months ago." Thank God for my first college girlfriend. Learned a lot about evangelical subculture, and most of the lingo was still current. Handy thing about a subculture that doesn't like change.

"Want a tip?"

I shrugged. "Sure."

"Tone down the whole Pharisee act. Just be you."

"Oh, that'll work well."

"Really." She fixed me with this look of great sincerity.

Time to let the co-ed win.

"Okay." I gave her a shy half-smile, looked at the ground, nodded my head a bit.

"Good. Now, the fun stuff." She returned to the door she was about to lead me through, the one heading north, and continued with the tour.

We went through into a snack bar, with a mail room

on the far side. She told me about the food, and how it was better than everything they served in the cafeteria, but more expensive.

Past the mail room, there was a staircase that led back up into the main annex, which she pointed out as we passed and wound down a long ramp past the psychology department labs and offices.

This was her department, her major, so I got the detailed tour. This was the room where they did the IQ assessments, this was the suite where students did practice therapy sessions. Down another hidden stairway was where they kept all the old equipment, and a door in the back of it led to the end of the library under the Annex. The psych department was the same office where they did the detainee processing back in the day, and there were still some old Army tabulating machines back against the walls. I had to resist the urge to let my inner tech geek study them, and then a second urge to pull out my phone and see how much those machines were going for on Ebay.

She regaled me with the history of the psych department, how they had to fight for funding every year because there were still people in the denomination who thought that psychology was somehow anti-Christian, and that anyone who went to therapy was admitting that God wasn't enough for them. How her professor, a Dr. Hunter, was a hero for how she fought for it every year so they could keep turning out graduates that went on to get their Ph. Ds from

Stanford.

After the in-depth tour of the psych department, we peeled around to the cafeteria, where I got a description of the food, full of minced oaths more creative than anything I heard as a Catholic kid trying to avoid getting smacked by my mother, the priests, and the penguin powers that be.

"...and don't even get me started on what happened when His Grubbiness got here last year." She was leading me out through the music department, on the bottom floor south side of the wing west of the Annex. She kept keeping her voice low so nobody else would hear us. "If I wasn't a junior already, I'd transfer out."

"Why's that?"

"Ugh. You don't even want to know."

"If I'm gonna take classes here I do."

"What, you want the whole story?" She rounded another corner to a staircase, started heading up.

I shrugged. "Why not? I mean, if it's not worth it..."

"Trust me, it's not."

"Why not?"

"You want the whole list?"

"Sure."

"Buy me dinner."

"What? It's not even..." I pulled my phone out, checked the time, "...five yet." Shit, she'd already burned two hours on me and we hadn't even covered half the campus yet. This was going to take forever.

"Your call. I gotta go to work at seven."

We mounted the top of the stairs, hung a left.

"That's the chapel in there," she pointed at the door across from us, "and this is where the big classrooms are. Theology and history mostly, but all of the lower division pre-reqs get taught in here, since they're the only rooms big enough." She waved at a series of rooms on the left. Open doors, all of them.

As we approached the second one, I could hear a familiar voice. The kind that carried.

Oh hell.

"That's Doctor Stride's history class. You want to get in there if you're a student here. Professor Aichen is the only other one that teaches it, and it's insomnia therapy when he teaches it."

I hugged the wall, then took a big step past the door, hoped to hell Tom wouldn't spot me.

If I hadn't been doing this thing for years, I wouldn't have been able to resist looking inside to make sure.

Just brazen it out, Lantham. Your neighbor won't see you if you don't look like you're worth looking at. You're just another plainclothes academic walking through the halls on a busy evening.

He didn't shout.

Didn't even change his cadence.

That was close.

Once we were past the next classroom door, so I was sure he wouldn't be able to pick out my voice, I said: "Okay, you got me. Where do you want to go for dinner?"

BETSY BOUGHT A TURKEY club and a San Pellegrino Lemon.

I had a falafel and a Coke. Between you and me, I gotta ask: Who in the screaming blue hell puts sugar in tahini sauce? I swear if I was in the mob I'd send a wiseguy around to acquaint the bozo that ran the snack bar with the concept of middle-eastern justice.

Not that I'm middle-eastern, but any geopolitical region that comes up with falafel, kebabs, and baklava is a region whose culinary honor is worth defending.

Betsy did not appreciate my reaction to her favorite restaurant, but since I was old and surly and buying the food, I just shrugged at her.

"First thing you need to know if you want to go to school here," she said, "Is they're going to make you sign a contract."

"What kind of contract?"

"A lifestyle contract. You promise that you won't drink, or smoke, or do drugs, or look at porn, or have sex, or...no, I think that's it. I think. I always forget one of them."

"Yikes."

"Right? I mean, they say it's all about biblical values, but how many of those things are in the Bible?"

We sat at one of the el cheapo round tables next to the vending machine. The geography of the place was such that I couldn't watch all the doors, so I angled the napkin holder in front of me so that I could tell if someone was walking up behind me.

"Well, the sex thing." I said. "I'm pretty sure that's in there."

"That's the only one," she said.

Betsy peeled the butcher-paper wrap back from one end of her sandwich, took the first bite. Made a vaguely orgasmic face. Obviously loved every ounce of it. "Real food. So nice."

My ass was not in love with the el cheapo mucho uncomfortabulo plastic seats. Those things are designed for people at least a foot shorter than me. I looked like Shrek's skinny cousin teaching a kindergarten falafel workshop.

Two bites into her sandwich, Betsy made eye contact with me, and just about spit her food out mid chew. She covered her mouth before she lost anything to the table. "Oh my God. Oh no. Oh, I'm sorry."

"Um...what?"

"You look like you're sitting on a tack."

I shifted in my seat. "Not really built for me."

She stood up, shouldered her purse, gathered her food into her hands. "Come on. I got a better idea."

"Okay..."

She led me toward the door near the stairwell, but turned left and led me down another staircase, this one open. It doubled-back on itself, taking us down one level into a long lounge with televisions, ping pong tables, a pool table, a really old grand piano with chipped paint, and an ugly-ass white linoleum floor, and couches.

Lots of couches. Much better. And a view of the green space out back through a series of arched windows in the brickwork.

"Here," she waved gallantly at one of the couches.

"Perfect." I took a seat on the left corner of a brown tweed job. It had seen better centuries. I'd lay good money that it also moonlit as a quicksand pit. But at least I had leg room.

She sat down on the orange overstuffed opposite me. Enough naugas died making that thing, it's no wonder they went extinct in the seventies.

I took a bite of my falafel. I chased it with a swig of Coke to cover the sugar in the tahini. "So, His Grubbiness. You said a year ago..."

"Oh my gosh. Yes." She swallowed so she wouldn't talk around her food, dabbed at her mouth. Practiced habit. "Okay, so enrollment's down, and there haven't been any new endowments in years. So the old president, Dr. Stevens—and there's this big thing about it—the denomination kicks out Dr. Stevens, they bring in their fix-it guy..."

"His Grubbiness."

"You got it. And that's when it all goes straight down

the tubes."

"Like how?"

"Well, we're suddenly moving to the butt-end of nowhere. Like, next year..."

"Wait, what?" I pulled my phone out.

"I know, right? We've been here for twenty years, the school *owns* the building, and we're suddenly moving to Nowheresville, California where nobody in there right mind is going to want to go to school. And that don't even *start* on what he did to the psych program..."

"Wait," a male student, walking by us, stopped mid-stride. Loose plaid shirt over a tank top, tall enough that he might actually be able to look me in the eye. "Are you talking about The Move?" You could hear the capital letters.

"Yeah. Clarke Follett, this is Jim Lewis." Betsy patted the couch beside herself. "Jim's a history major, works in the President's office. He knows *everything*. Clarke's thinking of enrolling."

Jim's eyes went wide. "Why, for God's sake?"

I looked around, nodded my head like I was impressed with the place. "Why not?"

He settled down next to Betsy, just far enough away that I couldn't tell whether or not they were a couple. "You haven't told him?"

"I just started," she said.

"Well, I hope you like commuting to Weed."

"*Weed?*" Calling that place a "town" would be a crime against language. Founded back in the gold rush by people who thought it would grow like a weed. It sits in a strip along I-5 way the hell up near the Oregon border, right in the shadow of Mount Shasta, in the middle of a valley filled with cinder cones and rocks and a little bit of scrub grass and not a hell of a lot else. Shows you what happens when furious optimists name towns.

If you've ever been out on the road in this country—at least an hour outside of the nearest real city—you've run into a place like it. Land costs about a tenth of what it does in any urban area, but it doesn't matter, because the groceries cost so much more and the jobs pay so much less that you have to have a special sort of stubbornness to even think about living there.

So who in the hell puts a college out there?

Someone looking to save a boatload on raw land, because I guarantee you they won't save much on the construction costs.

Yeah, Ted, you're gonna be moving in a year or two when the new buildings are built. Sorry about that.

But I couldn't tell the kid that *that* was enough to throw Tom off his stride, so to speak.

No, I was willing to lay money that the black bag operation was what had him in a tizzy. Academics have to go job hunting all the time, and college professors, doubly so.

Not that I've ever been a professor or dated one, I've just noticed that any job that pays that badly and demands that much tends to attract two kinds of people: people that like the work, and people that like to be important. Anytime you get a workplace with those two kinds of people, you get a political environment that sits somewhere between "toxic" and "radioactive biohazard" on the interpersonal poison scale.

And any job like that has an attrition rate just one or two notches shy of "holy fucking Christ, get me the hell out of here!" (or, "I sure don't want to hang around with these jerks" if you're using language that my client and his family consider appropriate).

In the movies, the heroes leap over obstacles like that with fast talk and lots of charm. The real world doesn't work like that. The real world sucks.

Jim nodded with great conviction. "I shit you not."

Betsy popped him in the shoulder. "Language."

"Yeah, yeah."

"Why Weed?"

"Tax incentives."

"I thought SF had a whole special tax structure for higher ed."

"They do." He pursed his lips, like he wanted to see if I would ask the obvious question.

Figured it would be rude to disappoint him. "So what's the real reason?"

He looked around, like he wanted to make sure nobody was looking. "I don't know. That's what I've been trying to figure it out."

Betsy patted his thigh. "That's why he took the work-study job."

"Come again?"

"Well," Besty said cracking open her San Pellegrino, "He's here a month, and he starts with the 'cost cutting' measures. First he cuts the basketball team..."

"Effective immediately, too. Poof, there goes my scholarship," Jim said. "I have to get a job to start saving for next semester."

"And then the work-study position in His Grubbiness's office opens up..."

"So I take it, and," he lowered his voice, "get this. He's got me raiding the archives."

"Archives?" I asked.

"Mm," Betsy grunted through her drink. "Bottom floor under the men's wing."

"Raiding the archives for what?" That tahini was gonna give me a sour gut later, I knew it. I gave up on the last half of the falafel as a bad idea, wrapped it up like I was gonna save it for later.

"Hell if I know," he shrugged. "I'm just bringing these banker boxes up, and Mrs. Paxton is going through them—she came with him from some college in South Dakota—and then they go back down and I bring another set up."

"Okay, so he's doing an audit, right?"

Jim shook his head. "I don't think so."

"Why not?"

"They didn't send them all back."

"Documentation they need for the audit."

Jim shook his head. "They shredded them."

"It gets worse," Betsy said.

"Oh?"

"They were sleeping together," she whispered. "Mrs. Paxton and His Grubbiness."

"Now, come on, we can't go spreading rumors..."

"You told me they were—"

"I said I *thought* they were. She was always staying late, and he had a bedroom in his office."

"That seems like kind of a giveaway," I said.

"Well, it was supposed to be because he's still got his family in South Dakota, and they haven't moved out yet, so he stays here to save the school money. But."

"Tell him what happened on Halloween." Betsy said. Something about her tone told me this was more than just garden-variety student paranoia. Not that I didn't already have a good reason to suspect nefarious haunted these hallowed halls.

"Oh." A conspiratorial look came over his face. "So I'm changing for my workout, and I realize I forgot to leave the key for the file room, so I schlep all the way back up the hill, all the way in there," he pointed behind him, upstairs and west, as if he could magically finger the President's office through umpteen layers of masonry. "I figured I'd just slide the key under the door. But when I get there, I hear them shouting at each other."

"Them..."

Betsy jumped in to clarify: "His Grubbiness and Mrs. Paxton."

"Right." Now Jim's face looked genuinely dark.

Troubled. Like this was the part of the story he really didn't want to be true.

"What were they shouting?"

Jim shook his head. "I couldn't hear a lot of it. Most of it was swearing. But Mrs. Paxton was going on about the denomination and an audit and something about buildings and said 'we're never going to get away with it,' and then said something about quitting while they were ahead. I put my ear up to the door, and I could hear His Grubbiness, talking reasonable, you know that kind of tone people use when they want to calm someone down? Couldn't hear the words all that clear, but it sounded like he wanted her to trust him cause everything would be fine."

I finished off the last of my Coke. Crushed the can down in my hand. Pure habit.

But Jim thought it was some kind of comment on what he was saying.

"Exactly, yeah, just like that. I tried to hear more, but I heard the custodian next door and figured I'd better get out of there before he saw me."

"Some Halloween scare," I said.

"I know, right?"

"Sounds like something crooked's going on. Have you thought of calling the police?"

Jim shook his head. "No way, man. No way."

"Why? You already lost your scholarship..."

"Forget it. Just no, okay?" He shook his head, leaned back in a frump.

I looked at Betsy, who gazed at him with the kind of strained pity that made me wonder, again, what kind of relationship they really had. Felt like halfway between siblings and lovers.

"He can't make any waves," she said. "His family can't afford to send him to another school. Besides, it's not like they'd help anyway."

"What do you mean?"

"Well they didn't to anything about the murder, did they?"

"Wait...*what?*" What the hell had Tom Stride gotten into with this po-dunk postsecondary paragon of pedagogy?

"Betsy, come on..." Jim shifted in his seat. Sweating a little bit despite the absolutely dead-boring sixty-five degree temperature of the room.

She ignored him. "Right after that, Mrs. Paxton disappears. Then they announce the college is moving next year. Then, two weeks later, guess what's in The Brazier?"

Their campus newspaper. I'd seen copies of it laying around here and there during my tour.

"I have no idea."

She lowered her voice now. "Mrs. Paxton was found in front of her new house in Weed, right on the new campus. Raped and murdered." She shuddered. " Her husband got arrested for it, even though he was out of town when it happened. They said it was a contract killing, but they couldn't find the guy he hired."

"You're serious?"

"You can check," she leaned back and took a loud slurp from her barely-touched lemonade. "Seriously. Pull out your phone. Search the Internet."

"Okay..." I figured a normal person would check, so I played like I was a normal person.

Sure enough. Mrs. Darla Paxton, found raped and murdered in front of her house. Just left out on the lawn with her throat slit. The police thought it was meant to look like a rapist was holding the knife to her throat and lost control of it, but the character of the slice said it was clearly the work of someone who'd done it before.

No DNA at the scene. The rapist had worn a condom—the news declared it with certainty, which probably meant they found latex residue on or in the victim.

I whistled. "Looks like the cops did do something."

"Yeah, but to the wrong guy."

"Well, if you're right and his wife was sleeping with her boss, he'd have motive."

Betsy gave me that squinty look again, only this time there was something else behind it.

Then she chewed on her bottom lip.

Then her brow settled down low over her eyelids, and her jaw set firmly.

Shit.

"You don't really want to go to school here, do you?"

"Well, after what you've just told me—"

"No, I mean you weren't ever interested in coming in

the first place." It wasn't a question this time.

So I leaned forward. "What else do you know?"

"That depends. Are you with the denominational guys?"

"What denominational guys?"

"They came through about a month ago, after Mrs. Paxton died. Some kind of review..."

"Yeah and they didn't look friendly," Jim muttered.

"Well, I'm friendly."

"So who are you?"

I could keep it up, or I could play the excitement card. They felt like they were up shit creek, people in trouble always want Mighty Mouse.

I slipped a hand into the hip pocket on my BDUs. Pulled out my wallet. Opened it. Took out my license. Handed it to Betsy. "Keep this quiet."

She half-cocked her head, then looked down at the card. Her eyes went all anime. "No way."

"Way."

She handed my license to Jim. Didn't even look at him. Stared at me instead. "Why are you here?"

"Just trying to find out what's going on."

"For who?"

"That would be the 'private' part of 'private detective.' But there's nothing saying I can't try to bring some heat down for you guys. If His Grubbiness is half as dirty as you guys are saying...well, who knows."

Jim handed the license back to me with a "What *exactly* are you saying?"

Now it was my turn to lower my voice. "You want him brought down? I've brought down people that make this guy look like a used car salesman."

They were on the fence. I could feel them dithering, something else was going on, right on the tips of their tongues, and they were scared of saying it out loud.

"It'll make my client happy," *I hope.* "Tell me everything he's done."

"Everything?"

"No matter how silly or small it sounds."

The two of them bounced back and forth for the next few minutes. They thought it was weird that he wore spats all the time. And that he was always flying out for days and weeks on end, when the school was supposedly in such dire financial trouble.

"And then there was what he did to Professor Walker," Jim said.

"Professor Walker?"

Betsy gritted her teeth. "My faculty advisor. She was going to write me a recommendation for grad school."

"What happened?"

"She ran the pregnancy center."

"For abortion counseling." Well, anti-abortion counseling, but there was no sense getting political about it, not with someone I needed information from. And seeing as how I don't have a uterus and I grew up Catholic and I'm no ethical philosopher, I figure I'm not really obligated to have an opinion on the subject.

"Right. And what happened to her?"

"Nothing. Yet. They're not renewing her contract after the move, so she has to move up for one semester and then find another job, or she has to quit and lose her pension vestment."

"That's shitty."

"And they moved the pregnancy center to the new campus in Weed."

"What, already?"

She nodded. "Just this week."

"So a student turns up pregnant..."

"She talks to His Grubbiness, and he excuses the coursework and puts them on a bus."

"Who would do that?"

"People who don't want to get expelled or lose their financial aid," Jim said.

"Please tell me you can't top that."

Betsy shook her head. "That's it, I think. He's just, I don't know, creepy. People just do what he tells them. Even when you know better, you talk to him for five minutes and you just suddenly want to, I don't know, do what he wants you to."

I looked at Jim. "He's like this with everybody?"

Jim nodded. "Yeah. I don't know what it is, but he's got that thing."

"Charisma."

"Yeah. Yeah, that's it. Lots of it."

"Look, you work in his office..."

"Yeah?"

"You've got a cell phone?"

"Yeah."

"You want to help me bring him down?"

"Sure."

"Good. I need you to do me a favor."

6:10 PM, TUESDAY

EVENING HOURS, THE COLLEGE was hopping. Tom Stride was in the annex talking to some students.

Well, listening to some students. I didn't see him till I was all the way in and heading toward the main door.

Straight toward him.

I spotted him when his attention was on a short college boy, clear eye line, but he didn't look up. I swerved left and hooked back up to the east hall, went all the way along to the lounge where Grandpa Roy's tulips were still sitting on the desk.

Made it out, got to the car. Now I just had to pray Jim came through.

BAY AREA RUSH HOUR. Rachael described it to me once as a river of shit.

She wasn't wrong.

I still had one stop to make before I got home.

But it meant I had to wade through 880 traffic all the way.

880. One of the Bay Area's two worst nightmares. The 101 of the East Bay. The kind of road God

sentences hapless sinners to wander through in an eternal rush-hour on the way from nowhere special to nowhere in particular, because the exit you want is always under construction.

Took me two hours to get from Silver Avenue to Davis Street, then I had to skip Davis because the ramp was, predictably, closed for construction. Had to go all the way down to Marina and double back to get to the new San Leandro Kaiser campus.

This time of day they were gonna be busy. No sense going in the front door. I took the easy way in, circled round the gigantic glass-filled campus to the ER loading bay doors in the back.

Three ambulances, all just sitting there. Their drivers inside, no doubt, making a delivery that was a hell of a lot more urgent than what I needed.

But, this time of day, it wouldn't take long before someone came out to restock a vehicle.

I parked, fished the vial of yellow goop out of the cup, pocketed it. Got out of the car, leaned back-to-the door, enjoyed the noisy diesel fumes from the snail's pace freeway forty yards behind me. I hadn't gotten my dose of carcinogens today. Good time to catch up.

Didn't have to wait long. A pair of paramedics strolled out, efficient and quick, but not in any kind of hurry. They went to the nearest AMR van, opened the back door.

I adjusted my hat, moved my wallet to my right jacket pocket, then strode to meet them.

"Hey," I shouted when I was a couple van-lengths away, "you guys on a call?"

"Not at the moment," the taller of the two, a broad-set black man going gray around the temples, grunted at me. The other one, a young white guy with the bearing of a trainee and some fancy ink crawling up his neck, was already scrambling into the back.

"Mind if I borrow you for a second?"

"We ain't day laborers, pal." He released the wheels on the gurney, pushed it into the back of the ambulance to get strapped down.

"Just got a quick question. Pay you twenty bucks for the consult." I reached the van, stuck my hand out. "Clarke Lantham."

"Darell Boggs." The black man shook my hand. "What do you need?"

I pulled the vial out. "Wondering if you can tell me what this is."

He took the vial, looked at it. Swished it around. "Plasma."

"Blood plasma?"

"That's the stuff."

"Thanks." I took the vial back. Stuffed it in my left pocket, brought out my wallet with the other hand. I pulled the twenty out and handed it to him.

"Hey," said the kid in the van, "What about me?"

I shrugged. "He answered first. Next time maybe. Thanks!"

NOTE DUMP TIME. I could hear Klepto barking and whining from inside the house when I parked, but if you don't offload your notes at the first chance you've got, you risk losing things. Human memory isn't a recorder, which is why I illegally record everything.

Klepto would have to wait, bless his little white furry socks. I felt like a heel doing it, but you do what has to be done, or you don't do it for long.

Once I was in the office, I couldn't hear him, which helped. Out of earshot, I could pretend I didn't know that he knew I was around and not paying attention to him.

Stashed the plasma in the fridge. It'd keep for a few days. If I found an actual crime at the back of this I'd need to hand it over to whatever cops had jurisdiction. If I didn't, I'd use it to teach Nya how to do blood typing.

One of these days I'll be able to afford a rapid genotyper. Another few years, they oughta be cheap enough to put in my little crime lab. Then all that boring forensic training won't get in my way anymore, but at least I'll have managed to burden a new generation with useless knowledge.

Desk. Computer. Found a note from Nya:

Gone clubbing. Gonna sleep at Rachael's. Call if you need me.

After a day like today, a night at home alone would work just fine. Dinner, a game of fetch, a nice walk, maybe some laptop work while I caught up on this season of Penn & Teller.

So, the notes. First impressions. Action items.

First impression? I needed to meet Frank Gruber. Had to arrange it somehow. Look him in the eye. Get the measure of him. They way the kids described him, he fit a certain type. We get our share of them around here, I've known a few myself. Slick operators—slick enough that you gotta respect it.

Sometimes you have to shoot them too. Just like with tigers. Gorgeous as life itself, twice as dangerous. One of them charges a kid, you shoot it. But you kinda wish you didn't have to. Better to keep them alive for study, right?

But if he was what I thought he was, then anyone who worked at that school was standing in line to be fleeced and didn't even know it yet.

It also wouldn't hurt to get eyes in his office and ears on his phone lines. He was running some kind of blood plasma subscription service for God-knew-what reason.

The more I thought about it, the more this guy gave me the creeps. I've known three people with that kind of charisma before. One of them was a serial killer. The Broadway Slasher, the papers called him. I knew him as

Deputy Captain Leonard Garrity. Fooled everyone in the Oakland PD for seventeen years, inspired loyalty like nobody's business. One of my mentors. Collaring him made my career in homicide.

And ruined my life.

Then there was Charlie Sternwood. How he managed to cast his spell over Nya, and her father, and her boyfriend, and her friends, and get them into that business out at the beach house in Half Moon Bay, I'll never know. Bad news. Bad news all around.

The other one, well, I was too young to remember much, but he left my mother in a hell of a spot with three kids and a three million dollar fraud charge which she only got out of because a good cop cared enough to do an actual investigation instead of just shuffling her case off to the District Attorney, like his boss wanted to do.

I went into law enforcement because of that cop.

So action item one: get everything I could on His Grubbiness. Run a background check with the social security number that kid Jim was going to get me. Engineer a meet. Try to get a measure of just how much of a problem this guy was.

Action item two: Find out everything I could about Trubody college. Press releases, trade papers. Did denominations have magazines? There would be some kind of public or semi-public story about this move. Might give me an angle to approach His Grubbiness.

Action item three: Hit the road. Up to Weed. Talk to

the local cops there. Flashing my Sheriff's shield ought to get me enough professional courtesy to find out how much weight to lend the rumors that the college kids were spreading.

Action item four: Read up on black market blood plasma. Figure out why someone would want regular deliveries. Why it might be worth enough to fly in special, or to pressure a professor into black-bagging it.

Pressure him? Or pay him off? Was Tom Stride getting ready to do what my old man did back when I was five years old?

My stomach hurt. All the sitting. The traffic. The bad falafel. This case was wrapping me up in knots.

Would've been easier if Nya was home.

Or if Rachael was still here.

Or if Erica wasn't still dealing with that whatever-it-was up in Napa.

I could still hear Klepto barking inside the main house. He'd be sitting with his nose pressed against the media room window, looking out across the patio to the office, wondering where the hell I was and why I hadn't come to see him yet.

Well, I had my action items in order. Still a couple hours worth of recordings to transcribe, but that didn't have to happen just this minute. Maybe I could give them to Nya tomorrow. Have her do it while I ran a background check on His Grubbiness.

I closed down the office lights, locked up. Headed across the dark patio. Tripped the motion sensors. Big back yard, takes a little while to walk across. Good reset time, gets me out of work mode every time. Now I could unplug, get some real dinner, give the dog some attention.

Real life, kind of a nice thing to have around when you need it, right?

I rounded the north corner to the back door, keys out. I fumbled them into the lock.

"Clarke!" Teddy's hoarse whisper came from the hemlock tree behind me. Just about jumped me straight out of my skin.

"Jesus, Teddy, what the hell..."

"You followed Dad today."

"Yeah. How did you—"

"He saw you."

Oh, fuck. "He did?"

"Well, he said he saw someone who looked just like you at school today. I don't think he knows it was you."

Well, there's that at least. Deep breath, Lantham. You're not gonna have to risk a fist fight with your neighbor tonight. "You could've led with that. What the hell are you doing over here?"

"Oh, come *on*."

"Come on what?"

"You followed him again. You went to the school. Cool place, isn't it? I love it when he takes me. Or used to take me." He stepped out from the bush. He was wearing shorts, despite the forty-degree winterish chill. Oh, to have a nine-year-old metabolism again. "What did you find out?"

"It doesn't work that way, Ted. You're a client, I gotta write up a report and—"

"So you found something! Come on, I won't tell..." He sang it, that kind of beguiling whiny sing-song that only kids can think will work, and then it does, because you realize they've got more energy than you do and can whine until you crumble like cheap concrete.

"I don't know yet. Really."

"You know something though."

"Okay, you promise you'll keep it quiet?"

"Duh. What, you think I'm a blabbermouth or something?"

"The school is moving next year. Some people are going to lose their jobs."

"Like Dad?"

"I don't know. He probably doesn't know yet, he's just worried."

"That's it?"

"That's all I know right now. I'll dig around some more, though. Give me a few more weeks, okay?"

"Weeks?!"

"This isn't like TV, Ted. Stuff takes a while."

"Ooookaaaaay." He looked at the ground, scuffed at the patio concrete.

"Now get out of here. I gotta make dinner."

"Can I play with Klepto?"

"Not tonight. I got other clients, I'm gonna be working for a while yet." Not true, but I really didn't need him in my hair right now.

He left. Wasn't happy about it, at least not till he made it through the gate and ran off to his next round of mischief.

Me? I opened the door. Ninety pounds of teenage hellhound jumped out to greet me.

A dog this big, you gotta train. If you don't, they do a Dino to your Fred Flintstone every time you come in the house. Liable to knock you on your back and kill you just because he's happy to see you. He just about killed Erica that way, and a dead Fed is not the kind of parcel you want turning up on your doorstep.

So I trained him to stand on his hind legs and lick me in the face. He wasn't quite tall enough yet, so I held my hands out for him. He'd get there, though. He got the size of his mastiff mama and the personality of his pit bull father. When he's full grown I'll be able to rig him up to a chariot and save a bundle on gas.

I took my licking. I had, after all, asked for it.

"Yes, boy. Good boy. Yes, I'm glad to see you too." I let him go, snapped, pointed at the back yard. "Go to the bathroom."

He whined, but did like I said. I waited for him at the back door, then waved him back into the house. He zipped up the stairs and went straight to the kitchen, picked up his food bowl, brought it back to meet me just as I got to the top of the stairs.

"Yes, dinner time. You got it." I took the bowl from him, scooped him a bushel or two out of the kibble bag in the pantry, then investigated the possibilities in the leftovers department.

Settled on some spaghetti left over from a few nights ago. Nuked myself a helping, drowned it in Parmesan and red pepper flakes, and settled down in the TV room to let my brain unwind for a while.

Only lasted about twenty minutes. Once he was sure I was done eating, he jumped into my lap, and as big as my lap is, he still doesn't fit. He planted his ass on my left knee and pawed my shoulder, and whined.

"Okay, okay, you're right."

And so, there was fetch. And a walk around the block.

And, all the while, the wheels in my head kept going round. This whole business was bothering me, and the more I thought about it, the more angles turned up that didn't fit.

What kind of lever did this guy have on Tom Stride? Had he promised to make sure his contract wasn't dropped if he helped with the black bag operation? Or were he and Stride in on it together—maybe they were old friends from way back? Or was it blackmail? Did Tom have a mistress? Some other skeleton rattling around in his closet?

It sounded ridiculous. The Stride family was the full-on *Leave It To Beaver* package. Two point two kids, middle class, more-or-less white, home in the suburbs, churchgoing, lived in a house that would command upwards of three quarters of a million if they put it up for sale.

Assuming they owned it. They'd lived here longer than I did, it was possible they were renting it on a sweetheart deal they'd landed back in the recession or something.

Did Tom know about the murder? Did he know the real story? Was he some kind of accomplice?

Despite what I'd warned Teddy about, the last thing I wanted to do was shatter his image of his father. I hadn't had a father. Mrs. Lantham did a hell of a job as a single mom, but when I was his age I'd have killed for a Dad that gave half as much of a shit as Tom did for Teddy. Whatever else about their way of life I didn't get, or didn't really approve of, or couldn't imagine myself putting up with if I was stuck in it, I didn't want to ruin it.

And if I didn't tread very carefully, that's exactly what I was going to do. Ruin the life of a family that didn't need it. For no good reason.

At least, I hoped for no good reason.

I was more wound up when I got home than when I'd left, so I set up the laptop in the TV room and checked my email.

Best part of that house, the media room. Takes up the whole back of the house, enough room for three couches, got windows wrapping around the corner looking out on the office and the back yard, a bathroom right off it, and French doors to protect the rest of the household from the sounds of my B-movie addiction.

Got lucky, too. Bought the house at the bottom of the market. If I'd waited another six months, I'd have had to move out to Stockton just to find a place I could afford.

One of these days, I needed to thank Rachael for twisting my arm on that one.

Laptop. Email. A note from Jim, the janitorial student.

With two photos attached.

One was a letterhead from the property company in Weed.

The other was a pay stub. For Franklyn Gruber.

With his Social Security Number. And his home address, still in Kansas.

Quick reply to Jim:

Got it. Excellent job. I'll take it from here.

And I did.

I started running it against my databases. Biggest single expense in this job, those databases. Most of them require a PI license to even join them, though there's no legal requirement. It's a marketing ploy. Helps with the exclusivity—and the ridiculous subscription fees.

After about an hour I had his employment history.

Pastor of an Evangelical Missions Association church in North Texas, starting about twelve years ago.

Then headmaster of a half-dozen Christian Academies—which in this case was a euphemism for "private elementary schools."

Then three postings in four years at denominational colleges and grad schools.

Dude got around.

He got the job at Trubody last summer. The old president was promoted to some grad school on the east coast. Talk in the denominational press about problems with falling enrollment. So far, all of it was pretty much by-the-numbers, just like the story I'd gotten from Betsy.

Except that, for such an impressive resume, Dr. Franklyn Gruber didn't have a past that reached back before his first posting as pastor.

His doctorate came from a diploma mill. American Patriot University, which, according to Google Maps, was a residential house in the suburbs of Mobile, Alabama.

"So who the hell are you, *Doctor* Gruber?"

The front door rattled. I barely noticed—but Klepto did. Two sharp barks and a gallop around the corner to do sentry duty. Then the sound of excited scuffling and a lot of thumping of his tail on the living room carpet.

I checked the clock. Two AM.

"I'm back here, Nya. Early night for you, isn't it? Dud night at Bondage A-Go-Go?"

No answer.

"Nya?"

No answer.

Prickles up the back of my neck. After that merc tried to poison Klepto a couple months ago, I take those prickles seriously, even in my own house.

I pushed the tray table away from the couch, reached for the end table where I'd left my holster. Quiet as I could. I'd already announced my position, I didn't want to give away that I was changing it.

Then, a voice I hadn't been expecting to hear. "Clarke? Could you come out here please?"

Erica Ellis.

I took a second. Got my heart rate under control. Backed off the .45.

"Yeah, sure," I bellowed. But with a smile on my face. Normally I'd be offended by the Feds knocking down my door at two in the morning, but this one gets a special pass.

I headed to the door at the top of the stairs, through the kitchen, toward the living room at the front of the house. "I wasn't expecting you back until...whoa."

There weren't any lights on. Couldn't see much of anything.

The blinds were half-open. The sodium street lamp outside painted a grid of yellow light across the sideways wingback in front of the windows.

And the woman leaning back against it.

The yellow played across her red hair, her freckles, the fluff on her vulva, like they were glowing from inside.

"Surprised?" She purred.

I was.

I walked to her, knelt beside her. Dragged my fingers from her toes to her crown.

She shivered. "What are you doing?"

"Looking for gaps in your armor." I bent down, took

the side of her neck in my mouth. She has a thing for vampire books. I never said I was above cheating. It worked, too. She moaned, and shivered like she couldn't breathe. "Mmm, think I found one."

"Bastard," she shuddered.

"Mmm mm, my mother was married. Just because my father didn't notice isn't my fault."

Talking to a woman's neck when she's that turned on, especially a woman who's got a hot-spot on her neck...not such a good idea. She started laughing.

Uncontrollably.

"Stop, stop, stop, that tickles!" She batted at my face. I retreated.

"Sorry." Times like this, it's easy to lose yourself in the giggles too, but if that happened Klepto would want to get in on the action, and I didn't have the energy for the Three Stooges routine that would ensue from the two humans—one of whom wasn't wearing a stitch—trying to convince the one dog that this was human time, and not play time, and no, you can't sniff that, and don't lick that either, and please for the love of fuck go lay down already, and finishing up with me having to leave the room with a hundred pounds of excited puppy panting in my arms wanting to play Wrestlemania with the weird humans who kept changing their skins all the time.

And just being aware that would happen made me break down in giggles too.

So much for romance.

Erica wasn't going to be put off, though. She took advantage of my moment of weakness, grabbed my shirt in one hand and my left hand in the other, and rolled me over onto my back.

Hard flop. Knocked the wind right out of me.

She, naturally, landed on top, like all the good training manuals said you should.

Then she switched herself around, facing my feet.

She found my buttons. Opened them up.

Frisked me. Read me my rights.

Stripped me for prisoner inspection.

I had the right to stay exactly where I was.

Any movement I made would be turned against me on the living room floor.

I had the right to shut up and keep my tongue busy doing something useful.

If I failed to shut up she would shut me up before she asked the rest of me any questions.

Did I understand these rights?

Since I was busy trying to breathe and keeping her happy, I settled for Morse code on her clit.

I have no idea if they still teach Morse code at Quantico, but I figured if she didn't get the message, she'd still receive it well.

She did, too. And Klepto didn't ruin things. Anytime Klepto came sniffing around she shooed him off without even using her voice. She'd obviously been working on a secret signal when I wasn't around. I'd have to ask her about that.

Not that I said anything about it at the time. Not with her all over my face. My mother taught me never to talk with my mouth full. Though I'm pretty sure she'd be horrified if she figured out that I only followed that rule during sex.

Something about living alone. Or more-or-less alone. You never realize how lonely it gets until someone shows up and reminds you that humans are social animals, in as animalistic a way as possible. Even though rest was exactly what I wasn't getting, she felt like rest, and smelled like home, and touching her unwound the knots in my neck like someone cutting a bungee cord.

I was glad she wasn't looking at me just then. Glad her attention was somewhere else. For a minute, the relief got too sharp, and I completely lost it.

She thought I was just having too much fun to keep licking. And I was okay with that. If there's one thing you don't want to do in front of an FBI agent, it's cry during sex. Especially when you have no idea what the hell you're crying about. They might waterboard you or something.

Granted, that's more or less what she was doing to me anyway. So I got ahold of myself, then took hold of her hips, and got back to cooperating like a good citizen.

Even though I understood my rights, she managed to get me undressed anyway, and without missing a beat with her mouth. The woman has talented toes and a hell of a reach.

And that gave me a problem. Even being a pretty

open-minded guy—and if you are going to survive as a single man in the Bay Area you kind of have to be, or you'll never meet anyone—there are a few kinks I've never really been able to get into.

Like rug burn.

My knees and elbows were a lot happier with me when I spotted an opening, so to speak, and rolled her off, picked her up, tossed her on the couch, slid under her so her knees were around my shoulders, and slid onto her and into her.

So was the rest of me.

So was she.

You know how when you go visit the house you grew up in, and you find out that the new owners didn't tear down your tree house in the back yard, and your hand prints are still in the front walkway, and you feel, for a few minutes, like you're eight years old again, and you've got adventures to have and nothing to worry about?

Well, when Erica looked me in the eyes, and held my gaze while we moved, until neither of us could breathe anymore, and still held my eyes while we came, and came down...

Well, it was like that.

We stayed there for a while, too. Long enough that my arms started to get a little sore, and so did my left thigh, from being thrown out over the edge of the couch so my toes could get traction on the carpet like that.

Long enough that Klepto got a little worried and nosed in between our bellies and started snuffling.

"Eiiieee! Klepto, stop. Down, down, NO NOT THAT KIND OF DOWN! Go lay down. Over there. Go on. That's good. Good boy." I sat back on my haunches.

Erica reached up to the back of the couch, where the couch blanket lived, pulled it down and tried to stuff it under her ass. Not a gracious move. She wound up standing up, re-folding the blanket, laying it on the couch cushion, then sitting down on it again. She's like that. Very fastidious. Didn't want to leak on the upholstery. Goes with the job, I guess. Kinda breaks the moment, though. I'd have rather dealt with the mess later, if there was one.

She hugged her knees to her chest, rested her cheek on one of them, looked at me with a smile.

I smiled back. A little half smile. Not a big deal, really. "Where the fuck did that come from?"

"I missed you."

"And you came all the way down from Napa at two in the morning?"

She shrugged. A happy sigh. No, not quite happy. Relief. Hell of a stressful assignment, I guess. "Guess I couldn't sleep."

"Can't blame you. Stuck in Washington like that. All those politicians."

She wrinkled her nose at me. She does that when she doesn't approve of my attitude but thinks it's cute anyway. Never met a woman who could disapprove of me in a way that made me want to kiss her before.

"I hate it when you're gone, you know?"

She shrugged. "Yeah. I hate being gone."

"I'd marry you if I thought it would help."

"Are you proposing to me, Mister Lantham?"

"Not yet. Just thinking about it. How long'll you be in town?"

She smiled. "A couple days."

I nodded. It's always a couple days.

"But then," she said, "I'll be back indefinitely."

"Really?"

"Desk duty. Liaising with DHS at the Port of Oakland."

"First good news I've gotten all day. Well," I ran my eyes over her body, "second, I guess."

She bapped me on the shoulder.

I caught her arm and pulled her on top of me, and welcomed her home all over again.

7:00 AM, Wednesday

RUMBLE RUMBLE RUMBLE.

"Clarke?"

Rumble rumble rumble shake.

"Clarke." Sounded like Erica. Had to be.

But Erica isn't dumb enough to try to wake me up before I've gotten my ugly sleep.

Roll roll shake shake rumble rumble.

"Clarke wake up."

"Arensdubmlkfmmpfuck off."

Thump thump thump thump. From far off.

Dog barking. Or a series of mortar rounds detonating a few blocks away. Hard to tell for sure.

"Clarke!"

"For Christ's sake, just get it already." Somebody was at the door. Either that or I was stuck in that nightmare where the monster in the fridge was sending a flock of sea gulls to pluck out my eyeballs.

Don't ask.

thump Thump THUMP.

Then she poked me in the ribs.

"Ow. Fine. Fine..." I pulled my face out of the glorious, soft, and now tragically inhospitable feather pillow that I'd been pleasantly smothering myself with. Another twenty minutes and I might have suffocated enough that I wouldn't have to deal with mornings ever again.

I found some pants in the living room where Erica'd yanked them off me last night, pulled them on and kicked the rest of our clothes into a pile under the wingback. I didn't bother with a shirt. I figured whoever-it-was could just deal with my nipples. That's the price you pay for waking a guy like me up in the morning.

Didn't think to peek through the blinds, or I might have changed my mind about that.

"Come on, Klepto, shut up, will ya?"

He was jumping up and down at the door and barking like Cthulhu's bastard son was trying to come through and swallow his soul.

I snapped, pointed at the couch. "Klepto. Couch."

He laid his ears back, whined, then spun in place once and slithered around behind me before mounting the maroon velour like a gurney going into an ambulance.

Dead bolt. Latch. Knob. Daylight.

And one very annoyed looking Tom Stride standing on my porch.

"Can we talk for a minute?" It was more a politely worded subpoena than a request. I waved him in.

"Have a seat on the couch. Don't let Klepto lick you to death. I'll get a shirt."

I got a shirt. Not a great shirt. Not even a good shirt.

But it covered my nipples and my belly button and didn't have the word "fuck" on it, so I counted it as a win. I kissed Erica on the way back out.

"Tom Stride's here. This might take a while. We'll be out back."

"Mmm. They're coming home to roost. I warned you."

"Yeah, yeah, I'll make the coffee if you stop gloating." I patted her hip and blundered back to the living room.

Stride was still standing there, by the door. Dressed for work—blue pinstripes, orange paisley tie, the whole bit. Kind of a stuffy guy with a seventies-throwback thing going on. So much for the hospitality. Maybe he didn't want to wrinkle his suit. Maybe he just didn't like dogs.

I made eye contact, waved him to follow with me. Led him through the kitchen, mumbled "Want some coffee?"

"No, I'm fine."

I whistled, sharp upslope. Klepto-speak. Amazing the kind of whistle language you develop when you've got a dog and you're too lazy to teach it much English. As long as I was going outside I might as well bring the mutt. He bounded along right after us, wound round us, beat me to the bottom of the back stairs.

"So what is it you need, Professor?" I led him through the door, rounded to the right and went out onto the big concrete pad that passed for a patio. The sky was angry gray. Smelled like rain. Better make sure to pack a hat and an umbrella when I went out, just in case.

I got goosebumps from the chilly breeze ripping through the paper-thin fabric I was pretending to be dressed in.

"Why are you messing with my family?"

"Messing with your...huh?" Rule number one, always play dumb.

"That was you at the school yesterday, wasn't it?"

So much for that stupid hope that Teddy wouldn't rat me out. "Yeah, I was there."

"Why are you sniffing around my workplace?"

"Got a client who's got some suspicions about your new boss."

He let out a breath. The kind of breath you hold when you're winding up to hit someone and you're not sure you've got it in you to lay on the pain. "The denomination?"

I shrugged just enough to let him think he was on to something, but I couldn't confirm it. "You know. Client confidentiality..."

"Bout time they got interested," he nodded. "Well, that's good. Here I was worried Teddy had you following me around or something. You know how he's always skulking around, bothering you."

I chuckled a companionable chuckle. "Aw, he's not a bother. You've got a good kid there. Polite too. Always stops tailing me when I ask him to. Might make a hell of a cop one day."

"Well, you'll let me know if he turns into a problem."

"Of course."

Tom nodded. Pursed lips, chin pulled in. Looked like he wanted to say something more, but then stuffed his left hand into his jacket pocket and walked toward the driveway—I guess so he didn't have to go back out through the house.

"Hey professor."

"Yeah?" He stopped. Half-turned back to me.

"You're not happy with your new boss."

He shook his head. "There've been some...rumors."

"About the murder?"

"Among other things."

"Like what?"

Stride looked around, like he was scared someone was listening. He looked undecided for a minute, then seemed to make up his mind. His shoulders hunched in, he took two quick steps toward me like he was trying to shrink from view, in case there was anyone around with a sniper scope trained on him.

"Tell me one thing," he spoke low. "If you can prove there's something shady going on, you'll take it to the cops."

"My girlfriend's an FBI agent and I..."

"Don't give me that crap, Lantham. I know a cop's only as good as his conscience."

"If I find something that can put someone away, then yes. I'll take it to the cops."

"You don't have any kind of confidentiality thingy

that..."

I shook my head. "Nope. Not this time."

"Even if your client doesn't want to prosecute."

"That's not how this works. It's...look, I'm running on four hours sleep and I haven't had my coffee. Can you help me out or not?"

"That depends," he mumbled. "What do you need to know?"

"Well," I crossed my arms over my chest. "Where are you during your office hours? Your students haven't been able to find you." Figured it was better not to let him know I'd been tailing him, if I could help it.

"Running errands. His Grubbiness—you have to have heard the nickname..."

"Yeah."

"His Grubbiness told me there's gonna be a lot of restaffing next semester. I'm up for renewal, and there isn't another school in the denomination on this side of the Rockies. So I...well, I begged him, no sense pretending it was anything else."

"And?"

"We made a deal. He needed someone to run some errands for him a few times a month. Medicine deliveries. Said he was too pressed to find a student who could be trusted, and the denomination was sending someone down in April, and if I could fill in, make his life easier, he could see that my contract was renewed. Well...I'm not wild about moving to Weed. Louise really isn't. But it's close enough that I could drive it, maybe.

Sleep in my office during the week, come home on weekends."

"You do what you have to." There's my philosophy of life, right there. Maybe Tom wasn't a bad guy after all. "What's worse than murder?"

"Huh?"

"You said 'among other things.'"

"Oh, that. It's just rumors. Nothing anyone can prove."

"I live on rumors. They're better than peanut butter." Just as fattening, too.

He looked around again, lowered his voice so much I had to strain to hear—not an easy feat when Klepto had taken an interest in a squirrel in the plumb tree out by the office and wanted the whole neighborhood to know about it.

"They've been saying he was sleeping with Mrs. Paxton," he said it with a special kind of contempt. The sort I normally reserve for dirty cops and politicians. "And he had some kind of interest in the company we bought the land from."

"And that's why you're moving to Weed."

"Why else would anybody move to Weed?"

I shrugged. "Looking to make it big in the diazinon business?"

"What?"

"Never mind." Clearly I'd done too much landscaping to pay my way through college. "Look, you want to keep your family in the Bay Area, right?"

"Least until I get the kids through high school."

"You willing to do me a favor, no questions asked?"

"I don't like the sound of that."

"Oh, don't worry, you're gonna like the favor even less."

"What?"

"I need to get Nya into Gruber's office."

"How'm I supposed to do that?"

"She's a hell of a secretary."

He eyeballed me. Stood full up. Still not as tall as me, but then, who is? He looked at me long and hard, like he was trying to get the measure of me. If he asked, I could've saved him the trouble and told him it was six foot three.

"Come on, Tom. If this guy's as dirty as everyone thinks he is, I can bring him down."

Klepto lost interest in the squirrel and trotted over to us. Took a seat at my right heel.

"You'll give me your word on that?" Tom asked.

I leaned to the side a bit. Scritched Klepto between the ears. "Swear to dog."

"WHAT WAS THAT ALL about?" Erica, dressed in the thin white tank top she wore as an undershirt and some high-cut black panties that did amazing things for her narrowish hips, bleared into the kitchen in search of the coffee I'd just finished brewing. She also had one sock on to keep her foot warm, but had given up on looking for the other one.

"Tom Stride. He's going to be very useful."

"You're still doing that case?"

I handed her a cup of coffee, double-sweet. Why anyone would do that to coffee, I've got no idea, but anyone with hair that red's got a right to be a little weird around the edges.

"Yeah. In the free minutes. You know."

"And he didn't punch you?"

I took a sip. Good stuff. Arabian this time. Nya picked it up at a little roastery she found in Berkeley. I'd have to tell her to keep up the good work. "Nah. He's working for me."

"You're joking."

Shook my head. "I have god-like powers of persuasion."

"Mmm...right until it blows up in your face." She kissed me. Takes a lot of talent to be patronizing when you're kissing someone, but she pulled it off.

"Well, that's why I carry a big gun and date a Fed."

"Would you cut it out with the Fed thing? God."

"Can't help it. Local cops got this thing. Part of the brotherhood."

"Riiiight."

"Well, in this case it matters."

"Oh?" She circled round the dining table in the middle of the kitchen, opened the fridge. "You got any eggs?"

"I think we're out. Got some leftover spaghetti in

there."

"Ugh. For breakfast?"

"That's why they call me civilized."

"Uh huh."

"So, yeah, I'm gonna need a favor. Business."

"What's that?"

"I've gotta ID my bad guy. He's running under an alias, don't know what his game is yet. If I get you some prints, could you run him through the system?"

"No."

"Come on."

"Don't you have AFIS civilian access through one of those database things of yours?"

"Yeah, but it takes up to a week. And it doesn't touch everything."

"Sorry, babe," she closed the fridge. Reached up top of the fridge for the fruit bowl. "Felonies. Like Rivers says: This is the FBI. We have rules."

"Come on, don't give me that official business crap..."

"It's not crap. I thought you were the big civil liberties guy."

"After all the help I've been to you and Rivers..."

"Look, just, don't ask again. Please? Don't fight with me on this. It's not my call to make. Funding's so thin they're watching everything right now. You know what I saw last time I was back in Washington? Headquarters is falling apart. They can't even afford to fix the building. So yeah, every nickel, so don't even ask."

"Okay, okay. Peace. I had to ask."

"Sure."

"Want some bacon?"

She smirked. "That's almost as good as an engagement ring."

7:00 PM, WEDNESDAY

ONCE YOU GET NORTH of Redding, you're on your own. According to a lot of the locals, you're not even in California anymore, you're in the revolutionary state of Jefferson, where nobody gives three shits about what they do in Sacramento, where they make laws based on the money flowing in from LA and the Bay and are perfectly happy to fuck over anyone who lives outside of the megacities.

Gorgeous country. Volcanoes everywhere. Enough pine trees to make enough Pine Sol to disinfect the whole goddamn solar system.

Remote, too. Even on I-5, which stretches from Mexico to Canada and in most places doesn't ever see enough of a break in traffic for a coyote to cross the road without getting smeared all over the tarmac.

And that's where I spent more than seven hours heading for—well, you have to budget time to stop and take pictures in country like that—right in the middle of that big gorgeous nothing. A little town that I'd been hearing way too much about lately.

Weed. A nothing town at the edge of nowheresville. A truck stop, a few thousand people, a whole shitload of rural routes, and a whole lot of nothing. About all it had going for it was the view. Gorgeous mountains around it. Great view of Shasta. And with all the fresh snow it looked like something out of another world.

God bless El Niño, right?

I'd gotten going pretty much after I woke up again, got myself presentable, briefed Nya and gave her the recordings to transcribe, and had a bit of breakfast. Then it was road.

Road road road and more road.

By the time I could actually see Mount Shasta, I was zoning pretty bad. The road twists like sailor's rigging up there, which normally I'd love driving over, but this time it was all I could do to stay on the road.

Blamed the short night. I can't do that shit anymore and not pay for it. Don't know if meeting Nya civilized me or if passing thirty-five just made me old. Either way, after Erica left for work I crawled back into bed for a couple hours. Woke up at eleven and had a shower, but even so I only got about six hours total.

The whole way, I'm running voice searches on the web, trying to figure out how blood plasma plays into everything. What could make it worth all that trouble?

My first thought was doping. Athletes—especially endurance athletes like runners, swimmers, and bikers—will do it to get an edge in competition. Some of them will use drugs to crank up blood productions, others will use plasmapheresis—that's where you take blood out, separate the plasma from the corpuscles in a centrifuge, and then return one of them to your body—to up their blood density.

I almost married a doctor once—you pick up some of the lingo.

But the whole point of blood doping is to increase the oxygen carrying capacity, and oxygen is carried by the corpuscles.

Corpuscles are what make the blood red.

Plasma is everything *but* the corpuscles.

So much for that theory. I needed another one.

What else can you use blood plasma for?

Well, injecting too much of it can screw you up, for one. It carries carbon dioxide, so you can get carbon dioxide poisoning if you get too needle-happy—but it takes so much to do that that, near as I could gather, it was only a theoretical danger. Disease was a bigger one. You didn't screen the plasma right, you could get some nasty shit in your bloodstream.

Which didn't make it any more special than unprotected sex, really.

So I dug. And dug. Way the hell down into the depths of all the latest medical research. Blood thinning was an important application, but you didn't usually get transfusions from other people for that.

Then I ran across the first interesting little article. *SBF: As a Vehicle for Gene Therapy.* SBF, or Synthetic Body Fluid, is a sort of lab-made blood plasma, as it turns out.

Now, I've had a few brushes with this subculture before. Mixed in among all the people like Tom Stride, who are basically good people who care a lot more than your average bear about the kinds of things that God gets up to, you find a couple other interesting sorts.

You get the conspiracy nuts, always looking for the next sign of the apocalypse.

You get the political nuts, who believe that Jesus won't come again until the United States takes the laws of ancient Israel that the Bible talks about and makes them the law of the land. They get a lot of play in the press, because they shout a lot in TV interviews, and it makes for good entertainment.

You get the people who think that money is a sign of God's favor, so they spend all their time on get-rich-quick schemes. They love their MLM schemes, buy a lot of gold, invest in penny stocks, and die poor.

Then you get the health nuts, who are all about muscular Christianity. They take this one Bible verse, the one that says something like "Your body is the temple of the Holy Spirit," and they dedicate all their energy to being ultra-healthy, falling for the latest fad diets, gobbling up supplements, doing anything that might make them live a few days longer or get sick a little less. It's like they think the Holy Spirit will spend more time in their temple if they keep it nice and clean.

Then, for all of those nutty types, you get the cynical sons of bitches who make a fortune playing on their fear and greed. These guys—and, sure, there's some women, but they're mostly guys—are usually hugely charismatic. They could talk four legs off a camel and then convince it to run a marathon. They'll get into anything that smells the slightest bit like money, and the less real it is the better. After all, if it's real, eventually they have to deal with regulators and cops checking on the quality of their bullshit.

So was Gruber running some kind of quack gene therapy operation? Buying blood plasma on the open market and re-selling it to gullible rubes as some kind of radical gene therapy, or a cure for cancer, or something like that?

Well, it gave me somewhere to start, anyway.

Trouble was, I was so wrapped up in trying to stay on the road and come up with a good theory that I blew straight past Weed and didn't realize it until I passed Yreka, which is an hour further north.

That'll teach me to drive sleepy. Ugh.

In my defense, Weed has approximately two exits and one sign, and sits on a stretch of road that always reminds me more of an air strip than a freeway.

I took the nearest available exit, realized that I was tired enough that I'd need to fill my coffee tank before I headed south again—and then probably get a room for the night. For a case with no expense account, I was really running up a hell of a losses tab. My tax guy was gonna love me. Rachael would've given me hell, but she was hell and gone and I didn't have much hope of seeing her again anytime soon.

Shame. I'd gotten used to working with a partner, and Nya needed bucket loads more training before I could lean on her the way I'd gotten to lean on Rachael before she winked out of existence like a bad special effect.

Yreaka's got two exits. Just off the south exit—which is where I got off—you can loop left for one of the town's only two 24-hour gas stations. Coffee there didn't used to be half-bad. Figured it was worth a try.

Coming up to the corner of Moonlit Oak Drive and Fort Jones Road, I got into the left lane. The streets were clear, but the not-very-dirty-yet snow banks lining up on the sides told me they hadn't been for long. I pressed my hand to the glass in my driver's door, I just about got burned from the cold. Well below freezing out there. The streets were only wet because of the traffic and whatever they were using to de-ice the pavement.

It was a long light. Long enough for me to decide I was hungry as well as thirsty, and I didn't really want to eat in the car when I was already too late to do anything useful in Weed when I got there.

There was an octagonal building across the way with a baby-blue-and-white sign on it, lit with a warm yellow light in the winter dusk. "Murphy's Family Eatery" it said. Diners like that are basically fast food with atmosphere, but fuck it, I wanted atmosphere.

Hung a left. Swung right into the generous parking lot. Got out of the car and hurried inside before my nose froze off.

Nothing quite as dry as subzero mountain air.

Between the altitude and the temperature it sucked the moisture straight out of my nostrils in the forty-five seconds I was out there. Another minute and I'd probably have had a nosebleed.

Not my finest hour.

The building looked like it was built as a rustic steak house back in the seventies. Rough-hewn timber archway over the door. Open beams in the ceilings. Polished pine logs making up all the header pieces on the banisters.

All that great ambiance, and the morons who ran the place now had decorated it like a third-rate Denny's knock-off. Formica counter tops with steel flashing trim. Same kind of tables. Like someone had tried to build Mel's Diner in the middle of a logging camp.

Smelled good though. Whoever was working the griddle knew their way around the iron. And they had classic rock playing on the radio. I could think of worse things than eating steak and eggs while listening to Led Zeppelin and Styx sailing away to heaven on a stairway.

The sign said "Please Seat Yourself," so I did. Took a menu from the box at the waitresses station. Blew past all the tables to the bathrooms at the rear, left the menu in my coat pocket while I did my thing. The road is hell on the digestion, let me tell you. Nobody's meant to sit that long at a stretch.

Washed hands. Grabbed a booth in the rear corner, away from the front windows, with good eye lines—force of habit more than anything else. You spend enough time dodging bullets, you start habitually checking sight lines, grabbing the high vantage spots.

It's a good habit to get into.

It's a better habit when you remember to actually check your eyelines every few seconds instead of diving into the menu like it was the latest Patterson novel.

"What can I get you, hon?" I jumped when I heard the waitress's voice.

I jumped again when I realized it sounded familiar. Throat went dry. A voice I only heard in my sleep these days. A voice I'd know anywhere. My toes started itching.

Glanced up. Rachael was looking down at her pad. Hadn't made me yet. Looked a lot different than usual. A disguise—good enough that I might have mistook her at a casual glance, if I hadn't heard her voice.

It probably only lasted about two or three seconds, but for about the next six hours I sat there, choking back relief, and rage, and joy, and some kind of massive yawning black pit of emotions I didn't ever want to have the words for.

She was dressed in a powder blue button-up shirt and black slacks with a lace-edged farmer's-wife apron, like you'd expect from someone serving food in a place like this.

Her name tag said "Daisy."

She had a different nose. Her hair was blond instead of the usual purple of blue. She'd let it grow out too. Her tits were bigger than they used to be—probably put falsies in. Change your profile, changes your center of balance, changes your gait. A little thing like that can fool some of the FBI's crowd surveillance biometrics.

Nobody does that unless they really don't want to be found. And here I was. Just showing up here, in her secret hiding spot? That would piss her off. Enough that maybe she'd never come home, and I'd never be able to figure out why the ever-loving fuck she'd skipped out on me and Nya right when things were settling in, and the business was going well. Right after she'd just risked her life to save my ass.

It didn't make sense when she did it. All these months later, and it made even less sense. And my arm still ached from the half-load of buckshot back in December, which I'd never have taken if Rachael hadn't bugged out like that. She'd gotten me that job out of guilt for bailing on me, and then she wasn't there to back me up. For weeks, I'd wanted to wring her neck for that one. If it was hurting this long I probably had nerve damage. That meant more doctors, goddammit.

But the hell of it was, she hadn't just been my assistant, or my student. She was the kind of friend you don't find. Anywhere. Ever. She was a partner—not my business partner, but the kind of teammate I used to have on the force, before that shit all went south. Only partner I ever had that got out of the job alive, too.

Cars and partners. Two things I never have good luck with. Once upon a time I'd have added "girlfriends" to that list, too, but Erica seems to have finally ended that losing streak.

Rachael tapped her pencil on her pad, ready to take my order.

Food was the last thing on my mind. I couldn't even remember why I was up here.

"Coffee, steak and eggs, and a big side of what the hell are you doing here?" I didn't use her real name. Figured she had her reasons for not using it, whatever they were.

She looked up at me. Stared blankly. Struggled to control her breathing. I couldn't tell whether she was gonna deck me or turn and run.

She didn't do either. Just stared at me with those deep brown eyes. Then she hissed: "Lantham?"

"Call me George, just for shits and giggles."

She looked around, all furtive-like. Then muttered. "The steak's shit."

"Salad then. Caesar. Chicken."

"You got it, honey." She scribbled something tore off a ticket, put it down in front of me, then scribbled something else, spun on the heel of white low-top sneakers, and strode fast back toward the kitchen.

The ticket read *We should talk. We close at ten. Meet me outside.*

AFTER A SHOCK LIKE that, you don't taste the food. You just eat it, and then get your coffee thermos filled, and then go out to the car and put the seat back and try to nap. Try not to think about it. Try not to feel anything.

This case had been interesting up till now. My favorite kind of case. The one where I don't have a damn thing at stake. The kind where I'm just swooping in to save the day.

So much for that.

Goddammit.

Then you go out to the car. Lay down. Do what you can to nap. Try not to look into that yawning black pit filled with feelings you don't have words for.

I wound up tossing and turning. Doing anything I could to get away from thinking about Rachael.

Thought a lot about Tom Stride.

And Teddy.

I'd been both of them before.

I'd been the kid who couldn't figure out why his Dad was suddenly disappearing from his life—I remember that more than I remember my actual father. Like losing a hand. After a while you're more aware of not having a hand than you are of what it used to be like to have one.

And I'd been the poor schlub pinned down in a shit job with an asshole boss who had me over a barrel, and not enough sense to just walk out the front door. Sure, I didn't have a family to support at the time, unless you count me. I do like to eat, and that's gotta count for something. Tom's solution was to jump over that barrel and try to find safety on the other side. My solution had been to put the boss's wife over the barrel and have a little fun with her.

Either way, someone gets fucked.

Me, I got fired from the only job I ever wanted. Tom Stride was going to get to hang on to a job that he clearly didn't want to keep, because every other option scared him worse.

At least, that's the way it would be if nobody put His Grubbiness away.

All I had to do is connect him to the land deal, and the school wouldn't move. Tom Stride would get to keep his job. Teddy would keep snooping around with his junior detective agency. Everything would be fine.

Even better if I could connect him to that murder.

Thinking about that murder? That's what finally put me to sleep. Nothing makes the world worth living in more than a good problem to solve.

9:55 PM, WEDNESDAY

THE ALARM ON MY phone woke me up at five-till-ten. I dug around in the back of Francine (my Subaru's name—long story), came out with my jacket. Not really thick enough for the fifteen degrees my phone said it was outside, but I'd rather risk frostbite on some dead cow's hide than on my own still-living skin.

I walked around the parking lot to get my blood pumping, work the road kinks out. Didn't really work. Mostly my blood wanted to hide in my gut, and who could blame it? I was about to talk to Rachael.

And I had no bloody idea what I was gonna say.

Turns out it wasn't all that brilliant.

"Hi." I said when she came up and made pace with me. Backpack slung over one shoulder of a ratty gray nylon parka she must've gotten at the local Salvation Army for a buck ninety-five. She'd changed from her work sneakers to her biking boots—I could tell without looking by the way they clomped on the pavement. Made her sound like a two-legged horse.

"Hi."

"So, you said we need to talk?"

"Yeah. Mind giving me a ride home?"

I didn't.

So I did.

Only took about five minutes, during which we said exactly nothing to each other.

Felt kind of like riding in the car with a corpse. The ghost of someone you used to know. Used to care about. Just sitting there in the passenger seat.

She lived in a detached garage behind an old ranch house that now sat on something approximating a residential street. A lot farther away from the main house than you usually got with detached garages. Good privacy. Looked like it had once been a stable, then turned into a garage, then turned into an AirBnB unit.

Optimistic move, that one. Yreka has about as much tourist appeal as the back side of an Idaho potato farm. It's the kind of place photographers can have a great time, and everyone else will go psycho from cabin fever.

According to my headlights, it needed a paint job. It looked like an aspen shedding its bark.

There was a healthy wind whipping across the plain. Felt like Jack Frost was trying to claw my skin off.

"Good pick. No chance of snoopers." No chance of visitors, either. Rachael used to give Nya a run for her money in the social department. The two of them used to tear up San Francisco's kink clubs three nights a week, come home early in the morning and still be up for working a full shift the next day. I'd lost count of their conquests and play partners, and that's just the ones I'd met over the years. To go from that to hermitage takes something radical. Something I didn't know she had in her.

"Thanks." She let her pack down next to the door, closed it behind us. turned the lights on after we got in. It was all oranges and yellows and browns and smaller in here than it looked from the outside, even if you accounted for the fact that there had to be a bathroom behind the rear wall.

It looked like an old hotel room. A little card table. An old tube TV. A queen bed on a Hollywood frame, the orange crocheted bead spread mashed all to hell and gone.

There was a portable makeup station at the card table in front of the little wooden chair. White plastic tri-fold mirror with built-in lights. Spirit gum, latex, powder, brushes, they all sat in front of it. Recently used.

Rachael peeled her coat off, tossed it on the bed. "Just pile your shit over here. I'll be a minute. Sit down, read a book or something."

I tossed my jacket onto the bed. She headed to the makeup station.

First it was the white sponge wedges. Rachael used them to rub the makeup off her cheekbones. Then she opened a little brush-bottle. Acetone hit my nose. Nothing else in the world smells quite like it. She dabbed it around the edge of her nose, then started to wiggle the skin.

Twenty seconds, and the nose was gone. She'd done a hell of a job building it or getting it built—it had flaps that ran the full width of her face, and laid all the way up the bridge of her nose to between her eyebrows.

"I didn't know you knew stage makeup."

"High school drama. Noses. That kind of thing. Wounds, too. I was hot shit at the wounds."

"Color me surprised." Never in my life have I met a woman with a deeper love of recreational violence. I think that's why she made a good partner.

Rachael plucked the prosthetic from her nose. "Lantham, for fuck's sake, stop staring. I know you watch all that behind-the-scenes shit on every movie you've ever watched. It's not like you haven't seen this before."

I shrugged. Bent over, grabbed my knees. Started working my hamstrings. I groaned while I stretched.. "What can I say. You did a hell of a job. I wouldn't have recognized you if you hadn't said anything."

"Thanks. So how'd you find me? Cell phone? IP traces?"

"Nah. Dumb luck."

"Right."

"Seriously. I was headed up to Weed for a snoop. Got road hypnosis. Overshot."

"I don't believe in luck."

"Like hell you don't."

"Not where you're involved."

"Well, I guess you're just gonna have go to shopping for a shiny new worldview next time you're down in the Haight."

She set her sponges down, started working on her boot buckles. Six little buckles up each side of her boots. Not exactly a quick-release setup, but guaranteed to stay on if she ever laid her bike down on the freeway.

"Weed, huh."

"Yeah. Gotta check out a new school they've got going in. Might be tied to a murder. Cover-up, corruption, the usual old tune."

"You get all the fun stuff." She kicked her shoes off, set them next to the door. "How's Nya?"

"You've probably talked to her more recently than I did."

She chuckled. "You really don't trust her, do you?"

"What do you mean? Of course I do."

"Right." She took her shirt off, threw it over the makeup chair. She wasn't wearing her gun, but she did have new ink on her back. Sanskrit, black, above the water lily that wrapped around her left side from her spine to her sternum under her left breast. She always knew how to find the good tattoo artists.

"What's the new ink say?"

"'If you can read this, you're probably Hindu.'"

"Cute."

She unsprung her bra. Two gel falsies thumped against the floor. She threw the bra on the chair. I looked at the TV. Not that she'd mind me looking. She'd been after me for years now to let her model for one of my photography projects. But I did. There are some people you just don't want to see naked, because you don't like the way it makes you feel.

I was right, too. She didn't care. She kept stripping right on down to skin. Then walked past me to the bathroom.

Even her pubic hair was blond.

"What's the deal, Rache?"

"With what?" She stopped at the foot of the bed, shuffled through the pile of clothes.

I nodded at her pubes. "That's a long way to go for a disguise."

"Well, I'm not dead, Lantham."

"Why all the trouble?"

"Christ, Lantham. Cause I don't want some nosy fucker poking his nose into my business, okay?"

"Then why did you ask me here instead of telling me to get lost?"

"You were already lost." She fished out a sweatshirt out of the tangle of cloth, threw it over her shoulder, kept rummaging.

"Oh for fuck's sake." I got up, grabbed my jacket. "I did not come to the ass end of nowhere to put up with your shit—"

"I'm undercover, Lantham. Work it the fuck out. Jesus."

"What, did you get a job with Pinkerton's?"

"No." She found a pair of yoga pants, shrugged, bent over to put them on.

"So what's the case? Who hired you?" She wasn't looking at me, so I had an excuse not to look at her. Not that it mattered now.

"Nobody hired me. If I hadn't stumbled into this thing I'd be having a hella good time somewhere a fuckload more entertaining than bumfuck NorCal. What the fuck are you looking at? Lantham?"

I was looking at the curtain behind the TV. Didn't seem believable as a native interior design feature. For one thing, it wasn't gold, orange, or brown. It was blue. Didn't exactly clash, but you could tell it wasn't put in here by the same person who put the rest of the room together.

I nodded towards it.

"Oh, that."

I looked back at her, just in time to see her tits disappearing from view. I didn't know quite how to feel about that. Good thing I grew up Catholic. Learned young that anytime you've got an emotion you can't identify, it's worth assuming it's something you ought to feel guilty about. Saves a lot of time. It's why we have lower therapy bills. If you know you're gonna feel guilty no matter what you do, you don't waste time and money on shrinks.

Rachael tugged her sleeves up to her elbows, walked to the curtain. "That's my murder board."

"Your...holy shit." 'Board' didn't do this thing justice. There was more information crammed on that thing than there is on some hard drives. "That's not a board, that's a fucking wall. What are you, tracking a serial killer or something?"

"Definitely an 'or something.'" She pointed to a "Missing" poster of a young black boy. "I found this kid when I rolled into town..."

My phone rang. I looked. Erica. "Hold that thought. Just a sec."

Tapped 'answer.'

"Hey, how're you doing?"

"Eh. It's been a day. But I'm work-from-home the next two days. Piles and piles of paperwork. You at home?"

"No, I'm on the road. Won't be home tonight." She sounded like an old bit of leather that's been dragged behind a truck.

"Don't tell me it's more shit for that Stride thing."

"Hey, we had a deal. You don't razz me about my clients, I won't razz you about what your employer gets up to in spite of all its 'rules.'"

She chuckled. Always a warm sound. Made me ache all over. "Fair enough. When'll you be home?"

"I don't know. Tomorrow. Day after at the latest."

"Mind if I set up camp at your place?"

"Sure. Go for it." Then I stopped. Something in her tone.

"Thanks." There it was again. Sounded almost...fragile? Fragile wasn't in the Erica Ellis vocabulary.

"Are you okay love?"

"Eh. It's been...I can't talk about it right now. Give me a long rubdown when I see you again?"

"Sure."

"I gotta get going."

"Love you."

"Love you too."

Click.

"Trouble in paradise?" Rachael said. Sounded like she really gave a shit, too.

"No. Why?"

"I've heard you when you're in love."

"And?"

She shrugged. "You're not."

I squinted at her. Couldn't tell whether she was joking or not. "Fuck you."

"Yeah, well," she muttered, "maybe that'd help."

"Excuse me?"

"Sorry. It's been an interesting few months. You figure things out."

"Well, keep 'em to yourself when you don't know what you're talking about," I growled.

"Now there's the surly Lantham I remember."

I stood up and walked over to the murder board. Stood next to her. Close enough to loom over her properly. "Erica and I are fine. We've been busy, and I've got my mind on other things right now. Is that okay with you? Or do you want a notarized document to that effect?"

"Suppose I'll just have to take your word for it." She looked straight into my eyes. Didn't back down. Didn't flinch. Just smirked. Like she'd gotten my goat. Oh yeah,

I was gonna strangle her all right. Kinda missed that feeling of constantly bubbling irritation that she inspired.

"You're a bitch."

She smiled. "I've missed you too."

I shook my head, an excuse to break eye contact before she saw down into my soul. I don't use it much, and there are cobwebs in there, and I don't like anyone seeing it before I've had a chance to clean up for visitors.

"So, you were saying. This kid..."

"Zarek Woodfork. Yeah. So he went missing..."

She told me the whole story. Everything that had happened since she rolled into Yreka three months ago. "And then they all just showed up again. Every one of them. Well, except one." She tapped a photo with the name Quentin Greenaway next to it. "I don't know, Lantham. I figured I had the best place in town..."

"You sure did a hell of a job." My voice sounded more impressed than I meant it to—not that I wasn't. I was. I just like to play it cool. "All the victims, all the info on them? Fuck, Rache, I don't know how you did it, but I'd be hard pressed to pull this together in this kind of a setup." I waved around the room. "And the undercover work? With the cops and one of the victims already knowing your face and your voice? That's ballsy as all hell."

"Well, it's gotten me fuck-all." She left the board, went back to the bed, flomped backwards on it, stared up at the ceiling like God was going to give her a secret decoder ring.

"Don't short-change yourself."

"I don't know where to go from here. I mean, it's like, whoever was doing this suddenly died or something—except that he would've had to be alive to dump them all in the snow like that, and knock them out so they never saw anything. I mean, who does that, Lantham? Who the fuck, really? Who the fuck gets up in the morning and says," she switched to a deep Loony-Tunes doofus voice, "'By golly gee, I love having a dungeon full of children to drug up and stick needles in and hug and love and play with and call George, but I just can't afford any more Cheerios this month, so I guess I'll have to just go and leave them out on the freeway and hope they find a good home.'" She sighed. Rolled back onto her shoulder blades, then did a kick-up off the bed to land on the floor.

That's the kind of trick only short flexible people can pull off. I spent five years trying to learn, just so I could look cool in the gym.

"Show off." Even at my most flexible and most svelte, I always wound up buckling my knees or smacking my back onto the floor. I suppose it's only fair. Short people can't loom.

"Absolutely." She went back to the murder board, then squatted down to the cabinet under the TV, opened it up. "You'll condescend to some Gentleman Jack?"

"If you don't have any scotch."

"No scotch. Are you kidding? Do you know how

hard it is to find good scotch around here?"

"Um...go to the liquor store?"

"Why, Mister Lantham," she said in an oh-so-sweet country girl voice, "Daisy Pickford is not the kind of girl who'd be caught dead in a liquor store. Think of what it'd do to her image!" She pulled the bottle out from the cupboard. "Besides, the nearest BevMo is in Redding and the best the local dirt merchant's got is a ten year Glenmorgaine."

"Ain't a bad drop."

"Doesn't fit the rules." She set a couple tumblers up on the table, poured a few too many fingers in each one.

"You have learned well, young grasshopper."

"So if you didn't come up here looking for me, why are you up here?"

"I told you. Got a case."

"You said. You didn't say what it was." She handed me a glass. I took it. I was too tired to drive anywhere anyway, and I'm not above sleeping on the floor when I'm drunk enough.

"All right, but only cause you bought the good stuff. Well, for Tennessee Whiskey, anyway." I took a sip. Smoother than I remembered. Heat, but no hard bite. I silently paid my compliments to the first folk of Tennessee. They did get damn close to replicating the Scotch they so dearly missed from the old country. "You remember Teddy Stride?"

"What, the little kid across the street? The creep who's always trying to peek through my window?"

"That's the one."

"That kid's gonna grow up to be a serial killer, Lantham."

"Nah. Gonna grow up to be a snoop."

"Hmph, just as bad."

"Gee, thanks, Ms. Pot." I was already halfway through the tumbler. Good stuff. Relaxing, too. Not the alcohol—it hadn't been in my system long enough for that, and it takes a shitload to get me drunk—the ritual. The nose. The shop-talk.

God, I'd missed shop-talk with her. Felt like slithering into an old frumpy sweater after a long day out tailing weirdos.

"Learning from the best." She plopped down on the bed beside me. Patted me on the back. "Self-loathing is a job requirement in this business, right?"

"Good work, grasshopper." Another sip. Another dash of sweet-vanilla-charcoaly-warm-smoothness in my mouth. "So, Teddy has this problem with his father..."

And then it was my turn to fill in the whole business to her.

She listened. Even took notes. Like we'd never stopped working together.

"Plasma?" She asked. Slurred a little bit. She was on her fourth, and she's got a liver that's smaller than my hand when I stretch it all the way out. "Blood plasma?"

"Yeah. I think he's trafficking in the stuff. I'm not sure how that plays into anything, but it's...I don't know, kinda creepy."

"So what's your next move?"

"I've gotta do the tour. Head down to Weed. Talk to a title company, get a history on the parcel the school's building on. You know they still don't have their property records properly computerized up here?"

"Welcome to Jefferson." She raised her glass to me.

"Then...the murder, obviously. Gonna try the professional courtesy lever, get a look at what the cops found. And there's something about this pregnancy center thing that's creeping me out, so I'm gonna drop by for a visit, check it out..."

"You'll never get in."

"What?"

"You're not pregnant. You want to see the inside of a place like that, you need to go in as a patient. And, well, I hate to say it, Lantham, but you're kind of dickish."

"Hell of a sweet-talker, aren't you Rache?"

9:30 AM, THURSDAY

RACHAEL FOUND THE PLACE on the Internet. Took a bit of digging around in student forums, finding the places where college kids traded info on the Q-T, but we had a lot of road to do it on—and, since we were in a real work car, she had the laptop station all set up on her side of things, so she didn't have to fuck around on a phone screen. It had an address on Old Stage Road, a trail running along the foothills that paced I-5 a couple miles to the west.

The snow was melting fast. Patches of ground poked through everywhere. We were also a few hundred feet lower here than they were in Yreka, and that makes a difference in how much snow fell in the first place.

We pulled up across the street from it. Three beige portables slammed together into a single triple-wide unit, and a dumpster. The whole unhygienic-looking mess bordered a construction site, with a slapdash wooden sign out front with "Trubody College Pregnancy Counseling Center" and another that said "Future Home of Trubody College."

"They're running a clinic out of this place? How is that even legal?"

"It's not a clinic."

"Uh, Lantham, it says 'Pregnancy Counseling' right on the parking lot sign." Well, it wasn't exactly a parking lot, but it was a bare patch of gravel-and-mud that could pass for it in a pinch.

"Trubody   College   is   a   Religious   Right establishment."

"So what the hell is the point of this?"

"Well," and this is where my nasty little research fetish comes in handy, "the basic idea is that if you give a pregnant girl counseling and prenatal care and job training you keep her from having an abortion."

"So they send them up here to bumfuck nowhere and stick them in a shed to hide their shame." Any more vitriol in her tone and she'd have blown holes in the windows.

"That's why I'm here. They used to have the place on campus, which is where they usually have them at the schools that have them. Having it this far away ruins the whole point of having them on campus in the first place—which is to help the women keep their education going..."

"You mean keep the customers from quitting the program."

"Yeah. So they move it up here last fall. And the school doesn't re-locate till next year at the earliest. Doesn't make any sense."

"Doesn't it?" The tone in her voice made me look back toward her. She wasn't looking at the building. She was looking at me. "Who else used to isolate women out in the boonies and propagandize the hell out of them?"

I shuddered. "Yeah, I've been trying not to go there."

We looked across for a while longer, each of us thinking. "His Grubbiness is behind this," I said. "But what the hell is he trying to get out of it?"

Rachael shook her head. She had nothing either.

Bloody brick walls. Gotta love 'em.

WE COORDINATED OUR stories. Headed inside. The place smelled like iodine and carpet cleaner. Definitely a clinic, and not just a counseling center. Figured they must have some doctors around to do amnios and blood draws and pelvic exams and ultrasounds and stuff like that.

I sat down on a cushy checked-fabric sofa. Rachael went to a service window cut in the wall next to the only door that didn't lead outside, asked if they were open to the general public. Played her Daisy Pickford role to perfection. I was her boyfriend who'd been urging her to have an abortion, but she didn't feel right about it, so convinced me to come along and talk to them.

We waited ten minutes. I read an article in *Christianity Today* complaining about the return of social nudity, and a rejoinder by another columnist talking about how the ancient Christians had been avid social nudists, so maybe the faithful should take their panties off rather than getting them in a bunch about it. Guess the Bay Area way was spreading. God bless the Internet.

My phone buzzed. Text from Nya.

Got job interview with Gruber today at 4. Will keep you posted.

I sent back: *Roger. Good luck. Be sure to lay on the charm!* Charm was Nya's native surplus commodity. She could corner the global market.

A woman in a white coat came for Rachael. Then, a minute later, a man in a deliberately-casual sport coat came for me.

He said his name was Roger. No last name. He led me into a boring office with pasteboard walls and sat me in a fake leather chair that wasn't designed to hold anybody for long. Then, with great sensitivity and salesmanship, he gave me *the talk.*

I won't bore you with details. It had a lot to do with being a man, and God's view of sex before marriage, and ended with photos of a developing fetus and talks about how criminal and despicable it was to snuff out a young soul before it had the chance to grow up and know the love of God and the wonders of life.

Nothing I wasn't expecting. But then, I wasn't expecting to find anything interesting. I did expect Rachael to find something interesting, maybe. I figured I was just a diversion.

Still, I'd come all this way. So I made noises like he was gradually winning me over. Talked about how I used to be a churchgoer, and I'd backslid in the last few years—Catholics have lapses, while Evangelicals backslide. Little markers like that are what tell people whether you belong in their club or not. It's a short-hand, happens in all kinds of closed subcultures. People actually care more about speaking the lingo than they do about what you actually think. That's why pastors who get caught fucking the music director's wife or snorting coke off a crucifix always get hired back.

About forty minutes later, we were closing in prayer. When we got up to leave, I figured I didn't have anything to lose, so I took a flyer.

"Roger, one thing that I can't figure out about all this."

"What's that?"

"Well, the school doesn't open for another year, so why send the students all the way up here? I mean, I'm glad you did. I don't know what we would have done if you hadn't been here, me and Daisy, but...don't the students lose class time?"

He smiled. A salesman's smile. "It's cheaper," he said. "And we can give all our medical care in house."

"So they..,oh!" I pursed my chin, made like I was thinking it over. "They aren't tempted when they go for prenatal..."

"Exactly. It's safer this way. And everyone's accountable. Accountability, you know, it's an important thing."

"That's not a bad idea."

"And the students don't miss out. They just take their classes over Skype for the few months they're up here. We house them all on-site, everyone has space to work, and it's beautiful country, plenty of quiet contemplation, especially compared to what they're used to..."

He went on for a little while longer, more sales pitch stuff—how they had made good on the terms of their grant for the clinic, how they were adding more staff in a couple months, how they had a state-of-the-art blood lab and could give excellent pre-natal care, about how there was an on-site birthing center, and if there were any serious problems there was a hospital within easy air-lift distance. And, of course, the adoption service they offered, and they still had their arrangement with UCSF for extraordinary problems.

I thanked him. Went back to the waiting room. Rachael wasn't there yet.

Asked the girl at the desk—very pregnant, very young. Obviously a student here for treatment, and putting in work-study hours at the only post available. Rache would be a while yet. I oughta cool my heels.

"I get antsy in waiting rooms. Okay if I walk around, look at the construction?"

"Sure. Just don't go past any of the hard hat signs."

"Thanks."

MORE HOURS THAN I expected up here. Chewed up the whole day. If I was going to get home tonight—and I really didn't want to spend another night in Rachael's bed if I could help it—I was going to need to trim my itinerary. You can do that, almost always, if you're willing to spend the money.

You've got no expense account for this, Lantham. You can't just drop big checks on people to get answers out of them.

That's my subconscious talking. It's smarter than me, but I don't listen to it very often. It was right in this case, too, but I could find ways to economize when I did the books. Hell, this year business was shaping up to be good enough that I could probably use the loss just for tax purposes.

Okay, I know it's rationalizing, but that's what humans do. And despite the otherworldly height, I am still human. Or, at least, that's what my GP keeps telling me.

So I walked around the construction site to see what I could see. And, while I did it, I trimmed my itinerary. Starting with a few calls to local title companies. Did anyone in town want to make a quick two grand? Because I'd pay that for a quick, comprehensive search of the history of the new Trubody College site.

No sir, we don't do that kind of thing, was the first reply. That property isn't for sale, and we aren't in the business of invading people's privacy.

So much for the 21st century, right?

Second company. No sir, that's against corporate policy. But there was something in his voice. Something that suggested ambition. A little note of hope.

"Is this call being recorded for training purposes?" I asked. Technically they were supposed to warn me before hand. Recording someone in California without demonstrable consent is a felony. I should know. It's one of my favorite laws to break But I didn't want to get the guy in trouble.

"No, we don't record our calls."

"Then maybe we should put our heads together. I'm sure we can come up with something that will meet both our needs."

Bribery is like sex—you can close almost any deal if you get the approach right.

It was gonna cost me sixteen hundred bucks plus the normal two hundred dollar search fee, but I'd have the complete history of that parcel in my email box by day after tomorrow. It would take that long to scan it all in.

All the time I was on the phone, I was combing through the construction site. Most of the activity right now was excavation. They were leveling the site, digging trenches for conduit, clearing brush. Looked like they'd only gotten their permits a week or two ago.

It was going to be a big campus, too. Easily as big as the current place, but with more parking here and there on pieces of plywood backed by two-by-fours stuck into the ground. Below the maps were more technical drawings, and a large-printed grid number so that the build crew wouldn't get lost.

The soil was poor. Red. You can smell barren dirt when they turn it up, and this was all pretty lean. They were going to have to pull in a hell of a lot of ash or cow shit or fill dirt just to landscape the place.

Then again, judging by the scale of this operation, I didn't imagine budget was a huge concern.

How the hell were they paying for all this when the school back in SF was facing falling enrollment?

The old building, you idiot.

That old building had to be worth a hundred million easy on today's market. You could build a lot of pagodas with that many clams.

I wound up hanging around the north end of the site longer than I should have. There were a few buildings beyond the border—an older California Ranch-style residential place, and a bunch more portables. Had to be the housing for the students they'd shipped up here, and, going purely on the fact that they were on the same piece of property, the place the den mother lived.

There was also a sign declaring the north end of the property to be the future home of the Trubody College Biomedical Research Institute.

They were digging trenches like it, too. Massive things, for drainage and utility pipes and access pumps.

Trubody Biomed? In Weed? That had to be a joke. Like the Institute for Creation Research opening an evolutionary biology school with Richard Dawkins as dean.

I took a pick of the sign, just in case it came in handy. Then I wandered further north, toward the houses.

Ranch-style house. That had to be where Mrs. Paxton lived, when she was alive. She was den mother up here. Big front yard, all scrub. Little gravel path up from the driveway to the door. Culvert over the drainage ditch. A little cross with flowers at the base sat beside the path halfway up to the front door. So why the hell was she killed?

People don't kill for a lot of reasons. They kill for passion, greed, and reputation. The husband had motive on at least one score—she was sleeping with her boss, if there was anything to the scuttlebutt—and I'd lay good money that he had motive on number two. Most people that age have life insurance.

I knew from being a cop that it wasn't hard to pin a murder on a husband. And it's usually a good idea. Ninety-nine percent of all murders in the United States are either gang violence or a grudge-kill of some sort. People don't get knocked off by strangers, and contract killings are statistically non-existent.

Statistically.

They do still happen.

Mr. Paxton was supposedly out of the country when this one happened. So whoever did, it had to be a hit. That meant there were some funds knocking around somewhere. A wire transfer, or a large cash withdrawal. Something that would buy a hit man for an evening.

She was raped, too. And had her throat slit. Up close and personal stuff. So it had to be a special kind of hit man.

But as for the hire, the husband was the safe bet. We just needed to make sure it was the right one.

We. Listen to that. Less than a day back in contact with Rachael and I was thinking in teamspeak all over again.

Oh well. That's what last hurrahs are for, right? Let you leave things on the kind of terms you don't mind being nostalgic about, instead of terms that make you want to beat the living shit out of the friend that left you in the lurch.

No cars in the driveway. Probably a good bet nobody was home. There sure as hell weren't any neighbors.

No one around to catch me doing a little trespassing.

I wanted to get a good look at the rest of the grounds. The portables back there had to be the dorms, right?

There were four of them. Two sets of two. The nearer set faced the open dirt back yard, had windows spaced in a way that suggested that it had about a dozen single-bed rooms in there. Had a couple cars parked near it—the sorts of second-handers from the nineties that you expect college kids to own. The other one didn't have any windows.

Both sets were still on their trailers, just jacked up and strapped down with the wheels still on. The windows on the inhabited-looking one had curtains and pop culture stickers, little figurines and cacti sitting on the sills, and stained-glass hangers with bible verses on them affixed to the glass with suction cups.

Sure looked like the kind of stuff you'd expect in a dorm room.

But they hadn't always been dorms. These portables had been here a while. Maybe a year. Maybe more.

Enough that they had moss growing in the wheels and rust on the rims, and dandelions peeking out from under the tires.

So they'd just recently turned into dorm rooms.

So what the hell had they been before then?

I called up the title company and added the Paxton house address to the title search, offered the guy another five hundred bucks for the trouble. After I mentioned money, he didn't seem all that annoyed.

There was movement inside. Figured there must be some student prisoners up and about in there. So I walked around to the other building, the one without windows. File storage, or a construction office.

Turns out it did have windows, just not many. A couple near the front door, but they were blocked by closed blinds. Going round the back side, everything was blind. Just a double-wide door with a wheelchair ramp leading up to it. ADA compliance even out here. Gotta love it. Back here, I could crouch down and take a real look underneath. Nobody would see me.

Fingers in the ground. Yeah, pretty soft. Even if you took away the snow, and there weren't even the slightest wheel marks anymore from when these had been rolled into position. They'd been here through at least one full go round of the wet/dry seesaw that California calls "seasons."

"What were you before you were you?" I mumbled at the buildings.

Whatever it was. They weren't going to tell me.

From where I was, on the north end of the structure, I had a pretty safe getaway back to the road. Just had to head directly east, bearing a little north so that the one tree that was back here shielded me from view until I was just an innocuous retreating figure in the distance.

That tree had a downed branch.

I just about tripped over it.

Knocked straight off the limb, not even at a join. Like something had hit it where it wasn't used to being hit.

Squat down. Pick it up.

The wood was green all the way through. Oh, it had been sitting out in the weather for a fair few days already, but it had fallen in the prime of life, not as an old dead thing.

Which meant something knocked it off. Something not very sharp.

I looked at the ground under it.

Tire prints. A day or two old. Big ones. Like, box-truck big.

Took a couple pictures for my notes. Dictated some thoughts on the walk back to the clinic.

Rachael was waiting for me on the front steps, about ready to come unglued.

11:00 AM, Thursday

"WE'RE RUNNING OUT OF time," I said. "We need to get down to the police station.

"Like hell we do. We need to get the fuck out of here."

I motioned with my head for her to follow, but she peeled left and headed toward the dumpster.

Trotted to catch up. "I thought you said we needed to go."

"Yeah, well, there's something you need to see first. Give me your phone."

"Why?"

She held out her hand. "Gimme." Then. "You still using the same swipe pattern?"

"New phone. Left-right mirror from the old one."

"Got it."

She tapped at my phone. Came to a stop in front of the rusty galvanized steel dumpster. Looked around like she was checking for cops.

"Remember that picture you showed me last night?"

"Um...not really."

She smirked. "You liked it that much, huh?"

"Bah. I was tired. I don't remember things when I'm

that tired. You know that."

"Mmm mm, so many glorious possibilities." She handed me the phone. It was the photo I took of the plasma vial.

"Okay, yeah, I remember it."

"Boost me up." She made to scramble into the dumpster. It wasn't tall enough to present much of a problem for her if she was using it, but it was one of those shaped like an inverted cone. Not a lot of purchase for a good scramble. Still, she didn't *need* the boost.

"That's not a good idea. It'll be full of sharps."

"I'll be careful. Come on."

I boosted her up onto the lid. She squatted down on one half, lifted the lid over the other half, laid down on her stomach, and reached down in to rifle.

"Shit, Rache, be careful in there will ya?"

"They use sharps disposal bins. All I gotta find is a biohazard...ah hah! Here we go." She came out with a little tub with a big biohazard sticker on the side.

I helped her down, she took her jacket off and folded it over her arm, hiding the tub.

"Let's get out of here before they get antsy."

I PULLED OVER A quarter mile up the road.

"Come on, Rache. What you got?"

"I think...yes. Look at this." She pulled out a discarded blood vial. The kind of vial you'd expect them to go through in the bajillions at any clinic in the world.

It had a label on it.

The label had a little device on it. A maroon cross, made up of four little flattened football oblongs around a blank center. Like some post-structuralist wanted to suggest a red cross without actually infringing on the American Red Cross's trademark.

"Let me see that picture again." I said it mostly to myself, since she wasn't holding my phone. I pulled up the gallery app, checked out the photo of that vial. "What the fuck..."

They were the same labels. The same vials.

"Rache, you never worked as a candy striper, did you?"

"No. Why?"

"If the labels come at the factory then...wait, no." I thought back to the last time I had my blood drawn. Closed my eyes. "They take the blank vials, and they print out labels, don't they? Then they stick them on after."

"Duh. Look at the labels." She held up two discarded vials from the tub. Each one had their labels at a different angle. "And that's not all. Check this out."

She reached into her pocket. Pulled out a sheaf of hand-outs. They had titles like *God's Plan for Pregnancy. Completing a Family: Your Baby and Adoption. Honoring the Life Inside You.* That kind of stuff.

The last one was about pre-natal care. It talked about not drinking, not smoking, all the standard stuff. It had other not-standard stuff in there, from right out of the

Victorian era, like a section on abstaining from sex for the health of the baby.

And then a care schedule on the back side.

Now, I've never been a mother. Haven't been a father either, as far as I know. But I've known a lot of people who've managed to reproduce from time to time.

I don't remember any of them getting weekly fetal blood draws.

"Wait...what? What the hell is a fetal blood draw?" It said right on the form that it was to monitor the development of the baby—they assiduously avoided the word "fetus" everywhere, even though they used "fetal" a few times—so that there could be early interventions in case of any diseases or "growth problems" (birth defects?) so that you would have a healthy normal baby that you could provide with a loving environment in a Christ-centered two-parent home.

"I don't know. Want me to look it up?"

"Yeah. And we'd better get on the road to—"

Buzz buzz.

"Hold on." Caller ID listed a 415 I wasn't familiar with. Click the button, phone to ear. "This is Lantham. Go."

A shaky tenor said "Clarke."

"Stride? Is that you?"

"Yeah. Look. I know what we talked about, but I've changed my mind."

"Changed your mind about what?"

His voice dropped to a whisper. "You've got to stop.

The investigation. You've got to leave it alone. Please."

"I can't do that. Nya's got an interview and..."

"I'll tell him who she is," he snapped. "And you'll be out anyway. I'll tell him I heard..."

"Tom. Tom. TOM. Shut up. What happened?"

"I can't risk it. They've got guns."

"Who's got guns."

"The guys at the airport."

"Stop. Hold on. Back up. What airport. Tell me what happened."

Silence.

"Come on, Tom. I'm your neighbor. I'm your friend. My girlfriend's an FBI agent. One of my clients is a cop. I'm not going to let anything happen to you." When talking to a panicked civilian, always use a calm, even voice.

"I can't have the police involved. Promise me you won't get the police involved..."

"I can't promise that till I know what's going on. Take a deep breath. Look, if you're that worried, if you want me to buy in, you gotta give me something. It's a big deal to drop a case. I have to know why, and it could cause me a lot of trouble."

He took a deep breath. "He had me run another errand. To the airport. To pick up another cooler..."

"And?"

"They had guns, Lantham. The guys in the airplane. This little Lear jet, and these two guys...I mean, they looked like drug guys you see on TV. They spoke

English fine, and they had sport coats on, but when they moved..."

"Did they say anything?"

"No. And I'm not going to either. I'm heading down to turn in my notice. I'll get a job at a movie theater or something..."

"Did you get a tail number?"

"I...well, yeah, okay, I took a picture of the plane when I was driving in, cause I thought, you know, it might be useful for you, but I deleted it."

"You got your phone with you?"

"Yeah."

"Is it turned on?"

"Yeah."

"Turn off WiFi and your mobile network."

"Why?"

"Just do it. For five minutes, okay? Are you somewhere I can call you back in five minutes?"

"Yeah, I'm in my office."

"Okay. Sit tight. Nothing will happen. I might have a rabbit in my hat. I swear I won't do a thing to put you in jeopardy, okay? Just give me five minutes."

"Okay."

I hung up. Swearing so much I might as well have been Rachael.

Who was looking at me with a question that didn't need any words.

"My new asset's about to flip. And this just got a lot bigger." I selected Erica's number, the phone dialed. She picked it up.

"Hey. Wasn't expecting to hear from you..."

"This is business. I just stumbled onto something that might be in your court. You don't happen to be at the office do you? Is Rivers around there? I don't have his direct number on me." Ronald Rivers was her boss, SAC of her team, and he was the man to take something like this too if I wanted speedy action on it.

"Um...no, Rivers isn't here but..."

"Can you give me his number? I'm kinda pressed."

"Sure, sure. Hold on."

Three seconds.

My phone buzzed.

Message received. Vcard attached.

"You're priceless. I love you."

"Love you too." She sounded distant, but I didn't have time at the moment. I'd probably interrupted her in the middle of a particularly riveting report form she had to fill out in order to be allowed to restock the tampon dispenser in the women's bathroom. Better to get out of her hair.

Hung up the phone.

Opened the vcard.

Called Rivers.

Ring ring.

"Special Agent-in-Charge Ronald Rivers."

"Rivers, this is Clarke Lantham."

"Lantham. How are things?" Rivers is one of those Feds without a sense of humor. Warmth in the voice isn't in the job description. Imagine Robert Stack spent his life hooked up to an enema machine, and you get an idea of just how buttoned-up this guy is.

"I might have something for you. Stumbled across a witness who might be on the end of some kind of trafficking scheme. What would it take to get him witness protection?"

"What is it, drugs? Counterfeit goods?"

"Human organs, I think. Bodily fluids. Illegal gene therapy. Something like that."

"I don't know if it falls under our jurisdiction..."

"Interstate shipment of illegal goods, possible human enslavement..."

"Okay, yeah, we'd take that case."

"And what about my guy?"

"If he's got information that cracks the case, we'll cover him."

"I got your guarantee on that?"

"Yes."

"Great. Cause if this winds up being as big as it's looking right now, this guy's going to be your star witness at the trial. What do you need from me?"

"What have you got?"

I gave him a quick run down in general terms-no names, no specifics. Just in case.

"Hmm...that's something. Could be a long investigation..." He thought for another couple seconds. "You get me a crime, I mean a real Federal crime that you can prove happened, and I'll take it over and protect your man, even if we can't take down the racket."

"Thanks. I'll be in touch in a couple days."

Hang up.

Dial Tom Stride's cell.

"Hello?"

"Tom?"

"Yeah."

"I just checked. We can get you into witness protection. All you have to do is lay low, don't attract any attention to yourself until after the arrests happen. Don't let them know anything is wrong—not Gruber, not the customers, not anybody. Once they've got you separate, they'll take you into a side room and you'll be offered protection."

"Won't that...won't we have to move?"

"Yes. I don't know to where."

"But my parents...our whole lives..."

"You're witnessing a crime, Tom. And a cover-up. And there might already be other people who are suffering because of Gruber. You're a moral guy. When you see the men who fell among thieves, do you cross to the other side? Or do you go out of your way to help him?" Thank God for Sunday school lessons about The Good Samaritan.

Silence.

I could hear him swallowing. Then a mumbling, like maybe he was praying.

"All right. I'll do it. You better be right about this."

"Tom, if I have to die to do it, I'll make sure nobody

harms Teddy or Beth or Erin."

"You give me your word on that?"

"Yes."

"Okay."

"Now, turn off the phone. Don't turn it back on today. Nya's going to be there for an interview this afternoon. Give it to her to take back to my office. I'll have it back to you tomorrow morning."

I hung up before he could second-guess himself and back out.

"Shit."

Rachael said: "He didn't go for it?"

"Oh, he went for it. I just have to get home and..." I looked at my dash clock. A little past noon. "...I'm gonna be wading through Sacramento traffic and probably get to bed at a zillion o'clock."

"Unless we split up the job."

"What do you mean?"

"I can talk to the cops here. You can go ahead and get back."

"What about your case?"

"Eh. FBI's on it now, I guess. I mean, they have to be, right? With all those kids coming back?" She sounded resigned, like the thought of diving back wore her out almost as much as the thought of giving it up depressed her.

"How bout I come back next week and we kick some trees, find out what we can knock loose."

"You're on."

9:00 PM, THURSDAY

SACRAMENTO TRAFFIC HAD 5 backed up all the way north of 505. Sunset over the delta hid behind some promising overcast. The clouds broke while I was on 680. By the time I got home, I was ready to dive into bed and never come out again.

But it wasn't an option. I'd gotten a note from Nya on the way home:

Didn't get the job. He didn't trust me. I'm sorry.

I'd sent back *No problem.*

Then she'd sent *I got his fingerprints, though. And Tom's phone. I left them on your desk.*

Rolled into Castro Valley at around nine. Erica's panel-side PT Cruiser was in the driveway when I got there. The lights said she was in the media room at the back of the house.

Deep breath. Heart flutter. Any night I get to spend with her is a special occasion lately. And that she can still make my heart race like that? I figure that's a good sign.

Not yet, though. I parked across the street so Klepto wouldn't hear me, snuck through the gate without so much as a creak, and skirted the security lights' sensor range.

I needed to visit the office first. Do the note dump and deal with Tom Stride's phone.

The trick with pulling a photo off a phone, or off anything, really, is to *not write anything to the media* after you've accidentally deleted something. That's why I had Tom turn off all his data channels—most phones go out and fetch things when you're not looking, and those things write to the flash memory, and they can overwrite the media where the deleted files are still hiding.

As long as he hadn't done anything after we got off the phone, I should be able to recover it.

Found the phone on the desk, with a post-it on it that said

Submitted fingerprint to AFIS. Query number CI85732434D.
—Nya

One less thing to worry about.

I plugged into Tom's phone. Woke up my computer.

Ran photorec. Still the best photo recovery software in the world if you can stomach dealing with the command line.

It turned up about four hundred files. Guess Tom was fastidious about deleting pictures he didn't want to keep.

I checked the file sized of the photos, then filtered the results to exclude anything that definitely wasn't a photo, then bitcopied the files that survived the sort off to my hard drive.

Then I pointed my image browser at the folder, and

told it to assume that everything in there was a jpeg, no matter what its filename was.

Some things I didn't really need to see were in there. Like sex pictures that Tom had been trading with his wife—I knew it was his wife he was trading them with, because I knew what Beth looked like, and she kept showing up in the deleted pictures, and no other naked people did.

Well, if I ever had to buy Tom a cock ring I knew what sort he liked. Ditto for getting Beth a vibrator.

But I did find the photo I was looking for. One plain white Lear jet.

With tail number.

Took me a few minutes to run the number. I got the same company as before:

International Sierra Charters.

I'd bounced off them at the beginning of this case, but back then I hadn't had any reason to think that the company itself could be crooked.

But what if Gruber had a stake in the ISC? Or what if this whole operation was being run by the people who ran it?

That was something I could sink my teeth into.

But I'd need to do it tomorrow. I had an Erica inside, and I ached all over just thinking about her.

The original meaning of the word "passion" is "suffering." There's a reason they use it to describe being in love.

I FOUND ERICA ON the media room couch.

She was not-watching *Archer*.

She didn't look good.

I slid onto the couch next to her to kiss her hello, then stopped. She'd been crying. It was all dry now, but her eyes still had that red, heavy, overworked look.

"What's wrong?"

She looked at the floor for a minute. Then said, "I'm sorry."

"Sorry for what?"

"I haven't been...you know how I've been up in Napa?"

"Yeah?"

"I haven't been up there working."

"You..." All the usual thoughts. Other boyfriend? Secret husband? Friend in trouble? Someone blackmailing her? Chasing down an off-the-books personal vendetta? "What have you been doing."

She choked up. She took my hand, held it between hers, like you see people do for children in the hospital.

"This. I've been doing this. For my Dad. He's...they...a month ago they told him he was terminal..."

And she gave me the whole story. How he hadn't wanted her to bring me because he didn't want anyone to see him "like that." How he was determined to beat it back no matter what, and to hell with all the doctors and their "stage four small cell" bullshit. He was going to beat it if it was the last thing he did.

How he'd used his titanic personality to bully his doctors into agreeing to some crazy surgery and gene therapy, and how they'd had to take him off chemo for the last two weeks to make it safe for him to go under the knife, and how the cancer had grown like crazy in the meantime.

"Now he's in surgery. They won't even let him have visitors for the next three days. They don't want him to get an infection." She kept shaking her head, like she was chiding herself for being a wreck. You get that a lot in this job. You wear a gun, wear a badge, you're charged with keeping order. You gotta be the rock everything else breaks against, and never lose your head. Sooner or later, you start believing you don't have a right to be a human being anymore.

The rest of what happened? Private stuff. Boring too. Death is a lot of drama that ends in the world's biggest anticlimax. Suffice it to say that she was the woman I was going to spend the rest of my life with, come hell or high water, and I didn't give a good goddamn about anything else. Not the case, not the way the dog was trying to get in between us to claim his share of my attention, not the fact that I was completely hammered from all the driving and investigating and hangoverness, nothing.

THAT'S WHERE THE CASE sat for the next few days. Erica worked from home. I helped Nya work through the pile of background checks that had come in from a couple of our regular clients. This time of year is as bad as the holidays for employee turnover. That means we get a big cash infusion, which means we have to scramble for our quarterly taxes—but it does mean we've got more leeway for the kinds of stupid expenses I've run up chasing Teddy Stride's nightmare fuel.

Two days on, I got the criminal inquiry on His Grubbiness back from AFIS. No criminal record, nothing else that I didn't already know. As far as the world was concerned, all I was allowed to know about Franklyn Gruber was his employment history.

The world could suck my big fat hairy toe. Nobody just comes into existence at the age of forty-five. They especially don't just wink into existence in a position like pastor at a church big enough to pay you a salary that leaves a paper trail. I know a case of identity theft when I see it.

And you can tell what kind of identity theft you're looking at by what the records look like. Say you're a refugee, and you buy an identity on the black market from a broker. You're going to be shopping for something with a history. Same if you're looking to run a long con where someone's gonna be peering in your background—you steal the identity of someone who's got a background that'll enhance your credibility. All you have to do to get away with it is not apply for something that'll attract attention. Like a passport. Or a job at the firm where your victim already works.

But if you're trying to disappear and you want a

completely clean slate? You steal the identity of a dead baby.

Gruber had stolen a stillborn's life, or...

No, Lantham. That way madness lies.

One of these days, I'll listen to that little voice.

But not today.

Today, I had to find out who Gruber really was. Because I knew damn sure now that he hadn't been born "Franklyn Gruber."

Or at least I needed a plan to find out.

Someone who'd been living under a false identity this long—and the same false identity—must have really needed to disappear. Or avoid detection.

I could only think of four sorts of people who fit that description: domestic violence survivors, wanted criminals, foreign spies, and members of the witness protection program.

Gruber didn't strike me as the kind of guy who would be running from an abusive wife—or husband—too much charisma. Too much dominance. People with god complexes tend not to wind up on the short end of the club.

That left three categories. Foreign spies were, by definition, un-find-able. You wouldn't be much use as a spy if Uncle Sam had a database of sleeper agents. So if that was Gruber's game, I wasn't going to be able to prove it. Best I'd be able to do is eliminate the other possibilities and report him to the DHS as a suspicious person.

But that wouldn't protect the Strides.

To do that I needed actual evidence of an actual Federal crime.

Either way, I needed to run a background check through the Federal databases. The kind I don't have access to.

But I might know someone who does. There's a data miner who's gotten me out of trouble on more than one occasion. He charges the kind of rates that would make Satan cry "predatory pricing," but if it's on a network somewhere, chances are he can get to it.

This is one of those phone calls I made when I was out throwing the ball for Klepto and Erica was inside. It's basic courtesy: if your girlfriend's a Fed, you don't talk about committing Federal crimes in front of her. That makes her an accessory, which doesn't look good on a resume.

"Twinkle twinkle little dear, what are you doing in my ear?"

"Hey Earl, it's Clarke."

"Silly boy. Your dulcet tones are laid down in my synapses like mother's milk."

"Remind me never to interrogate your neurologist."

"How has suburbia warped you?"

"It's got me thinking about the FBI."

"You've *got* to get back to the city."

"Right now I need to find someone in the witness protection and want lists. What can you do for me?"

"Nothing this week, honey. The big old eagle's got

his ears in my lines after I stepped back out in public with Personae. We're rebuilding all our links up here at Skullcrusher so they won't catch us rummaging in their jockeys."

"Okay, now the real answer."

"Sorry, sweetie, that is the real answer. I can get you next month if it ain't urgent. Job like that'll cost you thirty smackers. You understand."

"Don't like to expose myself unless you've got some coverage."

"You're all talk, you are, Clarkie boy."

"And don't you forget it." There was no way I could afford thirty thousand bucks on a job like this. No way in hell. I was gonna have to find something else. "I guess I'll give it a pass this time, old buddy. Take care of yourself. Don't let them catch you with your hand in the cookie jar."

"Honey, I *am* the cookie jar. Ta-ta!"

MY MOTHER DIDN'T THINK movies were a good influence on young minds. Especially after she was left to fend for herself. I figured Dad must have left her for an actress, given how intent she was about keeping us away from movies during my elementary school years.

Which meant that everything I saw was either at someone else's house, or it was *The Sound of Music*. Over and over. Strychnine for young neurons.

There's a reason I got this sickness in my melon. No wonder I can't sleep at night unless I've got a case.

In that movie, the Reverend Mother said that when God closes a door he opens a window.

Now like any good Catholic, I'm not quite sure how much God wants to bother with my doors and windows—big guy, big responsibilities. Got other things on his mind, way too much to worry about without the problems of a Lantham clogging up his inbox.

My inbox? Alternates between constipation and diarrhea. The minute something gets it moving everything just sort of gushes out.

Like the solution to my blood problem.

Let me put it to you this way:

If you're trying to figure out why someone would be moving blood plasma on the sly, and all the customers you know about are seriously wealthy residents of one of the most expensive cities in the world where everyone is seriously loopy for the next big thing, then what do you need to know?

Right. You need to know what the next big thing is.

If I could phone a friend about the witness protection thing, I could phone a friend about the plasma thing.

Except I didn't exactly have a friend in that business.

But I did have a couple reliable enemies who owed me a favor or three.

THE CLOUDS CLUSTERED AROUND Diablo low enough that you couldn't see its peak from the freeway, and the Alaskan weather that had rolled in over the course of the morning had me breathing smoke. The old, dead volcano that towered over Danville would probably get some powdered sugar on it before the day was over.

Appropriate for the kind of town where sweetness-and-light was the third most popular drug behind Ritalin and cocaine. It was a white powder kind of town. With the kind of money moving around out there, you'd expect either that or a politician infestation worse than termites in a woodpile. In these neighborhoods, you got both.

Nya used to live out here. I was actually on the way to the house where I first met her. Bleeding out in the guest house out back, doped up on drugs. Bad business all around. Made me look at Danville in a whole new light. Once upon a time I thought white-bread towns like this were basically where boring people went to do boring things. Now?

Well, now I know what boredom does to people with

money.

When I lived in Oakland, it took forever to get out here. From Castro Valley, it's just a quick cut through the canyons.

I didn't bother with the freeway. Just snaked north up San Ramon Valley until I got to Diablo. More fun that way, more interesting shit to see.

More time to get into the right frame of mind.

The last time I'd been out here, I'd faced a shotgun to the face. I didn't expect I'd get a warmer welcome this time. The old man had a lot to be afraid of, or he did last time I checked.

Like the people that had killed his son and ruined his name.

Last thing he'd want was to see me again. But if I thought he'd answer my calls, I wouldn't have hauled my carcass over all that tarmac

The clouds broke wide open just before I parked in front of his house on Ackerman. I didn't have my trench with me. Didn't expect rain. Especially not rain that cold. My hat and leather jacket weren't enough to keep the cold damp off even in the few yards between my car and the front door.

Not really the kind of place you'd expect a Nobel Prize winning molecular biologist to live, if that's the kind of thing you think of a lot. But this is where he lived. He won his Nobel for work he did on IVF in graduate school way back in the early 1970s. Then he went on to start the de-extinction movement, which he called "Species revivification" in the early days when I met him. He worked out how to bring extinct species back from the dead. And he did the first proof-of-concept, too, which is the reason I met Nya. But that's a long story.

Doctor Richard Sternwood was his name. And, the last time I saw him, he was a shadow of his former towering genius. Huddled beneath a bottle and behind a gun, waiting for another attack by the people who killed his son to get at him.

Sternwood's house was a low long affair, a ranch house built to the kind of scale to serve a ranch of about eighteen thousand acres. Made you wonder how many gunmen were hiding behind all those windows.

No hedges out front either. No cover. No way to sneak up on the door without being seen by people inside. Or neighbors.

Like a bug on a plate.

Not that there was really a reason to worry about that kind of thing now, but every time I come here I'm stuck back in that first night, where I wound up hiding behind the shed from Sternwood's son who was trying to put Nya in the ground. Puts me in a bad frame of mind.

I spotted six cameras coming up to the door.

Electronic RFID keyless entry plate.

The door looked like heavy oak, but when I bruised my knuckles on it I heard the faint ring of an iron core.

Last time I'd been here I'd given Sternwood a lecture

on proper security. Guess he listened.

"What do *you* want." His raspy Gandalf-y voice came through a speaker behind the RFID plate.

"There's only one way to find out."

He didn't say anything for almost a whole minute.

Then the door buzzed.

I pushed in.

Not a squeak.

The living room floor was white marble, broken up here and there with green-and-gold throw rugs. The couches were green and gold too, and the end tables and coffee tables and little display columns for vases were all marble. Looked like someone had looted the Parthenon. There's this theory in architecture, used to be big in Victorian design, about having a formal room for receiving guests.

Makes for a very cold home.

Like a beetle's carapace. Hard and brittle.

I found Sternwood in the kitchen. Grey silver hair, cut close, wide shoulders, looked like he used to be a football player—but old now, and a little dumpy. He was hunched over an Asus tablet, reading something, back to the water-smeared window. He looked better than last time I saw him. He'd lost the obsessive frailty, the haunted look. He had a spark of life in his eyes again. He'd had that same look when I'd first met him. The kind of look that said *I have more important things to do than waste my time with you.*

I stood my drippy carcass in between two sides of an

archway made up to look like Doric columns and said. "What's up, Doc?"

He didn't look at me.

"Looks like you're doing well for yourself."

He didn't even grunt.

I really hate this guy. He's a rude sonofabitch with the professional ethics of a salamander. And it's because of him that I wound up as the go-to investigator for weird shit in the Bay Area, which is how I can afford a mortgage around here. And, of all the brainiacs I've run into over the years, this guy out-brains them all.

That didn't mean he was gonna give me the time of day.

"Okay, fine, I'll get out of your hair. I just got a question for you."

He shook his head. "Not one of your lackeys, Lantham."

"You're only alive because of me. Just pretend I'm a debt collector."

He looked up at me, finally. "You need a better suit for that work."

"I'm working on a budget here. What do you know about plasma?"

"Which plasma?"

Right. Because there was also a physics plasma and a sci-fi plasma. "The blood kind."

He put his tablet down. "You're looking for more than the Wikipedia definition."

I walked across the much-more-homey hardwood

floor, joined him at the table. Didn't sit down, because I didn't want to piss him off, and the old man is big on manners. And I filled him in.

"I thought about it being one of those mail-order health scams," I said, "but you don't get armed men to guard shipments of those. And you don't sink god-knows-how-much money into plasmapheresis and disease screening and all the rest that you'd have to do for shipping real plasma around. You'd just fake it, wouldn't you? Or buy plasma from a blood bank? So I gotta wonder, what would make perfectly healthy people inject themselves with plasma on a kind of regular schedule."

He chuckled. Shook his head. "Gun jumpers. Always with the gun jumpers. How do you keep finding them?"

"Gun jumpers?"

He pursed his lips. Nodded like Obi-Wan. "Just so. Every application for plasma is therapeutic. Treats blood disorders, helps with hemophilia by increasing the available clotting factors. It's basically free—doesn't cost a lot on the open market."

"There's an open market?"

"The only tissue it's legal to sell. It's how the Red Cross stays in business. You give them blood, they sell it to hospitals. Not a bad business model, getting people to give you the things you sell."

"So that's where Facebook got the idea." That'll make me think twice about giving blood to the Red Cross." Then a thought hit me. "If it's an open market, why smuggle it. What kinds of special blood are there?"

"Rhesus negative, I suppose."

"That's for babies though. Whose blood types don't match their mothers." I had learned a few things dating a pediatric surgeon all those years ago.

"Close enough. Not much call for it outside of neonatal intensive care." He got up from the table, headed for the fridge. "Want an apple?"

"No. Thanks though."

"Can't get enough of them myself. Easiest way to stay young, eating apples. Not exactly scientific, but it makes you feel healthy, and the attitude helps." He pulled out one of those newfangled designer apples. About six colors blended together like it was designed by Kandinsky the night he went nuts with the paint thinner. "Got me back on my feet."

"What are you up to, doc? New research grant?"

He waved me away. "Not important. We're talking about your blood, remember? Why did you come out here?"

"I figured you'd know anything new that hadn't hit the mainstream yet. Maybe some crazy next-gen thing."

"Like the SENS people?"

"The *what?*"

"Strategies for Engineered Negligible Senescence. They do anti-aging research. Organ replacement, targeted genetic therapies, tissue rejuvenation. Their motto, modest though it be, is Live Long Enough to Live Forever."

"Snake oil?"

He shook his head. "Optimistic, maybe. But it's bearing good fruit."

"You're telling me that they're finding ways to reverse aging." This is the kind of thing you read about in science fiction. Not the newspapers.

At least, not anywhere or anywhen else.

Sternwood bit into the apple. I could smell its honey-vanilla sweet all the way across the room. "This is just chemistry," he said pointing at the apple. "And so is this," he said, pointing at himself. "The SENS Foundation believes that since we are a chemical process, we can be repaired like any other chemical process that breaks down. Enhanced, too. They have some ideas that would have had me burned at the stake as a young man." He shrugged. "Times change. But what you have there," he nodded to the vial of plasma on the table, "That might be a pirate therapy for reversing the aging process."

"Right."

"First broke last year. Transfusions from younger mice to older mice made the older mice younger—and the reverse as well. Older blood made the younger mice older."

"You're pulling my leg."

Doc Sternwood shook his head.

"How?"

He shrugged. "We don't know. Not yet. But if that plasma you've got there is from a child, or a teenager..."

A morbid thought flashed across my brain. "...or a fetus?" The words were out of my mouth before I realized I'd said them.

"Or a fetus. You might be dealing with someone who's trying to get a jump on the rejuvenation market."

REJUVINATION. REAL REJUVINATION.

Age reversal that isn't some bullshit scam. If this keeps up I'm gonna have to hand in my detective's license and try to time travel back to the thirties—back when detectives were real detectives, and you didn't have to worry about science fiction eating your job and your life.

Not that my inner geek wasn't jumping up and down for joy that I lived long enough to see this kinda crazy shit, but it's the kind of thing that makes you wonder how much longer you're actually going to fit the world you're walking through.

Sternwood's a creepy guy.

Even creepier seeing him on his feet again and moving around with purpose—not that I'd hope the guy stayed kicked and bleeding forever, it's just that when he's at full steam he's one of those people who move the levers of the world (literally). Keeping tabs on him is a matter of "keep your friends close and your enemas closer."

Creepiest, though? That's the little thought that flew across my synapses back in his kitchen. The notion that Gruber was running a subscription service for people who wanted to mainline blood from fetuses made my skin crawl.

Sternwood said it could be from anyone young—it could be from college students. But that prenatal care book they were handing out at that clinic in Weed told me that they were pulling this stuff straight out of the kids in utero. Hard to get it any younger than that, right? And the younger they were, the more you could charge for their amazing anti-aging powers. If this horse shit actually worked, who knew? Maybe it could even reverse balding or un-gray the gray hairs...

Oh, Lantham, you twisted son of a bitch.

Give me serial killers and child molesters any day of the week. The kind of garden-variety sickos that made for all the interesting parts of history class. But this?

There is some shit I just don't want to know about.

5:08 PM, Monday

I FOUND KELPTO AND NYA and Erica all at home. Klepto was standing guard at the driveway fence, waiting for me. I wrestled him for a minute, left him on a patch of lawn on his back, thumping the ground with his tail while I headed inside.

After about four steps I heard his tags jingling behind me.

Inside. Up the back steps. Found Nya was in the media room with Scuttlebutt, her orange tabby, perched on her shoulders.

Scuttlebutt eyed Klepto with a "don't you dare" kind of look. Klepto didn't even notice. He was completely interested in my apparent lack of interest in the kitchen and the sacred cupboard wherein dwelt the holy bag of kibble.

I said hi to Nya. Earned a smile and a hug. She told me Erica was in the front room, probably needed me, so in I went.

Nya was right. Erica was in the front room, curled up on one corner of the couch, her phone perched on her knee, a cup of coffee gone cold on the end table next to her, and her work laptop open on the coffee table, which she wasn't paying any attention to.

She didn't look at me when I came in. She just said "He hasn't called."

"Your Dad?"

"Yeah."

"Have you tried calling the hospital?"

She shook her head. "An hour ago. No love."

"Want a drink?"

"No. No, I want to be sober when he calls."

Made sense. Still, it made my guts feel squirrelly. Here was a woman whose job was to hold it together in the face of any kind of sick shit the world threw at her, and she was worried she wouldn't be able to hold it together.

Guess I'd feel the same way if it was my mother going under the knife at the ass end of some really shitty odds.

"Backgammon?"

"No I...hell." She reached for her coffee, took a sip, then spit it back in the cup.

"Here. I'll warm it up for you."

I took it from her. Kissed her quick.

Ninety seconds in the microwave. Just enough time to feed Klepto.

Making a dog happy, that's easy. Dogs want food and attention.

Making a Fed happy? That's trickier.

I did bring the backgammon board, coaxed her into a few games. Not quite fair, since she was distracted, but I was playing for shit.

My mind wasn't on the game. It wasn't even on Erica.

It was on Franklyn Gruber.

A pastor with no past. A president with other things on his mind than presiding. Maybe a murderer. Definitely a con man. And maybe...maybe someone stealing from the young to feed the old.

And maybe using the product himself. If his hair was any indication, it was working.

I had to connect him to a crime. A Federal crime. But selling blood wasn't a crime. Unless...did you need some kind of special license for that?

What if I could connect him to the murder? Contracting a murder was a crime. But he'd have to have worked across state lines for it to be a matter for the FBI.

I had to figure out who he was, and how he was connected to those armed thugs on the charter plane. Was he the mastermind of this whole scam? Or was he a franchisee, working with a syndicate of some kind, and trying to build up his own supply lines to cut them out?

I lost six rounds of backgammon trying to figure that out.

As she was setting up round seven, Erica said "You're not letting me win, are you?"

"No. No. Just got a case stuck in my head."

"Stride's? Still?"

"Yeah." I took a stack of pieces from her, started

lining them up in my outer table. "The kid was right. Something seriously screwy's going on, and it's got jack shit to do with his parents. If I can prove there's some kind of crime, Rivers might be able to get some protection for the family, but if I can't, I'm gonna have to leave it alone and hope they don't get chewed up when the real cops arrive."

"I told you to steer clear." She sounded tired all over. But it still needled.

"Yeah. Yeah you did. And I told you I couldn't do that." It came out a lot sharper than I meant it to. And now that I was going, I couldn't reign it in. "You get to pass things up the chain when your case is done. I don't get to do that. I deal with the shit the cops can't. Sometimes it's boring. Sometimes it's nasty. Usually it just sucks."

"So just be a cop."

"Be a cop. Easy. Except I'm dealing with the same kind of shit in the Sheriff's department. I don't even get to be a cop anymore. Not a real one. I fucked that one up big time, and I've gotta live with it. That's my bed. Built it myself, get to lie in it every day."

"That's not fair, Clarke." She was starting to pick up steam. Trying to stop herself, and me. "You've got a job as a cop again. You can shut all this down and be just fine..."

"It isn't enough. You don't get it. That's what's different about us. Yeah, we both carry a badge, both carry a gun, but we're not the same." I put the last piece down, looked straight into her eyes. "You enforce policy. It's all politics for you. This year, it's illegal to move some product through the port, so you watch the port and put people in jail because they're selling things some fucking politician doesn't approve. Next year, that same thing'll be legal again, and it'll be something else. You think you're a cop? Look at your badge, sweetheart. You're a bureaucrat..."

She smacked me so hard that I just about ate carpet.

And she didn't say anything. Just calmly picked up her dice and put them in the cup, and shook them.

I rubbed my jaw. Picked myself up. Proceeded to take my subconscious out into the back alley and rough it up like a deadbeat player from an underground card game. "Guess I deserved that."

"You think?"

"I'm sorry. I...ah, fuck it, there's no excuse..."

"Go ahead, say it. Can't be any worse than anything you've already said."

"Something about this case has me by the short hairs and...I guess I'm looking for a fight." For the record, the whole part of the relationship code about honesty being the best policy? I'm pretty sure that's bullshit. At least, it's never worked that way for me so far. "I'm sorry."

"Forget it." She rolled the dice. She was pissed. But it was more than that. She had this helpless rage in her eyes, the kind that comes from trying like hell not to lose your shit in the face of a world that's determined to take everything from you.

Thirty eight years on this planet, and I've never felt like such a fucking heel in any of them as I did at that second.

Buzz Buzz

Erica's cell rattled on the coffee table.

She had a handful of game, so I grabbed it, passed it to her.

"Damn. This is it." She looked at it for a split second, then pointed her green eyes at me. I nodded. Took the board off the couch, put the game away in the hall while she answered the phone.

"Hello?" She said.

I popped back into the living room in time to see her face fall, and her right hand go to her ear. She stood up and walked out the front door and started pacing back and forth across the front porch.

I watched her for a bit at the window, but she waved me off and went down the front steps.

Then, a moment later, her car pulled out of the driveway.

I should have gone after her.

I actually started to.

But I didn't know where she was going. And I didn't have a tracker on her cell phone.

Erica was gone, and there wasn't any calling her back. Probably up to Napa, where her Dad was in the hospital. I'd have to wait a little while, and call her, find out what was going on.

Didn't stop me feeling like a heel. Was gonna have to

make it up to her. I'm good at that. Dug myself out of trouble a few times that way. And she was worth it.

Oh well, might as well clear up and go take Klepto for a walk.

I picked up the dishes. Tossed them in the dishwasher.

Went back for the hardware. Looked around, found Erica's laptop bag, opened it up and set it on the coffee table.

Unplugged the power supply, picked it up.

The screen was still unlocked. She was logged in to the FBI mainframe. Probably better log her out.

I sat down, put my hands on the keyboard...

She was logged into the FBI mainframe.

And she wasn't coming back any time soon.

I looked at the apps. Lots of hooks into lots of databases here.

But that mainframe, it was a goldmine. And it just might solve a few problems.

She had security clearance. An authorized query was routine as daylight and dusk.

If she had access to...

She did. The witness protection program.

No harm in running a query.

Just had to make sure the screen stayed unlocked. Easy enough.

TO DO THIS RIGHT I needed all the info out in

the office.

No problem there.

I went out the front door so Nya wouldn't ask any inconvenient questions.

Got to my office. Sat down at my desk. Klepto hopped up on my easy chair, curled up, propped his chin on the arm and looked at me as if to say *I hope you know what you're doing, buddy.*

Of course, being a dog, he was probably saying *Why are you fucking around with those stupid clickety boxes instead of doing something interesting, like finding a ball?*

Either way, I kept her screensaver from locking the screen.

Got the fingerprints and vital info.

Took about twenty minutes to find the right screen to enter in all the vital data, but I found it.

And I put it in.

Now all I had to do was wait. On TV this kind of thing takes about twenty seconds. In real life, a shitload of computers were now hunting through their memory banks on the kind of complex search that could take hours, or days, depending on the priority flag Special Agent Erica Ellis had on her account.

I killed some time by calling her. She answered. On the road to Napa. Her father wasn't expected to last the night.

Of course I'd come up. Sure. When?

Lunch time tomorrow? That would be fine.

Sure, I'd bring her things. Mine too. We might be a

few days? No problem.

That's what you do when the love of your life is dealing with tragedy, right? You drop everything?

I hoped so. All I really had to go on for models is the shit I read in books. Never thought that would be a problem, but now that I was making it up as I went along, I wasn't sure what had me more freaked:

Getting it wrong.

Or getting it right.

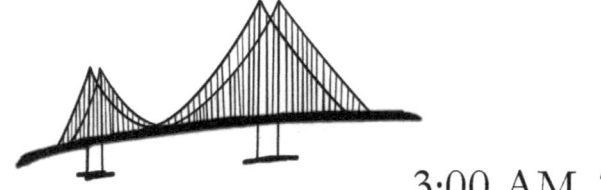

KLEPTO GROWLED.

The kind of growl he growled when there was an unfamiliar noise in the house.

I rolled off my bed with my gun in hand. Peeked down the hall.

Nya wasn't awake. I could hear her snoring through her door at the other end of the short hallway.

Every corner was deep shadows. Only filtered streetlight lit the house.

I crept to the archway leading into the living room.

Listened.

Klepto followed me, the warning click throbbing low in his throat.

So much for stealth.

Then I heard it. A creak on the rear stairs.

Klepto heard it too. His ears laid back flat and he bolted around the corner.

Aw, fuck.

Well, what do you do? I ran with my pistol pointed safe down, my gun flopping around on its magazine cause I hadn't had any time to put pants on.

I was halfway through the kitchen when I heard an

"Oof!"

I knew that "Oof."

"Rache?" I whispered. Didn't want to wake up Nya.

She poked her head round the corner from the stairwell. "Nice suit." Her smile said "teasing you," but her voice was flat and unfriendly.

"Give me a sec."

TWO MINUTES LATER, FRESHLY dressed in my grubbiest available clothing, I made my way into the living room.

She was standing next to the front windows, arms crossed, blond hair glowing in the street lamp light. Looking out on the world she'd just come in from.

I went to stand next to her. "What are you doing here?"

"Do you have a drink?" A shake in her voice. Like she was just keeping it under control.

"Yeah. Pick your poison."

"What's that salty Scotch you like?"

"Two fingers of Old Pulteney, coming up."

"Make that two flasks. We have to talk."

"That bad?"

"Worse."

"Give me a minute."

The liquor cabinet is in the media room at the back of the house. I had a couple hip-flasks, strictly for science-fiction-convention use only. Filled 'em both with the good stuff, spun the lids on, took them back to the front room.

She had a look on her face that I'd seen on other cops. Never on her, though. It didn't suit her. That hollow stare, like it was scanning the horizon for any sign of hope. Any sign of light. Any sign that God actually gave a shit anymore.

"I assume you're not going to want Nya to hear this?"

She nodded.

"Come on." I opened the front door, invited her out. Klepto tried to follow. "Klepto, couch." I snapped and pointed. He whined, but went and curled up on the couch and looked at me out of the side of his eye like I was the cruelest human being on the planet.

We sat down next to each other on the steps. The concrete was cold, the air was dry. California was still thirsty, the kind of thirst that a little bit of Scotch wouldn't be able to help. But it might numb up these two Californians enough to talk about the worst kind of thing you ever have to talk about to your junior partner in this line of work.

How do you like that? I still thought of her as my partner.

"How did it happen?" I handed her a flask.

She spun the top open. Took a long drink. Longer than is healthy. Then she coughed. "Warren. Ben Warren. Rat, it said on his jacket." She took another drink, then hung the flask from the end of her hand, resting over her knees. She was looking down at her hands.

"Was it clean?"

She shook her head. "I don't know. Doesn't feel clean."

"Never does." I took a swig myself. A sip, really. Scotch this good was for sipping, not drinking. "So run me through it. You talked to Paxton?"

"I did. Mister Paxton. Mister 'Call Me Toby.' He was...not someone who belonged in there, Lantham. Not that kind of man. He was happy to have a visitor. Really sweet old man."

"What did he say?"

"When I mentioned his wife...he cried, Lantham. He fucking lost it right there. You would see him pulling himself together. Like his heart was on a string, and he had to reel it back in. He swore up and down that he didn't kill her. And he had...he had this...this *look*. In his eye. You just knew he had to be telling the truth." Even though it was vacant and flat, her voice throbbed, like she had a lump in her throat she was straining to swallow. "And he was relieved, too. Like he was glad someone believed him. His lawyer didn't. Didn't even want to talk to him."

"Public defender?"

"I think so, yeah."

"Shit."

"Yeah." She took another drink. "Then he said that the cops knew it wasn't him, and *they knew who did it*, and they weren't gonna do anything about it. A local biker.

Dope dealer. Bad guy all around, you know? Ben "The Rat" Warren. They actually arrested him first, but didn't hold him."

"The nickname. Think he's a CI?" Some cops'll bend the law well past break point to protect a reliable confidential informant, and there've been more than a few CIs over the years who've built a business on that kind of arrangement.

"It's a good bet, isn't it?" Drink. "Well, I found him at this shithole dive. Still smells like dead cigarettes."

"Quite an achievement." Been over twenty years since they outlawed smoking in bars in California.

"Yeah, I know, right?" Drink. "And this guy, Lantham. This *guy*. Wasn't hard to spot. Looked like that part the cat left out to rot when it dragged in the juicy squirrel head. I hustled him for three hundred bucks on eight ball, then did double-or-blow-job." I shuddered. Anyone who goes up against Rache when she'd got a cue stick in her hands deserves what he gets. "He was totally into it. Rolled over like a puppy. I scratched on the eight ball, and we went into the alley out back and...well, you can guess."

"Rache?"

"He wasn't going to get caught, Lantham. Nobody was going to arrest this guy. He knew it. And he wasn't gonna talk. He laughed at my gun, Lantham. *Laughed* right when I was pointing it at him. I had him right there in front of me..."

"Jesus Christ, Rache. Tell me you didn't shoot him."

Please God tell me you haven't turned that fucking stupid.

"I flinched. He saw it. Pulled a knife. He got inside on me..." She pulled her jacket down, showed a big gauze pad over the back of the nape of the meat of her neck, above the collar bone. "I had to stitch it up. Don't worry," she held up her hand to stop me chiding her, "don't worry, it didn't go deep. I'll go to the doctor tomorrow."

"And then?"

"He was inside on me, so I went inside on him. I kneed him in the balls, then I came up with the barrel and clubbed him in the larynx..."

"Oh no..."

"He just...froze. His eyes got so big and...he started swinging his arms, and he knocked me over, and ran. Not very fast, just...right out into the street. Fell down on his face. I could hear him, you know? Trying to breathe? That wheeze like," she wheezed like she was going into anaphylaxis, "and...um...this drunk in a pickup came out all spinning wheels. Drove right over his chest."

"Oh, thank fuck."

"Thank *fuck*? Lantham, he's dead. We can't pin this on him if he's dead! And that poor old man in jail up there for..."

"Thank fuck because they'll never pin the murder on you. You'd have a hell of a time proving self defense on that one. Don't worry, though," I patted her arm, "It was a clean kill."

"Yeah. That's what I keep saying." She looked at me. Met my eyes. Like she wanted me to make everything okay. Like she wanted me to tell her that killing people wasn't so bad. That it got easier.

I couldn't, though. Cared about her too much to lie like that about something like this. So I slid over, and took her in my arms. Two seconds later, she was all snot and tears and was keening like a drowning elephant.

I just held on. It's all you can do. And, after a while, I joined her in blubber-land for a bit. I'd had a hell of a day, and besides, I've got my own pile of bodies behind me. Plenty of sympathy to go around when I really need it.

Took a while, but she did eventually run out of tears. The front of my shirt looked like something Jabba the Hutt would be ashamed to wear.

And Rachael? She'd been tarted up for picking up the killer in the bar. The road hadn't washed that off her. Now she looked like someone had smeared coal down from her eyes, but didn't notice.

"Well, one good thing" I reached out to her cheek, brushed the tears back, drew a streak of football-player war paint under her left eye. "At least it didn't ruin your mascara, right?"

She laughed, then. That kind of laugh you laugh when you don't have any reason to believe you'll have a chance to laugh again in the morning. Because you don't know there's going to be another morning. Because, sooner or later, no matter what you do, there isn't one.

Then another long drink. Another deep breath. I knew the drill. Backing herself off from the edge. Letting today's events lie for the evening. Or the morning. Or whatever.

"So how is it going with Agent Alliteration? You still in *love*?"

She said it like we were in middle school. Playground teasing. I bumped her with my shoulder.

"Yeah, yeah. Still in love, still going like gangbusters. I gotta head up to meet her in Napa tomorrow. Help her out with a family thing." I took a drink. Suddenly needed one. "Speaking of family, you know your Dad gave me a job?"

"Nya mentioned it. I'da told you not to take it."

"He offered it to me because you told him to take care of me."

"Sorry about that."

"Yeah, well, Cal's Cal."

She chuckled. "You could say that about anybody, Lantham."

"Nya's Nya, you're you, I'm me, Erica's Erica..." I trailed off. That was a sore spot I wasn't interested in poking at.

"Erica?"

"Yeah."

"I'm guessing it has something to do with Erica."

"Shut up, will ya?" I bumped her again, trying to play it light. Not sure how convincing I was, really.

"I thought you were in *love*. You're gonna marry her and have a bunch of little Lathamlets running around."

"Oh, yeah, we're in love." I took a drink from her flask. "That's how you get the FBI inside your home. Under your roof..."

"Damn, Lantham, I knew you had a thing about authority, but Jesus..."

"She can't talk about work, cause it's always classified. I can't talk about work, because I might put her in a conflict of interest..."

"It'd be the same if you were dating a lawyer or a shrink. You work in a confidential business. They work in a confidential business. That's how this works. That's what you wanted..."

"It's not what I wanted."

"So what *do* you want?" She sounded exasperated. Could hardly blame her. I have that effect on people.

"I don't know. I just wonder if it's enough, you know? Being in love." If it could ever really be enough.

Rachael put her right hand on my head. She turned it so I was facing her. And she looked at me. The kind of look that'll rip your soul out from under you. Eyes wet like sea rocks at low tide. Like something, somewhere along the line, had drained all the juice out of her. Everything was left poking above the surface.

"Rache? Really, no bullshit. Why did you leave? What happened to you?" I asked.

"I found out something...I found out..." she trailed off now. Like she didn't have anything left in her that could finish that sentence. Like the blood covering the cement back up the street was hers.

"What did you find out?" I whispered.

"...that being in love isn't enough."

Before I knew what happened, I was kissing her. Or she was kissing me. I couldn't tell which. Like we were made of magnets, and someone'd just taken us off our chains.

I pulled away. Shuffled through about six rejoinders, then gave up and said "Um...sorry."

"Yeah. Yeah, me too."

"Look...umm...about the Rat. You didn't say. Did he tell you how much?"

"Oh, yeah, that. Five k. The day after the job."

Big sigh of relief. "Thanks, Rache." I squeezed her hand like I meant it. Cause I did.

"Yeah. Look, you got my keys?"

"Nya hangs 'em on the hook by the phone."

She got up. Went to get 'em.

I stood. Waited for her to come back.

She melted right against me. Held on for a few more minutes.

I wrapped my hand around the back of her head. Massaged it a little. Hoping I could draw the tension away. "You'll be okay, you know," I said.

"Does it ever go away?"

"No more than the first time you had sex."

"Great."

"You'll be okay tonight? Don't get too drunk?"

"I'll take a bath."

"Better plan." I kissed her forehead. "Welcome home, Rache."

"We'll see." She looked up at me. Her eyes looked like I could fall into them and drown in an open pit of pain. Like the big wound of her life had just gotten ripped open and she wasn't sure she wanted to get it fixed anymore.

After a while, you get tired of those bandages. Everyone does.

Because some wounds hurt more when they're closed.

7:00 AM, TUESDAY

FOR THE FIRST HOUR of my day, the real world was back.

Bacon woke me. It does that. One of its many, many superpowers.

I had to wait for the bathroom, because Rachael was using it, even though she had her own place with a perfectly good bathroom just a little ways down the street. Hell, she could've used the other bathroom at my place, which was closer to the kitchen. That's where the real action is that time of morning anyway.

Then Klepto joined me in the shower and we both got a good scrubbing. I came out of there smelling a little less like rotting goat meat than I normally do. So far so good.

Then there were pancakes to go with the bacon. Nya still couldn't cook them worth a damn, but she's getting better. Klepto likes them now.

We ate together like it was an old company breakfast. Klepto underneath having the pancakes. Talked about things that didn't sting.

Until, eventually, we talked shop.

"You haven't lived. We made it right off the trees

here just after you left," I said while I was getting the plum syrup from the fridge. Rachael didn't believe I could cook, and there are some misapprehensions that don't add to your mystique, they just annoy you. I'd had plenty of annoyances recently. "You dated an evangelical in high school, Rache, right?"

"Francine the Fuckwad? Yeah, we had kind of a thing, why?"

"Those matching vials—the one from the clinic and the one from Stride. That's been bugging me."

"Why? Other than it's kinda creepy?"

"Well, if you're going to get into the quack medicine business and sell people blood to inject for some kind of miracle cure..."

"Sick." Rachael shifted like she was trying to take pressure off a hemorrhoid.

"What? You go to the clubs with Nya and do needles and razors."

"Blood *play* Lantham. Blood *play*. And it's only sexy because it's a taboo. You don't get off on the blood, you get off on the rule-breaking. Who the fuck would want to straight up inject themselves with someone else's bodily fluids for health reasons?"

"Well, from what Sternwood tells me..."

"Wait, you stalked to Sternwood?" Rachael looked at me like I was half crazy.

"That doctor?" Nya said. The room felt like it had stood up on pins and needles all of a sudden. "Gravity's father? Is he okay?"

"Yeah, yeah, he's fine, nothing to worry about. I just use him for a consult every now and then, since he owes me a few thousand favors."

"Oh." Nya let her breath go, and the room deflated back to normal. "Good."

I picked up the conversation before the interruption, because that's the way you have to do it when Nya's around. Otherwise you'll slide down the nostalgia hole. Just one of those things you gotta be on the lookout for with a Nya in the house.

"From what Sternwood tells me, it might be a real thing." I laid out the theory.

"Ugh. Just *ugh*. Gross, Lantham. God, I'm eating here." Rachael shook like she was trying to shake off a slug crawling up her spine.

"Oh, come on. I shrugged. "Worked for Mina Harker and Sookie Stackhouse…"

"Holy fuck. Lantham."

"Don't shoot the messenger, Rache, I just…"

"No. No. No. Oh fuck fuck fuck Lantham Zarek Woodfork."

"What?"

"When I talked to him that morning, in his bedroom. He whispered to me…he…oh fuck fuck Lantham holy shit he said…He said 'Don't let the vampires get ya.'"

"He did? Those exact words?"

"Yeah."

Boom boom boom. Like dominoes. "He was using the kids. Rache. He was keeping them there. The kids were his first strategy. No wait," I held up my hand to keep her interrupting. I was still letting the pieces all settle in my head. "There's a business opportunity. Maybe he spots it. Maybe it's a franchise thing. Whatever. He gets his customers. He works with this charter company. All he needs is product—or maybe they're giving him product, but he wants to start up his own operation. Either way, he needs to be able to get the blood somewhere. He figures, nab a few kids, keep them doped up on hypnotics or whatever—something that won't hurt the end user, maybe even give them a bit of a high when they shoot up...oh yes, that's perfect. The kids'll never remember a thing, so he just taps them. Like maple trees. Or dairy cows. Just squeezes out a little every few days..."

The girls were both looking at me like I was some kind of monster for even thinking of something like this.

"No, no, it makes sense. Listen. The secretary, Mrs. Paxton, she's his partner in crime somehow. Except she'd got her reservations—maybe she's the only one who can tie him to the kidnappings? He'd have had to do all the snatch-and-grab himself. He'd have had to manage the room on-site...no, that doesn't work. He'd have had to have a staff.Maybe only one or two people...The Paxtons? Anyway, Mrs. Paxton gets nervous, something goes wrong. Then everything changes. Something goes wrong. He has her bumped off and...oh my god. That's why he killed her." I looked across at Rachael.

She was nodding. "She dumped Zarek."

"And when that happens," I said, "he knows that it's just a matter of time before someone links the kids back to those portables behind the Paxton house, so he has her knocked off. Then he needs a new supply, or the rich customers will just go elsewhere."

"Wait, wait, behind the *house*?"

"Yeah, I think so. It's a good place for it. Isolated. No one around to really notice anything. Portables all over the place for the construction anyway. Here." I had my phone on the counter, so I went to get it. Opened up the gallery and pulled up the pictures of the tire tracks. "These were only a day or two old when we were up there. Around back, where the kids in the temp dorms wouldn't see them. I'll bet you anything that he had the kids taken out in a U-Haul and dumped by the road, and that's why they all turned up again."

"What about Quentin Greenaway?"

I shrugged. "Anesthesia overdose?" I filled my coffee. Figured I might as well since I was already up. "And right around the same time, there's that big accident with all the blood products on 5. It's his stuff. He loses the whole shipment. But he was tapping a lot of kids, so he had to be stockpiling—or meeting a hell of a demand, but let's say stockpiling,,." More chance we'd get a good connection that way. "Keeping stuff in the school somewhere down here. But now he's running thin. Starts bringing it down on planes. Meantime he gets the idea of the pregnancy center. Figures maybe he can charge a premium for fetal blood. So he moves it all up there on a dime. Sets out this radical schedule for blood draws, gets it all sent 'to the new school'..."

"Lantham, there's no way you can prove this."

"I don't have to. I just need to make enough links that the FBI will take it over. Just gotta connect Gruber to a Federal crime."

Rachael held up her fingers and ticked off "Kidnapping, enslavement, violations of child labor laws. You could even get him for the murder..."

"How? It all happened in-state."

"You think he didn't use the Internet to wire the payment?"

"Okay, maybe the murder." I raised my mug. "I think we just solved both of our cases."

"Yeah, maybe. Now we just gotta nail the fucker."

"Guess I got some typing to do."

"Um, Clarke?" Nya said. "That's not all you have to do." She pointed at the clock on the microwave.

"Oh, right. Shit. Look, I'll be up in Napa helping Erica deal with this...thing."

I took my coffee with me to pack. Got my laptop and my bag of tricks. In between intense comforting sessions I was pretty sure I'd have a lot of time to work up a good solid report to turn over to Rivers. Collate all the evidence, tie it up in a bow. Hopefully it'd be enough to get some protection for the Strides.

Last check. Phone. Coat. Hat. Tricks. Laptop. Overnight bag for me. Erica's overnight bag that she neglected last night. Toothbrushes...

Computer. Erica's computer, I mean. She'd asked me to bring it, and I'd left it out in the office. The bag for it was still on the coffee table.

I took it with me. Loaded everything else in the car. Brought the bag with me into the office.

Sat down in front of it to abort the query and change back her screensaver settings, since it didn't sound like I needed it after all.

Except that the search had yielded one result.

A younger version of Franklyn Gruber's face gazed at me from the right side of the screen. Long before his hair went white, and he'd had cosmetic work done on his brow line.

It looked very familiar.

Almost like the face I saw every day in the mirror.

I looked left.

Franklyn Gruber, it said.

Also known as:

Jack Lightfoot.

Dalton Gerton.

John Lantham.

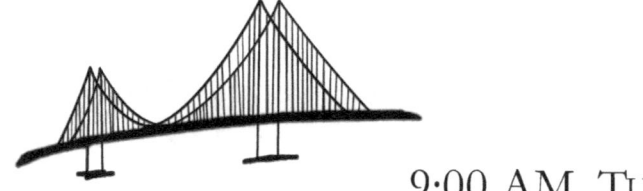

SO, YOUR FATHER IS alive. After all this time.

And he's been standing right in front of you for months.

You have pictures of him on your laptop.

You've got his face burned into your brain. The face of a con man, a murderer, a Jim Jones.

What do you think at a time like that?

What do you feel?

Like something reached out of the pit and hooked into your shoulders, and dragged you back down and under, into the long nightmare. Back into Dreamland, where the seagulls and the phantasms hang out. Where each new breath reminds you of something you've lost.

I spend a lot of time here. It's a sort of shadow world. Nothing real survives long. Nothing stays solid. Ghosts came up out of the past to haunt you, and friends ran out on you for no reason, and people died because there wasn't a less convenient time for it to happen.

One thing Dreamland had in common with Realityville, though?

Traffic. More people on the roads during morning

rush hour than you could find in the whole state of Oregon. The kind of traffic that Satan studies with a weather eye on days when he's looking for inspiration for the Circle where they punish everyone who participated in global warming.

The clouds broke again about the time I hit Richmond. Everything that was moving at a crawl gave up and started swimming through the carpet on its belly.

Left me a lot of time to think about a man I didn't remember much about. Fleeting impressions, if I worked really hard. The sound of a deep voice telling me to stop something or other. They weren't warm memories. They weren't cold either. Just disconnected facts. None of them meant much.

Just little drops, like the rain outside. Every time you think you've got your hands on one, it breaks apart, blends in with the background.

Jack Lightfoot.

Born in Texas, 1953.

1960. First arrest, age seven, for running a pyramid scheme in his elementary school.

1965. Second arrest, age twelve, for selling communion wine to high schoolers.

1969. Third arrest for a check-kiting scheme when he was sixteen. Rolls on a money laundering operation. Enters the Texas state witness protection program.

1971. Enrolled UC Santa Cruz, age 18 as "John Lantham."

1974. Married Marie O'Neil. My mom. Age 21.

1975. Graduated middle of his class, age 22, with a BA in Behavioral Psychology.

1976. First child, age 23. Clarke Lantham.

1977. Second child, age 24. Tricia Lantham, now Tricia Baedecker.

1978. Third child, age 25. Sam Lantham, now deceased.

1980. Age 27. Arrested, along with wife Marie, for pension fraud. Fled before trial. Marie stands trial, is acquitted.

1982. Age 29. Sued in Kansas City by the Church of Scientology for copyright infringement. Fled before trial.

1987. Age 34. Warrant issued for Dalton Gerton in Detroit for operating a pharmacy without a license. Charges of medical insurance fraud added before arraignment. Fled before trial. Fingerprints later identified Dalton Gerton as John Lantham, a wanted fugitive in three states.

1989. Simon Halifax enrolls in the University of Kansas as pre-med. Is later expelled for conducting research on other students without consent.

1995. Age 40. Picked up in New York for practicing medicine without a license. Indicted for insurance fraud. Illegal pharmaceutical business seized, along with marketing materials promoting the "only known cure for aging." Turns states evidence against the Gambino crime family. Admitted into witness protection.

After that, it was his cover identity in Texas. His home state. His old stomping grounds. The pastor, the principal, the headmaster, the administrator, all like I'd found in my normal background check.

My father the con artist.

Well, now I knew where I got the social engineering gene from.

I was going to turn him over to the FBI. And the FBI already had him. They'd be thrilled about that. Protected witnesses didn't usually go back into the business once they had a clean break. It happens, but the risk is a little less than a normal woman's risk of pregnancy on any given day.

I used to date a doctor. There's a lot of useless information rattling around up here. Or, at least, useless until the kids come.

One thing for sure, I didn't have to worry about living up to my father in the fatherhood department. Breathing in the same general area as my offspring for the full eighteen years will pretty much take care of that.

So now, lucky me had to take down his old man in order to make sure the neighbor kid and his old man could live long enough to get to hate each other during the teenage years, as God intended.

I wasn't sure how I felt about that, but "good" didn't come anywhere near the same universe. Numb, maybe. This wasn't my problem. It shouldn't be my problem. John Lantham hadn't been my problem since before I could remember.

John Lantham. Talk about one slippery motherfucker. All those arrests, not a single conviction.

Escape or deal, every time. So I didn't have to worry about more Catholic guilt of getting my own father thrown into the klink or onto death row. He'd have some kind of escape plan ready.

I let out a long breath. Didn't realize I'd been holding it. But it made sense. Last thing I wanted to do after all these years was sit down and have a heart-to-heart with the old man, catch up, have him hug me while I bawled my eyes out at him about why he abandoned us and left Mom holding the bag for all the evil shit he did.

And I didn't have to worry about any of that with this son of a bitch. I could do my job, throw him to the wolves like he deserved, and he'd take care of himself.

Just like I'd never been part of his life.

I LIKED THAT PLAN. I'd have stuck to it too, if I hadn't spent the next two days in Napa writing up my report and making a list of the stray bits of evidence I had to lock down.

Like that bank transfer to The Rat. If we could get him on that murder. Assuming he'd done it over interstate wires.

I could rely on Stride to connect him to the precious bodily fluids, and from there I could connect him to stealing the fetal blood without consent—there had to be a crime in that somewhere, though I was damned if I could figure out what it was exactly.

There was the kidnapping, though. I needed to be able to link him to the kidnappings. And if he was as slick as his rap sheet made him look, he'd be doing it all by remote control. Hiring it done. Plausible deniability. Using some kind of sneaky scheme to move the cash around...

This was gonna take a little more work, which didn't make me any kind of happy. It wasn't like I had the spare time to do it. Not with all of the death-and-dying going on.

Erica's old man was hanging on by bare threads. She was out with him when visiting hours opened at seven AM, and stayed with him through until they closed out again at seven in the evening.

Then it was three solid hours of "I don't want to talk about it, let's go see a movie" followed by another two solid hours of crying or fighting. Like happens.

Left me a lot of time to dig through databases, try to figure out any way I could to trace down connections that His Grubbiness might have to anyone or anything else in this case.

I just about went blind staring at the computer screen.

And Erica.

Yeah.

I've never watched someone I love lose everything before. And on a yo-yo schedule. First he was going to last a few months, then he wasn't going to last the night. Now he might last years. A passing infection that might have killed him was clearing up.

The uncertainty made it worse. Her Dad was as

much everything for her as mine was nothing to me. The kind of man who believed in his kids, did everything he could for them, and didn't take shit from the world. And he was falling apart right in front of her.

She didn't want me to meet him. He didn't want me to see him like this—frail and old, whithered up and worn out from too much chemo, too many surgeries, too many costly battles holding off old man death. At this rate, I never would get to meet him.

My children would never know what it was like to have a grandfather.

1:00 PM, Thursday

ADULTS SUCKED.

Teddy wouldn't let his mother hear him use that word, cause he didn't like getting thumped on the cheek, which kinda proved she sucked as much as the rest of them. They all sucked like all the black holes in all the galaxies in all the universe and all the other universes too. They didn't tell you things until after everything went wrong, then they got mad when you couldn't fix them, then when you fixed them they got mad at you for sticking your nose in adult business.

Like now.

His dad had left earlier in the day to go teach his classes, and then he wasn't going to come home. He was going to go on his stupid road trip to Yreka for some stupid ceremony, and he wasn't even going to let Teddy come with him.

So after his Mom got done telling him for the thirtieth time that he couldn't go to Yreka because it would be boring, and besides, Dad was going to be on the road by the time he could go to meet him, he told her to forget it it and walked up the road to talk to Clarke and find out what was going on.

Well, he'd been at if for months, hadn't he? He ought to at least be able to say *something* besides "Yes, the school is moving and your dad's not happy about it." Any idiot could work that out.

Besides, Clarke's house was always better. It was a place you could hang around, learn stuff about detective work by listening in. You could play with Klepto, which Teddy couldn't do at home because Aunt Nikki was allergic to dogs and she came to visit sometimes, so Mom wouldn't let them have a dog.

Lame lame lame lame.

And it made his own back yard—which Teddy had to admit was big enough to lose a battleship in and could be pretty fun in the summer—inexpressibly boring during the school year, when no one came over to play, even on weekends, because of all their stupid homework and Xboxing.

Not that Xbox sucked, exactly, it's just that it wasn't the only thing in the world, and Teddy couldn't get any of his friends to believe that.

But Clarke wasn't home, and Nya was too busy working to hang out with him. So he played with Klepto for a little, waited for a chance when Nya left the office to go to the bathroom or something, and asked her what was up.

Well, she couldn't tell him everything yet, because there was a lot of unconfirmed blah blah blah, but he shouldn't worry too much because Clarke was going to be able to get them witness protection.

So he said thanks, and threw a stick for Klepto, then ran off and jumped the gate, cause he didn't have a lot of time.

If Clarke was trying to get them witness protection, that meant that whatever was going on was serious. Like, bad serious. Worse than his dad knew, for sure, because Dad wasn't stupid and wouldn't keep going to work if he thought he needed a witness protection program. He had to warn him.

Dad wasn't going to be on the road until three—that was when his last class wrapped up—and he wasn't going to turn on his phone until then, if then. He never answered calls in the car, and he always turned off his phone during work hours. Something about respecting his employer's time, which he thought was very important, but Teddy didn't understand at all.

Since he couldn't call him, Teddy did exactly what any other kid on the planet would do when he knew his Dad was in trouble. He snuck out of his house, got on BART at the station four blocks away, and rode under the Bay to the Glen Park Station and walked the two miles uphill to the college.

THREE DAYS. RACHAEL HAD BEEN back in the Bay Area three days.

Three days in the place she'd missed all those months on the road.

Three days in her home—her real home, the condo she kept on Santa Maria Avenue just down the street from Lantham's house—petting Sir Seligman, blasting Lords of Acid, eating every ethnic food she could get delivered.

Three days of laying in *her* bed.

Of sitting on *her* couch.

Of soaking in *her* bath.

And in three days, she hadn't been out of the house except to go across the road and talk to Nya.

Just talk.

She hadn't had sex.

She hadn't gotten drunk.

She hadn't had a joint. Watched a movie. Gone clubbing. Tied someone up and whipped them raw.

She hadn't even used her vibrator.

For three days, Rachael had sat in her house, walked across the street, talked to Nya, come home, and stared at her bookshelf.

All those books—textbooks, her own books—they looked like they'd been painted on the walls. Pretty pictures, promising words, with nothing underneath.

Like everything else around here.

She felt like she'd left some part of herself in that shack up in Weed. Standing in front of that murder board, filled with the faces of kids who'd never been murdered.

The touch of the sea green flannel sofa on her skin. The crunch of an egg roll. The smell of coffee brewed really right. They felt real.

But just barely.

She wanted to pretend it was because she wasn't ready to come home yet. That she belonged back out on the road. That she needed to get back to Yreka, pull up stakes there, and head for Portland like she'd been planning.

But she didn't believe it.

Because when she slept, she kept seeing the fight over and over again. And it wasn't the parts that a real person—a good person—would be stuck on.

A good person would be horrified by Rat's body crushed under the truck's wheels. She would be stuck on the horror of standing toe to toe with a murderer.

A good person would be traumatized—shattered, even—by the fact that *she'd killed somebody*.

With her bare hands, even.

Well, almost.

Rachael wasn't seeing that.

What she saw was worse.

It was a reflection.

Of her face.

Her face, in that rat-fuck's eyes. She saw her reflection in the fucker's eyes, when they tussled for the gun.

"A clean shoot." That's what Lantham said. It was a cop phrase. It meant that the killing was all by the rules. You kill by the rules, you're a good cop.

And if she was a cop, it'd have been a clean shoot, because there were no witnesses, and because it's illegal to strike an officer of the law. No court in the country would convict a cop for shooting a man that stabbed her. They'd let her off even if he'd just slapped her.

But she wasn't a cop. She was a civilian. And she had lured the Rat out into an unwatched alley and pulled a gun on him.

And he fought back.

And a fight ensued.

And he died.

And for a civilian, that was murder one. Self-defense or not, she'd started it with premeditation. She'd introduced the weapon. And she'd struck the killing blow, even if the truck finished him off before his crushed larynx could.

And in his eyes, in that reflection, she'd seen the face of someone she didn't want to be. The face of a woman willing to do even this much to find a bad guy.

No. More than that.

The face of someone who knew what it meant to carry a gun, and was okay with it.

When you strap that on, her dad had said when he found out she'd gotten her permit, *you're saying "I have the right to live, even if someone else has to die." Don't ever pretend different.*

She'd ignored him.

She'd ignored him because it was obvious.

And she'd ignored him because good people don't think that way.

Good people carried guns to protect other people. They would sacrifice themselves, sure. They'd take a bullet for someone else. And they'd give a bullet to protect someone else. Good people, like the cops she'd grown up with. Good people said things like "You're a danger to innocent people, this moment, and you have to die so they can keep living."

But saying "I have more right to live than you do"? That wasn't the kind of thing good people said. It wasn't the kind of thoughts they thought.

That's the kind of thing that Mafiosos said.

It's what psychos said.

Except...that's exactly what *she* had thought. When she swung that weapon.

She'd seen it in her own face.

Reflected in his eyes.

I have more right to live than you do.

The world is better with me in it and you out of it.

I've decided this. I will make it so.

That's who she was, now.

Maybe who she had always been.

And she just wasn't quite sure she wanted to keep living. She wasn't sure that a person like her deserved to walk around free.

It wasn't like she didn't have options. She had a gun, she could do the job herself. And she had a phone. She could call the sheriff and let them haul her in, and let the State do the job.

She'd thought about it. She'd even picked up the phone a few times.

Each time she'd put it down, and gone across the street.

Because she was a coward.

Because she didn't want to embarrass her father.

And because, when it came right down to it, she deserved to live.

And Rat deserved to die.

And she was okay with that.

But somehow, she had to find a way to live with what that said about her.

12:00 PM, Friday

ENOUGH HOURS AT A database, you begin to think in weird ways. Your mind bends around corners. You get weird ideas. I took apart every piece of the public record. Followed my dear old Dad around in retrospect. Looked at the tax return of every non-profit he'd ever worked for. The business license for every year he'd worked in every county since his entrance into the witness protection program.

And then I did it again in his real name. Which brought me, the morning of my third day in Napa, to a little LLC. Lifelong Holdings, LLC, registered with the Nevada Secretary of State in 2004.

Lifelong Holdings, LLC had a director named John Lantham. With John Lantham's social security number. Its tax returns weren't public, but something it had done once was.

It had helped co-finance an aviation venture. Sierra Charters, Inc.

So His Grubbiness owned a piece of the charter company that was carrying his contraband.

Through a Nevada company.

I had my interstate link.

Just enough to take to Rivers.

But Erica called me first.

SHE WANTED TO HAVE lunch.

We met at a wine-country rustic restaurant, the kind of place where everything was finished in deep-stained oak and rusty steel, accented with old wine barrels, and decorated with bottles with faux-aged labels. It smelled like grilling steak, and everything was fifty bucks a plate.

She was waiting for me at a table by the window. I never sit by the window. After a while with people shooting at you, you stop sitting in places where you don't have good cover and can't make an exist. She was FBI. She'd had actual threat assessment training. She should have known better.

But she was also on the ragged edge. Her eyes were swollen, and rimmed as red as her hair. When you're in that kind of state, you forget things.

I kissed her. Sat down opposite. Ignored the prickles I got from sitting with my back to the door. "I won't ask how your morning was."

"Thanks."

A waiter arrived, like he'd been waiting for me to show up. He presented us each with single-sheet parchment menus. I took a quick look, ordered a fillet medium rare. Erica got the sole. We didn't get any wine. Too much driving to do. Back and forth to the hotel, back and forth to the hospital.

We made small talk for the next half hour. We talked

about the book we were reading together—some Nora Roberts thing, since it was her turn to pick. Good reads, but they all run together for me. Girl meets boy. Girl likes boy. Girl must overcome all the obstacles on heaven and earth to keep boy.

The food came. It was good. But it wasn't quite fifty bucks a plate good.

Then again, it's not like I was in a tasting mood.

Somewhere toward the end of the salad, she stared idly twirling the leaves on the tines of her fork. "I know it doesn't make any sense. But every time I look at him, it's like he's hiding under the bed somewhere, and the version of him I can see is just a puppet."

"Oh, Beaker, you say the sweetest things."

"Yeah. Exactly. He's...he's always been..." she shrugged. "Larger than life. God I hate that phrase. He was like you. Big, always on the move. It doesn't feel real."

"Your father he is not, hmm? Visiting you in familiar form, great master Yoda is." I used to do the voice pretty well. Got me points in elementary school. I couldn't quite pull it off anymore, but I got close enough to make her smile.

"I should buy him some green makeup." Then she chuckled.

"I think my work here is done." I cracked a smile, but as soon as the words were out of my mouth my mind was already outside in the Napa sunshine. You've never seen sunshine look so dark if you haven't looked at it while you're trying to decide how, exactly, you're going to ruin your own father.

Erica caught it. Of course she did. That was what she did for a living. "Where are you?"

Normally I liked the challenge of dating someone with all the same secret superpowers I have. Right now, though? I'd have given just about everything for a girlfriend who was as oblivious as my mother obviously had been when she started dating my father.

"Me? Nowhere. Forget it."

"I don't think so." She shifted to her left and craned her neck, moving her head so that her green eyes completely interrupted my view of the deliciously featureless asphalt parking lot and all the gray and black cars decorating its surface. right in between me and the window. I couldn't tell how much she was worried about me, and how much she was just glad to have something else to concentrate on.

"Really. It's...just this thing. I don't want to get into it."

She picked up her goblet—it was the kind of restaurant that hedged against the outside chance that Jesus might walk through the front door with a wedding party by serving its water in wine goblets—and took a sip. Then shook her head, just slightly, like she didn't have the fight in her to pursue it.

"Guess it's just as well." She set the glass down. Settled back into her chair, restoring my view of the parking lot. "You know, I don't know if I'd have made it through these last few days without you."

I snorted. "Course you would have."

"Okay, fine, I would have, but," she reached across the table, took my hand, "it wouldn't have been...well, it wouldn't have been pretty. Thanks."

"You don't have to thank me," I sighed. Maybe more than I should have. "It's kind of my job, you know."

"It means a lot. Having you here."

"Forget it."

"No. Clarke." She snapped in front of my face. I jolted away from my mental parking lot meanderings. "Don't say that. It means something. Don't...don't act like it's nothing."

She was right on the edge, and I had no idea why. And it made me edgy. Well, edgier. It felt...I don't know, indecent somehow, to be thanked for doing what any decent person would do. Today of all days, the last thing I wanted was to be reminded that the world was so shitty that just holding your partner when she was hurting was some kind of extraordinary admirable act of kindness.

But just like you show up, because that's what partners do, you don't escalate in public, no matter how much you want to. And I was still feeling like shit for that bureaucrat comment a couple days back.

"I'm sorry," I said. And squeezed her hand. "I'm just happy to do it, is all."

"That's the thing," she said.

"What?"

"I need you to go home." She looked like saying it

cost her something between a leg and a Fabergé egg.

"Why?"

"I can't tell you that." A little cloud flitted across her face—I hadn't realized that the demolished expression she was wearing was actually a poker face covering up something a hell of a lot worse.

Now she had my full attention. "Come on, Straw Dog," a pet name, on account of her being strawberry colored and a law dog. Always made her smile. "I don't care how bad it is. I'm not gonna squeal."

"I..." she ran out of breath. Her eyes were wet, first time since I'd gotten to the table. She swallowed hard. Looked out at the parking lot. Guess she'd figured out that it was a good blank depth to gaze into while you're chasing down the slippery shit that swims around in the dark corners of your brain.

She shook her head again. Swallowed hard again. Took another breath. Then another. Then gulped the air once. Looked down at the table. Then looked up at me.

The kind of look that says *I'm not allowed to think what I'm thinking. I'm not this kind of person. I don't do these kinds of things. I don't know who I am anymore, and I can't bear to let you know.*

I nodded. Only one reason Erica would give me that kind of look, when her Dad's sitting in the hospice clinging to life and refusing to die even though medical science says there shouldn't be anything left.

I squeezed her hand. "I know a couple reliable sources. No questions asked." There was no way he could pass scrutiny now. Not with a life expectancy. Not with such a muddy treatment path. No ethics board in the state would clear the doctors who signed off. She was going this alone—and her, with her oath, and more integrity than any ten cops I knew back when I was on the force.

She shook her head. "I already took care of that."

"When?"

"A couple days. He...we're waiting for my uncle to fly in. But I can't have you here. It..."

"I understand. Private thing. Family thing." It's not something you really want to share with people. Not when it's a felony. Not even when it's not. Killing your own father because it's the right thing to do? I can't think of anything more private. Who in the hell would ever understand, anyway? Certainly not the fatherless snoopy schlub you're shacking up with half the time. "I'll be at home if you need me. When do you have to go back?"

"I'm watching him tonight. They're letting me stay over on a cot. Are you sure you're all right?"

She'd caught a change in my face that my brain hadn't caught up with. When she said it, my brain did catch up, and it didn't like what my face was thinking. "No, not really. But I'll manage."

"Sweetie, if..."

I shook my head. "It'll keep. It's not life and death." Well, not at the moment. "I'll tell you all about it after...well, after."

"Then do one more thing for me?"

"What's that?"

Well, she did have a couple hours before she needed to head back. And, trust me, when you're staring death in the face that long, the only thing that helps is sinking into someone else's skin until you're so lost you can't feel anything but need.

8:00 PM, FRIDAY

AFTER WE FINISHED, WE showered. I knelt in front of her and touched up the trim on her pubic hair. She hates it when whiskers grow in, or when her bush goes wild. She's also OCD enough that getting it crooked will drive her to distraction.

It's one of our little rituals. One of the things I do for her because it makes her day better—or at least removes something that could make her day worse. Some men make bagels in the morning. Some get coffee or take out the trash. I trim bush. Doesn't matter *what* it is, you're showing her that she's important enough to take trouble over.

If she wasn't, what would be the point? It's not hard to get laid. Keeping it together when the world throws itself square in the middle of your relationship and tries to blow you apart? That's hard. And little things like this, they remind you that you're important to each other.

Especially when you've got bigger things on your minds.

The hospice was only a mile and a half down the road from the hotel. I didn't want to let her out of my sight. Didn't want to slip from the world of the two of us back into the world of shit. She didn't let go of my hand the whole drive.

It looked like it could be any other office building anywhere on the west coast. Bland. Ordinary. Like they wanted you to relax and think "Eh, this whole death thing? Sure, it's a pain, but then, so is junk mail, and we cope okay with that." As if losing the gods of your childhood to failures of metabolism was banal and completely uninteresting.

She held onto my arm for a minute before she went in. I held onto her head. Breathed in her hair. Told her the things you tell someone who you'd trade the world to be able to help. To make it not so. I'll be here when you need me. Don't forget to call. Be good to yourself, because you're still going to be here in the morning, so don't forget to stay fed and hydrated.

I think that was when I decided I was in this for good and all. Holding her there, that eon before she slipped out the door and into her own private hell, that's when I decided that I was going to ask her to marry me, for real, and not just keep talking about it as something to do "one day soon."

Sometimes you look death in the face and it eats a piece of your soul. And sometimes, it reminds you that you still have one, and its time is running out.

SOMEONE ELSE'S TIME was running out, too. Which I found out about when I was south of Keller on 580 and heading into the home stretch—that two mile stretch the freeway in the curves where, when traffic is light enough, everyone suddenly agrees that the new speed limit is 90, and the cops don't give a shit.

Some parts of the world still know what a road is for.

I was behind a 2005 Esprit geared down through that last corner by 98th and the zoo, topping about 93, when my phone buzzed.

Button on the wheel.

"This is Lantham. Go."

"Clarke?" A woman's voice. I couldn't place it. I'd heard it before, but not enough that I had it at the top of the rolodex.

"Yeah, that's my name. Who are you?"

"Oh, thank goodness. This is Beth." Beth Stride. Tom's wife. Teddy's mother. "Have you heard from Teddy?"

"No." Liquid nitrogen jacked into my jugular. The little hairs on the back of my neck started crawling south for the winter. "Why would he be calling me?"

"I haven't seen him since he went over to your house yesterday afternoon." Phone calls like this are the reason I can't have a real life. "I thought he just came home late, but I haven't seen him all day..."

Insurance sales. That's the career I should have gone into. Fuck with people, get their money, maybe help them out. All the things I like about this job, none of the downsides. Goddammit. "I haven't been home for three days. Just heading there now, actually. Have you called the cops?"

She gasped a little bit, but kept her cool. "Do you think that's necessary?"

"I don't know." Lying to neighbors. That's a legitimate hobby, right? I'd win a bloody medal at the next exhibition. "I hope not. Twenty minutes won't make a difference either way. I'll be there in ten. Is Tom there?"

"Oh, no. He's off to the groundbreaking ceremony in Weed..."

Groundbreaking. Right. For a site that's been under construction for months. "When? When did he leave?"

"This morning. Bout six."

I shoved the klaxons to the back of my head and kept talking, calm as you like. Keeps the civvies happy. "Okay. I'll talk to you in five...make that eight minutes." Had to leave elbow room for traffic lights.

TEDDY WASN'T AT my house.

Nya was.

"Yeah, Clarke. He was here. He wanted to know what was going on with his case."

"Shit. Tell me you didn't tell him..."

She looked at me like I was insane. "He's the client, Clarke."

"So you told him it'd all be in his report."

"Of course."

"And that's all?"

"Except that we were pretty sure we were going to

be able to get his Dad protection for..."

I turned around and bolted out of the office before she could finish the sentence. I threw myself into the car.

Nya ran out waving her arms, shouting after me. Wanting to know where I was going.

She could fucking phone if she wanted explanations. I didn't have the time.

I knew where Teddy was, because it's where I would be if I was ten years old with a hard-on for solving mysteries and beating the bad guys and saving the day. And I only had one hope in hell that he hadn't already landed himself in deep shit.

My phone had his cell number. So I dialed it.

Ring ring

Ring ring

Ring ring

Ring ri...

"Clarke?" He was whispering. "Is that you?"

"Yeah, Ted. Are you okay?"

"Yeah." He sounded terrified. "Yeah, except..."

"Except what?"

Dead silence. The line was still open.

Then in the background. "Come on, kid. There's no way out of this room. Don't jerk me around, you won't like what happens." A voice I'd never heard before. Except it had the kind of familiarity that made me shrivel and itch way down in my scrotum.

Some shuffling.

Then, Teddy's voice a ways away from the phone. "I'm here." Playing all innocent.

"What were you doing back there?"

"Nothin'." The kind of 'nothin' I used to give my Mom when she wanted to know what we were all doing in the clubhouse that required us to be naked with an enormous box of matches.

A long silence. The kind of silence that made you wonder if someone on the other end had gotten knife happy just to save time.

580 westbound, toward the City. Pedal to the floor.

I fumbled in the back seat while I slid out into the fourth lane, came up with the laptop bag. Plopped it on the passenger seat. Opened it up. I still had Teddy's phone's ESN, so I just might...

There was a fumbling sound on the other end of the line.

"Interesting. Clarke." That deep, unfamiliarly familiar, smoky voice had spotted the phone, and the caller ID. "Who is Clarke?"

Please, for God's sake Teddy, don't have my last name on that contact list.

"A friend of mine."

He held the phone to my ear. "Hello."

I put a smarmy-little-shit note in my voice, and said: "Hello, your Grubbiness." *If he doesn't fall for this, Lantham, you're screwed.*

"Are you on campus?"

"Not at the moment."

"Give me your ID number."

He fell for it. Thank God.

"I don't think so." I hung up. Pure instinct. If he thought I was a student, he might give me a few minutes while he looked up my number in the student database, so he could lever me into the office. With a campus that big, it might buy me enough time to get across the bridge before he figured out I wasn't actually a student.

Just do anything dangerous or stupid before I get there, John. I'd hate to have to kill you.

Which reminded me.

I keyed open the secret cubby behind the stereo face. Pulled out my primary weapon. I'd kept it close in Napa, but hadn't carried it. Didn't seem like I was likely to need it, and having a big hunk of metal digging into the small of your back gets old after a while.

Now? I'm back in "anything goes" territory. I need my little friend.

Checked the load. Full mag. One in the pipe. Two spare mags In the mag pouch that I kept velcro'd to the holster when I wasn't wearing it.

I might not have gotten many merit badges, but I internalized the fucking scout motto. This bastard wasn't going to catch me flat-footed.

Ring ring.

I ignored the phone. Pulled the laptop out of its bag. Unfolded its stand from under the glove box. Set it up. Plugged it in.

Ring ring.

If I didn't answer it soon, though, it would go to voice mail.

I put on that smarmy college student voice.

"Hello?"

His Grubbiness said: "Clarke Lantham Investigations?"

Guess Teddy couldn't keep a secret. Goddammit. "That's the rumor."

"Your friend has been causing me problems."

"I'm sorry about that. He's an excitable kid. Well, you know that. He hangs around there with his father often enough. Been trying to bug me to help him start his own firm. At nine. Can you believe it?"

"I'm afraid I can." That voice. Every time it made a sound another part of me turned inside out.

"Why don't you give him to his Dad, bar him from the campus? That ought to keep him from poking around."

"His father isn't here."

"Want me to come pick him up."

"If you would be so kind."

I was just passing the 13 split. I didn't have a traffic map on any screen in the car at the moment, but this time of night I was gonna have clear sailing all the way to South San Francisco.

Thirty minutes, give or take.

"I'm down in Santa Clara right now. I can be there in an hour."

"I'd be most obliged."

"Don't mention it. He's a good kid."

"And Lantham?"

"Yes?"

"Negotiations are a private matter." The tone was all he needed. Just the slightest edge under the gravity of an annoyed professor.

"I understand. I'll see you in an hour."

Click.

No cops. That's what that meant. No cops. No witnesses. I couldn't quite prove he was a murderer yet, but I'm a big believer in the strength of genetics. There's something in the meat between your ears, and some spots in your genes, that make you an effective killer. There's a lot of overlap between that and what makes you a good con artist. Smooth tongue, easy with the lie, the ability to just let things be, not obsess over them.

I'm an effective killer. I don't like it very much, but I'm good at it. I've got more bodies on my conscience than normal people could stay sane with, and it only bothers me a little. They were clean shoots. Every one of them deserved to die. Every one of them died by the rules. And most of the time, that's enough for me. Deep down in my bones, I'm still a cop, and those rules about a clean shoot are what make the difference between being a good guy and a bad guy.

Dad was a good con artist. He was willing to run a kidnapping ring and use little kids for their blood, and keep them drugged up while he did it. I had to assume he was a good killer. And I had to assume that he wouldn't be talking to me now if he hadn't caught Teddy calling me, and then heard my name.

So here's the call you make. You've got a killer. He's got a kid. And you're the one who's got a chance to spring the kid.

If you call the cops, you risk a hostage situation. Does he run with the kid the minute he sniffs them coming? Does he hold the kid and then surrender? Or does he kill everyone?

White collar criminals don't kill people, Lantham. That's what Rachael would say if I'd have thought to bring her along. Dammit.

And what would I have said to her?

"He's already hired it done," maybe. Maybe "He's capable of anything. Trust me. We have a history." I don't really know.

I do know what I said to the car.

"Call Rivers."

RACHAEL JUMPED WHEN SHE heard the shriek of rubber on the road out front. Sir Seligman flew off her lap in a fit of fur and claws.

Someone had just dropped their clutch like a hot rock.

And, as far as she knew, only one man in this neighborhood did things like that, and only in an emergency.

She raced for the door, opened it, looked out just in time to see Francine—Lantham's Subaru—flying low over the tarmac. Streak to speck in two blinks.

Her across-the-parking-lot neighbor, a Korean man whom she hadn't met yet, hung out his door looking for the source of the noise. When he caught sight of her he stared, which made her look down.

Turns out an oversized sweat shirt and a thong made for distracting outside clothes. Go figure.

She ducked back inside, pulled some BDUs on, then her military boots.

The sweat shirt she ditched in favor of a sports bra, tank, and leather jacket.

Then came the belt, with the holster.

She actually waited a whole thirty seconds before putting it on. It occurred to her that it could all stop right here. She could go back to being just Rachael. She could deal with never having to choose again whether to draw on somebody.

But if Lantham was peeling out like that, someone was in trouble—and if someone was in trouble, he was going to end up on the short end of the stick. He always did.

And she loved him. FBI girlfriend or no FBI girlfriend. And she'd be damned if she was going to let him go into whatever-the-hell-he-was-up-to-now without backup.

"Sorry, Lantham," she muttered, "But you're fucking stuck with me now."

She strapped the belt on.

Tucked the holster inside her waistband.

Took her Ruger from the antique cigar box on the desk where it lived with its spare mags.

Checked the load; full mag, one in the pipe.

The pistol went into its holster.

The mags velcro'd on the belt on her left.

She grabbed her keys from the coffee table, and ran out and across the street.

Nya was standing in the middle of the road, vainly waving her arms like an airport flagman after the disappeared detective. "Clarke! Dammit…"

"Where the…" Rachael reached Nya's side, just in time to be cut off by Nya throwing her arms out and groaning.

"He's...Shit. He just ran out like..." Nya looked at Rachael, her large eyes dark with worry—or terror.

"Where did he go?"

Nya shook her head. "I don't know. He was asking about Teddy Stride."

"Teddy like from across the street from me Teddy? The kid with the Encyclopedia Brown delusion?"

"Yeah."

"Why?" Rachael opened up the cell tracker program.

"He's our client..."

"Wait, what?" She looked up from the computer.

Nya was all shrug. "Our client. He hired Clarke for a job, and then Clarke came in here asking if I'd seen him, and asked what I told him, and then he turned around and ran off..."

"That doesn't sound good." Rachael ran past her, didn't get more than four steps when a shout stopped her.

"Was that Clarke?" A blond woman, maybe five two and a hundred pounds with uncomfortable-looking tits, was running towards them from Lantham's side of the street. Beth Stride. "Wait, Rachael? Are you back?"

What, did everyone in town notice she was gone? Rachael shook her head. "Just a clever trick of the light."

Beth huffed to catch her breath. So much for the theory that chasing kids around gave you plenty of exercise. "Was that Clarke that peeled out of here?"

Rachael nodded.

Nya jumped in. "He came in, asked about Teddy, then ran out like someone lit his shoes on fire. What's going on?"

"Oh my god..." Beth put her hand to her mouth, as if she'd just said something she was ashamed of. "Um...Teddy. I haven't seen him since he went over to your house yesterday." She went on. Said she'd called Lantham about it, and Lantham had promised to talk to her, but never showed up.

"Fuck me blue," Rachael said. Beth flinched, but Rachael ignored it. Any woman that had pushed three melon-sized humans out her snatch had no business being squeamish about anything to do with sex. That kind of childish bullshit was bad enough when it came from men, she sure as fuck wasn't going to put up with it from a woman. "He knows. Lantham knows where Teddy is and has gone to get him."

"How do you..."

"Trust me, you know Lantham long enough, you can read the guy like the top row of an eye chart." Rachael dug into her pocket for her phone, didn't find it. "Monkeybrain, you got your phone on you?"

Nya reached into her pocket, tossed a Samsung sports model to her.

From memory, she punched Lantham's number in. "Let's hope he's got his phone on him."

"He does," Nya said.

No ring.

"This is Clarke Lantham of Clarke Lantham

Investigations. Leave a message."

Rachael hung up. "It's turned off."

"Or he's on another call."

"Right." Rachael looked over toward the office, then back to Nya.

Nya caught. "We'll get a hold of him, Beth, and we'll let you know what he's doing."

Beth sighed a desperate kind of sigh. "Are you...I mean, should I call the cops?"

"Well, you know..." Nya started.

Rachael interrupted her. "You did that when you called Lantham. He works for the Sheriff's department..."

"He does?"

Rachael smirked a thin, barely tolerant smirk. "Doesn't like to spread it around. Cops tend to get shit on by their neighbors."

"We'd never..."

"Trust me, honey," some of that country waitress still hanging around in her speech patterns. Dammit. "If Teddy's been snatched, Lantham's already called the Feds and you'll be hearing from them in a few minutes—so you wanna hang out by your phone. Don't want to miss that call."

"And if he hasn't?"

"Then Lantham knows where he his and went looking for him. And if he doesn't call you before I get ahold of him, I'll break his fucking arms."

Beth winced again, then nodded.

Rachael didn't wait to see if Beth went back to her house. She bolted toward the office. Nya followed two breaths behind. Rachael burst through the gate, dodged around Nya's MINI, round to the broad side of the garage, ducked in the door. Hung a right into Lantham's office. She needed to find out where he was going, and if he wasn't answering his phone...

"Goddammit." He hadn't left his computer on the desk.

"What?" Nya huffed behind her. The redhead was built for power, not speed. She could break your arm just by looking at you, but she hated running enough that she never did it if there wasn't someone chasing her. Which is why she'd collected a few bullet wounds, and how Lantham had gotten at least two of his.

She jerked a finger at Lantham's empty desk.

Nya shrugged. "Took it with him to Napa. Still in the car, I think."

"Fuck." Rachael lunged out of Lantham's office, back into Nya's reception area/office situation. She circled the desk, with its computer screen and antennae-laden black plastic corporate-looking monstrosity of a phone.

Once upon a time it had been her desk, and Nya hadn't changed much since Rachael had quit. Rachael's little troll doll, which she'd leathered up with electrical tape and given a toy flogger made out of rubber bands, a toothpick, and more electrical tape, still sat right in front of the monitor like an impossible-to-take-seriously taskmaster. Had *everyone* been watching the clock, wondering when the fuck she'd show up again?

Rachael rattled her head, shaking off a mob of feelings sneaking up behind to mug her. She could deal with that kind of shit later, once she knew what kind of trouble Lantham was in. If his phone was off, she was going to need to find him, see where he was going.

She pulled out the return extension just under the lip at the left side of the desk. She used to keep emergency locator numbers on a sheet taped to the enameled metal. It wasn't there now.

"Shit. Monkeybrain, Lantham's still got the same ESN, right?" Rachael was pretty sure she remembered it. She sat down in front of the computer. She tried her old login. It still worked. She wasn't sure whether to be happy or angry about that.

"Not since Earl gave him that Blackphone." Nya emerged from Lantham's office.

"Great. Fine." Rachael poked around for the tracker program. "Where do I find the fuckin' ESN sheet then?"

"File drawer." Nya circled round, squatted by the drawer next to Rachael.

"What was the last thing he said?" There it was. Buried under the menu entry *Barely Legal.*

"He didn't tell me anything." She was rifling through the files. "Just came in, asked about Teddy, and ran out..."

"Fuck." Lantham wasn't exactly Miss Manners, but he didn't leave his partners in the dark. Something about this screamed 'emergency' to him, and on a whole other level than just 'urgent enough to waste good tires on.'

"Calm down. It's Clarke, he'll be fine."

Rachael needed bullshit reassurances like she needed a colonoscopy. She had her hands full chasing the adrenaline around trying to get a piece of her brain back. She needed some thought in her head other than *gotta find Lantham gotta find Lantham gotta find Lantham.*

"What the fuck was going on that Lantham took a job from the neighborhood wannabe?"

"I can't tell you that. Clarke will kill me. I...here you go." Nya pulled out a file folder, opened it up. On the inside flap were a string of unintelligible numbers, laid out neatly in two columns, some of them with lines drawn through them. The ones on the left were naked. The ones on the right had little three-character legends written next to them in pen.

Electronic Serial Numbers. Lantham's current crop of cell phones—the primary and the pre-paids—in the left column, people he liked to keep tabs on in the right column. She could see her own initials (REO), her father's (CEO), Nya's (NJT), Agent Erica Ellis (AEE), and a bunch of others she couldn't decode at first glance.

Rachael punched Lantham's primary ESN into the tracker.

The computer chewed on it for two full minutes.

Then, a map of Oakland appeared on the screen. A blue dot overlaid on it, moving along 580 westbound.

"Where the hell is he going?"

Nya studied the screen.

"He could be going to the school...but why..."

"School? What school?"

"You don't work here anymore and..."

"School. Like Trubody?"

"Yeah."

"Fuck."

"What?"

"Grab a laptop. And your stun gun." She stood up, closed the manila folder, tucked it under her left arm. "Cuffs still in the cabinet?"

"Yeah. Um...Twatmonster, what are you..."

"I'm on this case. We've been working the same one from different ends for the last three months. And if he's running out like this...." Rachael opened the olive drab cabinet that marked the border between Nya's office and the file room. Clarke kept his emergency cop stuff in here. Extra empty mags for his weapons, speedloaders, mag lights, batons, handcuffs, first aid kits. She grabbed two pairs of cuffs, stuffed one set in her pocket and held the other out for Nya.

Nya took the cuffs. "Clarke needs backup." She nodded. "I'll get my keys."

RIVERS WAS UNHAPPY. I had his crime—or, at least, I would as soon as His Grubbiness tried to trade Teddy for anything. My job was to box him into that corner. And play for time.

Rivers job was to get plainclothes agents into the halls of the school, so they could grab Gruber as soon as he came out of his office, without him ever knowing they were there.

I left the details of that up to the professionals.

And I left out the bit about knowing that Gruber was really John Lantham. I had enough reason to think he was dangerous already, there was no reason to drag that in. Would cause too much trouble for everyone all around.

There wasn't time to put a wire on me. We'd have to settle for an open cell phone line. I used a pre-paid from my stock in the glove box.

Stopped at the 76 down the hill to strap on my weapons.

The 1911 in the small of my back. Shirt un-tucked, hanging loose over it.

The .357 snubbie around my right ankle.

Extra mags and speedloaders in my bomber jacket along with the dental mirror, the buck knife, the evidence baggies, and the zip ties. Trust me, you don't want to know about my tailoring bills.

The pre-paid? I grabbed the smallest one I had. About the size of a credit card. Not much thicker either. I dialed the surveillance number.

"Okay, Rivers," I said, "I hope you can hear this. I sure won't be able to hear you." And I stuffed it down the front of my pants, tucked it between my legs where it wouldn't show even if he made me strip down to my jockeys to prove I wasn't wearing a wire. Here's hoping the thing could survive an onslaught of crotch sweat.

And whatever else His Grubbiness had in store.

I PARKED UP THE HILL, near the private school. Good view. Good chance to collect what passed for thoughts in my brain.

Fog was filling the valley, breaking over the hills in slow motion like the stuff that surfers' dreams are made of. Smack in the middle of all that creeping mist, the college's old brickwork facade stretched out wider than I could see from my spot up the side street, yawning at me like the castle for the knights who say "Ni."

The kind of big-picture view you want before you head into god-knows-what kind of fight.

All right, Lantham. Time to finish this one up.

I opened the laptop. Checked in with Teddy's cell phone.

It wasn't in His Grubbiness's office. It was somewhere in the girl's dorm wing. Weak signal, too. Couldn't tell what floor it was on. Just that he was somewhere in the middle of the wing, roughly between the stairwells.

I was only fifteen minutes early. It wasn't like I had enough time to go on a proper hunt.

But maybe I didn't have to. If Teddy was on that

wing, and Gruber didn't want anyone to find him, my guess was that he'd stick Teddy in a room on one of the lower floors, where no one ever went. What was it that Betsy had said?

Storage, I guess. It's locked anyway.

Somewhere nobody would happen by. Good place to hide a hostage. Better grab my lock picks, just in case.

They lived in a little fabric fold-over in the side pocket of my bag of tricks. I fished them out, stuffed them into the left rear pocket on my BDUs.

Now I just had to pray that my guess was right. I only had time for one side trip before I knocked on the door to His Grubbiness's inner sanctum.

Should have told him you were in Santa Cruz, Lantham.

Goddammit.

Better hope he doesn't have any guards on the kid.

Well, how likely was the guy to have any of his organized crime buddies on staff in this place?

Don't answer that question, Lantham. Get your ass in gear.

Jogged down to Silver. Had to take the long way around—actual crosswalks, since traffic was too heavy to jaywalk. Pedestrianism is one of the few unforgivable sins that carries a capital sentence in San Francisco. Not hard to understand in a town that bemoans the plight of the exploited, underpaid tech workers who are ruining the city by spending money all over the place and driving up prices.

Hey, what can I say? It's my hometown. It's got charm like that.

Up the west side of the big lawn. Considered going in the nearest door, the one by the girl's dorm, but decided against it. Better, maybe, to look like I didn't know where the President's office was.

So I strafed along the facade until I came to the arches and the annex, and made like a tourist.

Light traffic in there. My soft-soled sneakers smacked a hard flap-bang against the polished marble floor. Made it sound like I was bringing doom with me, because the devil don't deliver.

Which I was.

I spotted three of Rivers's people in the annex. Recognized them from the raid on Systems Analysis Foundry during the Chinese meteor job. But I didn't let on.

Neither did they.

If they had, I'd have told Rivers to pull them from the detail. I wasn't going to have Teddy Stride on my conscience just because the FBI couldn't hold its wad.

Down the stairs off the main annex, like Betsy showed me.

Left at the bottom.

Straight through the snack bar. Not crowded this time of day. Only the vending machines were open. I could hear noise coming from the rec room downstairs, but there wasn't anyone around to see me slip through the stairwell doorway.

The room was more dimly lit than I'd have preferred. Two florescent tubes were dim, and one was buzzing like a pissed-off wasp. Enough light from the next level up—and the voices of a couple co-eds talking excitedly about the best ever new vampire blah-de-blah—filtered down enough to make it clear just how much of a difference two floors makes.

That would be the difference between dorm and dungeon, in case you're waiting for the Cliff's Notes version.

I checked the clock. I had about five minutes before I needed to call the switchboard and ask for directions to the President's office. Might be just enough time.

Slip downstairs. Tried to step light enough not to make a creak that would attract attention from above. No mean feat on these old wooden stairs, no matter how much carpet they had over them.

It also didn't work.

One of the girls above said: "Did you hear that?"

The other one, in a deeper more Texan voice said: "What?"

"Shh. Listen."

I didn't move. Held my breath. I imagined them upstairs cocking their heads back and forth, trying to figure out if there was some dude in a William Shatner mask lurking just around the corner with a kitchen knife, just waiting for one of them to investigate the strange noise.

A door opened.

"Hey, Julie!" An overdone-swagger tenor. A freshman flirting with suave, for my money, and not very well.

The girl with the higher voice responded. With the extra noise, I figured I had the cover I needed. So I did something I hadn't done since I was about ten years old.

I propped my ass on the banister and slid down so I wouldn't make the stairs creak.

Gotta love old architecture.

The bottom level wasn't well-lit, but it wasn't completely dark. Safety lights in the corners gave it a nice dungeony feel. Good place for a haunted house.

I had three doors to choose from. One of them led back into the rec room area. I could see it through the little window set at eye level, but a little jiggle confirmed the door was locked.

Another door, directly opposite, led into the dark.

The third door led off to the north, under the girl's dorm wing. There were emergency exit lights at the far end of the hall, about fifty yards away, but nothing else.

Except for cracks of light coming from under one of the doors about halfway up the north side.

But that door was locked, too.

I dug into my back pocket. Found the picks. Selected a likely-looking pair.

Squatted down. Took me about thirty seconds to find and prop all five pins.

The lock popped like the cork on a champagne bottle. So much for stealth.

Still, you do what you can. Me? I stashed my picks and walked in, staying half-crouched and using the articulated stilts I call legs like shock absorbers.

Deep strides, quick pace, soft shoes. Stealth Lantham, that's what they'd call me if I was a superhero.

The deep pile maroon carpet didn't hurt either.

Fifteen seconds. Thirty-five steps. I stopped just outside the door with light. About halfway between the two ends of the corridor. Right where the tracker said it would be.

Three cheers for modern technology, right?

Of course, the paranoid Lanthamy reptilian brain I carry around in my skull didn't like it.

I pressed my body against the blank hand-plastered wall next to the antique wood door frame. Wasn't sure I was gonna like what I found on the other side of the door on my left. The .357 snubbie on my right ankle might make a decent stress ball, though, so I figured what-the-hell.

Rap rap rap

The snout of my .357 on the wood. Well, I wanted to give it something to do. Few things in the world worse than a bored revolver. Kept me out of the line of fire, you know, just in case there was some maniac with a buckshot machine on the other side of it.

"Hello?" Teddy's voice.

"Ted?" My blood pressure dropped back down into a range that might not tempt my cardiologist to buy a new Ferrari.

"Clarke!"

"Can you open the door?"

"No. No. He's got me tied up..."

That was all I needed to hear.

I turned the handle. Gave it a little nudge.

It swung like a coffin lid on rusty hinges.

Teddy was sitting on a matressless bunk with his back to a stained slat-board ladder with his hands lashed behind it. From where he was sitting, all he could see was the wall, no matter how much he tried to turn. Makes you wonder if the guy who invented duct tape had any idea what he was inflicting on the world.

Above him, on another unused bunk and not secured to anything, was Tom Stride. Eyes closed. Laying on his side. Still in his slate blue suit and tie. Hands duct taped in front of him.

He wasn't moving. Dead to the world. I was pretty sure he wasn't *dead* dead. Didn't smell right for that. There's a reason you've heard the phrase "stench of death." Dead people don't give much of a shit where they shit, and they do it a lot.

I could see his chest moving. Drugged and breathing, definitely.

"How long have you been here?" I crossed into the room. Shoved the snubbie into my right outside jacket pocket and reached into my left hip pocket for my buck knife. Snapped it open.

"Right after we got off the phone."

"Hold still. Sharp objects back here..."

A door creaked. Made me jump. My right hand automatically strayed under the fringe of my jacket so I could grab the .45 from its holster. I checked right.

The door right across the hall stood open.

I dropped the knife.

His Grubbiness stood in the doorway. Two-toned hair on top. Business suit dripping from his shoulders. A Glock subcompact in his right hand.

First time in thirty-four years I'd come face to face with him. The first time in all that time he was more than just a ghost. Fuzzy memories, filled with a larger-than-life grump who always knew how to turn a laugh, a face whose features were long since lost to the fog of memory and my mother's determination to burn all reminders, and a smell like cedar and cigarettes.

And he was just standing there. Looking at me.

My lungs had forgotten how to breathe. How can you breathe when the ghost behind your life stares through you?

What if he didn't know who you were?

A gazillion more thoughts tumbled from there, not a one of them had a thing to do with the FBI or my job or the investigation or the two hostages in here.

Three, now. Goddammit.

I took a breath. Opened my mouth. It couldn't decide whether to say "Hi Dad" or "Hello Your Grubbiness" or "You're under arrest, there are Feds all over the building, give it up now."

So he beat me to the punch. He nodded at my hand hovering at the fringe of my jacket.

"Don't even think about it." He inhaled as he said it.

Made him sound like a throat cancer victim talking through a synthesizer. An alien rasp that didn't sound a thing like he did on the phone. I hadn't seen anyone pull that stunt since I was ten and my buddies and I tried to make horror-movie voices.

I shrugged. "If you say so."

I moved my hand back toward my pocket. Well, what else could I do? The muzzle of that Glock was staring lovingly at my genitals. If this kind of thing kept happening to me, I'd start getting a hard-on every time I looked down a pipe. I really need another job.

Then, before I could make it into the pocket where I'd stashed my revolver:

"Don't talk," he inhale-wheezed. "Don't say a word."

Oh hell. He thought I was wearing a wire. No words from me equals no way to let anyone know I was in trouble. And no way for the eavesdroppers to ID him or voiceprint him or have it stand up in court afterwards, with that bloody alien rasp. *Goddammit, Ted, did you tell him my girlfriend is in the FBI?* "Lose the jacket."

Shit. No words, no jacket. He was taking away every beautiful plan before I could even get it rolling.

Well, I had three options. I could go for my gun or I could dive into the room, onto the bunk next to Teddy, and force him to come after me . Either of those would give me a chance to yell for Rivers, but chances were good that me and Tom and Teddy would all wind up eating lead before the Feds could rain down hellfire—lath and plaster don't stop bullets. Or...

Or I could play along until I could get one up on him.

His Grubbiness stayed put. Not stupid enough to move into grab range.

I needed to figure out some way to tell Rivers where I was while I stalled him.

So I shucked the jacket. Let it fall on the floor with all its glorious toys.

It hit the ground like a sandbag. You never realize how heavy you arsenal is until you hear it go smack in an abandoned wing of an antique college, loud enough to hear the slap-back echo from both ends of the hall. His Grubbiness smirked at the sound.

Great. Now he knew how much he'd pulled off me.

He inclined his head to his left. I was still standing sidelong onto him, he could see the .45 on my belt. Now he wanted me to give it up.

"Two fingers," he rasped. "On the ground. Slide it here."

So I kicked away my last noisemaker. Dammit. Unless I thought of something better, I'd end up having to take him down with my bare hands.

My hair itched. Breaking a little bit of a sweat. I'm normally a pretty cool customer, but that Glock, in that hand, with those hostages, and that ghost staring me down, that blew my limit. A bead of sweat rolled over my left eyebrow, dripped onto my eyelash. So much for my poker face. God knew what was happening to my balls. Here's hoping that pre-paid in my undies really was immune to crotch sweat.

I never took my eyes off His Grubbiness. I watched him for any weakness in the chest. Any sign of hesitation. Anything that might telegraph an opening.

But he stayed relaxed. Way more confident than a normal person would be in his position. His eyes were serious, but cool. Not angry. Nothing even annoyed. Just very very cool. I've seen that kind of cool before. In the eyes of the Broadway Slasher. If he was that kind of psychopath, I'd have to get him good and mad to make him crack.

The weapon in his hand beckoned me. "Come hither" with a three inch barrel.

I took a step.

It beckoned again, until I was out in the hallway.

Then it wordlessly waggled me further down the hall.

When I was two doors down, His Grubbiness hissed. No words, just a hiss.

I stopped. Turned. Found him pointing at the nearest door on the left side.

I opened it. Found an unlit room inside.

He nodded me into the darkness. Then he clicked his cheek and made a light switch flipping motion with his left hand.

So I turned on the light. Found myself in an unused dorm identical to the one where I'd just left the Strides.

"Strip," he croaked. "All the way."

Normally, I have the kind of relationship with clothes that birch tree has with its bark. They're fine for what they are, but I'm just as happy to get out of them. Usually in the presence of a particular redhead of a Federal persuasion. If there was a genre of stage magic that turned on how fast you could make clothes disappear, I'd be all over it.

This time, though? I wanted to stretch it out as long as possible. The longer there was silence on this end, the longer it gave Rivers to catch a fucking clue and start combing the place for me.

Assuming he'd even *heard* His Grubbiness. That croaking rasp might not carry through BDUs, underwear, and scrotal folds. For all they knew I could be roaming around the empty halls of the college and grumbling to myself like Rain Main.

There's only so long you can stretch out a belt, two high-top hiking shoes, a pair of black rip-stop BDUs, two socks, a long sleeve pullover tee, an ankle holster, and a pair of Monty Python boxer briefs. By my count, I managed to make it last almost a full minute. Not long enough to get me a good tip in any strip club I've every been to.

I tried to hide the underwear-phone, but skin-tight skivvies are even less forgiving of electronics than they are of cellulite. Earned me a good smirk, and a wave of the gun.

Last time this dude had seen me naked I wasn't far out of diapers. I wasn't exactly keen to repeat the experience. But that Glock didn't give me much of a choice.

My clothes and the phone stayed in that room, while His Grubbiness moved me along to the next one.

I went in. Turned on the light. He put me in the far corner from the door, followed in, closed the door behind us.

"Sorry about that, but I thought we should speak privately."

"Mighty formal of you."

"One does what one must." He leaned back against the door. "So, tell me. How's Marie?"

My blood washed cold again. I barely squeezed out "Marie who?"

"Marie Lantham."

Fuck fuck fuck fuckity fuck. "Should I know that name?"

"You should. She's your mother. Don't tell me she gave you up for adoption."

And that, your Honor, is all I know about the matter.

10:20 PM, Friday

THIS NEXT PART IS JUST between us. No public records. I can't say I'm proud of it, but it is what it is, and that's that.

I did my best to pretend I could still breathe. He knew who I was. How he knew who I was, I had no bloody clue. But he knew.

His Grubbiness's mouth twisted up in a little crooked smile. Almost a friendly one. Creepy too—looked way too much like the one that I got caught wearing by Nya's pathological predilection for phone photography.

"That Marie. I tell ya, kid, she was a hell of a woman," he said. "God, I haven't thought about that in thirty years. You turned out okay."

I kept my voice flat, did my best to be deliberately unimpressed. "Hello, John." Well I sure as hell wasn't gonna call him "Dad."

"How far away are they?"

"Who?"

"The FBI. Your girlfriend is an agent. You can't expect me to believe you didn't call them."

Goddammit, Teddy. "I wouldn't be very smart if I told

you that, would I?"

"You sure as hell wouldn't be very smart if you didn't."

I grunted. Almost a chuckle.

He smiled. Not the effect I was going for.

"Cagey motherfucker, eh? Your name is Clarke Lantham. You were born in September of nineteen seventy-seven. You have a brother Sam and a sister Tricia. Your mother is Marie." The cadence in his voice sent little weed diggers deep into my brain. Like hearing the song that played the first time you had sex with that cute girl from biology class back in high school. I swallowed, re-upped my poker face. "You live two doors down from Doctor Thomas Stride, Ph. D. in medieval church history and professor of history here at Trubody."

I set my jaw. Put a dangerous expression on my face, the kind that suggested I could eat raw steel and cook babies for dessert. "Teddy's got a big mouth."

He grinned. Shifted his weight. The way he was standing, I expected him to pop open a beer and light a cigar. "You know, seeing you on that bunk like that, I don't know, kinda makes me feel like I ought to tell you a story. It starts with a man named Brad. A good man, just wants to make good. Trouble is, he's got a shit job that pays jack shit—by the way, did you know that if you don't swear for long enough, it can start to warp your mind? True fact. Good to be able to talk straight—so he looks for ways to make a little money on the side. He's a prison guard. Keeps an eye on people for a living. And he's got a friend who asked him to keep an eye on a certain inmate, to see if that inmate got any visitors that might cause problems."

I already didn't like the way this was going.

"Well, he notices this blond girl who's got short purple hair on her ID. Dresses like a country bumpkin, moves like a cop. So he calls his client Jack, who thinks 'Santa Maria...Santa Maria. I know that street. I've been there to a barbecue at Tom Stride's house.' Well, something that close to home, you'd understand if he has to call a friend of his—let's call him Tony—around to see what she wants. By the time she comes out, the inmate is rattled and pissed. So Tony? He follows her around. Turns out she's looking for a guy named Rat who could cause Tony's friends a lot of problems, and she finds him in this dive bar. Well, Tony can't have that, so when they get in a fight, Tony makes sure that this rat doesn't make it out alive. He's got a big truck, it's a terrible accident. Nobody at fault. A horrible thing."

Between the cold and the cold fury, my balls had hidden all the way up inside. Handy, in case he kicked me when I choked the fucking life out of him.

"Then, being the stand-up guy that he is, Tony buys the surveillance tapes off the bar owner for a couple hundred bucks, and gives them to Jack. They show the whole fight, enough to send that pretty girl up to San Quentin for the duration. A hell of a shame if anyone ever saw them, so Jack decides to keep them, just to make sure everybody's nice and safe. No need to cause any more trouble."

Like he'd swung a wrecking ball at my gut. I was suddenly very glad he'd stripped me down to nothing and left that phone in the other room. I'd have shot him before I figured out how to dispose of the body.

His Grubbiness continued: "Turns out that pretty girl works for a guy named Clarke Lantham, who runs a PI firm. Except I gotta wonder, why the hell's he poking around this business?"

"I've been thinking of changing careers. Figured I'd go into the ministry."

"Trust me, *Detective*," he managed to make it sound like I'd failed at everything, the way he pronounced that word, "you wouldn't last. You gotta be one cold motherfucker to survive in this job. You were a good kid, but you ain't got the balls for it."

"That puts us in an awkward position, then. Me with no clothes and you with no way out."

He flashed a sparkly used-car-dealer smile. "That's the beauty of it. I figure we're in a position to give each other a hand up. You tell me what I need to know, and get me out of here, and I'll give you the only piece of evidence that ties your friend to that murder."

They don't make profanity for situations like this. If Rachael was here she'd start screaming "dude" and save me the trouble of looking for some.

You wouldn't be in this situation if you'd have brought her along.

Yeah, except I got used to her not being here, and it was an emergency.

Keep making excuses like that, you're gonna wind up a bit player in a Shakespearean family saga.

"All right. I'll get you out of here. You give me the tapes."

"That's all I ask."

"One thing."

"What's that?"

"How did you know I'd come down here instead of to your office?"

He pursed his lips. "I left a phone in my office for you. You were to hit send, and we'd have had a chat, and you'd have wound up down here. When I heard you picking the lock..." he shrugged. "You're quick, I'll give you that."

Exactly what you'd have done, Lantham, if you wanted to make sure you didn't get any attention from Feds you expected to ride in.

"Ten points for style." I inclined my head. Figured I'd get brownie points playing up to his ego.

He acknowledge it with a spooky mirror-incline of his own.

"So, Your Grubbiness..."

"Ooh...call me Jack."

"Fine. Jack, what do you want to know?"

"How far away is the FBI."

"They're in the building. They've got a perimeter. Don't know all the details."

"How many?"

"No clue. I spotted three on my way in here, but they tend not to screw around."

"How long until they know something's wrong?"

"If I was the SAC, I'd be worried already." I'd have been worried after hearing me talk to Teddy then go silent. I'd be combing the whole goddamn place for me, and trying to get a bead on that pre-paid cell, assuming it hadn't been killed by the crotch sweat. In fact, if I was the Rivers, I'd have my people sweeping the building now. If I could delay things another couple minutes...

And if I did that, it'd be Rachael in cuffs, cause His Grubbiness would trade those tapes for a reduced sentence. How could I be sure? Aside from the fact that he'd already gotten into Witness Protection once—which requires selling other people up the river—it's what I would do.

So far, everything he'd done is what I would do.

"Guess we'd better get moving. Stay here."

He opened the door. Slipped out. Closed it behind him.

I stayed put. Spent a full minute and a half counting my cuticles.

Doesn't take nearly a minute and a half to run out of cuticles, so I got bored pretty quick.

When the door opened, though, I'd have paid good money to stay bored.

Teddy came through. Pale enough you'd think he shits ghosts, but with the brave-face on that says *Don't ask me if I'm okay. I'm gonna handle it no matter how bad it gets.*

Hell of a nerve, that kid.

He was dressed in knee-length cut-off jeans, Converse hi-tops, and a Transformers 4 T-shirt, and, from the goosebumps on his legs, he was freezing.

Still, he got subjected to Naked Lantham, and nobody really deserves that.

He hung his head, like this was all his fault.

"He said to bring you these." Teddy held out a double-armful of Lantham clothes, piled up and unfolded, pretty much like I'd left them on the floor.

I stood up, took the two steps across the room, seized the threads.

"I'm really, really sorry, Clarke. I just thought Dad…"

"After what Nya told you, you thought he was in trouble."

"Yeah."

"What happened?"

I dressed. He filled me in. He'd come over on BART, hiked up the hill, found out that he'd missed Tom by about an hour, so he hung out with some students he was friends with, camped out in their dorm room overnight. When Tom's next class was scheduled, he went up to Tom's office. Tom was there, and Teddy tried to get him to leave, and Gruber came in right when Teddy was telling Tom about the Witness Protection Program and how he'd hired me.

Gruber went apeshit. Tom yelled for Teddy to run.

Teddy ran. Eventually he found somewhere to hide and called me.

He finished his story when I was tying my shoes. "It's not your fault, Ted." It kinda was, but he had no way to know who the bad guy was. Now, though, Gruber had all my weapons and all my toys and my phone. I might as well have stayed naked. "Don't worry. I'll get us out of this."

"I'll help."

"Okay. Don't do anything till I tell you. Swear?"

"Swear."

"And don't try to run or get away until I tell you. He's got a way to hurt Rachael and Nya, too, and I've gotta stop him so we're all safe."

"Swear." Serious as only a nine year old can be.

"Okay." I stood up, tossed him my jacket. "Keep warm. I'll be fine."

He wrapped it around himself like a cape. "Thanks. We gotta go out now."

"Lead the way."

THE SONS STEPPED into the hall, and into the sight of their fathers.

It felt like that. Like some epic, end-of-Star-Wars procession. For the first two seconds at least. Them, standing two doors down, Tom Stride still trussed up but now awake and bleary. His suit was rumpled, and not just from sleeping in it. There was ink splattered on the right side near the pocket, and blood higher up on the shoulder.

His nose was no great shakes either—swollen, along with the top of his lip. His right eye looked like someone'd smashed a cherry pie against it, and his cheek wasn't much better.

"And here I thought he drugged you," I said. I was tempted to say "Meet Jack Lantham, my dear old Dad," but I figured that the less these guys knew about His Grubbiness, the more likely he wouldn't try to make strawberry jam out of the two of 'em.

"He did. After he knocked me over."

Next to me, Teddy looked like all the demons of hell were gonna fly out of his face and eat His Grubbiness alive.

I put my hand on the kid's shoulder. Gave it a little squeeze. *Remember*, I thought as hard as I could, *I'm gonna take care of this.*

Then I locked eyes with His Grubbiness. "You didn't tell me you were a makeup artist."

"Call it a hobby."

"What's your exit plan?"

"Back gate."

"Won't work. They'll be watching cars going out."

"You got a suggestion?"

"Yeah. Send Tom to get his car, have him bring it around back."

A raised eyebrow. A little nod, like he was impressed. Then a head shake.

"You do it."

"They might flag me down."

"So don't get seen."

I took about three seconds to scroll through all the different possibilities. Then said "Your car. It's out back?"

"Yeah."

"What is it?"

"Twenty-eleven Town Car."

Well, at least I didn't inherit his taste in cars.

"I'll get that. Tom drives it out."

"Very nice."

THE IDEA MIGHT have been nice. The car wasn't. "Town Car" is a synonym for "Pretentious Prickmobile," so at least it made sense that it's what His Grubbiness would drive.

It had tinted windows, though. With any luck, we'd slip through.

Then I'd have some fancy footwork on my hands. I didn't believe for a minute that Jack was about to hand over the surveillance tapes. If they even existed.

My forearm against the cherry-black stained oak, my forehead leaning against it, and me looking out through the wiggly glass at the fog-socked valley.

Waiting.

Teddy and His Grubbiness filled the hall a few feet behind me like a pair of restless elements.

V.I. Lenin said once that there are decades where nothing happens, then there are weeks where decades happen. He was on to something. A few decades had happened in the last ten minutes, and the three minutes I was standing there waiting for Tom to return took another fourteen decades or so.

A set of four glow bulbs trundled through the mist. I straightened up. The Town Car headed for the bottom of the sidewalk running between wings of the building.

Deep black tint on the rear windows. Thank God.

"Yeah, it'll work," I said.

His Grubbiness grabbed Teddy's arm and manhandled him toward me.

"You should go into childcare with methods like that," I said. Hard to believe this was the same guy who read me to sleep at night. Then again, if he was the kind of narcissist I took him for, maybe he only liked kids young enough to worship him like a god. Maybe that was the real reason he took off and left my mother holding the bag for those fraud charges.

He grunted. Pushed his way past me heading for the door.

"Wait, Jack. Not till he's parked right up here. We want minimal exposure." I figured that as long as Daddy Dearest had my balls in the sling, I was gonna run this show. This was not my first goat-fuck, and I was pretty sure I was the only person here who'd worked with the FBI enough to have any chance of dodging their notice.

The Town Car glided to a stop a few feet from the corner of the building. About eight yards of sidewalk between the stairwell exit and the rear door of the car.

"Okay. Ted? Jack? We go out this door. Ted, you're in the front seat. Jack, you and me are in the back, curled up in the foot wells till we're out on the road. Got it?"

I turned to look His Grubbiness in the eye.

"You're the boss." Again with that fucking used-car smile.

I smiled back. Let him think I was getting into this shit. *Just keep that up Dad. Helps me hate you.*

"Now or never. Let's go."

I made sure I went out between them. Couldn't take the risk that Jack would run off with both the hostages.

We three pushed through the door.

Crossed the open space in that kind of fast duck-walk that drug dealers use when they're hoping the cops won't notice them.

Teddy and Jack circled round to the far side. I opened the driver's side door, swung in. Knocked my hat off on the way in, had to grab it off the pavement. At least it hadn't been raining.

The door closed with a sound like a pig's femur snapping. I huddled down in the driver's side rear foot well of the kind of faux-luxury shit-wagon that has "new car smell" air fresheners sewn into every seat so that when you get out your ass will inspire random strangers to make their way down to the Ford dealership and offer their oldest children in exchange for an automotive enema.

Jack and Teddy's doors closed. Teddy's seatbelt snapped. Jack huddled down, we wound up head-to-head. I considered picking my guns out of his pockets, but I didn't know if he even had them on him. If I was him, I'd have left them both in one of the empty dorm rooms, keeping them completely out of play.

And I had to hold my wad until we got the tapes.

Hold on, Lantham. You'll get the bastard. Just hold on.

The silence was thick enough that the gear shift sounded like someone dropped a forklift off a loading dock. The car lurched backward, then shifted again and crawled forward.

Thirty seconds later, I saw the shadow of the faculty parking lot gate inch by the car, and an inconspicuous-looking man in an A's cap, mirrored sunglasses, and a Raiders windbreaker gave the car a casual once-over. I recognized him as one of the low men on the totem poll in Rivers's team.

Rivers, this is one day I hope your team isn't on the ball.

The car stopped for a second. But no windows rolled down.

The agent in the windbreaker leaned toward the tinted window. The sunglasses slipped down his nose.

I held my breath.

The agent raised his hand, as if he wanted to shade his eyes to cut through the reflection on the glass.

The car rolled forward. Swung right.

And we headed down the hill, without a whisper of pursuit behind us.

WORKING FOR LANTHAM had given Rachael a burgeoning appreciation of architecture. She realized this about three seconds after walking into the rotunda annex of Trubody College and involuntarily half-shouting:

"Jesus fucking Christ!"

Only to realize, slightly too late, that those were not, perhaps, the best words to half-shout in a marble and plaster echo chamber sparsely populated with people who actually worshiped Jesus Christ and were committed to a subculture that, upon the release of *The Da Vinci Code*, spent millions of dollars to counter the notion that Jesus Christ might have had wife.

Not even her grandmother—for whom disapproval was more than just a lifestyle choice—gave looks that dirty.

"Excuse me, can I help you?" A very prissy, very buttoned-down girl about Rachael's own age was speed-walking toward them from the door to the eastern hall.

"Nope, I think I got it. Thanks!" Rachael rushed toward the western hall, Nya right on her heels.

"Hey!" The girl shouted, but Rachael ignored her.

The locator had put Clarke's phone somewhere in the westernmost wing of the college, somewhere in the middle. It hadn't moved in the last ten minutes. She hoped to hell he'd found who he was looking for, and hadn't wound up on the wrong end of a gun, or ambushed by thugs working for the crooked college president.

She broke into a run when she got to the hall running west. The night's dim was matched by dim lighting along the corridor. On her left was a flashing picket fence of dark wooden doors with official-looking plaques on them. To her right, a running guard rail separating her from a succession of brick archways housing plate glass windows looking down onto some half-fogged-in green space between the main wing and the west wing.

She'd made it almost all the way to the lounge at the far end when Nya shouted from behind her:

"Twatmonster! Stop!"

Rachael skittered to the stop on the green deep-pile carpet. Spun on her toes.

Nya was peering out one of the windows, leaning far enough over the railing that her head was resting against the glass.

"Quick. Look." Nya poked at the glass.

Rachael looked out the archway on her left, and down.

There was a luxury sedan of some kind down at the ass end of the green space where it dead ended into parking lot, maybe about forty yards away and forty feet down.

Three figures were scurrying along a cement walk straight to the car.

The first one looked like a little kid wrapped in a gigantic leather jacket.

The third one looked like a tall, middle-aged raver in a business suit.

Between the two of them was a skyscraper in a black fedora.

And now they were all ducking into the car.

"Shit shit shit shit." Rachael set off at a run, back the way she came. "Go go go go!" She hooked her left arm through Nya's right arm as she passed, pulling the stouter woman along with her.

"Twatmonster?"

"We gotta go..."

They burst into the annex, looped right, just in time to see a couple security guards stepping in through the front door with the co-ed that had accosted them a moment before in tow.

"That's them!" The girl said, pointing at the two of them.

"Fuck." Rachael said, and lowered herself like she was making a run at a pair of football linemen.

Nya had the same idea.

And Nya had the shoulders for it.

She checked Rachael to the side, and plowed right between the two security men.

They bounced off her. Rachael followed right behind her in the hole she'd left.

They raced down the granite stairs, across the narrow parking lot to the visitor space where Nya's MINI was parked, jumped in.

Nya laid tracks in reverse.

Laid more in first.

They nearly hit three students and a cat zipping around the last half of the crescent drive.

Hard right out of the driveway.

Another hard right at the light.

The MINI pointed straight down hill, just in time to see the ghost of a luxury sedan turning left at the stop sign at the bottom of the hill.

"That's them," Rachael said. "Don't lose them."

She fumbled her phone out. Pulled up the maps. Overlaid the tracker.

The tracker was still in the building.

"Fuck. His phone's not with them. Gotta keep them in sight."

"I got 'em." Nya gritted.

Nya ran the stop sign at the bottom of the hill. The MINI bottomed out, scraped like a leaf rake on a marble floor. The tires chirped as it pushed hard left.

"There," Rachael said. "Those lights. Looks like a Lincoln. What the hell is he doing in a Lincoln?"

"Shouldn't be hard to keep up with," Nya gritted.

Rachael wasn't so sure about that. Big boats like that had more horses than the RCMP. But maybe that bastard grubby guy wouldn't figure out he was being followed.

If Nya didn't crawl up his ass or tail him obviously. She obviously wasn't used to driving like this. Rachael'd assumed that, after she left, Lantham would have put Nya through the wringer. Training her up to be the new assistant. But Nya wasn't carrying a gun, and she didn't know what she was doing in a car chase.

Lantham really had been waiting for her to come back.

Fucking hell.

"Looks like they're heading for the freeway," Rachael said.

"Yeah, I got it." Nya tossed the car around another corner, closed to within a half-block of their quarry.

"Don't follow too close, you don't want him to spot you."

"Duh." Then: "Wait, Twatmonster, have you done this before?"

"Yeah, a few times."

"Okay. What do I do?"

"Stay about this far back. Let some cars get between you. Don't lose sight of him, but don't directly follow him either. When you get on a multi-lane road, follow in a different lane, but stay far back enough that you can get to any turnoff he makes, and make sure you don't get caught in a turn-only lane or something."

"That's it?"

"That's good to start."

"Okay." Nya licked her lips, like she was getting ready

to sink her teeth into a freshly-killed dear. "I can handle that."

"Well, don't get so into it you lose them." Rachael pointed at the entrance to 280 heading into the heart of the City, which Nya was about to blow by.

"Oh shit..." Nya jerked the MINI right, overcompensating, and scraped the underside of the car on the curb as she went around the corner.

"Goddammit, Monkeybrain..."

"I know I know, just...give me some space."

Rachael chuckled. "We're in a MINI."

Then she kept laughing. The kind of maniacal laughter that says "We're gonna die, but we're gonna have fun along the way."

Nya caught it too. Like their own private case of West Nile, passing back and forth through the cabin while 280 rolled away beneath them.

Until Nya took a half-breath, and choked like someone had shoved a lump of pure, unrefined, ore of distress down her throat. "Oh no."

"What?" Rachael checked left. Nya's usually-pale face looked like someone had drained the blood from it.

"Gas."

"How bad?"

"Quarter tank."

Rachael swallowed. Mileage was good enough in Nya's car that they'd probably be able to make fifty, sixty miles on the last quarter tank. Assuming they drove responsibly, didn't run into traffic, and more or less didn't do everything they'd just been doing. "Let's hope that boat is thirsty, too."

10:22 PM, Friday

HIDING IN THE BACK of a car. Hoping the adults don't see me.

Used to love doing that when I was a kid.

Finding out where they went when they left for the evening.

Watching what they'd do when no one was looking.

Listening to the conversations they didn't want to have in front of the children.

My mother used to take a drive with her friends, or boyfriends, or my father, when there was something she wanted to talk about in private. She pulled the same stunt with us kids when she needed to talk to us without our friends or siblings were around.

I saw, hiding in the back seat. And the trunk. Heard even more. Not something I've made a habit of since I was younger than I care to remember.

Well, not hiding out in cars at any rate. The eavesdropping, that sunk in.

Never thought that in all my life I'd be hiding in the back of a car with my long lost father, trying to figure out how to take him down without getting myself or any civilians killed in the bargain.

The bump at the bottom of the hill came just before Tom Stride said:

"I uh...Clarke? Doctor Gruber? I think we're clear now."

"Look in the mirror," Jack said. Man of many names, my old man. I figured the ones the students gave him really fit him best. His Grubbiness. "Are they following us?"

"I don't see anyone."

"Good." His Grubbiness unfolded himself, shifted up onto the rear passenger seat. The shadows of streetlights flashed behind him, lighting up the white ends of his hair like flashes of memory. "Get on 280. Head across the bay."

"Where we headed?" I asked.

"You're hardly in a position to ask questions."

"Oh, you'd be surprised at the kinds of positions I can get into when I put my mind to it."

He grunted. The kind of grunty half-laugh that Rachael made fun of me for doing. "Settle down. We're in for a drive."

I did. And we were.

We crossed the Bay Bridge in silence. No words at all except the occasional instruction to the driver. His Grubbiness and I watched each other across that wide back seat like two cats sizing each other up. We had a dozen entire conversations like that, sizing each other up, neither of us saying anything.

I figured he wasn't talking because anything he said

would expose him to more witness chatter. I didn't talk because I didn't want to talk family business in front of the Strides. Considering how seriously they took family, I figured I'd lose the ability to control them if they knew His Grubbiness was my father.

No matter what your odometer tells you, no mile is just a mile. A mile with a friend is shorter than a mile with an enemy. A mile in silence is longer than a mile in a conversation. But there are no miles anywhere in the world longer than the miles that pass between fathers and sons.

We passed a lot of empty miles before His Grubbiness softly gave the next direction. Studying him, watching the microexpressions on his perpetual poker face, I began to wonder if I didn't understand a few things about him he would rather I didn't.

Or maybe it was me I was seeing.

Either way, I hadn't expected to have so little reaction to it. Finding your long lost Dad is the secret fantasy of every boy that grows up without one—even when you know the guy you lost was a piece of shit. After all the years of fantasy, and all the years of forgetting, I figured if I ever ran into him I'd come over all misty, or pissed, or something.

But what I saw there across from me wasn't a world of missed possibilities. It was just a kind of blank mirror. A cardboard cut-out of a person. The shadow of some long-ago memory.

It wasn't a complete blank. There was real

determination there. A quiet kind of resolve. Out of character for someone who had spent his whole life rolling short cons over. Hucksters don't tend to be patient people, and his rap sheet didn't show patience.

But his face showed patience.

Lantham, watch yourself. You've just ruined his life and operation, and he's coming over all zen. This fucker's got another play up his sleeve.

And more than that before Tom said "We're low on gas."

The words seemed to stir His Grubbiness out of some deep, faraway place. The age lines, so faint as to almost not exist, wrinkled back into this dimension as he took his eyes off me and turned to look out the front window. "Go to the Arco on the next exit."

We were in Richmond, a few miles south of the tracks. I knew this neighborhood. Had a few fun high-speed chases through here from time to time. Might be able to do something with that.

The Town Car pulled to a stop at the Arco. On the wrong side of the pump, so Tom had to manhandle it into position. I could see his eyes in the rear-view. He looked beat. Bone-tired from the kind of adrenaline poisoning that most people never have to put up with, and no sane person enjoys.

I nodded at him. "Want me to drive?"

"I think you'd better stay back here with me," His Grubbiness said.

"Thinking's a hobby, is it?" I said. "Look at him.

How much more do you think he's got in him before he passes out at the wheel?"

His Grubbiness shrugged. "Grown man can deal with a car."

"Maybe. How far we going? You can't live all the way out here."

"What gave you that impression?"

"The tapes?"

"Ah, yes, the precious tapes." He settled back into his prop in the corner, one leg flopped half-Indian style between us, the other with a foot tucked under the front seat where Teddy was currently pretending to sleep. The forced snoring was a dead giveaway. Close enough to fool most people though. Certainly fooled His Grubbiness. Smart kid. "We've got about another hour to go."

"In that case, mind if I get some food? I don't think anyone here's eaten in anything like a lifetime."

"You? Sure. You can pump while you're at it. You," He looked at Stride's mangled face. "Tom, you stay put. Give me the keys."

Smart play. Now Tom and Teddy are grounded in the car, I'm on a blackmail leash in the mini-mart, and His Grubbiness can pump gas.

Tom grumbled. Ripped the keys out of the steering column. Handed them back to His Grubbiness.

I opened the door, patted Tom as I got out and mumbled "You said it, buddy." Quiet enough that I doubt he even heard me.

One step out the door, I stopped. Patted my pockets theatrically. Then I ducked my head back into the Town Car.

"Say Gruber, you didn't happen to hold on to my wallet, did you?"

 10:42 PM, Friday

NYA WAS A SHITTY tail artist. A *civilian* could have spotted her.

Any civilian.

She kept creeping up on the Town Car, then falling back, like her MINI was being towed on a ginormous invisible bungee.

After ten minutes of this kind of stupid behavior, Rachael mumbled "When we stop for gas, I'm driving."

"Oh, thank God." Huge sigh of relief.

"Really?"

Nya turned her head from the road, and it seemed to Rachael as if Nya dropped a mask from her face. The flat, alien-smooth features seemed to drop, and under those haunting eyes, a deep pit of exhaustion opened up. As if she was saying *I can't do this without you.*

Rachael laid her hand on Nya's leg. "Has it been that bad?"

Nya looked back at the road. She sniffed. A tear fell from her eyes. "Not bad. Just...well, he's Clarke, and...well, dammit...I'm not you."

"What do you mean?"

"I don't know. I just...you know about my father, right?"

Rachael tried not to roll her eyes. How could she *not* know about Nya's father, who killed three of Nya's friends and who Nya stabbed and Lantham shot? The wrongful death lawsuit harshed Lantham's mellow for months, and he only got out of it by blackmailing Nya's mother. That was after he'd spent God knew how many months or years fucking her and her friends.

"Yeah, I know about your father." The words felt cold in her mouth.

"Not like that. I mean...he fell apart before...well before the end. I couldn't stop it. I couldn't do anything about it. I never knew what was going on...anyway, that's not what I meant."

"What did you mean?"

"I mean he was alone when he came. And he almost didn't make it out. Every time he's alone, every time he's with me, he gets shot, or he almost dies, or something. He needs a partner, and..." More tears fell. Enough that Rachael wondered if Nya could even see the road anymore. "I tried to be you. God, I really did. But I'm not you. I just... I can't hold him together like that."

"Lantham's problems can't be my problems, honey. You know that."

"It's more than that. Clarke...ever since you left, he's been 'all good.' It's all 'all right.' He has what he wants, he's only a little moody. But he's not happy. He needs you...no, that's not it. Dammit. He needs *us*. He needs our family. Our team. And he doesn't know it. And it's killing him."

"Killing him?"

Nya nodded. "He's taking risks. Bad risks. He asked Erica to let him use the FBI database off the record—I mean, can you believe it?"

"Oh fuck. You're kidding."

Nya shook her head. "I can't keep up with him. Not without you here. I can't do it. I can't tail people. I can't go into the field with him. I can't do anything about it when he's in some gunfight in fucking La Honda. He won't tell me things because he thinks I'm stupid and won't understand, or he thinks I'll care too much and try to stop him, and...goddammit...and I love him more than anything in the world, 'cept maybe you. And I just...I'm gonna have to leave too if you don't come back. Please come back."

Rachael held her breath. She really had no idea what to say. Her own feelings where Lantham was concerned were still a complete mess, and this last week had been the kind of special hell she only ever got dragged into when Lantham was involved.

But the road was lonely. And she, too, had a knack for getting herself involved in things she had no business being near. Like the Woodforks case, or that business up in Reno that she'd been lucky to get out of.

After a couple miles she said "I'll think about it. No promises. Hey, you can always come to Portland with me."

"Portland?" Nya chuckled. "Never been there. Why Portland?"

"I don't know," Rachael said. "I've never been there either. Oh, hey, look at that. Looks like they're pulling off at Harbour. Get over, don't let 'em lose you."

While Nya worked the blinkers, Rachael reached into her holster, brought out her weapon, and checked the load.

10:43 PM, Friday

IN WHAT I HOPED would wind up being the worst mistake of his life, His Grubbiness had held onto my wallet. He tossed it to me.

I caught it. Closed the door. Walked to the little convenience store—thankfully still open even though it was edging eleven PM.

Turned around at the glass, more out of habit than anything, and scanned the neighborhood.

I saw a little pink MINI across the street at the independent gas station.

Nya, I don't know how you did it, but thank God.

A woman with long blond hair stepped out of the passenger side. Took a half-breath for me to realize it was Rachael. Sometimes, you roll snake eyes, and sometimes you come up aces. Maybe this was an aces kinda night.

His Grubbiness was at the swipey-pay kiosk. He wasn't looking at me.

Rachael was.

I waved. Held up two fingers. Made an "m" sign—I had a teacher in high school who taught us the ASL alphabet for the sheer hell of it—here's hoping Rachael could follow.

She tapped her wrist twice and gave me a nod.

Then I pointed at the Town Car, held my finger to my lips, and shook my head quickly twice.

Another firm nod.

Excellent.

I slipped inside before His Grubbiness extracted himself from the mechanical embrace of Arco's arcane robotic teller. Raided the shelves. Got bag of Nacho Doritos and another of Sour Cream and Cheddar Ruffles. Call it a fit of sadism. Three bags of beef jerky—protein is very important when you're a hostage—and four cokes. I took them to the teller and asked the bored fifty-year-old round black woman behind the counter if she minded if I borrowed a pen.

She flicked one my direction. I pulled my wallet out, handed her the company's Discover card—it was a business expense, after all. You can write off hostage food if you've got a PI license. It's the law.

I also slipped a business card from the outside pocket on my wallet. While the clerk totaled things up, I scratched out:

Rache-

FUBAR, hobbled. Do not tell Rivers no matter what.

Leave your baby behind the coffee cups.

Don't let Strides see you.

-Lantham

Not exactly legible, but.

"That'll be thirty eight twenty three." The clerk said.

"We don't take credit cards here. Debit only."

"Ah hell. Okay." I took the Discover back, handed her the company debit card. "How would you like to make a quick fifty bucks?"

"Wouldn't complain, that's for sure."

"See this business card?" I flipped it face up, slid it under the give a penny/leave a penny tray. "There's a woman gonna come through that door in about twenty seconds. Make sure she gets it."

"Why don't you give it to her?"

I took the bagged quasi-groceries and my receipt and card, and said: "Cause I have to use your bathroom."

She turned her head sideways at me, like she was trying to make what I was saying seem something other than completely ridiculous. I noticed she'd missed a bit on her left eyebrow, which was gray underneath the mascara she'd used to thicken and darken it up. Made her look even more perplexed.

I didn't give her time to figure it out. Ten seconds later I was in the bathroom in the little alley between the dairy case and the Icee machine.

Went ahead and took a leak, just to kill time. Then I recited the first ten verses of *The Raven* to myself.

That oughta do it.

Come on, Rache, don't let me down.

I opened the door. Poked my head out.

No Rachael out there.

I'd been in the store a little under three minutes. Much longer and I was gonna get His Grubbiness coming in here after me.

Stepped out into the store. The clerk looked at me and gave me a hopeful nod. I shot her a thumbs up, turned left, went to the coffee station.

I reached behind the cups. Found the baby. The .40 Ruger SRc I'd bought Rachael for her birthday. A bit small for my hamfists, but that made it easier to palm.

There was something under it too. Something flat and smooth and cold.

Clever girl. Rachael, you're a lifesaver.

She'd left her cell phone. Maybe even better than the gun. I palmed the gun and the phone in one grab. I stuffed the pistol down the back of my pants where I'd normally have kept my holster, the butt facing my right side so I could draw it fast if I needed to. Let my shirt fluff down over it. Then I slipped the phone into my left ass pocket as I drew my hand back out.

Thank God the food racks blocked the view between my ass and the clerk. I didn't have a jacket to hide under. Teddy was still sleeping under it in the car.

Bought a coffee to cover up my interest in the cups. Stood cocked to the side, half-facing the door, so nobody coming through would spot the phone or the carry. Paid my tab, requested fifty cash back from the clerk, just in time for His Grubbiness to stick his head in the door.

"Be there in a sec," I said. "Had a problem with my card."

I pressed the cash-back cash down on the counter, slid it off to the side. Pocketed the card, lifted the coffee, hooked the pseudo-groceries with my right pinky finger.

Joined His Grubbiness in the back of the car. Dolled out the food.

"No coffee for me?" he said.

"Figured you wouldn't trust that I hadn't drugged it."

"Thoughtful of you." He reached his hand across the seat like he expected me to give him the coffee.

I did. Cause what can you do? It was gas station coffee. Not even the quasi-premium shit they sell in the maroon cup for another two dollars.

If he wanted the indigestion, he could fucking have it.

With two aces up my sleeve, I could even afford to be gracious about it.

12:50 AM, SATURDAY

NORTH. NORTH. AND MORE north.

And when we started heading into the interior of the state, I got that sinking feeling.

Didn't help that my mouth was pasted in the half-vomity combination of cheese Ruffles and long dead Coca-Cola.

Tom started weaving at the Nut Tree, so we swapped drivers in the Genentech parking lot in Vacaville. I got the hot seat.

His Grubbiness got the passenger seat.

Teddy and Tom got the back. The kid snored. Sounded kinda like Klepto. Light wheezy rhythm, blended right in with the low whine of the road under the tires.

By the the time we left 505 for 5, the passengers were sleeping the sleep of the dead.

Or the soon to be dead.

At night, the central valley looks like a snowy waste strewn with little moving Christmas lights.

I'd given up asking where we were going. His Grubbiness wasn't going to give an inch. I guessed that if one of us managed to get free—especially Tom or

Teddy—he didn't want the escapee grabbing a passing CHP and bringing down the fury of the State of California on our heads.

If I was in his position, I'd probably have done the same thing.

Didn't matter anyway. I was pretty sure we were headed back up to Weed. Either that was his escape plan, or that's where he had the security tapes, or he was gonna use us to reinforce the foundation of his brand spanking new plasma supply center.

After a while, even he got bored of the radio, and the silence. He started making small talk.

"You know, I'm on to a good thing here. It's not too late to bring you in. Someone like you, cool head, you'd do well."

"So it really works, eh?"

"What," His Grubbiness said. "The plasma?"

"Mmm hmm."

"It really does." He ran his hand back through his hair. "A few years from now, it'll be standard medicine. Right now, it ain't available. That gives us a chance to make a killing. Lots of money, something priceless along the way."

"Priceless, eh? You got a hell of an opinion of yourself."

"Oh, not my services, my boy. Years. Time. The only thing you can't buy, or couldn't."

"You think you really conquered aging."

"Me? What do I look like, a lab rat? I just saw the

chance to get into a business that really works. For once in my life."

"Snake oil."

"No. Just experimental."

"I doubt your business partners would want someone like me."

"Built a reputation for yourself, have you? Fill in the resume."

"Oakland PD. Santa Clara Sheriff's Department. You remember the Broadway Slasher?"

"Yes. Yes, I remember hearing about that. Quite the local-boy-makes-good."

"That was ten years ago."

"It was all over the news. Fake name like Lantham? Easy to spot in the headlines."

Oh, joy. Another adrenaline surge. "Oh, it's a real name."

"If you say so." If you packed any more smug into that tone, the car would explode from over-pressurization.

"There's an actress out there with it. Ran across her on IMDB once."

"One person, out of how many million in the US? Ever meet another Irish Catholic named 'Lantham'? Course you didn't. Closest you get is 'Latham.'" He took a sip of his Coke, which he'd been nursing for the last thirty miles. "Course, keeping track of you was a fringe benefit. I picked it cause I wanted something I wouldn't get mixed up with anything else."

I felt gears meshing in my head. He was wrong, Lantham was a real name, I'd run into it here and there. Wasn't a common one, though. But *picked it?*

When do you pick a name?

Well, if you're a career con artist, you pick names like you pick boogers and scabs. It's just a compulsion, part of the life.

But you also pick a new name when you enter Witness Protection.

"Lightfoot." That was the other name in the file. "That's what you were born with."

"Pleased to meet you." Then. "I take it you've seen the file. That must've taken some doing."

"Eh, not much. You don't get far in this business without learning a few things about filing a request."

He chuckled. Like we were fellow scoundrels. "I bet you do, I bet you do. I hear she's quite the piece. Smart move, bagging a Fed like that."

I didn't realize he could say anything that would make me hate him more.

The first few thousand ripostes that crossed my mind all would have wound up with me driving us off a cliff just to rid the world of the fucker, so I took a breath, counted the ten ways I'd most like to disembowel him, and got back to the name thing. Nice. Casual. Polite. Meaningless.

"Fucking FBI, right?" I chuckled back at him. Pretty convincing, too, judging by his reaction. "So that first conviction...oh right. They put you through college. It was your deal."

"Hell of a promotion in life, wouldn't you say? Yeah, old Uncle Sam's been good to me over the years. Now I get to help out his people a little, filling the gap while the FDA drags its feet on every new advance that comes down the pipe."

"Who the fuck did you finger?"

"Oh, people. There's always people. If you're a good salesman."

"And you are."

"I'm still here." He let it hang there, like it was the answer to everything.

FOR BORING DRIVES, you can't do better than Interstate 5 through the Central Valley. Long and straight, with one slight jog every five miles to wake up sleepy drivers. The theory is that if you're dozing, the gentle curves will push you onto the rumble strip, wake you up before you can do any serious damage to the oh-so-delicate pasture lands that line either side of that long, boring ribbon of asphalt running from Baja to Canada.

I kept myself awake by watching Nya and Rachael in the rear-view. It wasn't a bad tail job, but they were staying close. MINIs have very distinctive headlights. Not hard to keep track of. Some small comfort in that. If I wound up needing backup, all I had to do was pull over and keep from getting shot for maybe thirty or forty seconds before they barreled right up next to me.

Of course, I had Rachael's gun, so mostly what they'd be good for is hitting people with the car. Still, having Rachael at my back again felt good. Made me think that we might all make it out of this thing without too many bumps and bruises.

A LITTLE WAYS north of Redding, he stirred out of his highway hypnosis. Climbing the mountains'll do that.

He looked back, like he was checking to make sure our passengers were still asleep. I doubt you could've woken them with a gong. Better for everyone. Thank god for civilian adrenaline tolerances.

"You never did answer my question back at the school," he said.

"What question?"

"How's Marie?"

"You left her in a hell of a spot."

"Ha. I made sure she got out of it."

"You made sure."

"Part of my deal."

Man, the bullshit some people peddle.

"I didn't want to leave you guys in the lurch like that. Just didn't have any choice."

"That's an old song, Daddy-o."

"No word of a lie."

"She's fine. Got married again. Had a good life, no thanks to you." Mom never dated again, leastways not so it stuck. Never could bring herself to trust anyone. She lives in a little commune in Watsonville now, gardens a lot. My sister Tricia keeps trying to get her to move back home—Tricia and her husband live in the old house—but Mom doesn't even want to see that place anymore since Sam died. The place where her husband abandoned her and her dead son had grown up has too many memories for her.

But I wasn't going to tell this motherfucker. He'd given up the right to the straight dope thirty four years ago.

"Glad to hear it."

"I bet you are."

"You really hate me, don't you?"

"Hmph. To hate you I'd actually have to give a shit. I just want to get those tapes."

"So that'd be a 'no' to the business proposition."

"Like I said, your partners wouldn't like me."

"You don't know that. They're pretty broad-minded."

"I'm engaged to a Fed," well, almost engaged. "They might worry that I'm a mole."

"Shame." Almost like he really meant it. "We coulda done great things. Lot of catching up to do. I got stories you'd want to hear." He sighed, like he was really upset that I didn't think he was the bee's knees.

Then, a couple curves later, all the smoothness back in his voice. "We're getting close. Pull off the next exit."

"Why? What's up here?"

"My cabin. You don't think I'd keep evidence in my presidential residence or at the college, do you?"

2:26 AM, SATURDAY

RACHAEL WASN'T SURE WHICH was more frustrating: driving the mountains in a car designed for it while following a land yacht, or knowing that Lantham and two of her neighbors were in that land yacht in some kind of trouble.

Nya didn't seem to care. The rhythm of the road had rocked her to sleep an hour ago.

Before that, they'd killed time with shop talk. Nya had brought her as up to date as possible on the case. Most of it was redundant with what Lantham had already told her, except for the surveillance photos of a man with white hair.

It was the same white haired guy she'd seen at the gas station, pumping gas for Lantham.

This was their bad guy.

And the more she and Nya looked at the pictures, the more they became convinced that Lantham was related to this guy, somehow. Same eyes. Same nose. Almost like they were brothers, except Lantham's brother was dead. Maybe this guy was a cousin, or an uncle, and Lantham was trying to convince him to cut a deal.

Why else would he play things out this far? Why else would he ride along for four hundred miles in a shitmobile with hostages, and tell her not to call the FBI?

Lantham, I hope to hell you know what you're doing.

Rachael rounded a broad, sweeping left turn. They were well past Lake Shasta now, climbing the long winding stretch toward Shasta and the high plains. A whole lot of nothing up here. Well, trees. The occasional volcano, but good fucking luck if you wanted gas after ten in the evening. Even the robopumps quit and went home to their families at night up here.

The brake lights on the Lincoln flickered. They blinked on and off like someone was quick-tapping on the brake pedal to get her attention.

Whoever was behind the wheel knew she was back here. It had to be Lantham. He wouldn't've told anyone else about the pursuit.

The blinker went on.

They were getting off. Some no-name road snaking off into the middle of the nowhere mountains.

"Oh, this can't be good."

Rachael geared down. She flashed the hazards once, to signal that she'd gotten the message.

Then she killed the lights, popped the car into neutral, and took her foot off the gas.

She rolled across the rumble strip to a stop on the broad shoulder.

Nya woke up.

"What's going on?"

Rachael pointed ahead, to the exit ramp and the Lincoln's disappearing tail lights.

"Oh!" Nya straightened up. She opened the glove box and fished around, coming out with a pair of knives—one folder, one straight two-edged throwing dagger in a a little sheath.

"What, are you going to slash the tires?"

Nya shrugged. "They just make me feel better."

"I'll bet. Just don't go doing anything forensic." Nya wasn't much of a gunswoman, but she was a holy terror with a blade. 'Feral' was the world Lantham had used. One of the things on Rachael's bucket list was to never see Nya on a genuine, life-and-death rampage.

The Lincoln disappeared over a rise at the top of the ramp.

Rachael put the MINI into gear and followed.

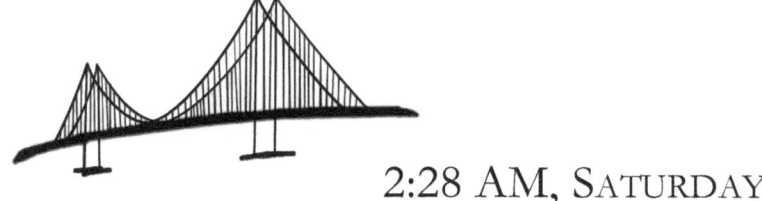

WE CLIMBED HIGH. UP high enough that while, sure, Pacific pines still grow, they do start to get a mite scraggly.

It's cold up here. Not a lot of oxygen, either. Okay, so no Denver resident would think it was thin, but for anyone who tends to stick around sea level? Not a lot of oxygen at all.

Not a lot of people, either.

Or guard rails, for that matter.

When we were about twenty minutes off the main road, His Grubbiness said:

"All right. We're gonna come to a driveway up here on the right. A little ways in, there's a gate. Pull up to the gate."

The way he said it made my gun itch.

Well, Rachael's gun, but it was pinch-hitting for mine.

The headlights painted streaks on my retina along with the asphalt.

It was an old cattle gate, with a sign on it that said "Private Property: Enter At Your Own Risk."

Not the kind of sign you want to see out in the middle of nowhere, on a cold after-midnight.

I slowed up gradually as I could, so I wouldn't wake the passengers.

His Grubbiness got out. Rounded the front of the car. He pulled a keyring from his pocket and squatted down. Fiddled with something. When he came back up, he had a large padlock in his hand. Then he reached over the gate.

The faint sound of wrenching metal squeaked through the cab's insulation, and the gate swung inward.

"Tom? Tom wake up. Don't move." I did my best to speak ventriloquist-style so His Grubbiness didn't get nosy.

"Hm?"

"Stay quiet. Don't wake Ted. We're here."

"Where's here?"

"Hell if I know. Up north somewhere. Keep your eyes peeled. If you get the chance, get Teddy and get yourself lost in the woods. There's only a few hours till light. Stay warm."

His Grubbiness stood by the gate, waved me through onto a gravel drive. He closed the gate behind me, then walked ahead of the car, leading me around a sharp bend to the left, a soft wander back to the right, and into a cleared space at the edge of a cliff.

Looked like a serious cliff. I had a clear view of Shasta, maybe forty miles to the north. Not a single tree poked up to disturb the view.

The drive ran between the cliff and the front of a small cabin built into the side of the hill. Bilbo Baggins meets Peter Prepper, designed by Frank Lloyd Wright. Even in the moonlight the place looked like something out of a Kincaid painting, if Kincaid was into Gothic vampire horror.

What? So I like Kincaid. So shoot me. Plenty of other people have.

No guard rails. Not the kind of place you'd want to go out for a stroll if you had an eye infection.

His Grubbiness was standing in front of the car in the blare of the headlights, back to the western sky. He stuck a hand in his right coat pocket, beckoned me with his left.

"He wants me to get out," I mumbled. "I'm leaving the car on. Get out of here if you get the chance."

"Got it," Tom said.

I opened the door, swung my feet out. The door was between me and him. If I wanted to draw on him, now would be the time. I could come up with the gun before he had a chance to get me. Maybe even wing him. With luck, I'd miss all the major arteries, and he really would just lose the ability to shoot straight.

Not a good plan, Lantham. Not a good plan. Play it out. Play it out and get those tapes, make sure he can't send Rachael up, then turn him over to Rivers.

I closed the door soft. No reason to wake up Teddy.

"Nice place."

"Thanks. I like it. Built it back in eighty-six. Thought I might need it if Reagan spooked the Russians too much. No major targets up here, as far as I could tell.

Prevailing winds all come in from the oceans. Figured I could ride out the chaos up here."

"You're kidding."

"What, you think I can't cover my ass, son?" A twinge of Texas coming through there? Well, he had spent god-knew-how-many years in the Midwest. "Where do you think you got it from?"

"You got me there, Pop," I couldn't resist mocking his twang. He didn't seem to notice. "Where are the tapes?"

"We gotta have a conversation first."

"That isn't what we've been doing for the past four hours?"

"Different kind of conversation."

"What, you wanna take bets on the World Series?"

"You see this place here?"

"Yeah."

"It's yours."

"You trying to buy me off?"

He pulled his hand out of his right pocket. It didn't have a gun in it.

It had a set of keys.

He tossed them to me. I snatched them out of the air.

"Call it an inheritance," he said. "It belongs to a corporation. The papers are inside. You can transfer ownership to yourself, just sign the ledger."

"What am I supposed to do with this?"

"I don't know, hunt fucking elk for all I care."

"You want me to go in there now?"

"No."

"Well what the hell are we doing? It's freezing out here."

"We? *We're* not doing anything. You're staying here. You'll go in the house. You'll call for a ride. And you'll hole up here until someone gets you. By the time they get here, I'll be gone."

"And the security tapes?"

He shook his head. "Eh, I don't think so. I think I'll hold on to those for insurance."

I took a couple steps to the left, getting away from the car. "That's not gonna work for me."

"You're in no position to bargain, son."

The wind kicked up. I shook my head. Scratched it with my right hand. Looked down at the ground.

Looked up at him again, dropped my hand to my belt.

His Grubbiness had the headlamp in his eyes.

"Thing is....I am." I drew Rachael's gun from my pants, brought it up, drew a bead on him. His hand strayed to his pocket. So what? Even if he could get a shot off, the chances he'd hit me were somewhere in that vast wonderland between fat, slim, and none. "I think I'll take those tapes now."

He shook his head. "Give it up, Clarke. A threat isn't a threat if it ain't credible." Mist curled out of his mouth like smoke. His hand moved slowly toward his hip pocket.

"Keep your hands out."

"Relax, kid."

I shook my head. "Don't mistake this for a negotiation, Jack. Tell me where the tapes are."

He smiled. The kind of smile you smile when you're holding all the cards. "Let's run through this a moment. You can't arrest me, you're not a cop. You won't turn me over to the FBI, because you know I'll cut a deal again. I've been in Witness Protection once, they'll put me in again. And you won't kill me."

"Don't count on it."

"Too many witnesses. Do you think Tom Stride will lie for you? He wouldn't even lie to protect his job. Face it, Clarke, there is one thing and one thing only that's going to happen here. You're going into the house with the Strides, and I'm leaving."

"Put your hands on your head. Kneel on the ground."

"I underestimated you." He gave me a nod that looked like respect. "You got some balls, kid, I'll give you that. But what about your partner? Those tapes'll look mighty sweet in court. You're gonna sell her down the river just for the collar?"

"He won't have to." Rachael stepped out of the trees by the edge of the house. "I'll take the rap, Lantham. Bring this fucker down."

His Grubbiness looked at me. Surprised. Almost proud.

"How far away is Rivers?" I asked her.

"What, you want me telling our prisoner how long he has to get away? What are you, stupid?"

Some people, the more they insult you, the more it puts a smile on your face. "Glad to see you too. Stride! Go!"

The Lincoln reversed deliberately.

Twenty seconds later, the Strides had disappeared around the bend.

With it went the light. All the light but the full moon—just enough light to spot a gun draw by.

"They won't get out of the gate," His Grubbiness said.

"No witnesses." I grinned at him as unpleasantly as I could manage. I've been told that grin could freeze gasoline. "Just me and my partner. Since this concerns her. So let's review our options. One, I kill you. Two, you give me those tapes, and I hand you over to the Feds. I'm not seeing a lot of upside for me to go with a three or four. Rache, got any cuffs with you?"

"For this asshole? *So* not my type."

"I meant to arrest him."

"Oh! Right. Sorry, it's been a while. Left 'em in my other pants."

"What good are you then?"

"Mmm...I could break his arms."

"That'd work."

"Cover me."

She strode toward His Grubbiness. Not in any big hurry.

"Jack, put your hands on your head and drop to your knees. You're under arrest."

He shook his head. "You're gonna have to shoot me."

If there's anything worse than getting your bluff called, it's getting your bluff called by someone who really deserves to be shot.

His Grubbiness was only about ten feet away from me.

Close enough that I couldn't afford to take my eyes off him.

A shadow caught my eye. Moving along at the edge of the cliff, out of His Grubbiness's sight line.

Nya. Moving like a hungry tiger. Coming around behind him.

"Lantham!"

His Grubbiness lunged for me. Covered the distance fast enough that he hit my hand before I got a shot off.

Oh, I got a shot off. It went wild. Somewhere, a few miles away, some drunk at a campfire would start bleeding from his leg or something.

My whole world was hands.

His hands on my arm. Trying to wrest the gun.

My hands trying to get control of the situation.

I stomped at his toes. I missed.

He twisted our hands, ducked down, stepped back into me.

Classic Judo move.

Too bad I never took Judo.

He got low enough on me that I didn't have any choice. I pitched forward.

Rolled over him.

Wound up flat on my back.

My diaphragm seized.

I couldn't breathe.

I lost my grip.

Two seconds. That's the difference between safe and dead. Not even long enough for Rachael to react, to come knock him over.

And now he had all the guns.

I could see his eyes, looking down at me. No expression in them. Nothing at all. Or maybe it was eighteen expressions mixed together into a muddled gray nothing.

Rachael's gun, in his fist, pointing at my head.

"Stay back!" he shouted. "Stay back or I pop your boss."

My lungs decided to work again. Then my spine. A quick glance left showed me how close Rachael had gotten. Another half second, she'd have been on top of him.

Goddammit.

"Get up, Clarke," he said. "You didn't hit that hard."

Actually, I did. And if he wasn't doing such a good job keeping his eyes on me I might be able to take a poke at his nuts.

"Come on, kid. Up and at 'em."

I rolled onto all fours. The ground had enough loose

gravel to be interesting. I grabbed a couple handfuls. Stood up.

"Your move, daddy-o," I grunted.

"You." He snapped to Rachael. "Over here."

He stepped back. Well out of range, so I couldn't do to him what he'd just done to me.

I couldn't see where Nya had got to. I didn't dare scan around. If His Grubbiness spotted my eye line, he was liable to start pulling the trigger.

Rachael sidled over to me. Then she stepped into the line of fire.

"Get out of the way," he said.

"You want him. You go through me."

Oh for fuck's sake. First she buggers off for months, now she plays hero. God save me from self-righteous twenty-two year-olds.

I stepped up right behind her. Put my closed fist on her waist.

"Rache, please."

"Fuck you, Lantham. Just...fuck you."

I shrugged at His Grubbiness. While I did, I mumbled: "When I move, grab some cover."

"Where?" she grunted back.

"Wherever you can."

"Are you nuts?"

"Maybe." I stepped around Rachael. Spoke up. "You still have no exit," I said. "No car. Let's go inside, turn on the heat. You give me the tapes. I'll trade you something. Maybe some of the evidence I've got on you can go away, make it easier for you at the trial. You can tell me about your cons, I'll tell you about my cases. We'll have a glass of something. Maybe a bottle. And when the FBI gets here, you'll go quietly. I'll even visit you in prison."

He shook his head. Gave me a big smile. "You think they'll lock me up, son? You really do? I'll be out in time for your next birthday party."

"We'll see about that." He was too far away to run at.

He wasn't too far to throw at.

I took one step. Flung my left hand at him.

The gravel showered at him. He ducked. Reflex. Anyone would.

I followed it up with the second handful, just as he was looking back.

It caught him right in the face.

He tumbled backwards. Squeezed the trigger. A reflex. Caught me in the left shoulder. Just a graze. About as much damage as barbed wire. Burned like a fucking branding iron.

I dove for him. Couldn't close the distance.

But before I could scramble after him, I heard an unholy scream. Like a screech owl wrapped around a rabid dog.

Rolled to my feet. Nya was on him, wrapped around his back like a spider monkey, stabbing the shit out of his gun arm, screaming loud enough to scratch fingernails across my eardrums.

Two more shots. Rapid succession.

Wild shots. He was waving his arm, trying to get her off. Trying to shoot her off.

He was screaming too, and lurching.

Another stab. Nya got her knife in deep, twisted it. Bent down. Bit into his neck. She was gonna chew his fucking head off.

Rachael's gun clattered to the earth. The two of them kept stumbling around.

I dover for it, grabbed it in a roll, came up at the edge of the cliff with the two of them in my sights.

His Grubbiness was dancing on the edge in a blind pain-filled panic.

"Nya, stop! I got it. Get off!"

One foot went too far. He slipped. Tottered over backwards. Nya hit the ground on her tail bone, hard enough to shatter her sacrum.

She yowled again.

I broke into a run.

He was still yowling. Thrashing, grabbing on to her, trying to keep himself up by getting a grip on her clothes.

Her shirt tore free. He slipped again, almost all the way over. Caught ahold of her ankle.

Like hell.

I caught her by the arms, lifted her, threw her a few feet behind me. Maybe she'd get another bruise, but she wasn't going over the cliff with this motherfucker.

The motherfucker who had tapes of Rachael.

Which the cops would find when they searched his property.

Wherever he had it stashed, they'd find it.

Nya hit the ground. She groaned.

His Grubbiness bellowed for help from just over the cliff's edge.

I can't pretend it was noble. I can't pretend it was reflex. But I did toss the gun away, lay down on my stomach, slid over the cliff.

And found myself looking down a two thousand foot drop as sheer as a pair of nylons. Only a few little outcrops right past the lip, and them only sticking out five inches or so before it plunged down a couple thousand feet. I could see the little windy ribbon of I-5 snaking through the mountains a couple miles off.

His Grubbiness dangled by his left arm from a lip. It was big enough for both his hands, but it was sticking out further than the rocks below.

His feet were kissing sky.

His right arm flapped around. He kept reaching up to get his fingers around the rock.

But Nya had shredded his right arm to shit. He looked like a vulture with a broken wing.

Even if he could reach over his head, which he couldn't, he was never going to be able to lift himself up.

I stretched my hand out. I could just reach.

"Nya! Rachael! Grab my legs!" She had the kind of horsepower in her thighs that could keep a VW from going over the cliff.

They latched on. One of them on each ankle.

"Hold on, Dad." I scooted forward. I could just

barely touch his fingers. "I need another four inches, guys! Four inches!"

They lowered me. "Come on, Dad. I got ya." I wrapped my right hand around his wrist. "Grab on."

He looked up at me. Locked eyes. Naked terror smeared across his face, stripped off all that car salesman charm.

He jiggled his head. A little trusting nod.

He took a breath, heaved himself up as far as he could on one arm—which wasn't far—and reversed his grip.

Ever try to lift two hundred pounds of live weight with one arm? Ain't easy.

I slipped forward again. I could hear Nya and Rachael digging into the ground.

"Come on," I grunted at him. I hauled. Dug my knees into the ground. "Scramble up!"

He flapped his useless arm, pulled up hard against me.

I pushed against the ground with my stomach, pulled my chest back, walked my hips back.

A couple centimeters at a time, we started pulling him back up over the edge.

After six inches, he was able to flap his right arm up over the lip.

Another six, he leaned his chest against it.

Another foot, I was clear of the top of the cliff.

"All right, Dad. I got ya. Last bit. Come on."

He smiled. He was going to live.

But it wasn't just that. It wasn't a smile of relief.

It was triumph. He was going to make a deal. Maybe he'd sell Rachael out, maybe he wouldn't. She had just helped save him. And sure, he might lose a lot of the money he'd made. But he wasn't going to jail.

He'd have his freedom within a few months.

He'd find another mark.

And he'd do it to them all over again.

Once upon a time he'd left my mom holding millions in fraud charges.

Then he swindled churches, schools.

He'd had his secretary raped and killed.

He'd framed her husband for the murder.

He'd knocked off the hit man.

And because he could turn over an interstate trafficking ring, he was going to walk.

And he'd do it all again.

My father, the hero. He could save anyone.

As long as it was himself.

"Dad?" I grunted.

"Yeah?" He said. All sparkle.

"I'll miss you."

"Huh?"

I flexed my arms, hard as I could. Pulled him up almost level with me. He got his knees on the granite. He was hauling on me for all he was worth.

A flicker of alarm crossed his face.

But not fast enough.

Quick as I could, I twisted my hands free of his, then

thumped my fists against his chest with all the leverage I could muster.

And, like a flagpole past its tipping point, he tumbled backwards into the empty air.

His Grubbiness. Mr. Frankly Gruber. John Lantham. Jack Lightfoot. My Dad.

Whatever you want to call him. It didn't matter.

He wouldn't be answering anymore.

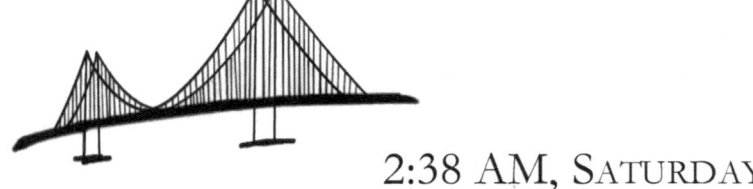

2:38 AM, Saturday

"OH MY GOD. LANTHAM..." Rachael said.

Which was odd. I didn't feel like any sort of god. Didn't feel like anything at all.

I pushed myself back onto solid ground, stood up.

While I dusted myself, Rachael crept up to the cliffs edge. Looked over.

"Oh my FUCKING GOD! Lantham!"

"Can it. We gotta move fast." Everything in the world was cardboard. A chessboard drawn in pencil. "Nya, you took a hell of a hit. You okay?"

"Yeah. Yeah, I'll be fine."

With her bones, I shouldn't've been surprised.

"Okay. I need you to get down to the Strides. Tell them that there was a fight, he shot me, then he escaped, and you've got to get them out of here. Take them home. Don't call the FBI. We'll take care of that. If Erica's home, don't mention any of this to her. In fact, don't go home. Go to Rachael's place. Got it?"

"Yeah. Yeah, I got it..."

"Lantham!" Rachael's voice was right on the edge of I don't know you or trust you anymore territory. "We have to call this in, we've got..."

"Goddammit, Rache, stop thinking like a cop. We call this in, and you and I are both going down for murder."

"Murder?"

"Yeah. Numero uno. San Quentin retirement home."

That shut her up. Her face went blank—Nya's did too. Well, blanker than normal.

"But, Clarke..." Nya searched my face, like she was looking for something. Then her shoulders dropped, like someone had just dropped a heavy load onto them. "Are you going to be okay?" She reached her fingers toward my arm, still leaking blood from the gunshot graze.

"I'll be fine. See?" I stepped toward her, slipped my arm out of the jacket, let her inspect the wound. "Just sliced me. Didn't go in."

She visibly relaxed about eight notches.

"Okay. Strides. Home. No FBI. The bad guy is loose. Got it."

"Good. Oh, and make sure you drive and they sleep or something. I don't want them finding their way back here, ever."

She nodded. "I got it."

"Oh, one thing..." I looked around on the ground, paced back to where I'd been standing near the Lincoln, kicked at the dirt. "Here they are. These keys, one of them unlocks that gate. Unlock it, then leave the keys in the dirt on this side of the gate. We'll need them."

"Okay."

"Rachael have your keys?"

"Yeah."

"Okay, good. Get going. We'll meet you at Rachael's place in a few hours."

"Twatmonster?" Nya pushed past me to Rachael, who was still simmering at the edge of the cliff. "Are you..."

"Just get out of here," she growled.

Nya did.

I watched her go. Waited to say anything until I heard the gate squeak.

"Give me one good reason I shouldn't leave you stranded up here," Rachael said.

"Because your life depends on what we do next."

"What the fuck are you talking about?"

"That guy right there? Do you know who he was?"

"Well it couldn't be Gruber. I mean, I *assumed* he was our collar, but I know you'd never straight-up *murder* a collar."

"It was Gruber. And he deserved it."

"*Deserved it?!* Who the fuck are you to decide he deserved it?"

"His son."

That was the point at which she officially lost her shit.

I couldn't blame her. I can't say I exactly had a good handle on where I'd last dropped a load of mine. Or anything else outside of that tunnel-focus a good emergency can give you.

But I explained, quick as I could.

And it didn't seem to make her like me any better.

"I did what I had to, Rache. I'm not saying it was the right thing. It was just the only thing."

"Why?"

I held out my hand, ticked a finger off. "When you killed Rat, we know it was a clean shoot, but a jury won't see it that way."

"Fuckin' figured that out for myself days ago, dumbass."

He had tapes of the fight where you killed Rat. The truck wasn't an accident, it was a hit. But he didn't keep any evidence of that. He just kept the camera footage that shows you hitting him and pushing him and getting him dead, then fleeing the scene. And you know how prosecutors work."

"Fuck me."

"More or less, yeah." I ticked off another finger. "He's killed two people *that we know of.* He's got a rap sheet longer than my dick on a warm day."

"So he'll go down for it."

I ticked off a third finger. "This is his second round in Witness Protection, and he's been stockpiling secrets so he can get a third if he needs to. That means everything—the murders, the kidnappings, the trafficking, the blackmails, it all goes away, and he disappears into a new life where he can do it all over again. I don't know about you, Rache, but I don't want that shit on my conscience."

"The system isn't perfect Lantham, you still don't get

to decide..."

"Well I fucking do this time!"

"Why?"

I held my hand up to her, the fingers ticked off like I was in the middle of forming a fist. I ticked the fourth finger down. "Because that son of a bitch? That was my father. And now that he knows where I am I'd always be looking over my shoulder. And I'm not going to spend the rest of my life living in the shadow of that piece of dog shit." I realized I was shouting, then realized I didn't give a good goddamn. "That man deserved to die, and if we don't want to follow his ass by the long slow road, we've got work to do, and fast."

Rachael's face looked like I'd just taken a hammer to her gods.

But she isn't the kind of woman that breaks, not under anything. She's the kind of woman that I wish I could be—well, you know what I mean.

Tears were spilling down her face like the blood spilling down my arm. But she didn't back down an inch. She didn't flinch. She didn't take her eyes off me. She just looked at me, like she was trying to figure out if I was still there.

"Your father." She said.

"Yeah, my..." And that's where I broke. *Dad? I'll miss you.* I hadn't been lying. I already did. Some little piece of me that never grew up, that missed him for the last thirty-four years. That part of me was missing him all over again. "My father...my dad. My responsibility."

I couldn't look at her anymore. I could barely stand. So I stumbled instead. Down the dirt and gravel driveway to the gate, to where I could use Rachael's phone—which I still had—to rummage around in the dirt for His Grubbiness's keys.

My keys.

Consider it an inheritance.

I found them by the gate, hiding in a nest of pine needles, right where I'd told Nya to leave them.

When I returned to the front yard of the little hobbit hole, I found Rachael still standing where I left her, but she wasn't looking at me. She'd turned around, watching the full-moon track its way over whichever-valley-that-was.

"Rache?"

"I don't want to talk to you right now, Lantham."

"Tough. We gotta work." I jingled the keys. "And fast."

She looked over her shoulder at me. "Tell me something first. How many murders have you covered up?"

"Counting this week? One. Or one and a half. I wasn't very popular with my brothers in blue."

"Cops don't murder people, Lantham."

"You know better than that."

She sighed. "Yeah. Yeah, I guess I do."

Keep your mouth shut, Lantham. Give her some space. Don't say anything that'll make her bug out again.

After about twenty seconds, I started to get itchy

feet. Last thing I wanted to do right now was look out at infinity and ponder my sins. If I wanted to do that, I'd go to church.

"Eh," I said, "It's a dirty business."

"So why do we do it?"

"It's what we're good at. Come on. We've got work to do." I made as if to go to the hobbit hole, but didn't actually move until I was sure she was behind me. Call it caution—I didn't want her running off with the car or jumping over the cliff. Guess I still didn't quite trust her like I used to.

She dithered for a second, turned around, squinted at me.

"We'll talk later."

"Yeah."

Then we crossed the bare dirt to the wispy wild mountain grass, and to the door. Not a round door like a proper hobbit hole, just an ordinary rectangular one with some serious locks on it.

I monkeyed around with the keys, found the one that fit the first deadbolt.

Started to turn it, but stopped.

"Rache, get out of the way and back."

"What?"

"Bobby traps. He's the type."

She got back, walked along the house until she was in front of the berm supports instead of in front of any part of the house proper. Or, at least, any part we could see.

I ducked behind the door frame. Wouldn't help me in the event of a bomb—but a shotgun blast, at least, wouldn't take any more chunks out of my hide.

And I used my left hand. That arm had already taken enough damage this year that it was basically made of scar tissue, so I figured that if I had to sacrifice one on the altar of doing my job, it was the best candidate.

I turned the key.

The bolt clicked.

It released.

No boom. This time.

I repeated the process with the next four locks.

That made the locks. But the easiest way to rig a booby trap is with a piece of string, a pulley, and a gun of some sort.

Okay, Lantham. What's the worst that can happen? It's not like you can kill your own father twice in one night.

Some days I really wish my subconscious would shut up.

The knob turned in my hand.

The latch popped.

The door creaked and swung inward.

The wind kept blowing. The moon kept shining.

My left hand would live to spend another day resenting my right hand for getting all the action.

"No boom. Oh, thank fuck." Then I raised my voice. "Rache! It's okay!"

"Don't forget trip wires." She said as she jogged back to me.

"Right. Trip wires." And me with my bag of tricks moldering in street side parking in San Francisco.

Rachael's phone would have to do.

Dug into my pocket. My left pocket, because I just love keeping phones on the side of my body that's collected enough lead to come back as a sewer pipe.

I laid down on my belly, scooted into the doorway, shined the light in.

Rachael joined me on the floor, and the two of us spent about three minutes trying to find a stretch of filament line that wasn't there.

"You stay out here," I said to her.

"Like hell I will."

"Hey, this is my house."

"Yeah, and the probate court just loves to legitimize inheritance to heirs who murder their way into their inheritance."

"That's not how it went down," I growled.

"No jury in the world would buy it."

"Yeah. I'll keep that in mind next time Rat comes up."

"Fuck you."

Now she was mad enough to not notice me slip in ahead of her.

Found a light switch just inside the door. Hadn't seen any wires coming in from the road. Come to think of it, I hadn't seen any wires on the road for the last few miles. This place couldn't be hooked up to the grid. Maybe there was a propane generator? I'd have to find it and turn it on if there was one. Or did it have solar cells up on top? If it did, were the batteries fresh or flat?

Figuring I had nothing to lose, I flipped it. The room lit up. And I lost the ability to breathe.

"Well, they're not in here," Rachael said.

She was right. The place was caked in dust—dust on the carpet, dust on the furniture, dust on the bookshelves. Nobody had been up here in a year at least. Aside from the little tile entry pad where we were standing, there wasn't so much as a footprint or a fingerprint anywhere in the room.

It was sparsely furnished. But it wasn't empty.

Two freestanding unstained pine bookshelves lived on either side of a fireplace.

They didn't hold books.

They held photos.

The same, exact selection of photos that still hung on the wall in the house I grew up in.

I knew them all by heart. Could spot them all, recall every detail, just from seeing them in the dim light of the single-bulb torchiere from halfway across the room.

On the left, photos of the Lanthams from before I was born. My parents wedding. My mom pregnant with each of us. The baby photos from the hospital. Right the way up through the day my Dad disappeared from our lives.

And then, on the right, the other photos. The ones from school. The ones from Sam and Trish's wedding. The ones of me in my police academy blues.

I fell back against the wall.

Did what I could to get ahold of my respiration.

I turned the light off, wiped down the light panel, shouldered Rachael out of the house, wiped down the door, and grumbled "Come on. We've got work to do."

2:53 AM, SATURDAY

RACHAEL WANTED TO TALK.

I didn't.

We locked the property up, got in the MINI, and then had to talk.

As soon as we left that building, the clock started ticking.

Now that I had access to a phone, every minute I didn't call Rivers was sixty ticks closer to an obstruction charge that could see me put away until my prostate decided I'd had enough erections to last a lifetime.

"Really, Lantham, what the hell was it back there?"

"Later," I said. "First we gotta decide where we're headed."

We could go North. Ask the bar manager whether someone really took the tapes—but it was late enough now the bar was long dead. And I didn't need to ask anyway. His Grubbiness described the incident closely enough that he had to have actually seen it.

"We've got the office at the school. The Presidential Residence at the east end of the school grounds. What else?"

"Safe deposit box?"

"Eh. Not likely. I mean, it's possible, but seems like a lot of trouble to go through."

"Unless he was going to trade them to you for an escape. The guy made plans, Lantham."

"Well..." I shuffled through the key ring he'd tossed me. There were the five keys to the house. A handful of other keys. All of them looked like house keys, with DO NOT DUPLICATE stamped into the brass. "No. No deposit box key here."

"What are those others."

"Institutional. They'd belong to school property. Like his office, the supply closet, stuff like that."

"School property?"

"Yeah."

"Like the portables at that construction site?"

"Genius." *I swear to God, Rache, if you bail on me after this case, I'm never speaking with you again.*

Twenty minutes to get back to the highway.

Twenty minutes north on I-5.

Ten or fifteen minutes off the main drag.

For those of you who aren't all that keen on math, that means I had to spend almost an hour sitting next to Rachael in that MINI.

My former assistant, Rachael Oldman, is not a subtle woman. She's got about as much of a poker face as Klepto. You want to know what she's thinking, all you have to do is contemplate glancing in her direction.

And right now, she was thinking about whether or

not she could work with me ever again, or be my friend, after what I'd just done. She was wondering if, all this time, she'd been learning from a secret monster. A man who could push a helpless person off a cliff—and not just any helpless person, but his own father.

Well, she didn't know my father.

Neither did I, for that matter.

And normally I'd tell her to go to hell. Because I don't answer to her. She could hang me out to dry, or become an accessory after the fact. It was all the same to me. But the normal Lantham procedure is not to explain myself.

I learned early on that explaining yourself means that someone's gonna leverage you.

Guess who I learned that one from?

But that's normally.

This time was different. This time...

...this time she wasn't sure I was still Lantham. Because she didn't know.

And if she was gonna stick around, maybe even come back to work, she deserved to know what she was getting into.

So I told her the whole story. Filled her in on everything. I told her things I hadn't told anybody else, ever. Things I'd overheard my mother talking about. Things I'd learned on that FBI rap sheet. Everything that happened from the time he kidnapped Teddy Stride.

After I told her what I saw in his face when he knew he was going to be safe, there was silence for about four miles.

"How long have you been a cop, Lantham?"

"We're not cops."

"You know what I mean."

"Yeah, I do. Seventeen years, it's been. Seventeen since I got into the Academy. But that doesn't matter."

"Doesn't matter. Right."

"Having a badge doesn't make you a good guy."

"No, doing the right thing does."

"And if he'd gone back under, into some new life..."

"That's not our choice to make."

"Cops make it all the time, Rache."

"Doesn't make it right. And we're not cops."

"No it doesn't. And you're right. We're not." Technically I was, but I didn't want to argue the point as I was only supposed to be an IA monkey and I sure as hell wasn't supposed to be covering up homicides, let alone committing them. "Cops enforce the rules. People come to us with things that cops can't handle. Or won't. And maybe..." this occurred to me as I was talking, "I don't know. Maybe I never was a cop. Not really. Not deep down. I guess...I guess I'm more like Mighty Mouse. I come in to save the day when everything is fucked. And the places I go, Rache, they're fucked beyond repair. The places where the system doesn't work. And it's my job to find out how, and why. People pay me to find the truth. And I make things a little better, if I can. Or worse. Truth is a brutal motherfucker. And if I'm careful I don't get too dirty. There's no

bleach that washes your soul here. No priests. No judges.
No review board to make you clean like when you're a
good tool of the system. Out here you're on your own.
And you have to deal with that one way or another."

"I see." In a tone as icy as the words sounded.

"I never said I was a saint, Rache. Never even said I
was a good guy. I'm just trying to do a job."

"If you say so. Right now your job's gonna get us
both done for obstruction and accessory, at best."

"Yeah. Yeah, maybe. This ain't legal. It maybe wasn't
even right. What I did. But I'm not going to look over
my shoulder, and wonder how many other peoples
blood is on my hands. I'll be able to look myself in the
mirror."

At least, that's what I was telling myself.

WE STILL HAD NIGHT on our side when we got
to the construction site. Quiet night like that, all those
stars in the sky, looked like Tinker Bell had bled to death
up there.

We had our pick of buildings, but my money—and
Rachael's—was on the portables behind the Paxton
house.

"One problem," I said as we rolled up on approach.

"What's that?"

"No gloves." No hat either. Bare minimum when
you're breaking and entering you don't want to leave
prints and hair. Fiber, we couldn't do much about, at
least not at the moment. But if the Feds were gonna be

combing this place for forensics in a few days...

"Maybe not. Pull in here."

I did. 'Here' was the pregnancy clinic. I pulled off the road instead, just in case.

"There's no cameras," she said.

"Well, none we can see, anyway. What you got in mind."

"Lantham, it's a medical clinic—right next to a construction site."

Which meant gloves and overalls, if we could swing three break-ins instead of one.

I liked the logic. The Feds weren't likely to give the construction site and the clinic the same kind of scrub they'd give the portables, if they gave them any at all.

"Nice thinking."

"You don't like it."

"No, I like it fine. We just don't have what we need."

"Like?"

"Lock picks, tac makeup, anything to disguise ourselves. Construction sites have security for insurance reasons..."

"Right. All that equipment laying around..."

"Exactly. And a clinic, with all those drugs..." I rested my elbows against the steering wheel, folded my hands in front of my face, leaned my chin against them.

"Fuck."

"But it's not a bad idea. It's a great idea. But..."

"But what?"

"But maybe you picked the wrong target." I extended

my left pinky finger, pointing with it through the windshield.

She followed it and spotted the dark hulk of the Paxton house.

"Nobody's home. We can get clothes and something to cover our fingers."

I DIDN'T HAVE MY lock picks. We had to break in the old fashioned way—with a pocket knife. Slide a little blade between the panes and pop the latch. The place had old enough windows that I could do it without gouging any vinyl.

We went in the front of the house. Living room window, right off the front porch. Easy entry, no risk of disturbing the girls in the dorm out back. No neighbors across the street, just an open field.

No witnesses.

We both went in, then I went out through the front door and popped the screen back in.

"No lights," I said. "We've got students in the portables back there. Check the bathroom for gloves. You're a size, what. Four?"

"Six."

"Nice."

"Thanks."

"I'll get us some clothes. Wipe down anything you touch." I said it while I wiped down the window frame and the door knob. "Don't make it obvious that anyone's been here."

"No suspicion, no warrant?"

"That's the idea."

I COULDN'T HELP BUT notice the land line next to the bed in the master bedroom. I picked it up, got a dial tone. If I actually wanted to get away with this, I was gonna have to go out on a serious limb.

I dialed Earl's emergency number from memory.

Earl wasn't up. Got his voicemail.

"Earl, it's me. I'm in the shit here. Gonna need some surgery. Life and death stuff. Details in the box in the morning. Get it done before lunch. I'll owe you my spleen."

It would have to do. If Earl could erase the cell phone location pings from Rachael and Nya's phones, then there'd be nothing to tie us all to the hobbit hole. Then, maybe, we'd skate by without getting sent up for murder. The FBI doesn't look for murderers. Murder isn't a Federal crime.

It's a hell of a thread to hang from, but it's what I had.

Well, that and Mrs. Paxton's clothes. She was a size twelve, back when she'd been alive, so anything that was actually meant to fit wasn't going to work.

I wasn't in much better shape where Mr. Paxton was concerned. He was short, even by average-guy standards. Twenty four inch inseam. Twenty-eight inch waist. XXL shirt. Feet like a bloody Barbie doll. Dude must've looked like an olive on a toothpick.

"Bad news, Lantham. And good news." Rachael shouted from the bathroom. "Which one you want."

"Thrill me."

"They don't have any gloves."

"And the good news?"

"She had nail polish."

WE WENT OUT THE FRONT, our breath fogging in front of us like steam engines. Our noses freezing like we were pressing it against cold lamp posts. We were over a thousand feet lower than we had been up at the hobbit hole, and circled round to the north side of the house, as far away from the dorm driveway as possible.

The house provided good coverage to the sparse trees. After that we played like we were kids doing cowboys and Indians—creeping up on the empty set of portables.

At least I hoped to hell they were still empty.

The stairs creaked underneath me. If the noise woke any co-eds up, and they looked out their windows, they were gonna see a pair of people straight out of a cartoon—me in a bath robe, pantyhose, my own high-top shoes, and a hair net. Rachael in a man's t-shirt tied around her waist with a boot lace, and pantyhose below under her US Army-style combat boots.

I had to try three keys before I found one that worked. Had to fumble with them—you never realize how much grip your fingerprints give you until they're covered in nail polish.

But it worked.

Even with flashlights, I wished it didn't.

The place was a wreck. Looked like it had been abandoned in a hurry and no one had come back to clean up. It smelled like urine and old panic.

"Don't touch anything. Just look for the tapes."

"I'm not an idiot, Lantham."

Well, at least she was acting normal. Maybe there was hope for us after all. Or at least for her. Never thought I'd find her bitchy abuse comforting.

I checked the desks in the front room first. Not a lot of A/V equipment. No tapes of any kind that I could find. No computers, either. No USB sticks. There were cables and power strips, though. Looked like they'd cleared out the IT when they cleared out the inmates.

There were medical supplies, though. Office supplies, too. Candy wrappers. Business cards.

A particular business card caught my eye. It had a familiar name on it.

Dr. R. G. Fender

Director of Strategic Investment

Oxford Capital Management Group

"Oh, fuck. Dad? Really?" Not nine weeks ago, when Cal Oldman hired me on as an IA auditor for the Santa Clara Sheriff's Department, he'd told me that he suspected a venture capitalist named Revell Fender of being involved with several of the high profile cases I'd gotten mixed up in over the last few years. All of them were cutting-edge tech stuff. All of them were potentially destabilizing to more than just their market sector. I still had a lot of boning up on geopolitics to do, but Oldman was convinced that Revell was the center of a big organized crime enterprise with major political aims.

I took a pen. A scrap of paper. Made sure I was writing on a hard surface.

Copied down all the info on the card.

Then, because I was rocking the pocketless housewife look, I twirled it up like a cigarette and stuck it under my hair net.

"Rache? Find anything?"

"They kept them here, Lantham." Tight, controlled voice from one of the back rooms. "This is where they did it. This is where they bled them."

"What you got?"

"IV trees. Oh god..."

"Rache?"

"I'm fine. Just...I found Zarek's bed."

"How do you know?"

"I just do."

"No tapes?"

"Nothing."

"Any rooms you didn't get?"

"None."

"All right. That'll have to do. *Tempus fugit.*"

BACK TO THE PAXTON house. To the bathroom. Stripped to the skin.

I was starting to get comfortable looking at her naked. Didn't know why it had taken so goddamn long. Never had it phase me before, not really, not with anyone else. Then again, I never had another employee that didn't care about stripping in front of me, and I don't have that kind of sexual harassment insurance. Nya's different, cause Nya's Nya. But this time, with Rache, it was okay. Maybe since she wasn't my employee anymore, I wasn't going paranoid about it.

Bagged the stolen clothes. Re-dressed in our real clothes.

Wiped everything down again on the way out.

Then, once we got in the car:

"Lantham, I need you to take me to Yreka."

"Yreka? Rache that's an hour in the..."

"TAKE me to Yreka, Lantham. That's where I live. For Christ's sake just...just take me home, okay?"

Guess she'd made her decision after all.

"What about the tapes?"

"You'll find them. And I'll owe you. I mean, where could he have put them? They could be in the construction office, I guess. Or back at the college. I mean, he wouldn't left them...oh my god."

"What?"

"They're in his car."

"Oh come on."

"No, think about it. He wanted to keep the leverage. He was gonna strand you up there and drive away himself. He knew that as soon as he was gone his shit would get raided. Anything in his name. So he'd want to keep anything he had for insurance on him, so he could get away with it."

"Doesn't make sense. If he had it on him, they'd find it, he couldn't do a deal."

"Not insurance from them. Insurance from you."

"From me? What kind of threat did..."

"You're his son. You killed him."

"Point taken. Okay. You want to make the call?"

"Yeah."

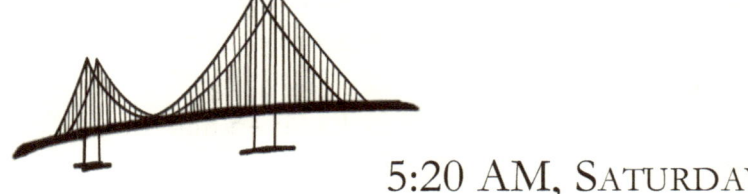

5:20 AM, SATURDAY

LANTHAM DROPPED HER OFF in front of her rented garage.

She'd hugged him.

He'd asked if she was going to come back.

She'd told him she didn't know. Maybe she'd wave when she came by to pick up her bike.

Then she kissed him.

Just a friendly kiss. She wasn't sure she could handle more. She was damn sure he couldn't. But she needed to do it, just barely.

Because she didn't know if she could go back. And she didn't want to miss out on him completely.

Maybe he felt that way too. He held her as long as she'd held on, and when she let go, he was crying. That quiet, even-breathing, tough-guy crying he did when he didn't want anybody to know he had feelings.

Yeah, she'd take care of herself. He'd better do the same or she'd hear about it and kick his ass.

And then he was gone. Off into the cold, through the last bits of the patchy, long-dead snow.

Rachael took the bag of clothes with her into her apartment.

She dropped them inside the door. Emptied her pockets onto the dresser. Dropped the clothes she was wearing, stuffed every stitch of them into that bag. Just about froze while she did it too. The house hadn't been on regular heat for a week. By the time she got the furnace on and into the shower she was sure her nipples were going to fall off.

The hot water made promises even it couldn't keep. Promises about making her clean. About keeping her warm.

They didn't make a warm for the kind of cold she was feeling.

Once she was dried and dressed as Daisy Pickford, she took the bag out behind the garage, to the barbecue. She doused the clothes in lighter fluid, set them on fire, and kept it going until all that was left was ash as gray as the pre-dawn sky.

DAISY PICKFORD HIKED THE mile to work in the morning. As far as her coworkers were concerned, she looked a little tired. She'd been gone because her sister's husband had taken sick. Now she was back in town to move away—she didn't know how long her sister would need her help, but it could be a while.

In the meantime, she needed a ride to the other end of town. She needed to rent a car. Could anyone help?

Susan, the manager who really hadn't wanted to fire her, was willing. It was only a couple miles down the main strip, but she couldn't imagine sending the poor girl back out into the cold.

Daisy said her goodbyes. Gave her hugs.

The last time Susan ever saw her, she was walking into the Hertz office with a big, Daisy-sized smile on her cute Okie face.

THE WHOLE APARTMENT fit in the back seat of the little red Chevy Vuze Rachael rented. The landlord wished her well, but he wasn't happy to see her go. Not a lot of housing demand in Yreka. Probably would take him forever to rent the place out again.

She packed everything in the back—her murder board, the rest of her Daisy Pickford clothes (all two non-work outfits and the one uniform), the saddlebags from her bike. Everything except her wallet and the little trophy.

An action figure, about three inches tall. From *Return of the Jedi*. Lando Calrissian, Jabba's Palace edition.

The action figure Zarek Woodfork had lost.

She'd found it laying, forgotten, on a urine-soaked cot in the portable behind the Paxton residence.

Where the vampires took his blood. And drugged him so he'd forget.

THE CURB OUTSIDE THE Woodfork house wasn't a curb at all. Just a ragged edge where lawn met road.

At that edge, a square, weathered, seasoned oak post stuck in the ground, and on top of it, a mailbox fashioned to look like a small oak wine barrel, big enough to hold a magnum bottle. It stuck out over the drainage ditch where the letter carrier might reach it without getting out of her car.

At around nine AM, a red Vuze pulled up on the wrong side of the street, its driver's window drawing even with the mailbox.

The window rolled down.

Rachael Oldman reached her arm out, opened the door, placed a tissue-wrapped action figure in the the barrel, and closed the door again.

Then, before anyone could notice or remark upon her presence, the Vuze rolled away again.

I CALLED RIVERS ON the way home from Yreka that morning. Wound up having to stop at a truck stop and sleep anyway, so I grabbed a pre-paid and let my fingers do the walking.

We'd been taken up to NorCal. He'd tried to dump us in the middle of nowhere. My assistants showed up, there was a fight. He managed to escape on foot. Nobody was seriously injured. A few scuffs.

But I was sure now I could connect him to things. I would swear out a warrant for him, for the portables behind the Paxton place. The FBI, of course, could expect my full cooperation. As long as they took care of the Strides.

Protective custody was a must. This was an organized-crime connected thing. It might take the FBI a while to crack it, but Tom Stride had first-hand knowledge of how it all worked, and the companies involved, and the mechanics of distribution. He was in serious danger as long as he was in the clear. There were some big fish behind this one. Based on what His Grubbiness told me before he disappeared, I was willing to swear it was old mob money from the east coast.

Not a traditional mob venture, I know, but business moves with the world, and the mob was hurting for places to make a buck.

Why would they get into blood plasma?

Why Rivers, didn't you know that health care is a growth industry? And regenerative medicine is going to be held up for years by regulatory hurdles? What with the card room business drying up and the Mexican organizations pushing the mob out of the hard drug trade, it was only a matter of time before they sunk their claws into not-quite-legal biomed. Diversify or die, right? Stands to reason.

Rivers bought it. Hook, line, sinker. And there never were any questions about where His Grubbiness got to.

And I buried those keys to the hobbit hole in a little empty easter egg in the back yard. Just in case I needed to go back there someday.

Rivers put an agent on the Strides while they were processed in. Took a few days, but I figured they had the leeway. Nobody would actually start looking for the Strides until there was an indictment.

All that was left for me was to alert Cal Oldman about the case, and tip him off about the Oxford Capital business card I found.

On the QT. Completely deniable. But it was one more point on the graph for an investigation that I fully expected to lead to a whole lot of nowhere.

RACHAEL SHOWED UP again, about a week later.

Showed up for keeps.

I asked her whether she wanted her job back, and she looked me in the eye and said "Only if I get to vote before we bump anyone off."

I don't think she was joking.

And it's okay. That's a condition I can live with.

AFTER THAT THERE WAS a lot of paperwork.

A lot.

Well, there always is. Whether it's on paper or not, someone always wants a report.

On this one, I wanted more than a report. I wanted to make sure I never forgot it. I figure life doesn't give you many clear lights to show you how to walk between the time you learn how to breathe and the time you forget again. And me? Well I had two now.

I had my brother Sam. Poor, deluded, venial Sam. Weak as cooked broccoli. Murdered because he didn't have the balls to stand up for...well, anything really.

And I had His Grubbiness. John Lantham. My Dad. Con artist. Blood dealer. Fraudster. Murderer. Rapist-by-proxy. An invaluable Federal Witness. One cold-hearted sonofabitch.

Me? Rachael used to say I do the right thing all the time. I'm a stand-up guy. Guess it'd make me feel good if I could believe it. I can't, though.

Truth is, I'm too cold-hearted to be a coward. And too much of a goddamn softy to be a complete bastard. And I like kicking ass and taking the credit, which you can't do if you're hiding from your own shadow or hiding from the cops. So I take the sucker's road, and play the white hat for the crowds, and all the time I'm really just walking right there between the ghosts of my Dad and my brother—too much of an asshole for one, too much of a coward for the other.

But you take what you can get. And, if you're smart, you start to get a clue, sooner or later.

Watching how Teddy and Tom held onto each other after it was all over? Well, it finally gave me a clue. So I called Erica while I was looking at it. Told her voicemail that I loved her. Told her there were things I had to tell her. Told her to call me when she could.

She did.

Her dad was alive. He was on the mend, even. Might last another couple years, and have them be good years at that. Nobody knew why. That kind of thing just happened sometimes. But she'd tell me all about it when she saw me tomorrow night. She had to go do a couple days at the office first, get set up for reintegration next week. Get up to speed before she was officially back on the clock.

A CASE LIKE THIS rearranges your head. Makes you see how things are. How you wish they were. Puts you face to face with the fact that you're getting older than you want to admit. That you'd better get on with life before you realize you wasted it.

For someone who never thought he'd see thirty-five,

I'm doing a hell of a job at staying two steps ahead of the grim reaper. What'll happen to me if I wait another twenty years to do anything about the things I thought Lanthams were never allowed to have. Would I turn out like His Grubbiness?

I've thought for a long time about how I would do things, if I ever met a woman I wanted to marry. I've had some near misses over the years, but I never quite got as far as popping the question—except that first time, with Samantha, when I did the boring-old pick out a ring, get down on one knee, embarrass the woman into saying yes gambit.

Didn't want to do that this time. Didn't want to get Erica a ring she thought she'd have to wear. She had the kind of job where a ring might not be workable at all, or she might have specific tactical specs.

So, on the way home, I stopped by Walgreens, and I bought a packet of pipe cleaners and a cheap watch in an expensive-looking box. Her ring finger was about as big around as the little segment on my left pinky, so I wrapped some pipe cleaners around it for size, tied a bow on them, then tossed the watch and put the temp-ring in the box.

Not a long trip home from Walgreens. Two blocks and change. I pulled into the driveway—first one home. Klepto was beside himself—not used to being left alone, he just about baptized me when I came through the rear door.

I propped the door open so he could go in and out.

He bolted out, eager to re-mark his territory and evict any squirrels and possums—okay, okay, opossums for you pedants out there—that had made it into the yard. Then went down to the basement, to the dirt portion, to clean up what I could smell halfway up to the main floor.

Note to self: make a deal with one of the neighbors for emergency on-demand pet-sitting.

Then, back up to the kitchen.

Washed my hands. Pulled a hunk of lamb out of the freezer, stuck it in a bowl of hot water to thaw. Grabbed the ingredients for flat bread and Greek salad. When Erica got here in an hour, she'd have fresh gyros and some Maréchal Foch, and mango slices for dessert. Butter her up just right before going in with the pipe cleaners.

I tossed Klepto little snitches of everything that wouldn't kill him, since I felt like a heel for leaving him alone for so long. Rationalizing that I couldn't help it didn't matter—dogs don't understand why they get left on solitary guard duty.

At least he'd had Scuttlebutt to keep him company.

The house hadn't been properly cleaned in a week, so I did a quick pickup of all the spare crap and brought the vacuum cleaner up from the basement. Opened the front windows. Took in the evening air.

Right now, about twenty-seven miles to my northwest, Teddy Stride's family was getting their new identities. In another couple hours, there would be a moving van in front of their house, and a removals team that would pack up everything they owned and take them away. I'd never see any of them again.

Small price to pay for Teddy Stride getting a chance to actually get to know his father. That's a chance I would have given up everything for at his age.

Difference is, his Dad is actually worth the trouble.

Mine wasn't.

I wondered how much bullshit I would've avoided if I'd figured that out sooner.. How many lies I'd not have told myself.

How many years would I get back if I could go back in time and tell my younger self just how much my father wasn't worth it. But that my future was.

I might have realized that I had a future.

Well, I knew now.

Now, I was gonna make something of it.

KITCHEN. WARM WATER. BREAD flour. Masa. Salt. Baking powder.

Knead until firm.

Pat out into pancakes.

Dust with flour and stack for cooking.

Cucumbers. Tomatoes. Salt. Garlic. Shallots. Mint.

Mince. Mix. Dash of lemon juice. Leave set.

The lamb was soft enough to cut.

Carving knife, freshly sharp. Cut into short strips.

Minced Garlic. Minced onions. Black Pepper.

Mint. Salt.

Toss with olive oil.

Cast iron pan on high.

Sear.

Deglaze with retsina.

Finish with lemon.

Serve covered to keep the heat.

I checked the clock. Erica was due in fifteen minutes. Just enough time to do the bread.

I heated the griddle to near red-hot. Patted each pancake out thin. Tossed it like a pizza crust. Brushed olive oil on it.

Threw it onto the griddle.

Stretched with my fingers. Careful not to burn the tips.

Flip. Repeat.

Land it in a bamboo basket. Cover.

Repeat with the rest of the bread.

Then candles.

Plates.

Silver.

Crystal.

And one more bamboo serving basket. This one with the ring in it.

Ding-dong.

One of the things I love about this house. Old, genuine, dangling chimes for the doorbell. Sounds like something out of an old movie.

But Erica should have been coming in through the back door.

"One minute!" I shouted. Gave my hands a quick run under the tap and brushed them off. Didn't want to get bread dough all over my doorknob.

Went to the front door. Blue hour outside. Gorgeous light. Made me want to go out and take pictures of something.

Not the stiff at the door, though. The sunglasses and suit were a dead giveaway, before he even pulled out the credentials.

"Can I help you?"

"Clarke Lantham?"

"Who's asking."

"Special agent Victor Argen, FBI." Credentials. Quick and efficient.

"What do you need?"

He reached into his inside coat pocket, whipped out a white A4 envelope.

He handed it to me. Nodded.

Turned around.

Walked away.

I looked at the envelope.

It read:

Clarke Lantham in clear, no-nonsense blue ballpoint.

My guts twisted themselves into a knot.

I walked out onto the porch. Leaned against the black wrought-iron railing. Tore off one end of the envelope.

There was a single sheet of A4 paper inside. Tri-folded. Laser printed.

It said:

Clarke—
I have been reassigned to D.C., effective tonight. It was the only choice I had.
You used my account to gain access to AFIS and God knows what else. I told you they were watching.
They're sick of your using your relationship with me and your working relationship with Rivers for personal advantage on private cases.
Misuse of classified access is espionage. They want to charge you.
This is what it costs to keep you out of jail.
Do not contact me ever again.
-Special Agent Erica Ellis, FBI

And, underneath the printing, some handwriting.

I loved you. Goddamn you. —E

I stared at the letter for a long time. When I finally looked up, there wasn't any more blue in the sky. Just that dull, brooding red of the city lights reflecting off the underside of the overcast.

Endless twilight.

Klepto found me out there, staring into space. I heard his tail thumping on the concrete porch.

I stood up, stretched, knelt down and gave him a pet.

He licked my face. All around my eyes. Then whimpered and nuzzled his snout into my chest.

"Yeah, boy. I know. She won't be coming around

anymore. Yeah, I'm gonna miss her too."

This is what you get, Lantham. These are the kinds of choices you make, for no fucking reason at all.

So much for happy endings.

I crumpled the letter I my hand.

Walked inside.

Closed the door.

Got the lamb off the table, scraped about half of it onto Erica's plate.

I set it on the floor for Klepto.

Then I went to the bedroom, stripped the bed, and threw the sheets in the trash.

After that, I got my cheapest scotch out of the liquor cabinet and went out to the office. Stretched out in my easy chair, pulled up the oldest episodes of *Star Trek* I could find on Netflix, and drained every last drop of gold out of the bottle.

9:36 PM, MONDAY

TODAY HAD BEEN Rachael's first official day back at work. After returning from her exile, she'd gone down to her parents' house and spent some time reassuring them that she hadn't gotten raped or mugged, that she hadn't wound up in a car accident or any serious trouble.

She only had to lie a little bit about that last part, but that was okay. She couldn't make her father an accessory after the fact.

She walked around the old neighborhood. Slept in her old room. Pretended for a few days that she was just fresh home from camp and ready to start school again.

It was a vacation.

And vacations end.

She'd ended hers by calling Lantham and asking for her job back.

He'd said: "If you swear that next time you need to have a shit fit, you'll talk about it first instead of slipping out in the middle of the night like some goddamn high schooler."

"There won't be a next time," she'd said.

"Yeah, right."

Well, he had every right to be pissed. She could think of at least six hundred ways she could have handled things better. She'd been making a list of them since that first morning she bugged out because she couldn't handle her own feelings like an adult anymore.

That's how you learned, right?

Her first day, she'd spent reading up on the cases in progress. It would take about a week to get back up to speed, and the big case Lantham mentioned wasn't even in the files. That one, he'd said, they'd get to when she was up to speed with the rest of it.

Must be a big one. Or really really secret.

When she'd gone home, though, she'd left her phone and her gun in the office.

Of course, she'd gone home to deal with a cat emergency and had gotten stuck there with Nya, but still, not an auspicious way to ring in her second chance at the Private Investigators' Hall of Fame.

She crossed the sodium-lit asphalt of Santa Maria—which took a couple minutes. Santa Maria was one of those residential streets that acted as an unofficial freeway.

Reaching Lantham's driveway, she saw that the light in his office was still on.

He wasn't supposed to be working late tonight. He was going to have Erica over and propose.

Rachael let herself in through the gate, skirted the edge of the sensor light field, made her way to the side of the garage.

The office door was standing open.

"Lantham?" She cautiously slipped in. Announced herself in case Lantham and Erica had decided to do the nasty on the lab bench.

Her desk—the one she now shared with Nya—was ten feet from the door. Her phone and gun were still sitting on it, right next to the bondage troll. Lantham's office was just to the right of the entrance to the main office in the converted garage.

And its door, too, was standing open.

Lantham lay inside, half-hanging off his easy chair. Spock's Brain was playing on the computer screen that he'd swiveled around from his desk.

An empty bottle of Johnny Walker Black and a puddle of vomit soiled the floor beside him.

"Jesus Christ. Lantham..." She stepped in, danced around the vomit, smacked his face.

He groaned.

"Oh, thank fuck." She'd never seen him this drunk. Come to think of it, she'd never seen him seriously drunk in her life. Anything more than a medium buzz and he switched to coffee. And not the fun kind of coffee either.

But he wasn't coming out of it. He was way the hell down the hole to blackoutsville. "Oh God, Lantham, what did you do?"

Well, she knew what she had to do.

And she just about got a hernia doing it.

She stripped his shirt off, left it on the floor with the

rest of the soiled shit. He could deal with that tomorrow.

Then, she hauled him up out of the easy chair. He wasn't fat, but at slightly-shorter-than-a-skyscraper he was heavy as all fuck. She turned around, pulled his arms over her shoulders, hauled him up to a piggy-back drag, and pulled him into the house.

Once they were in the front hall, she leaned him against the wall, stripped him the rest of the way, stripped down herself, and shoved him into the shower.

Hot water would help. It always helped her.

Klepto whined at the door, demanded to be let in. The shower was big, but two adults and a dog was definitely pushing it, so she ignored him.

Then, wetter than she'd planned on ending up, and still half-soapy, she dragged Lantham's stumbling, insensate, naked carcass around the corner to his bedroom, flopped him on the bed, covered him up.

Klepto hopped up and curled at Lantham's side, looking at Rachael with protective, suspicious eyes.

He might still be sick. He needed a bucket.

And he needed someone to sit up with him in case he aspirated.

Great. Normally he just exasperated.

First things first.

She left dripping tracks on the carpet, mumbling "I didn't sign up to be your fucking nursemaid, Lantham, why the fuck you'd go and drink that shit..." while she made her way to the kitchen, squatted down by the cupboard next to the sink, rooted around for some tupperware. Lantham had a couple big fucking popcorn bowls and...

...and why was there a wadded up piece of paper under the table?

Lantham never left paper wads on the floor.

She shimmied over. Reached under the table for it. Opened it up. Read it.

Rachael's stomach sank down past her toes.

She closed her eyes.

"Fuck."

Phone. Nya. "Hi, honey. Yeah. Look, can you stay there tonight? I'll be back tomorrow. No, I can't explain right now, just do me the favor? Thanks."

Assuming he didn't die in his sleep, Lantham would want his space tomorrow morning.

Rachael tossed the paper in the trash, took the bowl to Lantham's bedroom, rooted around in his dresser for a T-shirt.

It stuck to her wet skin like wrinkly lycra, but she'd dry. She kicked the heater on just to be sure.

Rachael picked a book off Lantham's headboard without looking at the title.

She turned the closet light on.

She sat on the floor next to the closet, with her back against the dresser.

She opened the book.

And she settled in for a long, long night.

THE END

Clarke Lantham will return in
The Bodies in The Basement

Acknowledgments

Lantham exists in a world not-too-different from our own—a few variations on reality exist in terms of geography, history, and organizations.

The Evangelical Missions Association and Trubody College, for example, are not a real denomination, nor is its structure or culture a direct Roman à clef of any particular denomination. They are a pastiche of the dozens of such organizations and schools I've worked with, at, near, or attended over the years, in official and unofficial capacities, as well as the ones my family and friends have worked with, at, and near. That said, I must admit I've never actually known anyone to use a church or a church-school as cover for a kidnapping and blood-theft ring.

That one I have to thank Peter Diamandis for. Mr. Diamandis tweets regular, and fascinating, updates on the biomedical sciences, and it was his twitter stream which first brought to my attention the experimental (and very promising) therapy of blood-factor transfusion from young donors to old, which accomplishes rejuvenation of aging tissues. Despite its use in the story as the economic motivation for a horrific criminal enterprise, the therapy itself holds great promise for both life extension and for the treatment of the diseases of aging. I will be following its developments with enthusiasm in the coming years.

Sue Baiman, Kitty NicIaian, and Elizabeth Snell did

yeoman's work proofreading and beta-reading the volume. Elizabeth Snell, particularly, saved me—and you—from a fate worse than Full House re-runs when she pointed out that the initial way I had constructed the missing children's case didn't pass the sniff test for small town life. Although her observation necessitated some fairly radical surgery on Rachael's storyline, the book is ultimately tighter and creepier because of it.

For this, and many of the other times she's noticed similar flawed premises in earlier books, she has my undying gratitude.

Author's Note

Lantham and I don't share a lot—he's tall and lean, I'm shorter and...well, not, and that's just the beginning of our suite of disagreements. One thing we do share, though is an obsessive love of architecture. When I was seven years old, I first had occasion to walk through the doors of an old army base on a hill in San Francisco—a building that you now know as Trubody Bible College—and I fell in love, not just with the amazing old building, but with architecture as a phenomenon.

The building as it once existed and as described in this book is now a memory, its west wings damaged beyond repair in the 1989 Loma Prieta Earthquake. One of the few extant examples of a vanishingly unique architectural period (the tail end of the period that brought us Fort Point and The Armory, both of which still stand in San Francisco), its facade and some of its original wings still stand, but the western end of the building has been swallowed up by retrofitting and redevelopment that, while adding a great deal of utility to an admittedly impractical structure, destroyed the symmetry and club-footed grandeur that the old building possessed.

Haunting its halls for a period in my youth was a formative experience for me, and I've been looking for some years to memorialize it as-it-once-was—and, as one might expect from a fellow architecture geek, Clarke Lantham finally gave me that chance.

This is one of those books that came together at just the right time to wrap a time capsule together. Klepto owes a lot to Trixie, a Malinois who's recently invaded my household and re-formed its rhythms. The last year has seen a number of trips to and from San Francisco from my new digs up on the Oregon Coast, including many late-night stopovers in Yreka and Weed—both towns sitting on the border between the major trade artery on the West Coast and country so vast, so gorgeous, and so empty as to give them the feel of outpost cities in the old west, despite their being modern, even hyper-modern, in every way.

Before In The Cloud, every Clarke Lantham story was born of direct, day-to-day experience around the Bay, growing as naturally out of the rhythms of my day as trips to the spice shop and sunsets over the Peninsula.

Now that I live a day's drive away, and can no longer hop in the car to go check out the fine details of a location, I'm finding the experience of writing Lantham's world more dream-like, more colored by nostalgia, and more relaxing that it used to be. Although Lantham's always been fun, writing him felt a bit like journalism to me in the early days. Now, it feels like balladeering. I don't know that it makes any difference to how it reads—I almost hope it doesn't—but I mention it here partly because these authors notes are a way for me to keep track of my authorial life-in-progress, and this book feels like one I might want to look back on in a few years and wonder "Why was is that that book came together at that time for me?"

Something else happened, too, that seems only to happen to Lantham novels: I wrote another book in the middle of this one. As happened to me with Silent Victor (where I stopped writing in order to write Smoke Rings before I finished Silent Victor), work on Blood and Weeds ground to a halt about halfway through, and my subconscious wouldn't let me finish until I wrote the next book in the series The Bodies In The Basement.

I have my suspicions as to why that was, but if I set them down here, they might serve as a spoiler, so perhaps I'll discuss them in the author's note at the end of the next book.

Finally, the destiny of the Stride family has been a matter of some personal concern for me. It seems that, as part of their witness protection and relocation deal, they're going to wind up in a small town on the Oregon Coast, where Teddy is going to get into all kinds of trouble operating his detective agency when the family is supposed to be keeping a low profile—you might even be able to read about it before too awful long...

Meantime, you'll get at least one more Lantham book before then, maybe two or three depending on how I do on my other big project this year.

Doing my part to keep the world mysterious and interesting...

-J. Daniel Sawyer
Lincoln City, Oregon
April 2016

Also by J. Daniel Sawyer

The Kabrakan Ascendency
The Orinthal Deception
The Hartman Gambit
The Reeves Directive (forthcoming)

The Clarke Lantham Mysteries
And Then She Was Gone
A Ghostly Christmas Present
Smoke Rings
Silent Victor
He Ain't Heavy
In The Cloud
His Grubbiness
The Bodies In The Basement
The Sky Miners (forthcoming)

Suave Rob's Amazing Adventures
Suave Rob's Double-X Derring-Do
Suave Rob's Rough-and-Ready Rugrat Rapture
Suave Rob's Amazing Ass-Saving Association

Standalone Works
Down From Ten
The Resurrection Junket
Ideas, Inc.
The Auto Motive (Forthcoming)

Collections

Sculpting God: Bedtime Stories for Adults

Frock Coat Dreams: Romances, Nightmares, and Fancies from the Steampunk Fringe

Non-Fiction

The Every Day Novelist

Business 101

The Every Day Novelist (forthcoming)

Writer's Guides

Science Fiction Weaponry: A Guide for Writers (with Mary Mason)

Throwing Lead: A Writer's Guide to Firearms and the People Who Use Them (with Mary Mason)

Making Tracks: A Writer's Guide to Audiobooks and How to Produce Them

About the Author

With the advent of his hard-boiled Clarke Lantham Mysteries, J. Daniel Sawyer's abusive behavior toward the English language finally landed him in serious trouble, and he now spends his days and nights chained to a desk in a vain attempt to write his way out of the loony bin. Unfortunately, his attempts have yielded further entries in his sci-fi thriller series The Antithesis Progression, the cabin fever comedy Down From Ten, and significant alterations in his medication. On the rare occasion that he slips his bonds, he escapes to the wilds of the San Francisco back country where he devotes his energies to running afoul of local traffic ordinances in his never-ending pursuit of the ultimate driving road.

Should you be so inclined, you can communicate with this shady character, as well as find stories, podcasts, articles, and other literary abominations at http://www.jdsawyer.net

www.ingramcontent.com/pod-product-compliance
Lightning Source LLC
Chambersburg PA
CBHW030924020726
47498CB00001B/101

* 9 7 8 0 9 9 1 5 4 5 8 5 8 *